LOVING HIM

HEARTS INTERTWINED, BOOK 1

DREA ROMAN

CONTENTS

Cover Design by Amai Designs

Editing by Miranda Vescio, V8 Editing

Trademark Acknowledgments

The author acknowledges the trademarked and/or copyrighted status and trademark owners of the following items referenced in this work of fiction.

Ten Things I Hate About You
We Bare Bears
"Bite," by Troye Sivan
"If I Could Turn Back Time," by Cher
Mountain Dew
Taco Bell

ACKNOWLEDGMENTS

Thank you, first and foremost to my alpha-beta reader Mel. Without you, none of this would be possible. Thank you to my fiancé, Ivan, for being excited for me and for only occasionally remarking on the number of gay sex manuals laying about the house. Lisa Caskey has been a wonderful self-publishing mentor, offering helpful and timely advice. Les Court Author Services provided much needed help in the nick of time. Miranda Vescio edited this novel for me and I appreciate all of her work. Amani Designs designed my beautiful cover and it exceeded my happiest dreams. My Facebook reader group, Drea's Dirty Divas, deserves a shout out. They have encouraged me all of the way.

My first novel beta readers were thoughtful and so very helpful. Thank you to Mel, Tash, and Kris. Kris, your insight helped me revise an important scene and I will be forever grateful. My cats have been very supportive of this endeavor even though it has meant they must meow with slightly greater volume in order to grab my attention. Thank you, Ra and Tibert. Bringing a story idea to fruition as a complete published book takes a village. I am incredibly thankful for my village. And, last but not least, thank you, dear reader for reading this book. I hope that you love Black and Aubrey as much as I do.

CHAPTER 1

The moment I see him sitting alone at a corner table, with his attention focused on the papers in his left hand and his right gripped around a coffee cup, I'm smitten. Even though he is halfway across the sunlit room from me, I can clearly see his face in profile as he blows on the coffee in his mug. His coloring is perfectly matched, creamy white skin, not too pale, but the kind that would freckle or burn but never tan. His dark auburn brown hair is cut in a tidy, well-mannered style, long enough to grip if the need arose. And, oh man, the need started rising in me as soon as I laid eyes on him.

He suddenly looks up and turns his head as if sensing my presence. His lips part into a sweet and welcoming smile, and I feel a warmth spread through me I'd never felt before in my life. The physical attraction is instantaneous, and if the widening of his crisp green eyes when they first meet mine is any indication, the feeling is most definitely mutual. But that isn't what causes that sunny, fizzy happiness to flow immediately through my bloodstream. There is something else about him, an innate goodness shining through, and I arch toward it, body and soul, like a sunflower follows the sun's progress across the sky.

I walk toward him, completely forgetting my original mission to grab a cup of coffee before getting down to business. Stopping about a foot away from his table, I relish how his head tips back so he can look me in the eyes. As he stands to greet me, I can see he is a little bit shorter than my own 6'2" height, probably around 5'11", which I've always found to be the perfect height difference. I won't tower over him and can easily stare into his crisp green eyes. I am so enamored with his presence that I do not quite catch the first words he says in greeting. We hadn't exchanged descriptions, but I knew he was there for me. It really wouldn't have mattered if he was my work meeting or not. I would have stopped and sat at his table anyway. He was like my opposite magnetic pole, pulling me toward him on an elemental level.

"Mr. Black?" He must have said my name twice before I noticed. I smile, and I can only say the devil made me do it because as soon as his hand reaches out to shake mine, I grab it and hold it firmly and purposely well beyond the appropriate amount of time. He doesn't try to disengage from me, but I can see a faint blush stealing across his features as his eyes drop to our joined hands. Lowering my voice to a purring growl, I say, "You must be Aubrey Davies." I see his pulse tick up in his neck, and I have to stop myself from leaning into his space and latching my mouth onto that spot. I know he saw me looking at his neck, and he must have read the desire in my eyes because his flash darker for a moment and he licks his lips.

I barely stifle a groan then reality suddenly returns, reminding me of our location and the purpose of this meeting, which is work, not eating this man up with my eyes and wishing it was my lips doing the exploring. I reluctantly release his hand and immediately thrust both of mine through my loose hair. It is a self-soothing gesture, but from the way his eyes follow my hands, I can tell he wishes he could replace my hands with his own. Shit, I have to shake myself out of this or this meeting will go nowhere but the backseat of my car. I'm taking much too long to respond to whatever question he asked me, so he calls my name again.

"Mr. Black?"

"It's just Black," I reply as I pull out the seat across from him and settle myself into it as he sits himself back down in his.

"But you go by your full name with your art?"

"Yes, I do, but please do call me Black."

"So, you're the artist known as Black, huh?"

I can't help but grin at that. "Well, I guess I am."

"One day you're going to have to change your name," he says, tilting his head playfully to the right as a sweet smile settles on his lips.

"And why is that?"

"So you can call yourself the artist formerly known as Black."

I immediately adore his silliness. I laugh lightly in response, and his smile widens, his brilliant emerald eyes crinkling up in the corners and twinkling. But we are here for a reason other than flirting, though I would rather flirt at this precise moment than discuss business.

"So, you are the new park planner?"

"That I am, Mr. Black." He looks at his papers for something. When his eyes raise to mine, I'm caught in his clear green gaze. "Or may I call you Ian?"

I stiffen at the name and am caught in a wave of unwelcome memories. Aubrey must have noticed my face freeze because his eyes cloud with concern. He automatically reaches across the space between us to place his hand over the fist I didn't realize I had clenched on the edge of the table. In a lowered voice, he asks, "Are you alright?"

I swallow hard and drop my eyes to where his hand is covering mine. I'm relieved he doesn't move it because the warmth of his palm against the back of my hand is calming the chaos of my mind.

"It's just Black," I manage to croak out, embarrassment flooding my system. Aubrey's eyes are kind, and he nods gently. He pats my hand once, pulling his own back and dropping it into his lap. He smiles at me softly and reshuffles his papers, deftly changing the subject while at the same time acknowledging my preference for names.

"As you know, Black, the city has commissioned a large metal statue from your studio. We are meeting today to finalize the plans for the design, construction timeline, and placement for the statue." His eyes return to his paperwork. "I've been given a list of possible designs, none of which would require further approval."

Having recovered my composure, due in large part to his kindness, I interrupt. "I've had a few new ideas about the design." He lifts his eyes, and a happy smile crosses his face. *Sunshine, his smile is like sunshine.*

"Luckily for you, I have the authority to approve. What do you have in mind?"

I'm captivated by his easy demeanor. I must take too long to respond while my eyes never leave his face. I swear I see that faint blush again, and I'm practically giddy with excitement over it. He raises his eyebrows expectantly, teasingly, and I can't help my widening grin.

"Plants, native plants," I answer, and he seems momentarily confused as if he's forgotten his own question. "The statue will be of a native plant, probably some sort of cactus or a succulent. I've done them before, including several for cities throughout the Southwest. While we may have more trees in Oakland, those types of plants thrive here, too. My plant sculptures have been particularly popular in Arizona. I did several for Tucson and one for Phoenix. I have photos of the finished sculptures, before and after erection. Would you like to see them?" I purposely threw in the word "erection" and I am not disappointed by his reaction. He is most definitely blushing now. As I hold his gaze, I am grinning like the Cheshire Cat.

He swallows hard and shakes his head lightly, then grins, acknowledging I got him by tipping his chin toward me briefly. He looks down at his papers again, skimming through a few before looking back at me.

"What do you think the city wants?"

I literally shudder. "A cowboy on a horse. That is what I did for them last time, but never again."

"Out of curiosity, what's wrong with cowboys and horses? They are pretty popular out here."

"Beside the fact that they're hokey as fuck? They are generic, boring, and, to be quite honest, a waste of my time. I've done one, and that was plenty. I'm more interested in the natural world and how I can represent that through metal." I sigh as I scrub a hand over my face and the scruff across my jaw.

"No offense toward Frederic Remington," I continue now that I seem to have his attention back on my words, "but I am not making another cowboy and horse monstrosity. If that is why the city hired me, they can stick it where the sun don't shine; and, yes, I mean it literally. They can literally shove that heinous excuse for art up their asses before I will make another one like it." I'm grinning, but I'm serious. Aubrey looks bemused.

"Well," he responds, sounding thoughtful as he taps his finger against his chin, "that would require gallons of lube. And I can't see the city authorizing the expense." He smiles, his eyes again twinkling. "I'm sure I can get the approval for your design easily, especially since it will be an original." He nods, "Yep, everyone's ass will be protected, don't you even worry about it."

A laugh is startled out of me and a look of pride flashes across Aubrey's face. I fall a little more in lust with him than I already was. But, I'm pretty sure, it isn't only lust. "You don't have a filter, do you?" My remark caught Aubrey as he was taking another drink of his coffee, causing him to sputter and barely avoid choking. He swallows hard, accidentally thunking his mug hard on the table. Since he is clearly not dying from my inappropriately timed comment, I press my advantage. I allow a slow smile to creep across my face as I stare into his eyes, which have widened in surprise. "I like it. I like it a lot."

You are not blushing, I tell the misbehaving capillaries in my face. *You are not blushing*, I admonish them, to no avail, as I feel the heat diffuse across my face. Black is grinning like the asshole he surely is. Yes, he's definitely laughing at me. His grin is devastating and handsome, soul shaking and so warm and welcoming, like a bubble bath. I clear my throat and shake my head as I realize I've been staring at his face for longer than is polite or in any way "hetero-conscious."

"Like what you see?" He drawls at me and his smile grows impossibly wider. Yep, he has my number, and damn it all if I'm not starting to blush again.

Get it under control, Aubrey! I sternly and a little bit desperately chastise myself. The man is hot with all capital letters, but work comes first. *But then, maybe play*, the naughty part of my soul whispers to me, *he looks awfully fun.*

"Shit!" I accidentally say. In shock that I've spoken aloud, my eyes shoot up to his face. I hadn't even realized I'd dropped my gaze. Now I'm staring into his dark brown eyes, completely mortified, my cheeks probably glowing like Rudolph's nose.

"Shit!" I accidentally say again. "Damn it!"

Then he laughs, a strong, welcoming sound which oddly relaxes me, and I laugh, too.

"Drinks tonight, then?" he asks.

He's completely and smoothly sidestepped the whole "I'm gay, are you too?" conversation, and I'm more relieved than I've been in my entire life. And also, a hell of a lot more turned on.

"Yeah, that sounds great," I reply, my voice sounding squeaky and a little bit high. I swallow, purposely lowering my voice as I struggle to get myself under control. My voice now comes out breathily, which in this case *is* an improvement, even if it clearly comes across as *interested.* "Yes, I would like that. Do you have any place in mind? I'm new here, you know."

He looks unbelievably relieved which calms me down considerably. How could a man who looks like an artist's rendering of Odysseus—all tall, tight muscle, with shoulder-length black hair, dark brown eyes you could drown in, and a smile he must have stolen off an angel or Lucifer—ever be nervous about landing a date? Now my mind thinks it's a date and I have to back up the mental trolley a bit. *He just asked you out to drinks, not to elope to Greece and go skinny dipping in Ouzo with him.*

My eyes are roaming over his face, and if I couldn't tell he was equally eyeing me, I would probably go up in flames from embarrassment. For a moment, we stare at each other, but all awkwardness seems to have evaporated. I notice the dark five o'clock shadow across his jaw. It's nine a.m. and he looks sharp otherwise with a tight black T-shirt tucked into black jeans that reveal his powerful thighs and probably cup his ass beautifully. But I haven't been favored with that view yet. I think leaving the shadow along his jaw was a choice. An image perhaps, it definitely goes with his shoulder length black waves. When he stroked his hands through his hair earlier, I'd had to stop myself from getting up and replacing those hands with mine. Yeah, I'm in real trouble here.

I clear my throat and realize we have been staring at each other, without talking for at least a full minute. I lean a little closer myself, drawn in by him. I can smell his cologne and coffee, and his eyes look like bittersweet chocolate from this vantage point. He leans forward as well, and we seem like opposite magnets, pulled toward one another. A soft smile plays on his lips, and it's different than the smiles he has favored me with thus far. It has a shy and earnest quality to it, and my heart flip flops over. This man is very dangerous to me, and I couldn't be happier to find out exactly how.

"Do you like wine?" he asks softly. Our faces are dangerously close together now, especially considering we met two seconds ago. I take another breath of his unique mixture of scent and pull myself back into my chair. He mirrors my move and leans back in his chair. The devilish grin is back on his face, and I grin ridiculously.

"Of course I do."

"Well then, I know where I'm taking you tonight."

"Good. I can't wait to find out." Even though I've known him less than half an hour, I'd let him take me just about anywhere.

Aubrey looked like a goddamn work of art and I wanted him to be *my* art. Realizing the depth of my reaction to a man I met a mere hour ago should have freaked me out, or at least given me pause. But, it didn't. I refused to consider why. Just for the moment, I will let myself just be. I will feel this...thing... for lack of a better word, and let it float me up out of the cavern of my despair for a while. I won't over think it,. I'll just go with the fizzy joy of sunshine that sparks through my bloodstream when his eyes meet mine. No need to think beyond that. I'm resolved, I realize, a little stunned.

I look up from the coffee cup and glance at my watch, only to notice I've been staring into my mug for the better part of half an hour. Ironing out the details of my contract with the city hadn't taken long, and after that, I didn't have a reason to delay Aubrey from his tasks for the day. From the full planner he had on the table, his day must be packed. Mine, on the other hand, is quite free, unless I want to start sketching that cactus, which I don't. I don't want to do anything other than think about Aubrey.

His yellow tie had stood out brightly against his blue button down. The color fit him, I muse, sunshine and sunflowers. If I were to paint him, I would have to incorporate sunflowers. Pulling in a sharp breath at the direction of my thoughts, I shake my head to clear it. I haven't thought about painting in years, and I won't be treading down that road of thought now, especially not when I have someone so much more appealing to think about.

Aubrey left as soon as we settled on the wine bar for tonight. I grin as I scoop up the cold coffee cup, unfold myself from the seat, and saunter over to the dirty bin near the condiment nook. I deposit my half full cup in the plastic container, a rare occurrence of lax caffeine consumption, and head out the door. The warm sunshine hits my face, and I'm sure my smile would look sweet to anyone who saw it. The sunshine feels like Aubrey's gaze, and I'm over the moon with joy that I will see him again in a few short hours. I fish my keys out of my jeans pocket and walk briskly to my car. A few short hours, I assure myself. Then, I'm having wine with Aubrey Davies.

CHAPTER 2

*I*t really wasn't the smartest thing to ask Aubrey out before our business meeting was even over. But I cannot make myself regret it as I wait for him outside of my favorite place to relax, Tilly's Wine Bar and Grill. Tilly's is one of the few places from before I still frequent, here and the coffee shop. Coffee and wine, that's my lifeblood right there. I grin at myself and glance down at my watch. Early, I am fifteen minutes early. I lean against one of the columns of the outdoor patio. I chose not to change clothes because I doubt he will have the time and I want us on even footing. Shaking my head at that thought, I'm not even sure what that means, "even footing." God, I'm nervous now and I just want him to show up so...so... So something can happen, I force my mind to complete the thought. So something, anything can happen, then I won't be in this restless holding pattern forever. I'm momentarily stunned at my own train of thought.

Arms crossed against my chest, I'm frowning down at the ground trying not to let my nerves get the best of me when a warm hand touches my forearm. I yank my head up, and there he is. I let go of my breath and a calm washes over me. He looks concerned and a throb pounds through my chest as his face indicates the concern is for me. I grin at him, the joy back, bubbling up inside to calm the reservoir of pain ever-present inside me.

"Hello," I breathe out, allowing my gaze to drift over his face. "I'm glad you could make it."

His eyebrows quirk up and his look of concern is replaced with a look more teasing and playful than before. "Did you think I would stand you up? You're the best thing Oakland has going for it thus far."

"Oh really? Well, you've been here how long? A day or two? There are plenty of interesting sites to see."

"I'm looking at one right now." He's not blushing as he did at the coffee shop, and the confidence in his green eyes and satisfied smile pull me in. I don't have anything intelligent to say in response, so I push myself off the column. His hand falls away from my arm as I unfold them, and I almost grab it back. Too soon, Black, I admonish myself, too soon. Aubrey is looking me directly in the eyes, and I still don't have a response to his previous statement. His smile does not waver, in fact it deepens, the corners of his mouth curving more into his cheeks. Kiss it, I want to kiss the smile off of his face, swallow it down, and take it inside of me. He saves me from whatever unintelligent blather I might have managed to spout by winking at me and gesturing toward the door, "Shall we?"

"Yes, we shall," I reply, picking up his mock formality and running with it. "Gentleman first."

He laughs at that and is quick with a reply, "You have no idea."

I lead him around the patio, to the door on the other side. I open it and gesture for him to enter first.

"Thank you, kind sir," he quips as he enters Tilly's, the interior dark for a moment as my eyes adjust from the light outside. The sun has just gone down and the glorious reds and pinks of the sunset stream through the glass of the westward facing wall.

"Wow," Aubrey gasps, "that is a spectacular view. No wonder you like to come here at this time."

"I would love to see the sunrise, but only Tilly ever gets that view."

Aubrey hums his appreciation, and I can't help but smile at that. Another note to file away in my growing folder on him, hums when he likes something. I lead the way to a table near the glass wall. Normally, I would steer him toward a booth for more privacy, but I want to see more of him appreciating the natural wonder of the sunset. I can't believe the timing worked out so perfectly. I hadn't given a thought to the sunset tonight. Pulling out the chair with the best view, I gesture for him to sit in it.

"Thank you. My, my, aren't you the gentleman now."

I laugh as he sits in the chair. I step around to my own and slide in. "I'm glad you like the view. You can tell a lot about people by how they react to the beauty of the world."

"So this was a test of my artistic sensibilities?"

I laugh. "No, just good timing. I am an artist after all. I like to know how other people see the beautiful in the world. Or," I add, my thoughts suddenly turning solemn, "how they don't react to it at all."

"What do you mean?"

"People often walk right past the most beautiful sites, plants, flowers, sunsets, without ever noticing them. It's sad, and I don't quite understand as I cannot stop seeing them." I pause and wonder how the conversation deepened so fast. But Aubrey nods his head, his face reflecting a simpatico understanding.

"I know exactly what you mean. I will work for six months to a year on a park site, anticipating how everyone will react to the features. It doesn't matter what they are, I expect people to love them the way I have come to love them. But the reaction of the public often disappoints me."

Intrigued at this glimpse into how he views his work, I lean my elbows forward on the table and nod for him to continue.

"It seems selfish of me, I guess, but I want the people to see the beauty of the park as well as understand the labor that went into the process of creating it for them. Public spaces are for the community, meant to bring an extra dimension to our lives, whether that be a fountain to sit by on Sunday afternoons or trees for children to climb. That is the purpose of parks, but people do not seem to take them seriously. You know what they say, you don't know what you got till it's gone. But I don't want us to have to lose the spaces to appreciate them, you know what I mean?"

I grin at him, "Joni Mitchell would agree."

He laughs, "I'm sure she would."

"So, it seems we both believe people should stop and smell the roses more often."

"Not just more often," he replies, "every damn day."

"Agreed."

We sit in silence for a moment, but it is not awkward. The sunset casts glorious highlights across his hair and face. My fingers twitch for a moment, as if instinctively reaching for my brush. I avoid thinking about what that means by picking up one of the wine menus on the table.

"What do you recommend?"

"I recommend Tilly's expertise," I say, pointing at the menu. I look up to see Tilly making her way toward us from the bar. She doesn't usually come out to take orders, but I'm not surprised she has spotted me. It has been awhile since I was here.

"Black, you devil, I have not seen you in ages."

"I thought I would remedy that tonight. I will take tonight's house special. What would you like?"

Aubrey looks surprised at my question, and I almost laugh. He looks flustered for a moment, then randomly points to one of the red selections on his menu. "This one looks nice. I will have a glass of that."

"Sure thing, boys. I'll send Belinda right back out with those selections. It's good to see you, Black."

"You, too, Tilly." Tilly briskly walks back to the bar, chatting up customers along the way. She speaks to Belinda a moment, relaying our orders. My glances slides back to Aubrey who has a quizzical look on his face.

"I thought you said you come here often."

"I used to, and now, I have a reason to come back."

He blushes slightly, rightly understanding that I meant he is the reason I'm back here.

Ever the efficient wine steward, Tilly's right hand, Belinda, bustles up with our glasses, setting them neatly on the table in front of us. She grabs the card I offer her and runs off again with a wave before I can greet her.

"What should we toast to?" Aubrey asks as he slides his fingers around the stem of his glass.

I want to say something completely inappropriate, like "you," but since we just met, I offer "to life." He echoes me and clinks his glass against mine before bringing it to his lips to sip.

As I sip at my red wine, which turns out to taste quite nice, I consider feeling Black out with the general first date type questions, though I'm honestly too distracted by his presence to really care about his family or education or anything other than what his five o'clock shadow will feel like against my face, against my lips, my neck, lower. But since I do want to get to know the man, I swallow down my desire along with the wine and say, "Let's have some first date questions."

Black's grin pulls very wide and I realize what I just said.

"Unless of course this really isn't a date?" I'm embarrassed at myself. Twenty-nine years old and I sound like a teenager begging for reassurances from the jock who wants to fuck me on prom night.

"Oh," he replies, dropping his voice into a bedroom register, "it is most assuredly a date." He leans back in his chair, not taking his eyes off my now slightly red face, and threads his fingers behind his head. "I like the sound of a first date."

Now I'm so strangled up with desire, I find it hard to speak. I take a larger-than-normal gulp of my red wine then go with the first thing that comes to mind. "Let's go with standard gay guy questions, shall we?"

Raising a dark brow, he queries, "Standard gay guy questions, huh?"

I tap my fingernail against the stem of my glass. "As much as we want to believe otherwise, dating as a gay man is different than dating as a straight man even if you discount the difference in parts."

When he gives me a skeptical look, I point out, "Do straight guys ever discuss when they knew they were straight or share stories of coming out with their dates? 'Getting to know you' often involves more than just finding out each other's favorite colors."

His eyes crinkle in amusement and understanding. "Yeah, I get you. One of my lesbian friends believes your whole life is a process of coming out, first to one person and then another." He pauses a moment. "All right." He drops his hands from behind his head and makes a "come at me" gesture with his right hand. "Give me what you got."

"When did you come out to your parents?"

Black's visage fades to a slightly sad smile, and I want to kick myself for opening my mouth.

I stammer to apologize, "I'm sorry. Clearly, I asked the wrong question."

His smile quirks up a little and he shakes his head. "No, it's a completely valid question, and I want to answer. It's just that my parents passed away." He cocks his head to the left and looks up as if trying to remember a date. "Oh, almost 10 years ago now. They died in a car accident."

I set down my wine glass and, before thinking about it, grab his hand that is resting on the table. "I'm so sorry. You don't need to talk about this. Unless of course you want to?"

Black's grin pulls impossibly wider as he remarks, "Aubrey, you are something else."

I am startled by the statement, and for a second, I'm about to get offended.

"Oh no," he quickly rushes on, sensing my sudden annoyance, "I meant that as a compliment." He takes my hand from where it was laying on his right one and puts it in both of his. He starts rubbing the back of my hand then down my fingers and over my nails. Thank heaven I convinced myself I needed a manicure before going to another city. He looks me directly in the eyes and raises my hand to kiss the back of it. I swear to God if he keeps doing all of the sexy things, I am going to be rendered speechless. Or I might go up in flames right here in this wine bar. Then the bar would burn down around us and... I don't have any thoughts anymore because I am just too mesmerized by his lips touching the skin on the back of my hand. His smile turns more wicked, and he waggles his eyebrows at me. I can't help but laugh.

Throwing caution and my dignity to the wind, I laugh breathily and say, "Keep doing things like that and you're going to end up on top of me in the back seat of my rental car in about sixty seconds."

Black has the decency to finally repay all of my flustered responses with a slight blush across his cheek bones. I laugh at him in surprise and throw my free hand over my mouth and then speak through it, "Oh my God, I made you blush!"

That makes Black blush harder, and I am laughing way too loud for the place we are in. I am freed by his show of embarrassment far more than the alcohol. Black's smile is sheepish now.

"That's not hard to accomplish, Aubrey." A thrill runs through me when he says my name.

"Really?"

"I don't think you see yourself as the world does."

Now it is my turn to blush, again. "I'm not sure what you mean."

"You're gorgeous. At least half of the people in here are eyeing you right now."

I whip my head around then whip it back just as quickly. The look on Black's face is almost reverent now, and I swallow hard. Since it is literally true, I gasp out, "I don't know what to say to that."

A smile that's just a touch wicked sits across Black's face.

"You look like a biker on a romance novel cover," I murmur.

Black throws his head back and laughs loudly. I'm now wearing a silly grin as I not so smoothly down the last of my wine. I'm shocked I drank it so quickly when Black has barely touched his.

"I need another," I say, as I rise and try to remove my hand from where Black is still holding it. I tug it, and Black winks at me before letting me go.

"Hurry back," he practically purrs as I dash away toward the bar. This place is busy, but not packed, so I reach the bartender in a matter of minutes.

"I'll have another of the red. Sorry, I have no clue what I ordered earlier," I tell Tilly.

"No problem, fella." The muscled-up bartender smirks at me, but she seems to be friendly, so I smile back at her. I had not paid much attention to her when she took our order earlier, much more intent on watching Black at the time.

"New in town?" she queries as she turns away from me toward the wine rack. I study the biker insignia on the back of her leather vest. The words "The Sirens" are emblazoned the top of the vest in blood red letters. The siren curls up on a rock jutting out of the sea, her hair the same blood red shade. Her mouth is open on a scream, a fierce warrior's face blazing with defiance. For an embroidered piece, it is richly detailed. This figure looks like a cross between a mermaid and a banshee, her vibrant emerald eyes are almost intimidating. I shake my head at that weird thought. The biker bartender looks so out of place in here, and a question pops out of my mouth before I can think the better of it.

"If you don't mind my asking, how did you end up here? You look more like a biker bar chick." Tilly throws back her head and laughs, her triple set of earrings tinkling musically. When she recovers, she rubs one side of her partially shaven head. Somehow, I had managed to miss the blue color of the faux hawk running down the middle of her head.

"Bikers and wine bars mix better than you might think. I own the joint."

"I'm here for work." I belatedly answer her previous question and hope I didn't offend her with mine.

"Well," she replies over her shoulder as she pours more of the red into my glass, "I knew you had to be new *and* something special for Black to bring you in here."

I frown at that and, before I can think better of it, ask, "What does that mean?"

She turns with my glass of wine and holds her free hand up, in a placating gesture. Tattoos are sprinkled across the backs of her fingers on the hand that holds the wine glass and her other palm contains some sort of image I cannot quite make out.

"No offense meant there, hon. I am glad Black is finally back out there."

I'm puzzled and annoyed by her comment. It seems like information I should receive from the man in question, not his bartender.

"Thanks," I mutter as I pick up the full glass she has finally set in front of me. I'm almost desperate to return to our table. As I walk back, Black's dark brown eyes watch me the whole way, the intensity so deep my skin feels like it is prickling all over. I feel like I'm swimming in an ocean far out of my depth. But instead of feeling afraid, I'm exhilarated. My lips feel tingly as do my fingertips. As I draw closer to our table, I'm sure he's feeling something similar judging by the look on his face. Nothing in my life has felt this way before, like there is an invisible thread pulling us together. My head tells me to cool it, but every other part, my heart included, leans into the pull without hesitation. I have no clue what I'm doing, but as long as it keeps this man in my orbit, I really don't care. I sit in my chair again and it's like someone turned on a sun inside of me. I'm warmed, I'm delighted, and I want more.

CHAPTER 3

$\mathcal{A}$s Aubrey sauntered up to the bar for a second glass of wine, I watched the way his ass moved, a subtle sway to his hips, his cheeks practically cupped by his dark brown slacks. I'm wearing my usual attire, black T-shirt and jeans with combat boots. His cornflower blue button down has been unbuttoned at the neck, his bright yellow tie lost somewhere along the way. I imagine him yanking it off and throwing it away from himself and chuckle at the image. My dick doesn't think it's funny. My dick thinks it's hot as hell.

At face value, the day and our interactions have been. . . strange, off-kilter in the best way possible. I barely know a thing about him, and I'm dying to remedy that lack. I absentmindedly rub my chest over my heart. Looking down, I realize what I am doing. He hit me there, smack in the solar plexus, as soon as I saw him sitting at that table in the coffee shop.

I'm also dying to kiss him, amongst other things. I watch him the whole time, noticing his interaction with Tilly, the bar owner, was a little strained at the end. Weird. Tilly is usually friendly, in a gruff biker chick sort of way, so I'm surprised she didn't click with Aubrey. But as Aubrey turns and walks back toward me, all thought of that stops and all I can do is stare at his graceful figure. He is tall, lightly muscled, with a runner's or swimmer's body, but I recall the nice curve of his ass I greedily watched when he left the table.

His fingers are long and slim, his nails clearly manicured, but not colored. His grasp on his wine glass is firm, and I want to feel those hands all over me. He is not overtly feminine, but his features are softer than mine and the corners of his lips curl up naturally. His brows are almost delicate, and he takes this moment to arch them up at me, deepening the natural curve of his lips into a smile. Sunshine. For the second time since I met him, his smile reminds me of sunshine: warm, giving, comforting. But it doesn't just make me comfortable. It makes me almost squirm in my seat as my desire for him ratchets suddenly higher and I am unsure I will be able to find my ability to use language. At this precise moment, all my tongue wants to do is taste him, his lips and the alabaster skin of his neck his loosened button down has revealed.

Though I've had a breather now—long enough to put away the momentary sadness of thinking of my parents' deaths—I've become so entranced by his beauty that I'm unsure I will be much good at conversation. But, as soon as he sits down, I try to pick up our previous topic and finally answer his first "gay guy date question."

"My mom caught me kissing Bobby Banks at my fifth birthday party. A little early to go around kissing people, I know, but I have to tell you, Bobby Banks was a cutie."

Aubrey laughs, his smile drawing me in like the proverbial moth to a flame, or in this case, like a flower toward the sun.

"So, I didn't have much to tell. They always knew. My mom went out of her way to make life easy for me. She must have sought out advice from someone because by the time I was ready to tell her during my early teen years, I had no doubts my parents would accept me."

Aubrey nods. "So you knew you could trust them. That is really lucky."

I sigh, caught up in bittersweet memories. "I know. Honestly though, I didn't really understand liking boys instead of girls was anything out of the ordinary until I was about ten years old. Because I always liked watching everyone, imagining how the parts of their bodies fit together and how I could draw them, I never considered that there were some bodies I was not supposed to like looking at. As soon as I could hold a pencil in my hand, I was drawing everyone and everything I saw in the thick artist pads my mom started buying me when I was three and wouldn't stop drawing on the walls."

Aubrey takes another sip of wine and smiles softly at me, which encourages me in this impromptu walk down memory lane. "What happened when you were ten?"

Breathing deeply, I relay the memory of the first moment I knew my liking boys would not be acceptable to everyone. "Some politician on TV was railing against homosexuality. When I asked my mom what that meant, she told me some girls like girls and some boys like boys. I remember nodding because I still had a crush on Bobby Banks."

Aubrey laughs softly, "He must have been a real cutie."

Chuckling, I nod and continue my story. "Black hair, blue eyes, and alabaster skin. It was a lethal combination to my childhood self."

Aubrey grins at me over the top of his wine glass.

"I'm still quite partial to alabaster skin," I murmur, winking at him. A faint blush colors his cheeks, and he swallows a larger sip of wine, causing me to think incredibly wicked thoughts about those lips and that skin which blushes so prettily.

Shaking my head to refocus on the rather somber story I just interrupted with flirting, I sigh and pick the thread back up. "My mom explained that some people didn't want boys to like boys or girls to like girls. Though I could tell it made her upset, she told me some people wanted to make those people's lives harder. I must have looked horrified because my mother hugged me hard and reassured me that no matter who I loved, she and my father would always love me."

I pause for a moment, realizing I had not thought of my childhood love in years. Swallowing a growing knot of emotion, I look into Aubrey's bright eyes and find myself relating the most horrible memory of my journey into adulthood as a gay man.

"Things didn't turn out so well for Bobby though."

Aubrey's smile drops, and his expression grows wary. "Oh, no. What happened to him?"

"He tried to come out to his parents when he was seventeen. They threw him out of their house. I hadn't fully realized how easy I had it until that day. We were still friends, and he told me after school that he would never see me again because his parents were sending him away. I was so shocked. I ran home to my mother and she just held me and told me that she would never abandon me. Even though they'd always known, even though I had officially come out to them a few years before, I'd needed to hear that. Though I was always closest to my mom, even my dad tried to help once they found out how poorly Bobby's parents had treated their son. They wanted to offer to take Bobby in as we had an extra bedroom. But he was shipped off to a distant relative before they had a chance to speak with his parents."

I lean back in my chair and watch Aubrey's sweetly concerned expression, "So that's my story, Aubrey."

I draw out his name and his clear forest green eyes widen, clearly affected by my little tale and I can only hope by me. His brow is smooth, and his auburn bangs fall forward as he leans his elbows on the table.

"Thank you for telling me, Black."

"Your turn," I murmur, mesmerized by his aquiline nose, so pert on his face. His cheek bones are strong, and I think I might see some light freckles across them and his nose. It would be mundane and not very artistic of me to describe his lips as perfectly formed, but they are, not too full, not too thin, maybe a little wide, but as Goldilocks said, just right. He squirms and blushes under my perusal.

"What?" He croaks out, pink staining his alabaster skin again, and I want to lick it up. I imagine his blush tastes like strawberries against the cream of his skin.

"Coming out? To your family? Have you forgotten your own question?" I tease. Pleased, oh, so very pleased that he is as flustered as I am.

I suddenly realize my first question to Black is harder to answer than I imagined. I'm feeling silly, so I say, "Picture it, Cicely, 1912."

Black immediately laughs. "Do go on, Sophia."

Outrageously excited that he also grew up on *The Golden Girls*, I continue, "Actually, it was Chicago, circa 2001. I was a skinny thirteen-year-old with a bully problem." As I retell the story, I slip back into the memory.

"He called me a fag," I sob into my hands. My aunt pulls my hands away from my eyes and draws my gangly teenaged body into her lap.

"I'm sorry, honey."

"But I am."

"You're what, honey?"

"Gay," I whisper into her soft golden waves where I've nestled my head against her cheek.

"Thank you for telling me, Aubrey. I love you."

"You're not mad?" She laughs, softly at first, then almost chokes and starts to laugh harder.

"You really haven't figured it out yet?"

I pull back and stare at her smiling face and twinkling blue eyes.

"What?" I ask suspiciously.

Her grin got wider, and she shuffles me off her lap but holds my hands in hers.

"My best friend, Susan."

"What about her?"

"Really, Aubrey? Ah," she sighs, "the innocence of youth. Or rather the innocence of you, Aubrey. Susan is my girlfriend, has been since before you were born."

"But, but, you never said. And you never kiss in front of me. And she doesn't live with us." My mind is a clamor with unanswered questions. Suddenly, I feel angry and confused.

"Why didn't you tell me?" I pull my hands out of her lap, and go to rise, but she stops me with a big hug.

"Oh, Aubrey, I thought you knew. I'm from a generation that was still expected to hide. Susan and I have never been publicly affectionate, and I did have to worry about gaining and keeping custody of you."

I practically collapse against her as I realize what she means.

"You could lose me," I whisper, terror flooding my veins.

"Not likely, honey bunny. I've had you for ten years now. Family courts don't like to mess with easy cases like ours. Your parents were smart. They had a will with me listed as the guardian in case of emergency."

She smiles fondly at me again, managing to pull me into her lap like I am a toddler. I lace my arms around her neck and lean into her.

"Plus, I've known Judge Walters since we were both freshman sneaking around in the gym bleachers, kissing forbidden crushes. I caught him with the quarterback he was tutoring, and he caught me with the lead flag girl. Friends ever since. But, still, the law does not protect me, so I've had to be careful. But, Aubrey," she pauses to kiss my forehead and hug me tighter. "I really thought you knew. I'm sorry I never said anything. I guess you really aren't psychic, huh?"

"No, Aunt Patty Cakes, I'm not." She laughs. "But are you happy with how things are, Aunt Patty?"

"What do you mean?"

"If you didn't have me, then you and Susan could be out. You could live together and be a family."

She squeezes me tighter.

"Oh, Aubrey. I've very happy with the way things are. Susan is a pilot and is gone a lot. I'd be lonely without you. Raising you has been a highlight of my life. I'd never trade that for anything. It's still not that safe for us to be too far out. Our friends know and now you do. I don't regret anything. I do hope that your journey will be easier, but I can't promise it will be."

Black is now leaning forward, his elbows on the table and his chin in his hands. "You're a natural storyteller. I felt like I was right there."

I'm pleased by the praise and with the prospect of having done Aunt Patty justice. "My parents died in a car accident when I was three years old. Aunt Patty, my dad's sister, was my listed guardian, and she adopted me immediately. I guess I wasn't very perceptive as a kid, because I had no clue Aunt Susan was her girlfriend. They are still together, happy as ever. They are most happy when they are trying to fix me up with random guys. You would not believe the number of delivery men those two have tried to pick-up on my behalf."

We are both laughing, and Black responds, "You know what they say about a man in uniform."

"That he has a job that provides his clothes for him?"

"Exactly," Black quips.

"That is one thing we have in common then."

"Of all the things to have in common, dead parents is not exactly promising."

"Shush, Black. I'm trying to make a go of it here."

"All right then, *Aubrey*." He emphasizes my name in such a way that I can't stop laughing. He winks at me, nods toward my half empty wine glass, and thunks his now empty one with his middle finger. "I need to catch up with you."

"Fine by me."

"Will you come with me?"

"But, of course!"

We rise from our chairs, and I fall in step with him as he comes around the table. He's so close the air feels like it is sizzling and my skin is shivering, and I decide to stop cataloguing my physical responses to Black and just walk up to the bar with him. Black leans against the bar when we arrive, setting his glass down and nodding toward Tilly who is at the opposite end chatting up another patron. I take her responding nod to mean she will be down in a minute. I slide onto one of the bar stools and angle myself toward Black. He turns so he is facing me with a sweet smile playing across his lips. The desire to kiss him overwhelms me, and before I'm aware of forming the thought, I spit it right out. "May I kiss you?"

My breath stalls in my lungs for a moment when Aubrey asks softly, "May I kiss you?" I'm overwhelmed by how much I want this. His earnest face is closer to mine than it was before, but gentleman that he is turning out to be, he doesn't take what has not been expressly given. I breathe in a deep breath, the moment taking on far too much significance for me to handle. Then my wickedness is back, and I know exactly how to answer him.

"First of all," I whisper as I lean closer into his space, "I love that you used correct grammar." Aubrey smiles, but does not laugh, the moment apparently as heavy for him as it is for me. "And secondly, yes, you may kiss me."

Aubrey sets down his glass on the bar, leaning forward as I slide closer to him. He gently slants his lips against mine, firmly pressing into my mouth, his lips slightly parted. His left hand, which had been resting on the bar, slides up my forearm. His other hand touches my shoulder gently, lightly, as he pulls back to look at my face, gauging my reaction. I'm floored, all thought left my mind with the touch of his soft warm lips. I must look dazed as a small smile flits across the lips he just touched to mine. So much was in that small kiss but not enough.

He leans forward again, and I meet him halfway, his gentle motion slamming against my sudden movement forward. He gasps, tightening his hold on my arm. I take advantage of the further parting of his lips and sweep my tongue into his mouth. This time, I moan as I taste the wine on his tongue. I may have lunged forward into this kiss, but now I want to explore slowly, softly. Our tongues slide against each other, languidly, as if this isn't our second kiss, as if we've been doing this forever. Aubrey groans and suddenly shifts, tilting his head from the left to the right, chasing my tongue back into my mouth with his. His hand on my shoulder slides into my hair, fisting it at the nape of my neck. Before I can slide my arm off the bar and around him, I hear a loud throat clearing noise and slowly pull back, kissing his lips softly one more time before turning my attention to Tilly. She has an amused look on her face, one eyebrow cocked up.

"As hot as this is for me to witness, you might want to take it elsewhere before you attract anyone else's attention."

Aubrey's eyes go wide, and a blush sweeps up his neck and face causing me to laugh. He looks from me to Tilly and back again, his flush of embarrassment turning up my desire.

"Come on," I murmur, disentangling Aubrey's hand from my hair before I push away from the bar and offer him my hand. We barely behave ourselves on our way out of the bar. As soon as we hit fresh air, Aubrey grabs me by the face, backs me against the brick exterior wall of Tilly's, and proceeds to kiss me within an inch of my life. He consumes my mouth, tilting my chin down and his up, bridging our slight height difference as he leans hard against me. He still clasps my hand in his and presses our intertwined fingers against my chest as he nips my lips, licking my bottom one before plunging his tongue back into my mouth.

Somehow, we end up in the parking lot, leaning against a car I can only hope is his. I back him up against the passenger side and slide one hand into his auburn hair as I trace a path across his skin with the other. Starting with the shell of his right ear, I run my index finger over it then slowly down his neck and over his thudding pulse. He looks at me with those glittering green eyes, his lips slightly red from our kisses. I crowd him further into the car, bridging what little space existed between our bodies, pinning him against the door with my hips. He gives an involuntary cry as our groins come into contact, both hard, both aching. I lean in slowly as my grip on his hair tightens. The look on his face suggests he is in my thrall, but the exact opposite is true: I am utterly spellbound by him. I touch my lips to his softly as the painful throbbing in my chest accelerates.

"Aubrey," I somehow manage to breathe out. He nips at my lower lip, sending a shudder through my body. I hear a metallic clink and realize Aubrey has pulled the door handle. He pushes me back a step, almost roughly, as he moves forward to open the back door. Somehow gracefully, he manages to climb into the backseat without turning around or letting me go, pulling me in with him. I follow where I am led. Once I manage to pull my long legs inside the cramped backseat of his late model sedan, I yank the door closed behind me. Then, all bets are off. His hand finds its way into my shoulder length hair, his grip almost punishing. The slight pain only increases my desire, and when he nips my lower lip, I growl involuntarily. Aubrey moans into my mouth, his other hand having found its way under my T-shirt. He is stroking my chest, now firmly, then gently, his fingers almost mimicking what his tongue is doing to my mouth. When his fingers graze my nipple, I cry out, the intense pleasure shooting throughout my entire body. Aubrey chuckles into my mouth and pulls back slightly.

"Good to know, very good to know." Then he uses the knowledge to his advantage by running his nail lightly over the other nipple. I practically buck beneath him as the sensation slams through my body, my movement jostling him forward into my lap. "Black," he breathes against my lips, and his kiss becomes softer, sweeter, more earnest. I'm trembling now, and not just because of his wicked fingers on my surprisingly sensitive nipples. He slips his hand from underneath my shirt and slides his other hand from my hair. He keeps pressing his lips softly against mine, now with tongue, then without, and the moment swells with so much more than desire.

Aubrey pulls back, putting some distance between our heated bodies. He slips backward out of my lap and leans back against the seat. Yanking gently on the bottom of my shirt, he looks at his hands instead of my face and says, "As much as I would like to rip off all of your clothing and mount you right here and now, I think that would be rushing things a little bit. So maybe," he continues, his eyes finally returning to mine, "I should just kiss you goodnight."

I'm not sure where I found my voice, but it answers "yes" on a barely audible whisper. Aubrey smiles very softly, his eyes brilliant, practically glowing in dark of the night. He bites his lip, and the look on his face shifts to determined. "I want to see you again."

All I can do is whisper "yes" again. It is the only word I know.

"Not for work, I mean."

"Yes."

He grins at that, grabs my face, and kisses me again. "Now, you have to go home, and I have to go through a drive-thru because we forgot to eat." He giggles, and I finally find some more of those language skills I usually have at the ready.

"You were a distraction."

"No, *you* were the distraction."

"I stand corrected."

Aubrey slides his eyes down my body and aims a knowing glance at my groin. "I can see that."

"No, you can't. Not tonight anyway, you already told me to go home."

Aubrey groans and throws himself back against the seat cushions again. "Don't remind me. I'm being a good citizen by not taking advantage of the townsfolk."

I laugh hard and fall forward into his lap. I look up at him from this vantage point, and it is certainly a view I want to have again.

"So, have you had a good introduction to the great city of Oakland?"

"I believe I have."

"I have to go home?"

"Yes, you do."

"By myself?"

"Yes, by yourself."

"You're mean."

Aubrey laughs. "To you and me both."

I sit up and grab his face, a joyful silliness overtaking me, so I pepper kisses all over his face. He laughs and pretends to push me away, but his grip on my shirt keeps pulling me back in.

"I can't go if you don't let go of my shirt."

"That can't be true."

"But, alas, it is. I can't go around town shirtless either, in case you were intending to keep mine."

"Well, you could."

At that, I give in to my insane desire to tickle him and am rewarded with a howl when my fingers slip across his lower belly. I look down, seeing his shirt has come untucked from his slacks, allowing me to stroke his warm, flat stomach. Desire flares hard, and all I want to do is lay him out under me in that tiny back seat. I swallow hard to get myself under control. When my eyes return to his, I can see that he knows exactly what I was thinking. A naughty little grin ticks up the corners of his mouth.

"Later," he murmurs, and I nod, taking the word as a promise. He sits up and leans his forehead against mine, the gesture feeling intimate and special. He looks into my eyes and murmurs, "Goodnight, Black."

"Goodnight, Aubrey." I lean forward slightly and kiss his lips softly. It is so hard to part from them, from him. He lets me pull back and watches as I open the car door and slip out. He smiles at me and I smile back. I shut the door firmly and force myself to walk to my car. I don't allow myself to look back.

By the time I arrive home, I have a text from Tilly.

You forgot to close out your tab AND you forgot your card. Come by tomorrow to pick it up. Expect to dish on the auburn-haired cutie.

I laugh and roll my eyes. Auburn-haired cutie, indeed.

CHAPTER 4

og. Dust. Crackles of light and sound through the smoky air. Searching for. . . someone. A moan, a cry. A voice, pleading, "Black, please! Help me!" Aubrey's voice. But how is he here? He can't be here. A scream, a grind of metal and glass clashing against one another. Silence. Deafening silence. A final scream, *NO!!! No! No! No!* I scream myself awake, alone in my bed. Heart pounding, the sound of the blood in my veins echoes through my skull. I jerk myself upright and comb my hands through my hair. Before I realize it, I am pulling much too hard at the roots. *Deep breaths, Black. Deep breaths. It was just a nightmare.*

Since I am calming down, I cannot resist rolling my eyes at myself. *Sure, I'm calming down so well I'm trying to pull my own hair out. Yeah, that is an encouraging sign.* I try to remember the grounding techniques I researched online. I close my eyes and breathe deeply again, air in and out of my lungs. My heart is still thumping hard in my chest, but at least I can unclench my fists from my hair and let them drop into my lap. One small victory at a time, I think wryly. *Because being able to breath without panic is such a massive accomplishment.* Shove it, Black, I admonish myself. My internal voice is a negative asshole. I shake my head at my line of thought. *Great, now I'm holding two sided conversations in my own head.* I fist my hair in my hands again as the desire to scream rises once more, overwhelming me. A shockingly loud growl of anguish rumbles through my throat and out my clenched teeth. Not better, Black, calm the fuck down!

Giving in to this consuming rush of anguish, I scream, and it lasts such a long time that I am without air by the time it peters out. I fall back against my pillows, dragging lungfuls of air into my body. I'm not okay, and I have the sudden realization that yesterday I thought I was.

The coffee mug warms the palm of my hand. Looking down into the dark blonde liquid, I realize how cold I am even though it's a bright spring morning. Wrapping my right hand around the other side of the mug, I lift it to my lips to sip the dark roast and cream. My mind is blank, not calm, more like frozen. The nightmare shook me far more than I want to admit. Finally coming back to myself after the panic recedes is just as painful as the panic itself. "Fuck," I exhale softly. It has been over a year since I've had to deal with this, and I know exactly why I had that dream. Except. . . it wasn't a car crash that ended my life before. I suck in painful lungfuls of air as a tide of ugly emotion rises inside me. I have no choice but to breathe slowly, even though a vice is crushing my chest from the inside.

A long ten minutes later, I've calmed down enough to focus on my coffee and the sunrise just peeking over the trees behind my house. I hear a little scrambling noise and grin because it means Benny is back. I rise from my chair at my back-patio table and look out over the lawn to the bird feeder. Sure enough, a fat gray squirrel is sitting in the pile of bird seed munching away. Occasionally, he will look up and around, obviously making sure no wrens or warblers are diving bombing toward him. I raise my mug to the little miscreant as I walk over to the deck fence. Leaning my hip against it, I watch my fat and furry little friend pack away the seeds.

"Hey, Benny," I call, "leave a few for the birds."

Since he knows me and deigns to allow me thirty feet across the lawn from his breakfast, he just glances over his shoulder at me, a pouty look on his face. I laugh because the furred little thief has that haughty royalty look down pat. I toast him again, "Thanks, Benny, I needed the laugh." He twitches his tail and turns his back on me, diving his paws back into the pile of seeds and scooping little clawfuls into his mouth. I shake my head at the greedy little squirrel and take another sip of coffee as I watch the sunrise send streaks of pink and yellow across the dawn sky.

Because I have known Tilly for years, I know she is down at the bar bright and early. It is a little chilly this morning, and since I spent the last hour on my patio, I'm wearing my leather jacket when I stride into Tilly's. She is behind the bar, buffing wine glasses.

"Black!" Tilly practically screeches at me, and I wince.

"Oh, you didn't have that much to drink last night. Unless you two picked up one for the road?"

"No, we didn't. You got my card?"

"Now don't be rude, Black." Tilly comes from behind the bar and pulls the card from her apron pocket. When I step forward and try to take it, she pulls it back and raises an eyebrow at me.

"Fine, Tilly. What do you want to know?"

"Where did you meet him?"

"Work."

"Well, aren't you Mister Sunshine this morning. Trouble in paradise already?"

I'm still on edge from that nightmare, and I'm really not in the mood for this friendly inquisition. I yank the card out of her hand, surprising her. Slipping it into my back pocket, I turn on my heel to go.

"Black," Tilly calls after me, a concerned tone in her voice now.

I stop my forward motion and eye the door. Six more feet and I will be out on the street and free from this interrogation. But I know why Tilly is acting this way, so I turn around slowly. I sigh. "What, Tilly?"

"I'm worried about you, okay? Aren't your friends allowed to worry? I haven't seen you in here in close to a year. I know why you haven't been back. But suddenly you show up with a gorgeous new guy, who seems sweet by the way, and the two of you can't keep your hands off each other. Then, you arrive surly the next morning. Give a friend a break. I don't worry about just anyone."

I sigh, knowing I owe her an apology. "I know, Tilly. It's just hard, okay? His name is Aubrey, by the way. He's the new park planner for the city, and they want another statue from me. We met yesterday to iron out the details and . . ."

"And what?"

Good question, I think, good question. I shrug because I don't have an answer. That dream knocked me out of balance just as much as Aubrey himself did, and I really don't know what to think.

"Black."

"What, Tilly? What do you want me to say? It's hard and you know why."

"But you clearly like him. Even without the impromptu make-out scene up front here, and the one just outside, you had to like him to bring him here."

"Wait, you saw that? You saw us outside the door?"

Tilly laughs at my incredulous look. "It's not magic. I have cameras."

I laugh too. "And you were nosy enough to check what you could see."

"Yep."

"I don't know what to tell you, Tilly."

Tilly changes the subject on me, and I dislike this direction of conversation even more than the previous one. "Have you spoken to Gloria?"

I fist my hands involuntarily as a wave of pain crashes through me. "Really, Tilly? Right now? You are going to ask me that right now?"

"She misses you, you know."

I shake my head and turn to go. I can hear her boots on the floor as she follows me, so I stop in front of the door.

"I'm sorry. I shouldn't have mentioned it. But she's hurting too. That is the last thing I am going to say on the topic." She touches my arm and pulls, making me turn around to face her. "I'm happy for you. She would be happy for you."

"I thought you said you were dropping the subject."

She laughs lightly, "Sorry, bartender's habit, butting into everyone's business."

I sigh again and close my eyes for a moment. After that dream, Gloria is the one of the last people I want to think about right now. "It's fine."

"Do come back, Black. I've missed you. Bring Aubrey."

I blink my eyes open. Tilly has such a look of concern on her face I have to laugh. I scrub my hand over my jaw and nod. "Yeah, I probably will."

"One more prying question before you go."

I roll my eyes at that. "Like I could stop you."

"No, you couldn't. Your mood this morning isn't because of him? You two seemed on *good terms* last night." She's smirking now, and I can't help but laugh.

"Yes, we are still on *good terms*, as you so eloquently put it."

"Good! Glad to hear it!" She claps her hands once. "Now, get out of here and go kiss that man. You better come back around here soon."

"I will."

"Will what? Kiss him or come back?"

I laugh again. "Both." I grab her and pull her into a quick hug. She pats me once on the back. "Thanks," I whisper in her ear before I release her short form from my arms.

"You're welcome. Now scoot. I have way too much to do to stand here and flirt with you."

"As if you would. I'm not your type."

"Nope, wrong things in the wrong places, I'm afraid."

I turn to go as she makes her way around the bar again. "Thanks,

Tilly," I call over my shoulder. She nods, and I finally escape back into the sunlight. I pause on her doorstep for a moment and breathe in, slow deep breaths. I honestly don't know what I'm going to do about Aubrey, about anything. But the sunshine reminds me of him, and I can't help but smile.

CHAPTER 5

*L*eaning against the counter of my hotel suite's small kitchenette, I'm sipping my morning coffee when my phone rings. I glance over at where it sits on the counter. It lights up with a familiar name, so I smile and swap my cup for the phone.

"Hey, Aunt Patty."

"It's your Aunt Susan."

"Hey, Aunt Susan. Good to hear from you. What's up?"

"How's Oakland?"

"Fair to middling."

She laughs, and I can hear my Aunt Patty talking in the background.

"What did she say?"

"Patty Cakes says to bring home a man." My aunt cackles over the phone, and I can't help but laugh with her.

"Tell Aunt Patty I'm here to do a job."

"So what? Doesn't mean you can't have a little fun. Aubrey, life happens when you're not looking. But seriously, honey, we just want you to be happy. We don't want you to be lonely, so keep an open heart and open eyes. I'm sure that big city has lots of pretty boys."

"How would you know, Aunt Susan?"

"I have eyes. Just because I prefer a dame in a skirt doesn't mean I haven't noticed what's going on around me."

At this point, I am laughing so hard I almost drop the telephone. Scrambling to put it back to my ear, I laugh out, "Seriously, you two are a menace to society. And I love you for it. But, umm. . . I sort of met someone already."

"What?" Aunt Susan shrieks in my ear. Now I can hear Aunt Patty's voice more clearly. "What did he say?"

"He said he 'sort of met someone already!'"

"Give me the phone." Shuffling noises ensue, then my Aunt Patty's voice fills the phone line. "Aubrey?"

"Yeah, Aunt Patty?" I'm not doing a good job of containing my laughter.

"Don't 'yeah, Aunt Patty' me, you miscreant. What do you mean you 'sort of met someone already?'"

"Do you need a dictionary, Aunt Patty Cakes?"

"Aubrey!"

I lift my mug up to my mouth with my free hand, taking a sip and purposely leaving her

in suspense for a moment. "Yes, Aunt Patty Cakes?"

"You are a horrible child; do you know that?"

I laugh. "Yes, I do."

"Fine, don't tell me. I'm gonna hang up."

"I doubt it."

"Aubrey!"

I giggle again, then cut her a break. "He's the artist the city hired to create a sculpture for them. We met over coffee yesterday and well. . ."

"Well, what, Aubrey? Don't keep us in suspense!" Patty must have put me on speakerphone because now my aunts are tag team interrogating me.

"He asked me out to a wine bar. We had a nice date."

"Nice date? What does that mean?" demands Susan.

I take another sip of coffee before replying. "It means we had wine and a nice time."

Susan tries to cajole me for details, "And by nice, you mean something naughty, right?" I can practically hear her waggling her eyebrows at me. I grin at that.

"A gentleman does not kiss and tell, Aunt Susie Q."

"Sooooo...there was kissing?"

Aunt Patty is laughing now and so am I. "Nope, no more details for you two. I have to go to work. Plenty to do here."

"Hey! What's his name?"

I frown, contemplating how Black reacted when I called him by his first name yesterday morning. A look of incredible pain had crossed his face, and I felt stabbed in the heart by the expression. Sadness had radiated off him, and in that moment, I could do nothing but attempt to soothe him. I swallow my coffee and finally reply, "His name is Ian James Black, officially. But he goes by Black."

"Black, huh? Sounds sexy." Susan chimes in. Both women laugh, and I can't help but smile.

"I do have to go now, Aunties."

"Keep us updated. Take care." My aunts yell their goodbyes over each other, and a swell of love for the women who raised me fills my chest.

"Bye, love you."

"Love you, too, Aubrey." Before I can hang up, Aunt Susan has one last tidbit of advice for me. "Go be naughty!" I laugh and end the call. As I lean against the counter, I drink down the rest of my coffee as I think about Black: his eyes, his hair, his soft lips, and his strange aversion to his own first name. Shaking my head, I laugh at myself. I'm not going to figure it out now, and I am technically on the clock. I drain the rest of my mug of coffee, wash it in the sink, and place it in dishrack. Thus, my day begins, caffeinated with a tall, dark, handsome, and mysterious man on my mind.

The next phone call of the day is not nearly as pleasant. I'm reading contractor bids in preparation for a couple of meetings this afternoon when my phone rings again. This time, I recognize the number of the Oakland City Council secretary, Jenene.

"Hello, Jenene. How are you?"

"Mmm... I'm fine, Mr. Davies. But a few of the council members have expressed concern over the new design details you submitted yesterday."

"Which ones, Jenene? I submitted about a ream of paper yesterday. Oh, and by the way, call me Aubrey."

"Well, Aubrey," Jenene is hesitating as if she doesn't want to relay the information she has been tasked with delivering.

"It's fine, Jenene. What is the council's complaint?"

She sighs, clearly relieved I'm not going to shoot off my mouth at the messenger. "A few of the council members are not pleased Mr. Black will not be creating a new western style sculpture. His last one is incredibly popular, and they don't understand why we can't order something similar."

"Because the man made it very clear yesterday that he won't be doing any more work in that style. He has a line of sculptures featuring native plants which has already met with success in neighboring states. He promised to create a wholly original work in his new theme. I explained this all quite clearly in the paperwork I submitted yesterday."

"Yeah," Jenene's voice drops into a conspiratorial whisper, "you and I both know that. But Mr. Owens pitched a fit, and that set Mrs. Swift off. You know the drill. You've worked with these types of committees before."

"Yes, in fact, I have. So, what exactly do they want from me now? Black is unlikely to change his mind. He was very vehement on the topic yesterday."

"A proof of concept proposal would go a long way toward smoothing some ruffled feathers. Black is a very popular artist around here. Plus, he is well liked in general. I don't think it will take too much to persuade the council to see his perspective. Do you want to call him or should I?"

"No, Jenene. I told him I would take care of it, and I will. Does he have an up-to-date website? I can pull together the proof of concept file myself."

"Yes, I'll email you the link now. Thanks, Aubrey."

"You're welcome, Jenene. When do they want this?"

Jenene sighs and hesitates. "They want it today, by three."

It is my turn to sigh now. "I have two contractor meetings scheduled for this afternoon."

"Sorry."

"It is one now. Tell Mr. Owen I will have the proof of concept down to you by three. Let me guess. They want to speak with me in person?"

"Sorry!"

I roll my eyes then rub my temples absentmindedly. Is this bullshit giving me a headache?

"No worries, Jenene. It is par for the course."

"Well, no matter, sorry you have to pull all this together at the last minute. Are you sure you don't want me to call Black?"

"Absolutely positive. I already know my argument. I just have to type it up and pull some stuff from Black's website."

"Okay then. I'll see you at three."

"You, too, Jenene."

I angrily stab the end call button on my phone. Taking a deep breath, I roll my shoulders and sift through my list of contact numbers. I have meetings to reschedule, a mini-argument to write, and pictures to pull from the internet. This afternoon just turned into a grind.

An hour and a half later, I have a two-page proof of concept and a binder full of photos of Black's native plant sculptures. If I had the time, I would love to study them. Even at first glance, they are impressive. *Just like the man himself.* I chuckle as I grab up my keys and throw on my suit jacket. If these staid, old farts won't listen to reason, I will have to call in Black. But I really don't want to worry him. I sigh as I leave my suite. Today is not turning out to be as good as yesterday. I grin, and I let my mind wander to lustful thoughts as I head out the door to face the Oakland City Council.

The emergency council meeting to discuss the new sculpture design ate up my whole afternoon. I had to reschedule the two contractor meetings, and no one was happy about it. The sun set an hour ago, and I can't help but think about the one last night rather fondly. As I scarf down a BLT in the restaurant on the first floor of my hotel, I finally have a moment to scroll through my messages. Work, work, work, Aunt Patty. I smile at that one and click it open. I'm not surprised she messaged me, not after our phone conversation this morning. As usual, she does not disappoint.

The image of a muscular man, wearing only tiny red briefs, fills my screen. He is lying across a bed, facing the camera with a come-hither look, his finger crooked to call the viewer closer. The words "Let's get it on!" emblazon the bottom of the gif, and I almost choke on the tea I should not have swallowed while opening the message. Aunt Patty's message makes me laugh even harder, as it is her usual excuse for saying anything naughty: "Susan made me do it!" *Oh, my God!* I shouldn't be surprised; honestly, the levity is welcome after the day I have had. I scroll through the messages again, continuing to ignore the work ones. They can wait until tomorrow. I'm done for the day. Then I see a number I don't recognize.

Clicking open the message, I see it is a link to an Amazon listing. Curious now, I follow the link, and once the image loads, I start laughing again immediately. I close the browser and hit the call button. Only one man could have sent me that.

"Hello?"

"Nice one, Black."

"Aubrey, to what do I owe this pleasure?"

"You know. The link you sent me."

"Just in case anyone wanted to know how much a fifty-five-gallon drum of lube costs, I looked it up for you."

I snicker, and I can hear him chuckling on his end of the call. "Thanks, I needed a laugh."

"Long day?"

"Yeah."

"Full of all sorts of park related things?"

"Yeah, mostly petty squabbles. Nothing I'm not used to by now."

"By now, huh? How long have you been doing this, park planning?"

"Oh, are we back to the date night questions?"

"Well, in all fairness, we only got to one last night. But you sound tired."

"I am."

"Okay then, I'll let you go."

Not wanting to get off the phone with him so quickly, I answer his previous question. "Seven years. I started my business straight out of college. Haven't lost a bid yet."

"Really? That's impressive."

"Glad you approve."

"Really, Aubrey, it is quite an accomplishment."

Here I go again with the blushing and the man is not even here to see it. Shame that. He seems to like the blushes, almost as much as I hate them.

"Thanks," I reply lamely. I am too tired from the day to think of anything better to say. It would be too much to explain the whole kerfuffle the design change caused, so I opt to let him in on it later.

"Well, I should let you go to sleep."

"Yeah, you have a good night, Black."

"I will. And, Aubrey?"

"Yeah?"

"I'll see you later."

"Oh, you definitely will." His laughter rings in my ear for minutes after he hangs up. After I pay and exit the restaurant, I roll my shoulders as I make my way to the elevator. As the doors close, I suddenly wonder, *how did he get my phone number?*

CHAPTER 6

*I*t's been three days since I've seen Black, and I'm climbing the walls. I have plenty of work to do, but what I wouldn't give to hear his deep, rumbling laugh again. He has this grin, a slow smile that grows across his face. He is busy, I remind myself. Then inspiration strikes. He *is* working on a piece for the park I am in charge of bringing to life. I wonder if he would let me come to his studio to watch him work. I imagine his t-shirt stretched across his back muscles, slathered to his skin with sweat from the hot forge. Wait, does his work involve a forge? He's not a blacksmith, is he? Black the blacksmith. I groan at how much I love the play on words and the sexy images my mind is conjuring up of him beating a molten slab of iron into a long sword. *Sexual much, Aubrey?*

Before I realize what I'm doing, I've opened my phone to type him a text. Thank God, I have a better excuse to talk to him than just wanting a repeat of our bar date. Not for the first time, I curse myself for stopping our make out session in my rental car. I *was* right, but mmm, I want him so badly. And there it is. My raging libido aside, I realize, I really *like* Black. His laugh is mesmerizing. He surprised me with his wit and his appreciation of mine. Many guys have found me silly, not entertaining or engaging. But Black joined right in, teasing me back. Hmmm...as I've been considering my blazing inferno of a response to the tall, dark, and sexy man, my phone has lit up with a message.

From Black.

Would you like to come by my studio? We can go over my preliminary plans and then catch some lunch. 11:30 work for you?

I grin, and my head almost spins with giddiness. I consider my response then think to hell with it. He seemed to like my personality before, no reason to be formal or conservative now. So I answer truthfully and that truthfulness is enthusiastic.

Yes! My fingers were literally hovering over my phone to text you when, what to my wondering eyes should appear? Your invite! You're not a black-smith, are you? Because I think that would be too much. You've already got that artist thing going for you. One man can't hog all the fantasy elements, can he? That just wouldn't be fair for the rest of us, now would it? Details, kind sir, where are you and how do I get THERE?

I hit send before I can edit myself. He doesn't leave me in suspense for long as my phone rings mere moments later.

"Hello?"

His laughter greets my ear, and I'm grinning like an idiot.

"That was some response," he practically purrs, and already, he has me a little tongue tied. But, me being me, it only makes me want to play harder.

"The truth is the truth. And will set you free. But really, you are not a blacksmith, are you? You had me a little...um, distracted last we met, and I forgot to ask just exactly what kind of sculpture artist you are."

"A hungry one," he replies huskily, and I don't manage to stifle my groan before it carries across the phone lines to his ear. He laughs again, low and a little bit dirty.

"In that case," he replies, "why don't you *come* on over now. My studio is on Foster Drive. It's the large metal building at the end of block, just past the firehouse. Handily, it has my name on the side, Black Studios. There's a diner a few blocks over. We can grab some lunch after I," he pauses, clearly so I can fill in the blanks with all sorts of naughty, delicious things he could do to me, "show you how every-thing works."

I'm on the verge of panting at this point, so I barely manage to say, "Yes, that sounds great." My voice comes out breathily, and he laughs again.

"I do love it when you say yes."

My sassy tongue returns: "Good, because I do enjoy saying *yes* to you."

It's his turn to groan, and I laugh, beyond delighted and beyond turned on.

"I'll see you soon," I say, eager to wrap up this call so I can see and hear, and hopefully touch him in person.

"Definitely," he responds in a throaty murmur.

I hang up and jump to my feet, almost knocking my cold coffee off the corner of my desk. I'm too excited to care though. I grab my wallet and keys from my jacket pocket, and half dance, half run my way out of my suite door.

It takes no time to find his shop. His perfect directions aside, his name is on the side of the building in five feet tall metal letters. I park and stroll up the sidewalk to the heavy oak door. It is weather beaten and scarred with wide metal bands running across it. An old-fashioned brass ring door knocker sits at eye level, a dragon's head with the ring clasped in its toothy maw. Shaking off a shiver of anticipation, I reach up, grab the ring, and bang it against the oak three times. The door flies back to reveal a grinning Black. He looks me up and down, and the smirk on his face indicates he is happy with what he sees.

"You're fast."

"In another context, that wouldn't be a compliment," I tease.

Black laughs, stepping back, and sweeping his right arm out is a formal welcome "Come on in, Mr. Davies."

"Why thank you, kind sir."

I breach the threshold, and it takes a moment for my eyes to adjust.

Then, I am marveling, my eyes almost bugging out at everything within. Large sculptures of plants and even a few animals stand at odd intervals throughout the large, open warehouse space. Interspersed among the statues are several work benches, each covered with a variety of tools. In the far corner, I see tall metal bottles and a table covered in welder's tools. We have walked around a ten-foot-tall Saguaro cactus to stop in the middle of the shop. A surprisingly fierce looking squirrel stands in the center at waist height. As I turn in a complete circle, I give Black an appreciative low whistle. "This is impressive."

Black grins, the warmth of his smile traveling all the way up his face to his eyes. "Thank you, Aubrey. I do aim to please."

I chuckle. "So, you weld?"

"And cast bronze. I've messed around with wrought iron a time or two."

Laughing at his choice of phrase, I step up to the squirrel and pat him on the head. "And who is this?"

"That's a story for another day."

"It is sculpted from marble, isn't it?"

"Good eye."

"I do aim to please," I quip, repeating his earlier statement.

The squirrel's head and ears are so smooth that I can't stop petting it. Black looks highly amused at my affection for the marble animal.

"What? I like squirrels."

"I can see that."

"Sooo, do you have a forge?"

Black laughs and steps forward to pat the squirrel's head. "No, I don't have a forge."

He strides over to the corner with the tall tanks and turns around to crook his finger at me. "Come here."

"With pleasure."

When I come over to him to stand in front of the area that is clearly for welding, he surprises me by patting me affectionately on the cheek. I look at him, expecting I don't know what, and he just smiles sweetly and starts explaining the tanks.

"I have an oxygen settling tank here. When I was a kid, I thought it was an oxygen settle-yen tank, and I couldn't figure out what the tank had to do with Japanese currency."

I grin and try to listen closely as he explains the types of gases and their uses in welding. He is rattling off details about arc welding, MIG, TIG, and stick welding. But I'm not really listening. I am watching the joy on his face, the sparkle in his chocolate brown eyes, and the movements of his hands as he describes something about welding, metal, and art. He must have noticed my inattention as he suddenly grins more widely and snaps his fingers at me. "Earth to Aubrey."

I've been staring at his face, his hands, and I haven't heard a word he has said in the last five minutes. Blushing, I stammer an apology. "Sorry."

He laughs. "No worries."

I take the moment to ask, "Did you go to school for this or are you self-taught?"

"Both. I have an MFA with a minor in sculpture. I took some welding classes at the local vo-tech when I decided to try my hand at Godzilla sized pieces."

"Vo-tech?"

"Vocational-technical college. There used to be a lot of them around, but with the current focus on a standard B.A. for everyone, not many people attend them anymore. It's too bad. If I didn't want to be an artist, I could make a shit ton as an underwater welder."

"Is that a real thing?"

He laughs again, "Sure is, on oil rigs in the ocean."

"I learn something new every day."

"Glad to contribute to your ever-expanding bank of knowledge."

"Speaking of knowledge," I reply, as I tap my finger against my lips, "how did you get my number?"

"Jenene, the council secretary, gave it to me before we met."

"Well, artist currently known as Black. You've got me all alone in your studio. Whatever are you going to do with me?" I bat my eyelashes ridiculously at him, and he laughs so hard he seems to be struggling to breathe.

When he recovers, he answers, "I'm taking you to lunch."

"Yes," I respond breathily, "feed me."

"You make it sound so naughty. I like it."

I laugh and then a thought occurs to me. "Have you ever caught your hair on fire?"

Black smirks. "No. But, as precaution, I tie my hair back when I am welding." He gestures to the table on his left, the one bearing gloves, a welder's mask, various tweezers, pliers, strips of metal wire, sticks of metal, and a purple plastic pencil box. I pick up the box and open it to discover brightly colored hair bands.

"I can't catch my hair on fire, Aubrey. If it all burned off, then I wouldn't be attractive anymore and you wouldn't like me."

I giggle as I close his purple box and set it back on the table. "Who says I like you?"

"You did."

"Did not."

Black steps forward and I step back, side stepping to the other side of the table. His eyes light up, and he put his hands on the bench. I step farther away, and he begins to stalk me like a hunting cat around his work bench. He continues our flirtatious banter.

"You said it with your eyes."

"Nah, you just had a bug on your face."

"You said it with your fingers."

"Nah, I was making sure your nipples didn't get cold. It was chilly in that backseat."

I let him back me into a nearby corner. He slaps his hands against the metal walls beside my head and leans into me, forcing me to tip my head up a little to meet his gaze.

He looks at my lips and huskily states, "You said it with your lips."

"Did I?"

"When you kissed me."

"I don't recall."

"Would you like a refresher course?"

I smirk. "Yes, please and thank you."

He leans forward, his lips hovering over mine for a moment before he replies, "Since you asked so nicely, I can't help but oblige." His lips descend on mine softly, his tongue barely grazing my bottom lip.

"Remember now?" he murmurs against my lips.

"Hmmm... I might need another hint. What was your name again?"

Black grins then kisses me hard, his tongue doing wicked things against my own. He growls and nips at my bottom lip, pulling it a little before releasing it.

I sigh, and Black chuckles, "I learned that little trick from you."

I can't help continuing to tease him. "You're that artist guy who likes to sculpt horses, horses with cowboys riding on them."

Black growls much louder this time and proceeds to kiss me breathless. When he finally pulls back to look into my face, he is smirking. "Know who I am now?"

"Oh, yes, I do, Mr. Black. I think you would look cute bald."

Black laughs. He runs his hands down my arms and pulls me out of the corner by my hands. "I think it's time for lunch."

"I most assuredly concur, Mr. Black."

Aubrey and I walk to the local diner. Through the window, I can see it is well populated by elderly ladies in flowery dresses and a few slouching teenagers who look either bored or stoned. I hold the door open for Aubrey, and a waitress greets us as soon as we walk in.

"There's a booth free over there," she says, gesturing with an arm and smacking her gum. "Unless you want to sit at the counter."

"A booth is good," I reply, and she leads us over to the last open one alongside the window. We settle in to browse the menu, and I notice the blue flyer tapped to the glass inside the booth. It announces the county fair, and suddenly, I'm desperate to take Aubrey.

Gesturing to the little sign, I ask, "Do you want to go to the fair?"

Aubrey's eyes shoot up from his menu and a thousand-watt smile lights up his face. Sunshine, I think again.

He is vibrating with excitement. "You want to take me to the fair? Yes!" he practically shouts then covers his mouth with his hand, glancing around, a blush starting to form on his cheeks. He looks back at me and swings his hand to the side to uncover his mouth, not removing it from his face. "Yes," he semi-whispers. "I haven't been to a fair since I was a kid."

I'm enraptured by his delight. "Then let's go. It starts next Friday. I have an art class Friday night, but would Saturday evening work for you?"

He nods emphatically and then cocks his head to the left. "You're taking an art class?"

"No, I teach it."

His eyes widen and his face lights up. "You teach it? Wow!"

"I'm a man of many talents," I quip. "It's a sculpture class at the community college. They ask local artists to teach their specialty, and they pulled me in for the Spring semester. It's just once a week, but I'm liking it. I might do it again, if they ask."

"What do you teach them? Welding?"

"Oh, no, no," I chuckle, "it's a basic sculpture class, with clay." I pause for a second and waggle my eyebrows at him. "And naked models."

"Really?"

"No. It's mostly still life, bowls of fruit and whatnot."

"I thought you were supposed to paint bowls of fruit."

"You can, but where's the fun in that?"

"Well, Mr. Black, you certainly have impressed me."

"I'm ever so pleased to hear it, Mr. Davies. So, what about the fair? Next Saturday night?"

"Absolutely," Aubrey responds excitedly.

Our waitress comes back, and we place our orders. We both want breakfast, and the conversation doesn't return to the fair until after the waitress brings our plates.

"Isn't it a little early for the fair?" Aubrey asks between bites of French toast.

"It's always in early to mid-April."

"Not in Chicago, it isn't. You have to wait until May to play the games and eat the food."

"Let me guess, the food is your favorite part."

He laughs and points his empty fork at me. "You will just have to wait and see."

I laugh too. Lunch seems to be over in a flash. After receiving a phone call that makes him grimace and roll his eyes, Aubrey has to dash back to work. But he kisses me softly outside of my shop door, and I'm floating on clouds for the rest of the afternoon.

CHAPTER 7

The sights, smells, and sounds of the fair surround us: popcorn, cotton candy, funnel cake, twirling lights, barkers pitching their games as the people shuffle by. Waiting a whole week to see Black again had been torturous, but work kept me so busy and the promise of this date kept my spirits high. The time apart has not dwindled our ever-increasing attraction, though I must admit to myself the suggestive texts and the continuation of our "date night questions" via phone has furthered our connection in the absence of physical proximity. Even now, we hold hands as we wander down the promenade as if this were not new and we hadn't met just two weeks ago.

"Do you want a teddy bear?" asks Black as we stroll up to an old-fashioned knock down the milk bottles game.

"Nah," I answer, a grin pulling across my face, "but you need one."

He raises his eyebrows, his chocolate brown eyes twinkling: "I do? I need a teddy bear?" "Yeah," I answer laconically as I point out the largest prize in the booth, "that polar bear right there."

Black grins wider, looking a little surprised at my confidence.

"And I'm gonna get it for you."

"Three balls for five bucks," yaps the skinny, scraggly bearded barker.

I pull my wallet out and find a five, handing it over to the barker as he hands me the balls. Slipping my wallet back into my pocket with one hand, I look at the target, the five-level stack of milk bottles, determining exactly where to aim. I step up to the line, pretend to tug an invisible baseball hat, and wind up in a pitcher's form. The ball feels just right in the palm of my hand, and as it leaves my fingertips, I know it will hit true.

Bang! Dead center and all five levels of bottles come crashing down. The barker looks annoyed for a split second then pastes on his fair smile. "Congratulations! You win the big prize."

I straighten up and smirk at him, "I know. I want the polar bear."

He nods, takes up the metal hook with a long handle and pulls the bear down from the top of the booth. "Here you go." He hands it over to me, and I tuck it into my elbow.

A boy of about seven or eight steps up to my side and motions me down to his level. "How did you do that?" he whispers when his mouth is even with my ear.

"It's not magic," I reply solemnly. "Do you want me to show you how?" He nods emphatically, causing both Black and me to chuckle. Black had stepped off to the side, and now, I look up to see his grinning face.

"I have to show this kid a thing or two," I tell him as I stand back up, setting the bear softly on the ground beside me.

"Of course, you do," he replies, his eyes twinkling at me, his smile bright on his face.

I hand the boy my two extra baseballs and quickly show him a basic pitcher's stance. His first throw goes wide, but the second taps the edge of a bottle on the top row, sending three of them crashing to the ground. I cheer, Black cheers, and the boy's parents, who have been watching from beside Black, cheer and clap.

"Great job! You did it!" I exclaim as the barker retrieves a small blue and red plush crab and hands it to the boy. He is practically jumping up and down as he shows his parents what he won. They thank me, and I wave it off with a smile as I turn toward Black. Bending over, I pick up my bear and gently dust off the bottom.

I grin at him as I hand him my winnings. "I won you Ice Bear."

Black laughs as he takes the bear and hugs it. I'm terribly smitten with the gesture and lean in to peck his lips.

"I think you mean a polar bear," Black replies when I pull back.

I mock gasp at him. "Oh, no! Could it be you don't know *We Bare Bears?*" We must remedy that immediately!"

Black chuckles at my enthusiasm. "It's a movie?"

I shake my head in pretend dismay. "Oh, no. It's a cartoon, and now, we have to watch it. You'll be a fan of Ice Bear, I guarantee."

Black moves his bear under one arm so he can sling his other around my waist to pull me in close.

"How did you do that, Aubrey?"

"You didn't know it, but you brought a ringer. I played baseball in high school." I shrug my shoulder, enjoying the look on his face that says I'm blowing his assumptions about me out of the water.

"I wasn't good enough to play in college," I continue as I hook my arm around his waist and we stroll along the avenue of games. "But I didn't really care. It was fun, but it wasn't something I was in love with."

"What were you in love with?"

"My, my, aren't you sneaky with those turns of phrase."

"I do try. Now answer the question."

I laugh and throw my other arm around his waist. I pull him into me, close enough to kiss, but instead, I stare into his eyes for a moment then say, "No."

Black can't stop laughing, "You are one of a kind, Aubrey."

"Prove it to me with funnel cake."

"Your wish is my command."

We eat funnel cake with powdered sugar as we stroll along, watching adults and children play games. The lights of the Ferris Wheel twinkle at us from afar and I point it out.

"We need to go on the Ferris Wheel."

"We most certainly do."

It takes a few minutes to walk over, but there is no line. The carny motions us toward the seat once we hand him some ride tickets. We settle onto a bench, and the wheel starts moving up slowly. As we stop at the top, I can see the lights of Oakland spread out in front of us. Since we are the only people on the wheel, the carny leaves us up there for a while.

"Are you having fun, Aubrey?" Black whispers against my ear as he snuggles his nose into my neck.

"Yeah," I breathily murmur. "But…"

He pulls back to look me in the face, and I continue, "But we can't make out up here. What would the parents tell their scandalized children?"

We both laugh hard, and the wheel swings into motion again, taking us around and around as the colorful lights twinkle overhead, creating a warm, soft glow around us. The evening is perfect, and I feel content.

CHAPTER 8

*D*rumming my fingers on my welding workbench, I not so patiently wait for Aubrey to pick up the phone. I'm agitated for no other reason than the news my assistant Monica just gave me about my schedule for the next two weeks. I haven't seen Aubrey since our date at the fair and now I won't be able to see him for quite a while longer. Aubrey picks up on the third ring.

"Black! To what do I owe the *pleasure* of your call? And how is Ice Bear?"

I chuckle, some of my nervous energy dissipating, like so much smoke. Illusions, I think, recalling what fear means as an acronym: False Expectations that Appear Real. I would do well to remember that all the time.

"That was just what I needed to hear. Thank you."

"What? You needed to hear me ask about Ice Bear?" His voice changes, now laced with mock concern. "What happened to Ice Bear? Did he run away to be a sushi chef again?"

I laugh. "I have no idea what you are talking about. No, Ice Bear is fine, just *chillin'* in my workshop." Aubrey giggles at my bad pun.

"Don't let his hair catch on fire," Aubrey warns, now with sincere concern in his voice.

Laughing loudly now, I scrub my hand over my face before I answer. "No worries. He's sitting on top of your favorite squirrel, far out of the reach of any danger."

"Whew!" Aubrey sighs in relief, and I cannot help but laugh harder. Aubrey giggles again. "So, if Ice Bear is *cool*, then why are you calling *me*?"

"Do I need an excuse?"

"Noooo…but…"

"But what, *Aubrey*?" I ask teasingly.

He surprisingly draws in a sharp breath, and I scramble to apologize for an accidental offense. "I'm sorry. Did I say something wrong?"

Aubrey's voice is amused, bemused, and maybe even slightly embarrassed. "No…" he pauses for a beat or two, lowering his voice, "I really like when you say my name that way," he confesses slowly.

My face cracks ear to ear with a grin I couldn't hold back if I wanted. "I *like* saying your name that way, *Aubrey*."

Aubrey laughs at that, his voice returning to normal as he proves that turnabout is fair play. "Why did you call, *Black*?"

I groan purposefully to his peals of laughter. "You are distracting me."

"I'm good at that, aren't I?"

"Yes, yes, you are."

"I enjoy distracting you."

"I can tell. But, getting back to the reason for my call, I wanted to give you a heads up that I'm going to be out of town on business for the next week and a half to two weeks."

"You are? And you did?"

I laugh again. God, I adore how much Aubrey makes me laugh. I haven't laughed this much in years and painful thoughts no longer stalk my ever moment. "Yes, *Aubrey*, I wanted to tell you. I have to visit Yuma and Santa Fe to supervise the installations of a few works. Yuma just has the one large flowering succulent; a desert rose to be exact. The set of smaller animal and plant sculptures are headed to Santa Fe."

"Wow, Black, that is awesome! Do you at least get a little vacation time in?"

I fiddle with the little tools spread out on my bench to distract myself from my continued nervous twitch. Tweezers, pliers, wire, gloves. "No, no rest for the weary, I suppose."

Aubrey's laugh now sounds naughty. *"Or, no rest for the wicked I'd say."*

"Me?" I fake incredulity. "Wicked?" I love his laughter so much that I cannot stop trying to amuse him.

"Oh, yes, you are wicked. You are a biker on a romance novel cover, remember?"

"So you say."

Unexpectedly, Aubrey switches topics. "Oh, no! You don't mean the squirrel, do you? I love that one!"

An almost overwhelming rush of joy floods my system. Aubrey loves my work. "I couldn't have asked for a higher compliment," I barely manage to whisper out. "It means a lot to me." Suddenly, I feel like we are treading into dangerous territory, and I quickly scramble to pull myself back from the emotional ledge. Reeling from my emotional response to his compliment, I am silent longer than I realize.

"Black, are you alright?" Aubrey's voice sounds genuinely concerned and another wave of joy crashes through me, taking my breath away again.

"I'm fine," I somehow manage to stammer.

"Good." His voice brightens. I know he is trying to distract me again and I'm touched by the effort. "But, it isn't the squirrel, is it? It is my favorite one."

Laughter, welcome and freeing rumbles through my chest. Even if I had planned to sell the squirrel, which I had not, knowing how much he loves it, I would never part with it now. "No, that is part of my personal collection. Now that I know you like it so much, I won't ever sell it." Aubrey sucks in a shocked breath, and I smile softly because I know I made him happy with that declaration. I sigh and look around my workshop as if the structure and uniformity of my space will help me order the emotions colliding in my chest. I not so deftly change the subject.

"Back to my reason for calling, as I said, I will be out of town, likely until early May. I just wanted you to know," I finish lamely. Even though I'm the one who decided to call him, I'm still surprised that I have anyone who might worry if I didn't.

"That's so sweet, Black. At the risk of sounding like a fangirl, I'm glad you made a point of telling me."

"You're more like a fanboy."

Giggling, he teasingly queries, "And how so?"

"Unless that was a flashlight in your pocket when we made out in your car, I'm pretty sure you're a boy."

"Yes," his voice drops lower, seductive, "yes, I'm definitely a boy."

"Good, 'cause I just happen to like boys."

"Really? I never would have guessed. You must still be in the closet."

My jaw drops in shock, and I can't fight the laughter. Nor can I speak for a minute. "You are naughty," I croak out at him.

"Just the way you like me."

"Damn straight."

"I have an idea...for how we can bridge the yawning distance between Cali and those far off border states."

"Do pray tell."

"Date night questions. By my count, we've managed no more than four."

"Still trying to get to know me, huh?"

"You are a tall, dark, and mysterious man."

"I'm glad you noticed."

"Oh, believe me, I have. Here's what we will do: one question a day. We both have to answer via text. Texting gives you time to think. I'll pick the first question, you the next, and then we trade off. Sound like a good deal?"

"Excellent deal. Just so I know the exact parameters of our conversation arrangement, we receive or send the question, when? In the morning?"

"Yeah, and we have all day to come up with an answer. No skip-ping questions and you have to be honest."

I'm a little nervous about the last bit of the agreement. "What if we can't answer the question?" My voice is low now, a little worried.

"No problem," Aubrey's voice sounds caring, soothing even, "just ask for a new one." He pauses, his voice suddenly sounding unsure. "Unless you don't like the idea." He sounds like he is biting his lip or worrying it with his fingers.

"Perfect." I inject the word with enthusiasm despite my trepida-tion. He sighs in relief, and a small smile flits across my mouth. I allow myself the next confession before I can put on the brakes of self-doubt. "I'm glad I called you, Aubrey. Your idea is great. I look forward to your inquiries."

"So do I. *And* I get the first question."

"I'd expect nothing less."

Aubrey chuckles. "When do you leave?"

"Tomorrow morning, bright and early."

"I will have my question to you by ten."

"You slacker, burning daylight like that."

"Hey! I need time for the coffee to jump start my brain."

Laughing, I respond, "Me too."

"Well, Mr. Black," Aubrey slips into a business-like tone, "thanks for the update on your whereabouts and plans. I wouldn't want for you to misplace yourself."

"Thanks, Mr. Davies. I look forward to your official communiques."

"Me too. Goodnight, Black. I will be messaging you tomorrow."

"Goodnight, Aubrey." I hang up, far lighter than when I picked up the phone. I stand and stretch then gather up my things for home. Calling Aubrey was the right thing to do; I just don't want to think too deeply about why I found it so necessary to my own wellbeing.

Aubrey is clearly going easy on me with the first question. It popped up on my phone after my flight to Phoenix. My layover before the little plane skip to Yuma is long enough for me to write an entire essay on my favorite color. By the time the attendants call for boarding, I've written six hundred words on why black is the most versatile color in the world. Since Aubrey is so smart, I even include my own personal artistic diatribe on white vs. black as colors or non-colors. I'm smiling as I board the plane. I cannot wait to read his reply.

Aubrey does not disappoint in his response, teasing me for my color choice:

Is this why black is the only color you have in your wardrobe?

It is my signature look.

Well, Johnny Cash, you are going to have to bring some more colors into your life.

You already do that, Aubrey.

I laugh at the little embarrassed face emoji he sends as a response. A happy, smiling face emoji follows. Then, Aubrey's mini-essay on the virtues of purple fills my screen. Just as he is in everyday conversation, in writing, Aubrey is witty, urbane, and just a touch silly. I glance around the airport baggage terminal wondering if anyone has noticed my mile-wide smile or the little laughs I cannot contain as I read his answer to his own question. Even if they have, I don't care. But I do wonder what I look like from the outside. Can anyone see at a glance how much Aubrey is changing my life?

I stop abruptly at that thought. Uncharacteristically, I choose to just shake it off. There is no room for sadness or regret when Aubrey shines his sunshine nature my way.

"Coffee, coffee, coffee," I am excitedly chanting under my breath as I wait for my kitchen machine to finish its cycle. At home, I have the single cup pour mode, so I can start caffeine before the whole pot brews. But, alas, this suite is at least five years behind the times on coffee delivery systems, and I will just have to wait if I don't want to risk burning myself with hot coffee as I have already managed to do earlier this week. I am up a tad bit early for a Saturday morning, but I am so excited to receive Black's first question.

I am finally enjoying my first cup when my phone buzzes. I whip around perhaps too quickly, almost spilling my coffee on my bare chest. That would be unfortunate. I snort at myself as I rush over to the kitchen island to pick up my phone. When I click on the message, I smile at Black's lack of preface. Just as in face to face interactions, he is direct. God, I do love that in a man. And, now I have made myself blush. Shaking my head at myself, I ponder how to respond to this fresh query.

What is your favorite place in the entire world?

Hmm... Wow, that is a harder question than I would have imagined it would be, much harder than the softball I tossed him yesterday. I will have to think about this for a little while. Taking my coffee and phone with me, I settle onto the couch in the tiny "living space," as the extended stay hotel described it in the brochure. After two cups of coffee, sorely needed as I am out of bed two hours early in anticipa-tion of Black's question, my brain is finally firing, and I know my answer: Central Park. Because I prefer to be silly whenever possible, I decide to frame it just as I did my coming out story.

Picture it, New York, Central Park, 2003. I am a lanky fifteen-year-old boy on his first trip to New York. My aunties thought I could use some culture and experience, so one spring Saturday morning, we hopped a plane from dreary Chicago, only to land in an equally dreary New York, complete with fog and hordes of tourists just like us. We managed to lose ourselves in the subway system three times before we figured out which way to go. If it weren't for the help of a kindly beat cop who took pity on us, I am sure we would be lost there still.

Patty and Susan had a million stops on their "to see" list, but all I cared about was Central Park. I had read dozens of books on it: picture books, travel guides, historical narratives, even some poorly written romance novel set during the first construction phase. You can imagine how awkward that was for a gay boy to read. If anything, it provided further, though wholly unnecessary, proof of my sexuality.

Central Park may only be New York's fifth largest park, but I will always argue it is New York's most important one. This is even taking into consideration how eminent domain was used to remove the "unwanted elements" from the lands in the 1850s so the park could be built. But I wasn't thinking about any of that. My teenaged soul was in love with the bridges, Bethesda Fountain, and Belvedere Castle. It was the wrong season for Shakespeare in the Park, but I tried my hardest to drag my aunts all over the place.

Central Park sparked my imagination and made me want to build parks just like it.

I continue on for a few hundred more words, sprinkling my love and knowledge of the park throughout. A warm happiness fills me as I shape the details of my life I wish to share with Black. Just as I finish and hit send, a tell-tale buzz lets me know Black has sent me his composition. I am immediately enraptured by the loving way he describes the Redwood National and State Parks system.

My heart trips a little knowing how closely related what I love and do for a career is to the places that inspire Black, inspire his sculptures, inspire his life view and values. Black wraps up his text essay with a statement that warms me inside and out.

I cannot imagine my life leading me to where I am without these parks. Their plants and animals inspire me in my art, furthering my career as I try to pay homage to their beauty. They are part of my foundation, and Aubrey, it is special to me to know you care about these types of places as much as I do.

I swallow hard multiple times to stop myself from crying. Just two days in and I am floored by what Black is saying to me and what I am saying to him. Who knew finding out someone's favorite place and favorite color would lead to such a feeling of deep connection? A feeling which is frightening, overwhelming, and feels so very right. I hug my phone to my chest, smiling a goofy smile as I take another drink of my coffee. I couldn't form a proper response right now if I tried, so I settle in to reread his words, imagining him speaking them to me, his slightly growly voice comforting me, even though it is only in my imagination.

I smile wistfully at my phone, wishing Aubrey were here. My heart gives a little throb I refuse to analyze or second guess. Technically, I cheated with that question. After racking my brain for an hour at dawn, I could not choose a proper question. So I googled "gay guy first date questions" and found some good lists. Apparently, you can find anything on the internet.

Why couldn't I decide on a question of my own? Because I want too much. Everything, I want to know everything about Aubrey, even as part of my mind reminds me of the danger and fights my growing attraction to him tooth and nail. No, not just attraction, need. Since I need to know everything about him, my mind clogged up, and I couldn't think of a single coherent question. Or, I shake my head at myself as I reread his message for the third time over my second cup of coffee, I couldn't think of a single *appropriate* question. *Do you sleep in the nude, or do you have light little freckles anywhere else besides your nose? Why do you smell so good that the scent lingers in my nose long after we've said goodnight? Why is kissing you the only thing that shuts my mind up and lets me breathe again?*

Yeah, those kinds of questions were not the point of this little game. I frown at my coffee on that thought. Is it a game? I roll my eyes at myself and glance around, wondering if any of the other patrons of this dingy little coffee shop have noticed my unease, my distraction, or if they can hear the noise coming from the inside of my head. No, don't be silly, Black. *But I like being silly*, whispers Aubrey's voice in my head. I choose to smile at the thought because crying in relief, pain, wonder, delight, and fear would just not be appropriate behavior in a coffee shop in Yuma, Arizona.

The doorbell chimes, breaking me from my reverie and bringing in my coffee companion from the unseasonable warmth of a late April day. Well, unseasonable for Oakland, not for the Sonoran Desert where I currently am. I wave my hand at the portly park manager I have worked with before, signaling him to my table. Letting out a breath, I refocus my thoughts on work even as part of my mind bounces between joy and devastation, pondering what Aubrey is to me and what he could be.

Messages fly back and forth between us. Silly questions, deep questions, off the wall queries, and odd but lovely reminiscences trip from cell tower to cell tower, connecting us over the physical distance and seeming to pull us closer and closer on the emotional plane of existence. By the last day of Black's business trip, I'm angsty as fuck. Minutes trudge by and I reread another boring work email for the third time because I can no longer concentrate. "Fuck!" I push my chair back from my desk and glance at my watch. 3:23p.m. "Fuck it, I'm done." No one will know if I bounce from work early. It's not like I have a permanent office or co-workers to watch my every move.

The town council tries to fulfill that function, but they probably don't know they could keep electronic tabs on me and my progress. Even if they did know, it's doubtful any of them would know how. I chuckle to myself as I think of ancient Mr. Owens and cranky Mrs. Swift cyberstalking me. Yeah, I need a break and coffee sounds way too good right about now. Practically tripping over my own feet, I rush to escape down to the coffee shop that is quickly becoming my second home and office in Oakland.

As I am standing in a surprisingly long line, considering the time of day, I suddenly remember why I chose to pursue this Oakland job in the first place. It wasn't because the job sounded any better than those popping up closer to home. No, I had needed a change of scenery, maybe even a permanent change. Permanent. I ponder the word and let myself contemplate it a little after the barista takes my order and I wait too long for a simple cup of black coffee. Permanent. Even though it is far too early to consider that word and Black in the same sentence, I do anyway. A soft smile settles on my face and I almost blush. I really cannot wait until Black comes home tomorrow. Home, a dangerous thought to consider, but I push the nagging little detail aside in favor of considering all of the delicious things I want to do with Black when I see him again. We already made plans to meet at a local Italian restaurant for dinner tomorrow night, and I am more than ready to get my eyes and hands on Black again.

CHAPTER 9

There is so much about Aubrey that is just right, I think as I spy him across the street. He spots me, and a smile lights up his face as he raises his arm to wave at me. Suddenly, I'm paralyzed with fear over the bouquet of sunflowers in my left hand. I clench them in my fist and wonder if I should toss them away. Too late, Aubrey is through the crosswalk now, his strides happy, confident, and light. His smile grows wider as he spies the flowers in my hand. I get the pleasure of watching a faint blush steal over those perfect high cheekbones again.

"For me?" he asks in a soft voice as his smile widens. "You brought me flowers?"

He steps into my space and lightly takes the hand in which I'm holding the bouquet. He raises my hand and the flowers as he dips his head down towards them, all the while keeping his eyes on mine. He takes a deep breath in, and sighs. His eyes flutter closed for a moment, then pop open and now so bright they could be cut emeralds.

"*Thank you,*" Aubrey breathes, emphasizing each word so strongly that I feel like they're floating on the air between us, arrowing their way into my chest and taking up residence in my heart. "No one has ever brought me flowers before," he remarks in a marveling tone as he clenches his fingers around the bouquet and takes them into both of his hands. He smells them deeply again and closes his eyes for a moment as if memorizing the scent. "I love them."

His body sways towards mine a little, and I lean forward into him, raising my right hand to brush his cheek. His eyes flutter open just as I press my lips gently against his.

"Thank you," I whisper against his lips. He suddenly snakes his free hand up my chest and around my neck to sink his fingers into my hair as he pulls me in tighter for what turns out to be a hungry, dominating kiss. His tongue sweeps into my mouth and takes up residence, sliding against mine in strong strokes until I am returning his fervor. My free hand slides from his face and down his neck, and Aubrey takes in a sharp breath. I'm so hungry for him now that I feel like I've lost my mind. I bite down a tad too hard on his bottom lip. I didn't mean to and think to apologize, but his eyes pop open, blazing green, so I do it again. I'm not sure how long the moment would have lasted or where it would have gone because someone takes the opportunity to honk their horn at us from their position at the stoplight. Still we barely pull from each other's lips, so the guy slides down his window to yell, "Get a room!"

I'm still reeling from the kiss and Aubrey's reaction to the flowers, but Aubrey yells right back, "Already got one! Thanks for the tip!"

The driver speeds off angrily as the light turns green, and Aubrey laughs as he turns his face back towards me.

"Shall we proceed?"

"What?" I almost wheeze out as I seem short on oxygen to the brain, to the lungs, all of my body except my dick, which now seems to have all of my blood too.

Aubrey laughs and smirks. He pecks me on the corner of my mouth and pulls me by the hand in the direction of the Italian restaurant where we have reservations.

"Come on. I'm starving," he pretends to whine. "Feed me."

Lust flashes through me so fast I could swear my body heats two degrees in a second.

"You can feed me *that* later," he teases, tugging me along, as my body seems to have lost all ability of independent forward locomotion.

Dinner flew by in a flash. I barely recall what I ate. Something with pasta and maybe chicken? Maybe chicken parm? But I don't care. How could I possibly care when I'm holding Aubrey close to me, kissing his soft lips, touching his tongue with my tongue? The hotel elevator dings, and Aubrey squirms out of my hold. He intertwines his hand with mine as he steps out of the elevator into the hall and pulls me along behind him. Desire pulses through my veins, and I clench my fingers tighter around his. He throws a glance over his shoulder, and the look he gives me is a beatific mixture of affection, desire, and something more my mind refuses to recognize. A whisper reminds me I've had a similar look thrown my way before, but the thought flies away as Aubrey stops in front of a suite door.

"This is me," he murmurs, suddenly shy, ducking his chin and gazing down. Dropping my hand, but leaving it full of the bouquet of sunflowers, he pulls a card key from his back pocket, fumbling it as he tries to slide it into the door lock. I take advantage of the moment by leaning one hand against the door frame, shifting my body to line up against his back. He shivers at the contact, falling back a moment to lean against my chest. His head lolls on my left shoulder, his eyes drifting closed as his neck is exposed to me unintentionally. Taking advantage of the accidental invitation, I duck my head down to his pulse and lick it, grazing my teeth across the vein, feeling the thudding of his heart, his blood, there. He groans, and I can't help me but grin.

"You smell so good, Aubrey," I whisper as I trail my lips up and down his neck. "God, I can't get enough of your scent."

Aubrey squeaks, blushing furiously, so I can't resist dropping my voice lower and whispering into his ear, "I wonder if you smell this way all over."

He jerks his head forward, cursing as he tries to shove the misbehaving keycard into the lock. I chuckle against his pulse, playing my fingers up his side, along his rib cage.

"In a hurry, are we?"

Aubrey growls and the lock finally clicks over to green. Yanking the knob, he throws open the door and stumbles across the threshold, pivoting around, grabbing me by the shirt and hauling me powerfully into his suite and into his arms. Luckily, I stay enough on balance to kick the door closed behind me. Fisting my shirt harder, he yanks me further into him, devouring my mouth with his. A surge of caveman-like possessiveness washes through me, and I drop the flowers to the floor before I grab his ass, forcing him to jump up my body, giving him no choice but to wrap his legs around my waist. Our groins connect and we both moan and shudder.

In between kisses, Aubrey murmurs, "What do you want?"

I've backed him up against the entry hall, so I have him at my complete mercy. But, in truth, I am at his mercy. Sliding my lips down his jaw, I nudge his chin up and he obliges, bearing his neck to me. Running my lips back and forth across his pulse, I somehow manage to breathlessly reply, "Tell me what you want me to do."

At his sharp intake of breath, I pull my head up, expecting...I am not sure what. Aubrey's eyes flash fiercely at me, a radiant look of power settling over his features. I'm mesmerized by the dominance in his gaze. His hand, which had been fisting my hair at the nap of my neck, clasps my chin, holding it firmly. He kisses me strongly, slowly, completely in control, pulling me further under his spell. Leaning back, he grins an incredibly devilish smile and lick his lips. The tone of his voice vibrates with power when he says, "Carry me to the bedroom. Put me on my feet and take off all of my clothes."

A shudder ripples through me as I flash cold for a second then so very hot. His eyes are laser focused onto mine, and I couldn't possibly do anything other than what he just commanded. How we made it through the kitchenette and into his bedroom is a wonder to me. Our gazes never drop and the intensity surges back and forth, like the tide coming in and out.

When I set him down, he maintains the searing eye contact as he slides down my body. I groan and twitch when his clothed dick slides past mine. He doesn't blink, and his smile deepens. He chuckles softly and strokes my chin where his hand has been since I had him pinned to the wall. Unable to do anything else, I follow the command he gave me in the hallway, raising my hand to undo the pink bowtie that has driven mad with desire all night. He tilts his head up to give me better access and drops his hand to his side. There is a bare three inches of height difference between us, so I can easily see his eyes, dominance simmering in them.

My hands are shockingly steady as I slip his dark gray blazer from his shoulders, allowing it to slide to the floor with a whisper. Unbuttoning his white shirt, I allow my knuckles to skim against his chest as it rises and falls beneath the slowly parting fabric. When I reach his waist, I tug the bottom of the shirt from his slacks, losing a little bit of my patience as I roughly shove the shirt off his shoulders. I gaze at his chest, so nicely defined and practically smooth except for a smattering of red-gold hair between his pecs. When I detour from my appointed mission of clothing removal to slide my work roughened palms up and then back down his chest, Aubrey pulls in a shaky breath and shudders. His eyes drift closed a moment, then snap back open, the intensity in those pure green depths sending a corresponding shudder through my own body. I tell my wandering hands to resume their task of undressing him, so they slide over his stomach toward the belt at the waist of his slacks.

As my fingers stroke downward over his flat belly, he squirms and breathily laughs. I grin wickedly, remembering that he is ticklish. I will explore that later. I swiftly part the belt from its buckle and slide it from the loops. I hold his gaze, still grinning, as I purposely raise it high and drop it so that it thumps when it hits the floor. He chuckles softly at that, but leaves his arms and hands dangling loosely at his sides as they have been since I set him on his feet.

Returning my hands to the waist of his pants, I slide the trouser button from its hole and slowly pull the zipper down by its tab. Unhurriedly, I sink down to one knee, my head tilting up to keep eye contact with Aubrey as I hook my fingers into his pants and boxers, sliding them off his hips then down his athletically muscled thighs. Runners' legs, the thought passes through my mind and disappears just as quickly. When I reach his ankles, I realize he must have toed off his shoes while I was busy trying to remove everything else. He raises one foot slowly and then the other as I remove the pants and boxers from him.

"I'll leave the socks for now," I murmur, returning my gaze to his face. Moving his left hand forward, he hooks a finger under my chin.

"Come back up here."

I oblige because I could do nothing else. Though I noticed his fully erect cock as I pulled his boxers from his hips, I did not touch him anywhere, only accidentally grazing his legs with the backs of my hands as I took his pants down. Licking my lips with sudden nerves, I realize I want him to tell me to touch him. I don't want to take it for granted, but beyond that, I want him to guide me, to direct me toward his pleasure. When I have glided to standing again, he cups my face and gently kisses me with almost chaste lips, softly on the middle of my mouth then at the corners of my lips, each side in turn.

"Take off your clothes," he whispers against my mouth. "I want you naked."

Not having to be asked twice, I am practically frantic as I rip the buttons on my shirt open. When I keep fumbling, Aubrey laughs, the corner of his mouth quirking up, "So this is why you like T-shirts so much."

I can't laugh in reply as I am too overwhelmed by the need surging through me. Cursing, I finally rip the offending button down off my shoulders and throw it to the floor. Luckily, I wore no belt, so the slacks are easy to remove after I toe off my dress shoes. "You are just lucky," I somehow manage to breath out, "that I am not wearing my combat boots."

Aubrey laughs softly as he rakes his eyes over my body. It is not a quick perusal, but a thorough look sliding from my chest to my groin all the way down to my feet and back.

"You left your socks on too. Nice touch."

A soft smile hovers on his lips, but the dominance in his eyes has not waned and I find myself barely able to draw in breath as his eyes bore into mine. A thrill ripples through me. It's never been like this before. I've never wanted someone to take control of me and my body the way I want Audrey to do. His desire shot so much higher when I asked him what he wanted me to do. I marvel at the confidence and power that illuminates his face. Others might have taken my question less directly, but Aubrey understood without further elaboration. I wanted him to take control of me. Definitely a first for me, sexually speaking.

I'd always wanted that control of the sexual encounter before, even in relationships. A painful thought tries to intrude, but Aubrey picks that moment to weave his hand through my hair and yank my head back, his green eyes darker than I've yet seen them. He brings his mouth slowly to mine then he devours me, licking my lips, then sucking my tongue into his mouth as his other hand slides to my naked shoulder. Pulling back slightly, he tilts his head to the left, reminding me of a cat, and presses his mouth against mine again, but not actually kissing me. Lightly increasing the pressure of his fingers on my shoulder, he whispers against my lips, "I want you on your knees."

I cannot draw breath anymore, but it doesn't matter as I sink to my knees in front of him. Unable to bear breaking eye contact, I watch his luminous face as he smiles, his lips quirking up more on the left side than on the right. "Suck me," he commands, his voice smooth, even, and beautiful. "Now."

Dropping my eyes to the fully erect and beautiful cock before me, I've never wanted this so much before. The skin of his penis is flushed dark pink, and I can see the vein on the side throbbing with his heart-beat. Slowly, I lean forward and breathe in the intimate scent of him, a shudder rolling through me. Somehow, I manage words from some-where in my hazed over brain, "You do smell this good all over."

Aubrey chuckles, and I take this moment to glide my flattened tongue from the base of his cock to the tip. He makes a whining noise in his throat, and I can't help but grin as I steady his hips with my hands. He is circumcised, just as I am, so I tease the shining head by rolling my tongue around and around the edges. Aubrey whimpers, his hips bucking up involuntarily. His hand hasn't left my shoulder, his fingers digging into my flesh as I breathe warm breaths against his head, reveling in the shudders wracking his frame. We have barely begun, and like me, he is already fighting not to come apart. I flick my gaze up to his face to discover he has closed his eyes, allowing his head to loll back. He gently settles his free hand on my other shoulder, squeezing his fingernails lightly into my flesh. I slide my lips down his cock, licking the underside and sucking lightly as I pull back up. My fingers clench tighter on his hips. I haven't done this in forever, but Aubrey's little moans and the slight shifting of his hips forward tell me I haven't forgotten how.

Moving slowly, I glide up and down on his dick, varying suction, flicking my tongue over the slit in his head then swirling it around before sucking my way down again. I leave my left hand on his hip as I use the right to gently cup his balls and finger the smooth skin behind them. Aubrey whines in the back of his throat, the sound driving me crazy. I'm not deep throating him, but he doesn't seem to care. I can taste his precum on my tongue, and I swallow. Even though I don't have him down my throat, he feels the contraction around him and bucks up almost wildly. He is panting now as I move my hand up to stroke over the base of his cock in time with my mouth. He gasps, whimpering out my name, "Black!"

His grip on my shoulders tightens to nearly painful, his left hand sliding up my neck and back into my hair. "Black!" he cries out again, and I can tell he is much too close to coming. He tightens his grip on my hair as I take an upstroke and pulls me off of his dick and roughly up his body. He slams his mouth against mine, tongue swirling in, touching every corner, dueling with my tongue. Need rising ferociously in me, I growl into his mouth as I grasp his arms and walk him backward toward the bed. He hits the edge and sinks down slowly, taking me with him. We settle on the mattress, me lying between his legs, our arms wrapped around each other, our tongues dueling as we naturally seem to be slowing down. Aubrey doesn't seem to be riding the edge of orgasm anymore and our kisses turn more languid. Even though my cock is at attention and aching, I am loving the slower pace. It's not a race and now that I have tasted him, I want to savor. But a thought intrudes.

"We haven't talked about preferences," I murmur against his lips as I pull back to look him in the eyes.

Aubrey's eyelashes flutter down, then up, and his green eyes hold my own.

"You, I prefer you."

I'm a little overwhelmed at that statement, but he still has not answered the question. "No, I mean which..." I sigh now and try to force myself to continue. It's been so long since I've wanted someone I've forgotten how to do this. Aubrey senses my discomfort and kisses me gently. He reaches around me to grab my ass with both hands.

"Even though I usually play catcher," he says, arching his eyebrows at me, "I don't mind pitching either. As you know, I'm a pretty good pitcher." We both laugh at his reference to my teddy bear, and I've relaxed considerably. We were hot and heavy coming through the door and even up until now, but I'm glad we have slowed down for a moment.

"Which do you want, Black?" he asks, to my surprise, and I almost choke on the words. I can barely get them out even in a whisper. "I want inside of you."

Delight and need flash across Aubrey's face as he smiles. "Lucky for you, I want you inside of me too."

I'm sure in the moment that Aubrey means far more than sex, and whether or not I want to admit it, so do I. We kiss again, and it is no time before we are moaning and writhing against each other once more. Trailing my lips down his jaw, I grin when he immediately offers his throat to me. I nip at his pulse as it speeds up, indicating his need is rising as quickly as mine; the desire we momentarily banked, blazing once again.

"Condoms?!" I suddenly garble out against his neck. "I don't have condoms." I pull back, shuffling off of him until I'm kneeling between his legs. Aubrey smirks at me.

"Whatever will we do?" he drawls out, widening his eyes at me. He pulls himself up to rest on his elbows and winks at me. He glances toward his right, tipping his chin toward the nightstand next to the bed. "Why don't you check that drawer and see if we get lucky?"

He chuckles at his double entendre as I lean forward and reach out to pull the drawer. "Bingo!" he yelps when the drawer opens to reveal condoms and lube. I can't help but laugh. I grab the box and the bottle, tap the drawer shut, and settle myself back between his legs. He has raised a socked foot and is rubbing it over my right knee. I eye him suspiciously.

"Did you stock up?"

He pretends to look away. "Maybe."

I drop the bottle and box on the bed, lunging forward on top of him, grabbing his face and ravenously kissing him. I take him back down beneath me as he laughs.

"Of course, I did," he gasps out as I kiss down his chin, across his jaw, and back to his neck. I nip at his pulse and he moans.

"When?" I murmur against his pulse as my tongue laves across it, feeling the rush of his blood through his vein.

"No comment," he murmurs as I continue to suck at the delectable skin of his neck. He turns his head a little to give me easier access.

"You plead the fifth?" I bite down on his vein again, eliciting a deep groan of need this time.

"Black!"

I suck hard on his skin one more time before releasing it.

"Yes?"

He thrusts his hips up at me, his bare cock sliding against my naked stomach. It's still a little slick from when I sucked it earlier, and suddenly, I want more of his taste. I shimmy my way down his torso, kissing his clavicle and licking a nipple then his belly button on my way back down his glorious body. He is almost thrashes against me as I take his cock into my mouth once more. He screams my name again as I give him a few quick glides of my tongue and lips before popping off and crawling back up his body.

"You called?"

Aubrey sighs. "You know what I need."

I pull myself to kneeling between his legs, his socked foot once more stroking my leg. With as much finesse as I can manage, I pull a condom from the pack, rip it open, and slide it down my very hard dick. I don't usually like wearing them a long time beforehand, but I can tell Aubrey won't stand to wait much longer. Aubrey is watching me, his foot caressing my leg up and down, amazingly matching the rhythm with which he is stroking his own cock.

"Black," he whines, "hurry up. Finger fuck me within an inch of orgasm then fuck me for real," he demands, that surprising dominance sizzling in the air between us as his voice slides deeper. "Now." He pulls his legs up and back.

I can only oblige him by slicking everything with lube, my cock, my fingers, and his asshole which he has now bared to me. I'm being very liberal with the lube here, but this has to be good. It wouldn't do to hurt him, and I am determined not to do so. Nudging his legs open a little more, I touch him as I watch his face. As I pet and circle his hole, he moans and bites his lip, his eyes open and holding mine. I press my finger in slowly, but it isn't long before it's two fingers and I'm grazing his prostrate as I rotate my wrist with every thrust.

"Black," he moans out, his eyes having fluttered shut, his face flushed, the color of a blush stealing down his neck to his chest.

"Yes," I murmur.

His eyes pop open as his breathing turns to pants. "Now!"

I've never heard a better invitation. My fingers slip from him as he gasps, and I slide up his body, settling my elbows on both sides of his shoulders. I want to be body to body, skin to skin for this. Taking my cock in my hand, I begin to push myself inside of his loosened muscles. His breathing speeds up as I slide further inside of him. I don't want to pull back, as I take this stroke so slowly. He is watching my face, the skin of his neck and chest flushing, his Adam's apple bobbing as he swallows hard. Suddenly he shifts his legs, wrapping them around my waist, pulling me fully inside of him on that first, single stroke. We both moan and jerk. He is so tight and already starting to pulse softly around me. I'm so overcome with emotion and desire that I have to bring up a hand to stroke his cheek. He turns into the caress, kissing the tips of my fingers without dropping my gaze. My tide of emotion seems to be reflected in his eyes.

After Black slides into me fully, he stops, brushing his hand up my face and through my hair.

"All right?" he asks, his lips against mine.

"More than all right," I murmur back, because this isn't sex and hasn't been since he first asked me to take control. We are making love, and as I stare into his dark brown eyes, he stares back into mine, a slow grin stretching across his face, and a sigh escapes my body as he kisses me again. I bump my hips up slightly in response to his deep moan, and whisper a command in his ear, "Now!" He needs no second invitation to make me his and himself mine. He glides in and out of me, picking up speed and ferocity until we are both grunting loudly, our bodies slamming against each other. My orgasm is building beneath my skin and hovering just out of reach. I cry out as I score my fingernails down his back.

My legs had settled around his hips, but he suddenly grabs my left thigh, pulling up my leg, pushing it out, and suddenly, he's deeper than before. He's touching places inside of me I didn't know existed. "Black!" I scream his name as he pushes home. He holds himself inside of me, his cock pulsing and so hot even through the latex barrier. He is still for a moment, my impending orgasm humming harder and harder inside of me. His hands cup my face again, and I flick open my eyes. He is staring at me with an emotional intensity I have never experienced with a lover before.

"Aubrey," he whispers, dropping his face to mine for a surprisingly soft kiss. Then he is grinding his hips against me in a counterclockwise motion. The friction and pressure ratchet up the intensity and my balls ache with the need to come. His forehead rests against mine, and he watches my face as we both pant, chasing glorious completion as we push ourselves higher and higher. He switches the direction of his grind against me, inside of me, and hits my prostate at the exact moment that one of his hands slips from my face to grasp my cock firmly. I'm twitching hard as his rough palm slides up and down my cock and his hips are slamming into me again. Then I'm flying as my orgasm rips through me. I'm screaming his name, pulling him as tightly against me as possible as my cum explodes out of me, my ass spasming around his cock.

"Aubrey!" he chokes out, still watching me with his dark chocolate eyes as he comes inside of me.

That was the hardest orgasm of my entire life. A twinge of guilt ripples through me at that, but I clasp the feeling in iron jaws and thrust it along with the other memories into the black hole of despair at the back of my mind. I purposely imagine locking iron gates. The past is gone, and this man lying spent beside me is the present. No future, no past, only the present. Those are my rules. Suddenly, I want him again with a ravenous outstripping our previous ardor. But Aubrey is done and so am I. I hear him chuckle and turn to find him grinning at me. I cannot help the smile creeping across my face. I haven't smiled as much in years as I have since I met him.

"What?" I ask, taking in his sweat soaked hair and flushed pink skin.

"That was fun. Wanna do it again?" He waggles his eyebrows at me and I can't help but throw back my head and laugh. I grab him by the shoulders and pull him on top of me.

"I think we might have to settle for making out," I fake grumble against his lips as they meet mine.

"All right by me," he responds, and he proceeds to kiss me within an inch of my life. And I love it.

CHAPTER 10

We fall asleep snuggled next to each other. I awaken several hours later and slip out of the bed to visit the bathroom. When I return, Black is on his side in the middle of the bed. He is clearly a cover hog as well, with the blankets pulled in tightly to his chest. I slip behind him and under the leftover length of sheet. Wrapping my arms around him, I snuggle against his back and settle my face in the crook of his neck. I breathe in his scent for a while, feeling both drowsy and the first stirrings of new arousal. I run my free hand up and down his arm and marvel at how right he feels in my arms. He is still breathing deeply in sleep.

I hum a little against his neck and think about the evening. I would be lying if I said that I hadn't hoped that tonight's date would lead to sex, but I had no idea how emotional the whole experience would be. And when he asked me to take control? I've never felt so turned on in my life. I've never been that dominant in the bedroom, usually taking things as they come and rolling with them. But if that taste of being in charge was any indication of how it could be with Black, well, I just might have to take control more often. I grin against his neck at that and Black murmurs in his sleep.

Black, hmm… I wonder why he doesn't like his first name. Ian is a pretty name and it fits him well. Oh, alright, Black does work, meshing nicely with the artist vibe about him. While I've been thinking much too hard about his name preferences, Black has started to stir in my arms. Kissing my way up the back of his neck, I hear him groan. When I bite down on his earlobe, he moans, and I smile against the side of his face. If he's awake, then I want to play again.

But when I go to voice my invitation, the wrong name pops out of my mouth.

"Ian," I whisper into his ear and he stiffens in my hold. Equal parts surprised and not surprised by his reaction, I pull back and lean up to look over his shoulder and down into his face.

"Don't call me that, okay?" he murmurs gruffly, not meeting my gaze.

Alarm bells trip in my head, and my heart lurches painfully. This name thing obviously means more than I originally thought. But, completely uncharacteristically, I acquiesce without question or argument. Pulling myself over him, I nod and kiss him gently. I want to sob because something is very wrong, but I settle for distracting him by suddenly shoving my tongue down his throat. He groans hungrily, and I shiver in anticipation, forcibly pushing the issue aside in my mind, focusing instead on what I can do to this man to make him mine. As we come together a second time, it's languid and lovely, even as it stitches my heart up with too many dreams.

I don't like playing what-if games, but right now, my mind is playing one, *hard*. Aubrey lies sleeping beside me, having dropped off quickly after we drove ourselves to another earth-shattering climax. But my mind is racing. What if I'd met Aubrey two years ago? Would my feelings be the same? If so, what kind of man does that make me? And since when does a single night of sex wind me up in knots? *Be honest, Black, you really wouldn't know the answer to that question any more, would you?* I'd growl in frustration, but the object of my thoughts is curled up into my left side. Despite my brain's admonitions, I wrap my left arm around him tighter, drop a kiss on his head, snuggle in, and I know I can sleep. His even breathing soothes me, and my eyes drift shut. My last thought is that it wouldn't have changed this—I would have ended up in his arms no matter and my mind is just not sure what it thinks about that.

The roiling in my gut starts moments after I wake up holding Aubrey in my arms. He popped up, kissed my nose, and announced he was making me breakfast burritos and practically danced off to the kitchen, wearing only the boxer shorts he had somehow slipped back on without my seeing. I wonder if he was awake before me, just waiting for me to awaken. Part of me wants to melt at the thought, imagining him watch me sleep. Then, everything crashes in on me. A sense of guilt and betrayal suffuses me, crawling up my skin like a rash of heat.

What am I doing here? I swallow hard, my heart racing, my head feeling like I drank a fifth of Jack. I have to get out of here. Before... I can't even complete the thought.

I don't even know how I would begin to complete it. It was a mistake. No, I find myself shaking my head at *myself* and violently disagreeing. Being with Aubrey was not a mistake. Even though it was. Panic is bubbling up inside me. Beating at me-- I have to go *NOW*.

Ripping the covers back, I jump up, frantically searching for my clothes. The button down and slacks are on the floor next to my shoes. Socks are nowhere to be found, and I don't care. Leave, leave, leave NOW. The panic beats at me. Sweat is beading up on my forehead and down my spine. My breathing is shallow, and I have no way to fix it. My pulse is pounding in my head, in my ears; I can feel it in my arms, in my veins. My fingers start to twitch, an overwhelming desire to claw at my neck, my inner arms, anything to stop the itch that isn't really there. The tiny nerve endings in my skin aren't misfiring; my brain is.

If I could step back and be intellectual about this, I could tell myself this is a panic attack. Tell myself I should say something to Aubrey. But I can't, can't, can't. The word is chanting its way through my brain. My hands cover my ears, even though the sound is coming from the inside, from me. *Now, now, now!* I have to leave *now.* Shoes are finally on. Fingers shaking, I curl them into the palms of my hands, trying to still them. I walk out of the bedroom, which is, unfortunately, just off the kitchen. This hotel suite is not very big, so I can't escape without Aubrey seeing.

"Hi!" He smiles radiantly at me from across the kitchen and everything about him is too bright. Technicolor, I think. Bright paints required to get him right. *NO!* I'm going to come apart if I don't leave *NOW.*

"I have to go," I mumble, dropping my gaze to the floor. Despite my panic, I have enough sense to hide myself from the hurt I know I will see in those green eyes.

"Oh."

"I'll see you later."

"You can't stay for breakfast? It's Sunday."

I look up and his face holds a tight look, as if he's trying not to be hurt by my sudden change in demeanor.

"I'm sorry," I whisper. And because I can't help myself, even with the panic screaming at me to *LEAVE, LEAVE, LEAVE,* I step forward and peck him on the cheek. He stands there looking startled, confused, and worst of all, sad. He hasn't moved since I practically ran into the kitchen. Holding a carton of eggs in one hand and a frying pan in the other, he looks suspended, like a marionette whose puppeteer left him dangling in the middle of a scene. I can't keep looking at him or I will cry. Brushing past him, one last contact as my shoulder slides past his, I walk quickly to the door, throw up the lock, and duck out. But I can't forget the look on his face. It's competing with my panic for space in my brain, but I can't stop. Tears slide down my cheeks as I dash out of the lobby, slamming the atrium doors open in my haste. Home, I have to get home. *NOW.*

Hmmm... Coffee. My eyes practically roll back in my head as I savor my first sip of java for the day. It has been two days since Black and I had "done the deed," and I haven't heard peep one out of him. I don't really have much of an excuse for contacting him as far as work goes, but obviously, I have the excuse that we've been dating. Have we been dating? Was it just a lead up to some spectacular sex and then... Nothing? I hum again as I take another sip of my extra-large, super-strong, black-as-night coffee.

I know he was upset in the morning. You don't distance yourself that far from homemade scrambled eggs and not have some emotional reason, unless you have an ovo allergy. I grin at that. Ah, the excuses I will make for a gorgeous man. My grin turns to a grimace. It's not just that, I admonish myself. I like Black, a lot. More than I've liked anyone in a while. Maybe ever. I sigh and lift the lid off of my to-go cup to blow on the slightly too hot liquid. I'm preoccupied with cooling off my coffee, so I don't notice I'm no longer alone. The chair across from me scrapes along the floor as it is pulled out from the table, and I stop blowing on my coffee to look up.

Speak of the devil. Black slides his gorgeous, old self into said seat and settles his arms on the table top. Though my insides are jumping up and down and doing the hula, I keep my face neutral and blink my eyes a twinge sarcastically at him.

"Took you long enough, didn't it?" I quip sardonically. He has the good sense and good fortune to at least look chagrined, but I also see a hint of sadness there in his eyes. I'm not doing the hula inside anymore. My heart is thumping hard and fast, and I'm afraid of what he's going to say.

"I'm sorry," murmurs Black as he drops his eyes from mine to settle on his hands that he has steepled together on the table.

"Why didn't you call me back? Or return any of the half-dozen texts I sent you yesterday?"

"Sorry," he repeats, and his shoulders seem to hunch in as if he were trying to make himself smaller. I actually feel sorry for him, though I want to shake that feeling off. He was rude and hurtful, running off like that and then not responding back to me. After all the time we have spent together in the past month, it was shocking and painful for him to quick kiss me good-bye and practically run out the door. It was worse when he did not return my calls or texts. I purposely stopped myself at two calls and six texts. No point in pursuing the man if he really wanted to put as much distance between us as possible. But I really want to know why he left like he did.

With that in mind, I put my scrambled thoughts together and spew them out at him. "I know we're not in high school and going steady or anything like that." I force a lighter tone into my voice and laugh lightly. "But, give a guy a break. If you didn't have fun and you don't want to continue past this point or with more than the business relationship we're already in, you can certainly tell me, and I won't be bringing any drama. I'm a big boy."

Black's eyes shoot up to mine and he leans forward on the table, clenching his hands together even harder.

"Oh, no. That's not what was wrong. It's me. I just..." He pauses as if he doesn't really know how to continue. He takes a deep breath and pulls himself back into his chair. He seems to be trying very hard to regain his own composure.

"The truth is, Aubrey, I really like you."

My heart leaps up and starts tentatively dancing again. I'm sure I have a puzzled look on my face as I query, "Really? Then why did you run off instead of having the absolutely wonderful breakfast burritos I was trying to make for you? They, by the way, are the only thing I can cook."

I allow a small smile to creep onto my face because I'm beyond excited to see him. He hunted me down here and is clearly trying to apologize for running off. I'm not going to make it too hard for him to get back into my good graces because he's honestly already there, but I gotta make him sweat a little bit for it. He drops his head down and lets out a big sigh. I'd laugh, but I can see his eyes are screwed shut. Suddenly, I'm on high alert. I swallow hard.

"What's wrong, Black?" I call him his last name, even though "Ian" is on the tip of my tongue. I know he doesn't like that, and I am not about to send him running by calling him a name that clearly makes him uncomfortable. He sighs again, and blinks opens his eyes. I see a shy smile tugging at his lips and the effect is devastating. If I thought sexy slow smile Black was a heartthrob, well, I don't even have the right words to describe what shy smile Black is.

He moves his mouth around a couple of times as if to say something. and then he sighs again. All of this sighing is honestly giving me the giggles.

He notices my giggle and starts to laugh himself. "Fuck, why is this so hard?"

"It's not," I quip, "or rather, I'm not. I'm easy, very, very easy."

A wolfish grin flashes across his mouth for a moment before fading back into the shy smile. "It's been a long time," he finally declares in a rush.

"Since what? Since you got laid?" I waggle my eyebrows at him, and I'm genuinely having fun teasing him. He is most certainly dangerous for my heart. If I was disappointed at his disappearing act after a single night, I suddenly realize with piercing clarity, I am going to be totally and completely screwed if he does it again. I'm a little stunned to realize this man could easily break my heart in half. I lean forward, placing my elbows on the table.

"That is not a very good excuse, Black." He looks momentarily panicked, so I smile broadly because I really want to smile at him. Even though he made me upset, I really don't want him to be.

"Try again," I say, purposely taking a playful tone. By the relieved look on his face, I think he is catching on that I'm going to let him off the hook far more easily than I should.

He leans forward and puts his elbows on the table, mirroring my stance. His face is very earnest, and he surprises me by unclasping his hands and pulling mine into his.

"I'm really sorry, Aubrey," he practically whispers. "I got scared, and it's not a good excuse, but it's the truth. But I've spent the last two days kicking myself because…" he purses his lips, and I'm barely breathing as I wait for whatever he has to say. He's struggling to find the words to articulate what is on his mind and I take the time to roam my eyes all over his face. He looks tired, like he hasn't slept since we last saw each other.

He shakes his head. "I shouldn't have left like that. I should have told you…" He pauses again. "I should have said something. But I was overwhelmed. I should have just been honest. Aubrey… It's been a long time since I've felt this way. Everything has moved so fast, and I freaked out. And I ran away." He falls silent then, and I squeeze his hands in mine.

"Okay," I murmur, " I forgive you." Black visibly shudders and squeezes my hands in return.

I lean back, but I don't release his hands. "Do you want some coffee?"

"God, do I ever need coffee."

"Rough night?"

"You can say that again."

"Rough night?"

He smiles a genuine, full smile then and laughs. "Yes, rough night." He is toying with my fingers and lacing and unlacing them on the table. He is watching our clasped hands with rapt fascination.

"Black," I say softly. He looks up at me, an expectant expression on his face. I hate to mar his lightened mood, but I have to make sure he understands where I am standing.

"That can't happen again." His face falls a little, so I rush forward with my explanation. "If you are upset or unsure, you have to let me know. If you need space, just say so. Because I really like you, but I won't be able to forgive you disappearing like that again. I'm not a martyr, and I won't let you or anyone else run over me. I don't play it cool, ever. I just can't. Maybe I'm not built that way. So, for me, this, between us, is going somewhere. Where? No one knows, but I'm willing to see. I know it's awfully early to say all this, but," my tone lightens, and I can't help as I twist up the left corner of my mouth, "it is your fault, mister. You brought this conversation on yourself by running off. You can have slow, but you can't have on again/off again. Is that clear?"

A smile starts to spread across Black's face. "So direct, so dominant."

That startles a laugh out of me, and Black suddenly leans over the table and kisses me. A quick meeting of our lips, but my heart finally settles down into a funky, happy dance.

"Yes," he murmurs against my lips, nipping my bottom one as he draws himself back into his chair on the other side of the table. "I won't do it again."

"Good. Now go get yourself some coffee because you look like a truck hit you and you might fall over any second."

He laughs and rises, but comes to my side first, leaning down for a kiss. I tilt my head up to meet his lips. It is sweet and tender and just a little bit heartbreaking. It's perfect, but I know he still might break my heart into a million pieces. As he pulls back and walks off toward the barista and the hot, black coffee magic, I watch him knowing I might just have signed up for the biggest disaster of my life. But I can't bring myself to regret it.

CHAPTER 11

He forgave me. I turn the words over and over in my mind as I wait an insanely long amount of time for a simple cup of Joe. I still can't believe it. I glance over my shoulder to find Aubrey once again blowing on his too hot coffee. It's what he was doing when I walked in here today, where I knew I would find him. He's as addicted to the nectar of life that is coffee as I am, and this place is the closest shop to his hotel. The bored young barista plops down a too full mug on the counter and the hot liquid almost sloshes out on my hand. She turns to walk away, and I stop her by saying, "Excuse me. I asked for a to-go cup."

She huffs and rolls her eyes at me but picks up the mug and a to-go cup from beside the register, carelessly pouring the coffee into it. I can't help but admonish, "Be careful, you're going to burn yourself."

She rolls her eyes at me again, slaps a lid on the cup and hands it over to me, the bored expression on her face never changing.

"Thanks," I say, taking the cup. I walk over to the condiment station to add cream, no sugar. How Aubrey takes it straight black I don't know. My lips quirk up at the double entendre, "takes it straight black." Well, he has certainly taken me. The last forty-eight hours since I bussed him quickly in the kitchen, leaving him holding a frying pan in one hand and a carton of eggs in the other, have been hell on Earth. I didn't answer his two calls or his exactly half dozen text messages. I couldn't even bear to pick up the phone. I knew if I did, I would be back in his arms in a flash and the thought terrified me beyond anything in my life. *That's surprising*, my ridiculously unfair inner voice reminds me, *especially considering...* I practically scream in my own mind. That is the past, I remind myself for the millionth time in two days. This is the present, and Aubrey might just be the future. My heart thuds, and for a split second, I want to run again, but not for the reason I told Aubrey. No, everything is much worse than that. I push the thoughts aside as hard as I can. Once again, I breathe deeply and realize my hands are shaking. Damn it, I've taken too long at this. I grab the cream container and pour a generous amount into my cup before replacing the lid.

I stand there a minute or so longer, trying to calm myself down. Until I met Aubrey, I had not had a panic attack in over a year. And now I've had two. This thing with Aubrey has freaked me out. I spent the last forty-eight hours thinking, arguing with myself, going back and forth in mind, until I knew precisely one single thing: I wanted to be back with Aubrey. I would just have to deal with everything else. No way can I tell Aubrey the truth, but I reason with the part of my mind telling me I must. I will try to give him everything else and hope it is enough. Because, if it's not, I might really die of a broken heart this time.

It really should have been harder and more awkward than it was, but I couldn't spend another moment without Black beside me. Maybe it was all the texting we had done during his work travel or maybe it was how he had shown up at the coffee shop, his heart in his hand. And, I had no doubts it was his heart that had brought him back to me. It was becoming clear to me a battle raged inside Black between his heart and his mind. For some reason, those two essential parts of his self were not united in my favor. I didn't want to take it personally.

In fact, I knew I shouldn't, but I couldn't honestly help feeling disappointed that wanting to be with me wasn't as easy for Black to accept as wanting him was for me.

My head was clogged with all these thoughts as Black and I walked hand in hand down the street to my hotel. I hadn't said a word in invitation, but as soon as we finished our coffees, we had risen from the table almost in sync. Black had held out his hand to me and I had taken it because it felt like my life depended on it. We did not say anything as walked out of the café and down the street, nor do we now as we walk through the hotel's lobby doors, ride the elevator up, and exit on my floor. Still no words as I unlock my door with one hand because Black won't let go of my other one. After securing the lock, I lead him to the bedroom. Once inside, I turn to face him and slip my arms around his neck. He pulls me tightly to him, holding me, caressing my back. He drops his head, leaning his face against my forehead, his bright eyes gleaming sadly as if he doesn't already have my forgiveness.

I doubt he has his own.

"Aubrey," his voice sounds broken, lacking even the calm that he had held onto in the coffee shop. He slips his head down into the crook of my neck, breathing deeply, obviously taking in my scent as he always seems to do. I can feel him trembling against me, and all I want to do is comfort him.

"It's okay, Black," I breathe against his hair, kissing it, pulling his scent inside of me. "Let's just lie down, okay?" He nods against my neck but doesn't let go or move back. Though he is taller and larger, I am the one to nudge us toward the bed. I somehow manage to lean forward past Black to pull back the covers without him letting go of me. When I rise back to standing, I kiss his lips gently. "Get in. I will be right behind you." I kick off my shoes as I push him down to sitting on the edge of the mattress, and finally, he lets go of me. He nods once and makes quick work of his combat boots. When he finishes, he looks up at me expectantly, making me smile. I lean down and kiss him as I push lightly against his shoulders. "Scoot back." He complies docilely, his eyes never leaving mine, as if he is afraid I will disappear if he looks away for a moment. He scoots backwards across the bed. The sight would have been amusing if the moment did not feel so heavy. I climb in after him, fully clothed, just like he is. We settle on our sides facing each other and I pull the covers up to our waists. Then, I reach for him and he practically lunges for me, pulling me against him. He settles his face in the crook of my neck again and sighs. I smile softly as I settle my arms around him. I rub his back softly as I nestle my face against his neck. The sigh that escapes Black is long, making me sigh as well. Our bodies start to relax, and the stress of the last forty-eight hours seems to settle over us in drowsiness.

"Sleep, Black," I murmur against his neck. "I'll be right here when you wake up."

A sound close to a sob escapes his lips and a shudder rolls through his body. Whatever is trying to tear Black away from me must be very powerful to hurt him so. I tighten my hold and breath him in. He settles after a while, and eventually, I feel his breathing even out in sleep. It is only now that I sigh and relax against his slumbering form. I have no idea what comes next, but as I fall asleep, I hope I will be able to keep Black with me, and whatever is tearing him apart from the inside can be put to rest. My last thought is my heart won't survive if I can't find a way to heal his.

CHAPTER 12

$\mathcal{M}$ ay passes by in a blur of final construction plans, the buildup to the official groundbreaking for the park, and an ever-increasing number of dates with Black. And sex, lots and lots of sex. Not that I'm complaining. The man can have me anyway he wants me. And he does half of the time. The other half, I have him any way I want him. I have never had a partner before who was so completely in tune with and turned on by my needs. Needs I didn't even know I had before. But...sometimes he becomes very quiet and seems so far away. The moments never last long, but they worry me. On top of those moments of disconnection, I still haven't figured out why he doesn't want to be called Ian. Thus far, everyone I've met calls him Black.

Shaking my head to rattle the heavy thoughts out, I blink at my computer screen, barely seeing my work calendar in front of me. My phone rings, startling me so much I knock my mug of cold coffee off the corner of my desk. A wet stain of coffee widens below the mug on the carpet and I am surprised it did not break. Leaning over, I pick it up with my right hand as I grab my phone with my left. Jabbing the answer button awkwardly, I struggle to put the phone to my ear.

"Hello?"

"Aubrey, Aubrey, Aubrey. Whatever have you been up to?"

My Aunt Susan's chortle greets my ear, and I find myself smiling despite my worries about Black and our relationship. Relationship? Fuck, great, another thing to obsess over, the fact we have yet to define what we are doing with each other. *What you are doing with each other is fucking your brains out and having a hell of a time doing it.* I grin at myself, then realize I haven't heard what my aunt has been saying.

"So, I told your Aunt Patty that—" I cut her off mid-sentence.

"Sorry, Aunt Susan, I haven't heard a word you've said, head in the clouds I guess. How are you?"

Aunt Susan laughs. "Do you at least have a good excuse for being so distracted?"

Somehow the comment annoys rather than amuses me. "No, Aunt Susan, I don't. I'm just up to my neck in plans for the groundbreaking ceremony at the beginning of next week. I haven't had an update from a few of the contractors in weeks, and I just spilled my coffee on the floor when your call startled me. Nope, nope, not busy enough to be distracted at all." To say I am lucky in who my aunts are would be an understatement because Susan does nothing but laugh softly.

"Poor baby." And just like that, my tension breaks and I am laughing too.

"Thanks, Aunt Susie Q. I needed that."

Her voice is kind when she replies, "Just a bit too much stress, huh?"

"Yeah."

"How is your personal life treating you?"

"You get down to business right quick, don't you?"

More laughter, "Of course, I do. I know Patty is about to steal the phone from me so she can dominate the entire conversation. I have to pry the juicy tidbits out of you while I can."

"Why don't you just put the phone on speaker like you want to do anyway? Then you can tag team grill me."

"Excellent suggestion, lad. Okay, you are on speaker now."

"Hey, Aubrey! How are you?" Aunt Patty's voice chimes in brightly.

"I'm okay, Aunt Patty. How about you two?"

"Same as ever, fat and sassy," Susan interrupts.

"Susan! He wasn't asking you. We're fine, Aubrey. But it sounds like you are a bit stressed."

I blow out a breath. While I'd like to pour out my soul to my aunts, I'm not really sure it is the best idea. I take the moment to rise from my chair and stretch my back, the empty coffee mug hanging loosely from my hand.

"Yeah, I am."

"It's not just the park, is it, honey?" My Aunt Patty's voice is soft, soothing. As always, she knows immediately when I am upset. I laugh lightly and am grateful for these two women who comprise my family. Feeling like I might actually cry now, I sigh heavily before answering.

"No."

"Do you want to talk about it?" No, I don't, but I don't have anyone else to share this with. I might feel better if I let my aunts in on the situation.

"I guess." I walk into the kitchen, deposit the mug in the sink, and grab a roll of paper towels off the counter.

"So, things aren't going as well with Black as they were the last time we spoke?"

As I tear a few sheets off the roll and wet them at the sink, I ponder the question. "Well, yes and no. Something happened I really don't want to talk about, but..." I pause as I am unsure how to describe the situation without breaking Black's confidence. It is the first time I have ever hesitated to dump my relationship issues out on the kitchen table for my aunts to investigate and piece together like a jigsaw puzzle.

"But what, Aubrey?" Aunt Patty's voice is still soft, soothing, non-judgmental.

I sigh and pause for a moment. "I guess I could use to get it off of my chest. But no advice. I just need your ears."

"You have them," Aunt Susan replies, making me smile. She is always the bold one, but her love for me is fierce and protective.

I wring out the paper towels and walk back into my office area, dropping to my knees to clean the coffee out of the carpet. "Well, it is pretty obvious we click in a lot of ways. But... there is a hesitancy on Black's part. I know there is something he is not telling me. No, it is not cheating," I offer before they can suggest it. The thought of accidentally being someone's side-piece of ass, no, not someone's, Black's, slices through my heart like a blade. "Something bad happened to him, Aunt Patty." The tone of my voice has changed, surprisingly, the words much harder to push out of my mouth than I thought they would be. I feel like crying now and have to swallow hard to clear the sudden lump in my throat.

"I can feel it, the pain in him, just beneath his skin. It closes him up sometimes, and it takes all of my effort to reach him, to pull him back toward me. I know this all sounds vague and too emotional."

"No, Aubrey, it doesn't. You've always been so intuitive about people's feelings. You experience them right along with them, you with your soft and open heart."

Aunt Susan butts in, much more brash in her approach, which makes me smile, the interplay of their personalities so familiar and comforting to me, "So why don't you ask him what's wrong?"

"Because I know he won't tell me. He has this weird thing about his name—"

Susan cuts me off. "His name?"

"You remember, Susan, Aubrey said he likes to be called Black, his last name."

I nod as if my aunts could see me. "Yeah, I have accidentally called him Ian a couple of times and he freezes every time. A look of intense pain crosses his face and..." I'm practically whispering now as I scrub the carpet. "I really can't bear it."

"Oh, honey, you're already in love with him, aren't you?" Aunt Patty's voice is soft, but her words hit me like shrapnel from a bomb. I swallow, my throat suddenly dry. I lick my lips and look down at the crumpled-up paper towels, now discolored with coffee.

"No comment," I murmur because I really can't think of anything else to say in this moment as the blood rushes through my ears and the pit of my stomach drops out.

"It's okay, Aubrey." Now it is Aunt Susan's turn to comfort me. Swallowing hard again, unable to dislodge this emotional lump from my throat, I stand up and return to the kitchen to throw away the paper towels.

"I don't know what to do." My voice is cracking, and I am riding the edge of a sob. Tears threaten to overwhelm me, and I blink hard to push them back. Instead of returning to my office, I walk back into my bedroom and throw myself down on the unmade bed.

"I don't know that there is anything you can do right now, besides be there for him," Aunt Patty sagely advises. "He makes you happy most of the time, doesn't he?"

Now, I am crying. Trying so hard for my aunts not to hear my tears over the phone, I stuff my face into my pillow.

"Aubrey? Are you still there?"

Pulling my head up from my pillow, I dash my knuckles at the tears running down my cheeks. "Yeah," I manage to mumble out. Clearing my throat, even though the tears have not dried up, I repeat myself, "Yeah, I'm still here. And he does make me happy, Aunt Patty. Ridiculously so. On our third date, he took me to the county fair, and I won him a teddy bear."

"You did? Let me guess, the game involved baseball."

I laugh and realize I'm not so much crying anymore as I am hiccupping and sniffling.

"Yeah, the knock down the milk bottles game." I smile wide at the memory and pull myself into a seated position against the headboard. "You should have seen his face. He was so surprised and happy. He hugged it. He actually hugged it right away. He put it in his workshop on top of my favorite squirrel statute. He said he won't ever sell the squirrel because it is my favorite."

I'm babbling now, joy rising up in me as I think of all of the ways Black has made me happy, has shown he cares. "He always laughs at my jokes and usually gets my references. He brought me sunflowers on our first dinner date." Gushing, I'm gushing now, and I'm blushing as if my aunts could see me through the phone.

Aunt Patty chuckles, "I think you have your answer, Aubrey. It sounds like he's worth fighting for."

"Yeah," I feel rung out and exhausted but lighter than before my aunts called me. "Thanks for listening. I guess I just needed to get all of it out. Didn't realize how much it was weighing me down." I sigh and scoot myself down onto my back. I feel like I need a nap now. "He does make me happy, Aunties."

"That much we can tell. You wouldn't worry about him so if that it weren't the case. Hopefully he will feel comfortable enough with you to share his secrets soon. Sometimes, it just takes time to build enough trust with someone to pour out your past pains and disappointments. It sounds like his were pretty serious."

I sigh, feeling more relaxed and content than I have in days. "Yeah, you're right. I'll give him some more time. And, you know me, I'm nothing if not persistent."

"See, I knew we could cheer you up. And, despite the pain, we are happy for you. But I do have one last question before we let you go."

I should have been more suspicious considering it was my Aunt Susan speaking, but I walk right into it. "Sure, what do you want to know?"

"Is he any good in bed?"

"Susan!" I laugh my head off as Aunt Patty admonishes her girl-friend for, well, being herself.

"No comment, I'm never answering that question. On that note, aunties, I will talk to you later."

"Bye! Don't forget to call!"

"I won't. Love you."

"Love you too." I'm still laughing when I hang up the call. I slip back down into the bed and pull the covers up over my head. Exhaustion settles over me as I fall asleep instead of returning to work.

When I awaken from my nap, I find a text from Black asking me if I want to catch a movie. Grinning so hard my face feels like it might crack, I send back my reply.

Only if we can have lots and lots of popcorn.
His response does not disappoint.
Your wish is my command.
Smiling, I think, yeah, this man is worth waiting for.

CHAPTER 13

With the beginning of June comes the rainbow flags which start to sprout up on flag poles, in shop windows, sometimes even fluttering from those weird car window poles. Since I have had my nose stuck in my work for the past seven years, I have not paid much attention to Pride month before. But it seems a bigger deal here in the heart of Oakland than it was in my corner of Chicago or in any of the myriad cities I have worked in across the US. As I walk to the café for some black coffee magic on the first Saturday of June, a young hippie girl with rainbow hair and a tiny chihuahua hanging out in her backpack steps into my path, almost causing a collision.

"Hey!" She chirps cheerily at me as she presses a bright pink flier into my hand. "Happy Pride month!"

I can't help my smile as her happiness is infectious. "Thank you!"

Her smile grows impossibly wider at my response, and she starts chattering at me immediately. "As you can see here, this is a list of all of the activities for the month. Oakland has its official Pride celebration in September, but all the neighborhoods and suburbs host their own celebrations during Pride month. We even have a parade that goes down this street. You should definitely check it out."

Before I can respond, she jumps away like a happy squirrel, her dog seemingly lulled to sleep by the sway of her backpack as she jumps into another pedestrian's path to chat them up. "Hey! Happy Pride Month." I hear her greet her new captive audience, and I laugh as I continue down the sidewalk toward the café. Black is meeting me there as he always does on Saturday mornings. I peruse the flyer and am pleasantly surprised to see well over a dozen events outlined for the month. It all culminates in a local Pride parade in this neighborhood. I must not have been paying attention to where I was walking because I run headlong into someone shorter than me, almost knocking them over.

"Oomph, oh, I'm sorry," I spurt out as I look from the flier to the person I have almost flattened. Much to my surprise, it is Tilly.

"Aubrey!" she greets me, a flirtatious smile on her face as she winks at me. "Where's Black?"

I laugh because I recognize the question for what it is: snooping. "Now why do you think I would know that?" We both laugh because Black has spent every free moment with me since we met, including a few more trips to Tilly's place.

"Oh, I don't know," she quips, "maybe because you seem to be his favorite person in the world."

Caught off guard, I blush, *hard*. Tilly points at my face and doubles over with laughter.

I fake huff at her but cannot help laughing at my own expense. I am surprised when she pulls me into a bear hug, especially considering that she is 5'4" at most. When she lets me go, she notices the pink flyer in my hand.

"Oh, are you planning on attending any of the events? You really should. The Sirens enter the float competition every year. We haven't won yet, but there is always a first time for first place." Just like the hippie rainbow girl, Tilly's excitement is catching.

"I've never been to any Pride celebrations before."

Tilly looks surprised for a moment then she grins. "We'll just have to remedy that." Glancing down at her watch for a moment, she winces. "I'm late, but stop by the bar next Saturday morning, and we'll chat about it. Bring Black with you." Without waiting for any response on my part, she waves the hand with a palm tattoo at me and hurries on down the street, leaving me standing in front of the coffee shop.

I pull the door open and see Black seated at our usual table. If it is free, we sit at the table we first met at every time we come here. No discussion, no outright decision to do so, but I love the little ritual. Black already has his cup of coffee doctored up with cream, and he nods toward the to-go cup on the table across from his.

"All black," he teases, his eyes shining happily. Instead of sitting in the chair he just shoved out from the table with his foot, I stand over him, grip his hair at the nap of his neck, and drop my head to kiss him. He chuckles when I pull away. "Good morning to you too, Aubrey."

Grinning, I take the proffered seat and open the lid to blow on the coffee. Black continues to chuckle at me.

"What? They make it too hot here. You don't want me to burn my tongue off, do you? Then what would I kiss you with?"

Black just shakes his head and takes another drink of his doctored-up brew. Once I am sure the coffee won't scald my tongue off, I take a sip. "Umm, that is good."

Black chuckles at me again. "What do you have planned for today?"

"What? You expect me to plan everything? So lazy," I tease him. He grins at me and slips his foot against mine. "Are you playing footsie with me?"

He laughs. "Maybe."

"Hey," I interject as I remember the flier I set down on the table when I picked up my coffee. "This hippie girl in the street gave me a flier for Pride month events. We should check some out."

Black swallows his drink of coffee and looks at me thoughtfully. "Yeah," he says slowly, "we should."

I am becoming ridiculously excited. "Tilly invited us to the bar next Saturday morning. She didn't say, but I think she is planning something for the parade."

Black nods slowly, thoughtfully, a little quieter than I expected him to be. "She probably is."

I am a little disappointed by his noncommittal tone but decide to lay my cards out on the table. "I've never been to any Pride events before, not even a parade." I am feeling a bit sheepish now and I drop my gaze from his, ostensibly so I can sip my coffee, but really so I can hide my embarrassed expression.

"Do you want to go?" Black asks gently, and I raise my eyes to find his face soft, contemplative.

My heart flutters, and I forget everything other than how hard I am falling for him. "What?"

Black laughs softly. "I asked if you wanted to go to the parade. Tilly and the Sirens will definitely have a float there."

"You'll go with me?" I'm not sure why I'm feeling so shy about this. Maybe because I feel silly that I have never been to a Pride celebration before.

Black gives me that sweet and earnest smile that never fails to send my heart pitter pattering. "Sure, Aubrey, if you want to go."

"I do." It comes out breathily. I feel relieved, though I'm not sure why I thought Black would judge me. "I'm a Pride virgin. You will have to be gentle with me," I tease, suddenly feeling more like myself.

Black laughs loudly. "Oh, Pride virgins are my favorite kind."

We must have been talking too loudly because I hear a snort of annoyance from somewhere behind me. I turn and see an older woman glaring our way before she huffs and puffs her way out the door. When I turn back to Black, we both dissolve into laughter. As we drink our coffee and the conversation turns to other things, I contemplate how different my relationship with Black is from any other I have had in my adult life. Guys either don't like how serious I am about my business or find me too silly for their taste. But Black is nothing like them. He seems to like my silliness, my need to make people, particularly him, happy. He is as dedicated to his career as I am to mine. Thus far, we have had no conflict in that respect. Whenever Black seems lost in painful thoughts, I always try to pull him back to me with some joke or silliness. I watch him as I drink my coffee. We have fallen into a companionable silence. I wonder if he is thinking about me as I am thinking about him. Feeling a little bit feisty now, I pull my foot up his leg from his ankle to his knees. Black gives me an amused and interested glance.

"Are you playing footsie with me now?"

"Maybe."

Black laughs at my reiteration of his own response. "What do you want to do today?"

"Something fun."

Black smiles, rising from his chair to stretch. I eye him appreciatively as he pulls his arms above his head and bends his back to pull out the muscles. His shoulders are wider than mine, and he is all muscle from the distinct vee of his torso down to his trim hips and muscular thighs. Black clears his throat to get my attention back to his eyes. His expression is amused and wicked, his grin playful and a hint naughty.

"Do you like what you see?" he drawls, echoing what he said to me the first day we meet.

I can't help laughing as he strides to my chair and looks down at me like I am something he wants to eat. He takes my free hand and pulls me to my feet. He steals a quick kiss and we both grin and laugh.

"It doesn't matter what we do," I breathe out. "As long as I get to do it with you." Black's dark eyes shine brightly, and his smile is the sweet, shy, earnest one that I cherish.

"Ditto."

Barking out a laugh, I favor him with a suspicious look. "You did not just quote Patrick Swayze from *Ghost*, did you?"

Black laughs again, and we tease each other as we walk out of the coffee shop, hand in hand.

CHAPTER 14

The next Saturday morning dawns bright and sunny. I wake with a slight feeling of unease, no doubt because of the plans Aubrey and I made for today. I try to shake it off with a shower and an extra cup of coffee before I leave home to meet Aubrey at the café.

Aubrey smiles so softly and sweetly at me when he spies me come in the door. For a moment, my emotions overwhelm me, and I have to blink hard not to cry. Aubrey is so much more than I ever expected him to be. I just hope I can manage an even keel while taking him to all the events of Pride month. By the time I make it to our favorite table, Aubrey has his head tilted back expectantly, clearly waiting for a kiss. Obliging him because my need for the physical contact matches his, I linger a moment longer against his lips.

"Morning," he whispers against my mouth, his bright emerald eyes dancing. Straightening back up to standing, I tip my head toward the counter, indicating my need for coffee. He grins and nods. By the time the surly teenaged barista manages to give me my cup, Aubrey has come over to wait with me. He slips his hand in mine, and after I doctor up the cup of Joe with milk and sugar, which causes Aubrey to fake shudder, we walk out the café doors hand in hand.

It takes mere minutes to walk the early Saturday morning streets to Tilly's place. No vehicles grace the parking lot but Tilly's hog, so we must be the first to arrive. The front door is unlocked, but ever polite, Aubrey knocks first then pushes the door open and calls out "hello" as he leads the way inside. Boxes of float decorations grace the counters and the tops of the tables Tilly has pushed together for this planning session with the Sirens. Tilly stands behind the bar, tapping her fingers impatiently against the counter as she waits for her coffee machine to finish making the pot. Casting a glance over her shoulder, she grins sleepily at us.

"Good morning boys."

Aubrey walks to the bar and leans against it, immediately falling into conversation with Tilly. I look around the room from my vantage point near the door. Memories plague me, and I'm once again unsure this was such a good idea. After pouring herself some coffee, Tilly comes around the counter and nods toward the boxes.

"So, you guys up for the cause?"

Aubrey looks at me with such a joyful smile across his beautiful face I want to cry. But an uglier emotion crashes through me as I remember the last happy face I saw at Pride, just a few short years ago. I feel the blood drain from my face, and Aubrey's countenance falters. He looks like he is about to ask me what is wrong, when I practically yell, "No! We can't."

A confused look of shock, dismay, then vibrant anger light up Aubrey's face. *Beautiful* is my first thought. My second thought is *Oh, shit, what did I just do?* I don't have time to contemplate it as Aubrey's face hardens as he grabs my arm and starts pulling me toward the door.

"We will be right back," he somehow manages to sound pleasant as he throws that line over his shoulder at Tilly as he practically frog marches me to her front door. Before he shoves through the door, he pulls me to face him and grits out, "May I speak to you a moment?" But it's a declaration of intent and not a question, as he drops my arm and slams the door open, leaving me no option other than to follow him out into the sunshine.

As soon as that door closes behind us, I shove Black back against the same wall that I kissed him against that very first night.

"First, how dare you answer for me? Tilly asked us *both* if we wanted to help and you just said no, as if you would know my reaction. Second, why did you say no? Third, are you embarrassed by me? Or just in public?"

I cannot believe that Black, of all people, has done this to me. After all of those boring, staid motherfuckers who wanted me to mute myself, turn myself down, I cannot believe what Black just did. It's not like I am flamboyant as fuck, I like what I like and enthusiastically so. I just never expected Black to do the same thing to me that they had.

Black swallows hard, clearly fumbling for an explanation of his little outburst. "I did this before with someone important to me."

"So, what, I'm not important enough? Oh, fuck you, Black."

"No! Aubrey! That's not what I meant."

"Then what do you mean?"

Black hesitates.

"Oh, no, we are not doing this again. Fine, you do *whatever*. I'm going back in there to tell Tilly that *I will* be helping her with her float. You made a mistake introducing me to your friends if you didn't want them to like me."

I drop my hands from his chest and turn to go. But Black grabs me by the arm, stopping my forward momentum. I whirl back around and shake Black's hand off of my arm.

"What? Speak now, Black, or forever hold your goddamn peace! I'm done!"

Black grabs me again and pulls me close. I fight for a second then just stand in Black's grasp, staring him hard in the face. "What. Do. You. Want? I'm leaving."

"No," Black's voice is hoarse. "I'm sorry, Aubrey. It was automatic."

"Sorry isn't good enough when I don't know what the fuck *your* problem is."

"It's not you."

"Well, you could have fucking fooled me."

My anger is slightly diminishing, back down to a simmer from a rolling boil.

Black's hold on me tightens, as he brings one hand up to brush the hair back from my face. "I'm sorry."

"It doesn't count if you don't say what you are sorry for, and I swear to god, if you say because you are upset, then I will probably bite you and not in the way you like."

Black has the fucking audacity to chuckle at that. I try to struggle out of his grasp again, but his arms are suddenly like iron bands, pulling me into his chest. I want to scream, and I have to bite my tongue to stop myself. Instead, I quirk up my left eyebrow and say, with sarcasm dripping from my words, "Oh, are you going to kiss it and make it all better now? That doesn't work when all *I want* are your words, your words explaining what the fuck just happened in there?! You went white as a fucking ghost as soon as Tilly even mentioned the Pride parade and you tripped over your goddamn tongue to decline an invitation extended to *both of us*!"

"I haven't gone to a Pride parade since my parents died. It used to be something I did with my mother. My dad would wear one of those cheesy 'I love my gay son' T-shirts. It was a big deal to her, to them both, to show their support of me."

"You could have fucking told me that, Black."

"I know, I should have."

"So, why didn't you?"

"Because it hurts too much."

"Black, as I told you once before, that is not a good enough excuse. What the hell am I supposed to do if you keep hiding things from me? This was important. You knew Pride was coming up. You even knew I wanted to go, with you…to my first Pride parade. Hell, you were the one who invited *me*."

"I know Aubrey, I'm truly sorry. It just popped out."

"What I want to know is why?" Fuck it all, I'm crying now. This hurts far worse than I realized a moment ago. I was too blinded by anger, but now that is wearing off, my chest aches. I thought Black was different. I thought he liked me for me. Hell, I really thought he was falling in love with me like I'm falling in love with him. Well, you were wrong, Aubrey, for about the fiftieth fucking time. As soon as the word "no" fell from his lips, I felt the same as I had when other guys gave me side eye for my abundant enthusiasm and sass, or my stockpile of pop culture references. Disappointed, sad, and annoyed at being found to be "too much." But considering how I feel about him, the rejection in that word makes me feel so much worse. Part of me wants to just reason it all away, so what if he doesn't want to go to Pride with me? I can go myself. But that would be lying to myself, and I simply refuse to do that.

"I wanted to go with you, Black, to my first Pride parade." I'm practically whispering now, and my gaze has dropped. I can't stand to look into his eyes when I'm fucking crying over, well, fuck, I don't even know what I'm crying over because Black won't fucking tell me. Now I'm angry again, so I jerk my head up to meet his surprisingly worried face. He looks almost as devastated as I feel, and my heart kicks up for a moment. But then I harden it. No, he doesn't get to feel kicked in the gut when he's the one doing the kicking.

"Let me go," I seethe between my teeth.

"My mom," Black cries out and I'm shocked. First, I'm shocked he spoke at all, and second, I'm shocked that his shout sounds suspiciously like a real answer, not like the half answer he gave me a moment ago.

"What about your mom, Black?" I query him, looking him directly in the eyes. I want to see if he is truly telling me something important or if this is just a distraction, a deflection from the real problem.

Black pulls me even closer and lowers his head and rests it on my shoulder. I'm not resisting his hold any longer, but I sure as hell am not relaxing into it. "Spit it out, Black. This is your one chance to explain what the fuck you just did to me in there."

Black shudders and pulls me closer. I don't resist and find myself cradled against his chest, my head in the crook of his neck, mirroring his stance with me. "It's more than just doing Pride with my parents. My mom *loved* the Pride parade. She helped organize the first one in

117

this neighborhood and every single one after that, up until her death. I guess I forgot how much it meant to her and how much it meant to me until Tilly asked us to help. I haven't helped in any meaningful way since she died. I'm sorry, Aubrey."

I whisper against his neck, "Why didn't you say anything when we talked about Pride last week? When I told you I have never gone before? Why did you say you would come with me? Why did you *invite* me to go with you? Why didn't you tell me any of this?" I manage to pull back in Black's arms far enough to look him in the eyes. "You could have told me all of this. But you didn't and what I want to know is why? Why didn't *I* matter enough for you to tell me?" My voice is dropping to a whisper and the tears that had dried up at the beginning of his explanation are starting to flow again. I look him in the eyes as I state the heart of the matter. "Why didn't you want to tell me?"

Black sighs, and I swear that I see tears glistening on his lashes as he blinks at me. "It's not that, Aubrey. You matter so much. I didn't want to disappoint you and… Well, I thought I could handle it. Then, when Tilly asked just now, I guess the memories hit me and I lashed out. I'm really sorry, Aubrey. I really am. You have to believe me. I didn't mean to hurt you, and I am so fucking sorry that I did. Will you please forgive me?"

My heart keeps catching, keeps cracking wider and wider. I am so in love with Black that I'm drowning in it. I'm not satisfied with his answer because it tastes like a partial truth, enough reality in those statements to distract me from the core of truth I am positive this man is hiding from me. But, can I walk away from this, from him? Because that is what this moment feels like to me, a crossroads; either I accept his answer and continue trying to ferret the whole truth out of him, or…I walk away. And, with that thought, I realize I've already made up my mind. "Okay." It is a barely audible word, but when Black sighs deeply, I know he heard me. He is staring at me with such need in his eyes my heart breaks again, for him this time and not myself.

"I mean it, Aubrey, I'm so sorry."

I swallow and tell a little half-truth myself to match with the half-truths I am sure he just told me. "I know." But, I don't know. I don't know what to think, but in my heart of hearts, I do know what I'm going to do. "I forgive you."

Black gives a little cry at that, startling me. He drops his head back to my shoulder, almost like he is hiding his face from me. Then I feel hot tears and his warm lips against my neck. "I'm so sorry, Aubrey." He keeps repeating it, over and over again. I finally put my arms around him, and he slumps against me. We stay like that, crushed together, leaning against that familiar brick wall outside of Tilly's Wine Bar and Grill, for a long while. When we finally pull apart, I feel hollow inside. I'm not really sure what just happened here, but I sure as hell know it is not over. Black leans down and I meet him halfway for a tender kiss that kills me softly. His arms slide from around me, but he grasps my right hand with his left and leads me back inside. Glancing at my face for a moment, he clears his throat and calls out to Tilly, who is currently on her knees and elbow deep in a box of float decorations, "Tilly, we can help after all. What do you need?"

I just lied through my fucking teeth to Aubrey, and I cannot swallow hard enough to push down the bile that keeps rising in my throat. Oh, my parents did love Pride, especially my mother. She would tell anyone who listened she was the ultimate supportive mom long before Ellen DeGeneres's mother supposedly set the standard. I had pointed out to her on multiple occasions that Ellen is about two decades older than me, so of course her mom did it first, but my mom always waved it off.

Someone else had loved Pride just as much; the last person I attended with over two years ago. But I can't tell Aubrey about it. About any of it. The thought of speaking *those* words turns the bile hotter in my throat. I might actually throw up.

To make it worse, I lied about the last time I helped with Pride. I doubt Tilly will mention anything about past years, but if she or anyone else does, Aubrey will know I lied to him, and I doubt he will forgive me for it. But I can't talk about any of it without coming un-fucking-glued, and I can't, no, *won't*, go back there again.

I breathe deeply and count to ten as I watch Aubrey and Tilly chat away about design, pomping, chicken wire, and tissue paper. I'm a little bit shocked my gambit worked. I hated lying to him, but some things just can't see the light of day without destroying my whole world. I've been there once. A horrifying chill creeps through my veins as I realize that if Aubrey leaves me I will be back there again, on my knees, dying. I shake my head to dislodge the thought and push away from the bar to join Aubrey and Tilly as they plan "The Greatest Pride Float Ever," as Aubrey just christened it. When I slide up to him, wrapping an arm around his waist, he glances up at me and gives me a tremulous smile. I kiss his lips softly again; hoping, praying I can figure this all out before I hurt him one too many times and he walks away forever.

CHAPTER 15

Since my aunts called me out on being in love with Black and our subsequent disagreement over Tilly's Pride float, I am just a bit nervous about our date tonight. When Black picks me up for a quick drink at The Moose, I am unsure what to expect. The Moose and its owner, Chuck, turn out to be the exact opposite of any of the possibilities I had imagined. It wouldn't be fair to call the place a dive, but it is on the dark side with ancient wood paneling, a scarred wooden bar, and a small stage in the back corner. Okay, so not a dive is a bit generous, but the bar has a homey, welcoming feeling to it, and I can immediately see why Black would like such an establishment. I immediately noticed the "Ally" sticker in the front window. "Gay friendly, huh?"

Black laughs, "Yeah, Chuck is Tilly's dad." Black nods to the burly, barrel chested man behind the bar. Chuck must be in his sixties, and as he chats up a customer, I am sure that I hear a bit of an Irish brogue.

"Is Chuck from Ireland?"

"Yeah, former British Royal Air Force. I'm not sure when he immigrated, but Tilly was born here, like me."

"Oakland native, huh?"

"Yup, I can't keep any secrets from you."

The smile on my face freezes, and I purposely avoid eye contact for a moment by stepping up to the bar and dropping my gaze to the polished surface. Black and I both know good and damned well that he is keeping plenty of secrets from me.

Black is silent now, and I know he has realized the import of the words that just tripped out of his mouth. Damn it. I just wanted to have some quiet time with Black. Now everything feels murky and weird, just like it did after our fight at Tilly's over Pride. I shake my head as I step forward to place my palms on the scarred wooden bar, running my fingers over the polished top. Breathing deeply for a moment, I chance a glance up at Black. The expression on his face is pained, and it gut punches me. Fuck, I want to cry now.

Chuck saves both of us from conversations neither of us want to have at the moment with a cheery "Hello!"

He is standing in front of us, leaning his hands against the bar. I can see the resemblance to Tilly, the same mirth filled eyes and stocky build. Hell, Tilly even has his masculine hands, and his are also liberally sprinkled with tattoos. "I haven't seen much of you around here, laddie. How long's it been?"

"Too long," Black mutters in answer, and I chance a peek at him out the side of my eye. He looks a little pale and disconcerted. Before I can think of what to do next, Black is introducing me. "Chuck, this is Aubrey. You know the park the city is putting on in Danbury Ave? Aubrey here is planning the whole thing."

Chuck whistles and leans over the bar to give me a hearty slap on the shoulder. Thank goodness he was at some distance, or I'm sure he would have knocked me over with that "love tap." "Good for you." His next question is for the both of us. "What are you drinking?"

Black orders a rum and Coke. I'm not feeling like anything at the moment, my emotions roiling a bit too much in my gut for a drink right now. "I'm fine."

Chuck nods and grabs a glass for Black's drink from a shelf beneath the bar. I turn and glance around the room. Black and Chuck continue to chat as my eyes zero in on the stage and the karaoke machine a young man, probably in his mid-twenties, is setting up alongside a microphone stand and speaker at the front of the stage. I'm in a weird mood now, part sad and anxious, part restless. So, without so much as a glance at Black, who is still conversing with Chuck anyway, I wind my way through the tables and chairs toward the stage. The Moose is closer to packed than I realized when we came in the door. I stop at the foot of the stage, and the younger man catches my eye, even as he bends over to fiddle with the knobs on the machine.

"Want to sing?"

"Yeah," I mutter in reply, seized by a clawing need to express my uncertainty, my need, and my ever-growing love for Black. "Do you have contemporary songs or just oldies?" The young guy grins, his smile revealing dimples in his golden tanned cheeks. Pretty. Not my type at all, but the young man should certainly attract attention from all sexes and genders with that smile and those dimples.

"I have anything and everything you could ever want." He's flirting just a little which brings my attention around to the reason why I am standing here. I slip my phone out of my back pocket and pull up my music app.

Turning the screen toward him, I ask, "Do you have this?"

His smile grows a little wider, and he nods. "Sure, I most definitely have that song."

"Good. It's what I want."

He has been bending over the machine so long I wonder if he is getting a head rush. He clicks a few more buttons then straightens as he looks at me and hands me the microphone. "Ready when you are."

I blow out a breath and find Black still at the bar. He turns his head and his eyes catch mine. "Yeah, I'm ready."

The young man steps down from the stage, and I watch as the words appear on the screen. When the music starts, I am ready to pour my soul out through the lyrics.

"Since when do you feature karaoke, Chuck?"

Chuck shakes his red head which is generously threaded with silver. "That new kid Rylan insists it will be good for business. Hey, lookie there. I think your boy is about to sing you something."

Chuck laughs, and I seek out Aubrey. I didn't realize he'd slipped away from my side. But now he is up on the stage next to the karaoke machine. A young guy I can only guess is Rylan is bending over it, fiddling with the knobs. The machine kicks on with a whine, and the kid nods at Aubrey who looks a little nervous but blows out a breath, nods back, and lifts the microphone to his mouth as his eyes seek out mine. Rylan steps back off the lip of the stage and blends into the crowd around the edge. Pop strains filter through the speakers; I don't recognize the music.

The song is plaintive, seductive, and beautiful; a lover pleading for a kiss, but then begging his lover not to hurt him. Aubrey sways soulfully with the music, the overhead lights playing gorgeously off his hair, his skin, his lips so close to the microphone. I'm not the only one transfixed by his performance, by his beauty. At the first sound of his clear tenor voice, everyone in the bar seems to turn in his direction. He is looking at me the entire time, and I couldn't look away if my life depended on it.

When the song ends abruptly on the last refrain, the room is silent for a moment before a raucous applause breaks out. Aubrey hands the microphone back to Rylan who steps forward on the stage and speaks into it. "Thanks, that was beautiful, wasn't it everyone? Fantastic first song for our first karaoke Thursday. Who's next?"

A middle-aged woman with pink hair jumps up to grab the microphone from Rylan as her group of friends cheer and throw out song suggestions. Aubrey has made his way to me now, and he looks up at me, his face serious before a shy smile peeks out. My heart is hammering in my chest because the song was obviously for me, a comment on our relationship. He is begging me not to hurt him again, yet he is forgiving me at the same time. I have no choice but to lean my head down and kiss him gently as I take one of his hands in mine.

"What song was that?" I whisper in his ear as the pink haired lady belts out "These Boots are Made for Walking" to the cheers of her table of friends.

Aubrey turns to lean back against my chest, and I wrap my arms around him, settling my hands against his waist. The Moose isn't a gay bar, but we don't have to worry about public displays of affection here. Just like my parents, Tilly's dad embraced her when she came out. Anyone steps out of line at The Moose and Chuck caves their head in with his big ole Irish fists. Aubrey hasn't answered me, so I kiss his ear and repeat my question.

"I liked your song. You sang it so beautifully. What was it? I've never heard it before."

Aubrey sighs and settles back against me. He turns his head to look at me as if he is searching for something in my gaze. He must be satisfied with what he sees as he smiles softly.

"'Bite,'" by Troye Sivan."

"It was beautiful. You were beautiful singing it."

He faces forward again and snuggles further into my chest. "Thank you."

He's very quiet and my heart throbs because I know I'm the reason why. I want to apologize again for leaving him alone, the unnecessary problems I caused at Tilly's the other morning, the lies he doesn't know I've told him, and anything else I may have inadvertently done to hurt him since I met him. I know he has forgiven me for everything he knows about, but his song choice tonight shows me he's still hurting. I drop a kiss in the crook of his neck. Besides my obvious transgressions, I know I've been a bit weird more than a few times, pulling back, going quiet suddenly. Aubrey always notices, always finds some way to pull me back. But for the first time, it occurs to me all my issues have had an impact on him. It's not a happy or comfortable realization. But what can I do without breaking apart or breaking away from him? Pain slices through me at the thought, my arms tightening reflexively around Aubrey. And, as always, he senses my distress and turns in my arms, slipping his around my neck and meeting my lips for a kiss.

"Are you all right?" he whispers against my mouth, his eyes open, looking into mine.

"Yeah," I murmur, changing the subject back, stuffing my fear, my pain, my past back into the corner closet of my mind where it belongs. "It was a lovely song, Aubrey," I whisper against his mouth before softly kissing him again. We just got here, but now I want to be alone with him, to worship his body until he forgets my flaws, so I can pretend they don't matter anyway.

"Let's go."

He pulls back with a slightly surprised look. "But we just got here. I haven't even had a drink yet."

I answer him honestly, "I just want to be alone with you."

He stares into my eyes a long moment then smiles wickedly. He glances over behind the bar and catches Chuck's eye. "Bye, Chuck, I guess we're leaving. Nice to meet you."

Chuck laughs and waves us away. "Next time, buy a drink. I knew that machine wouldn't bring in no money, just American Idol wannabes." Aubrey laughs, taking Chuck's ribbing in stride.

"For sure. Next time I'll have twice as much to make up for it."

Chuck grins widely, his brogue coming on more strongly. "You better. I'm holding you to it."

Aubrey laughs in return, and I start tugging him toward the door. When we make it outside, I pull him to a stop almost abruptly, my feelings threatening to burst out of my chest.

"I won't," I barely gasp out, my eyes searching his face for any hint of understanding even though I've given him nothing, no key to understanding why I am the way I am, knowing I don't ever intend to do so.

"Won't what?" Aubrey breathes out.

"Bite," I say, almost choking on my emotions and meaning.

Aubrey smiles brightly, sunshine again, in the middle of the night. "Even if I ask nicely?"

I almost choke on my laugh and kiss him softly before pulling back to take his hand and lead him to the car. "Whatever you want, Aubrey. That is what I want to give you."

CHAPTER 16

When The Sirens roll into Tilly's bright and early on the third Saturday in June, they blow all of my preconceived notions out of my head. To be honest, I wasn't sure what kind of ladies would comprise the membership of Oakland's only openly lesbian motorcycle club. When I asked about membership, Tilly informed me that being LGBTQ wasn't a requirement but being an ally was. As it stood, most of the members were LGBTQ, but not all. Considering the lesbians I know best are my aunts, neither of whom were particularly masculine or overly femme, I had no idea what to expect from Tilly's group of friends. But I was floored by the wide spectrum of womanhood that flowed through the door. Sylvia, their president, breezed into Tilly's with the command of Queen Elizabeth the First as well as her hair color. It was clear her visage inspired The Sirens' insignia. At least six feet tall with sunset orange hair down to her waist and forest green eyes, she more than vaguely resembled the goddess from the famous Botticelli painting "The Birth of Venus." Introducing herself as "an accountant by day and hell-raiser by night," Sylvia owned the room immediately with her sheer charisma of presence alone.

As more of the women arrived, I realized how stereotypical my expectations of The Sirens were. I had expected more "butch" figures along the lines of Tilly with her muscled-up physique, tattoos, and faux hawk. Yet, the six ladies who showed up were a diverse group. A pediatrician named Tricia, a tiny Asian woman who apparently has black belts in three martial arts, brought a box full of donuts. Wanda, an African American railroad conductor for Amtrak, lugged in two containers of float decorations before running back out to pick up Kirsten from her night shift at the twenty-four-hour diner Black and I had visited for our first lunch date and several times afterward. Turns out Kirsten was our gum smacking waitress, her appearance waif-like, complete with white blonde hair, eyes the color of an iceberg, and a wispy, theatrical voice. While pouring herself a cup of coffee from the pot behind Tilly's bar, she explains to me she is working her way through college and had joined The Sirens for the sense of community. She had inherited her father's classic Harley and had been riding for as long as she could remember.

The last two ladies to show up are a couple, Louise and Carolyn. While Carolyn is the general manager of the local NPR radio station, Louise is an artist, a painter who seems to know Black quite well. I am intrigued and even caught off guard by how Carolyn greets Black with a long hug, whispering something in his ear that makes him sigh and nod his head. It is suddenly clear to me most, if not all, of these women know whatever it is that haunts Black, though most of them seem ready to steer very clear of the topic. Carolyn is the only exception, but her private moment with Black is as far as their history seems to take them. After patting him affectionately on the cheek, Carolyn joins the rest of us at Tilly's planning table in the middle of the dining room.

While the larger Oakland Pride celebration is scheduled in September each year, as the hippie girl mentioned to me, a few of the neighborhoods sponsor smaller parades and festivals during Pride month. The Sirens have placed in the float competition five years running, and this year, everyone is all in for a run for first place. As we gather around the table on which Tilly had a long sheet of butcher paper filled with drawings, diagrams, and measurements, a round of final introductions begins as not everyone has managed to get acquainted with me yet. When Sylvia eyes Black meaningfully, her glance shifting between the two of us as if looking for a confirmation of our relationship, I have no idea what Black is going to say. It isn't as if we have discussed labels. In fact, I have assiduously avoided saying anything more than what I told Black when he came back to me in the coffee shop. Beyond agreeing with me that we are "going somewhere," I honestly have no clue what Black is thinking about us.

As Sylvia stares me down with her all too knowing smirk as if she is daring me to deny or confirm what is clear to the entire room, I'm momentarily at a loss for words. But with a quick glance at Aubrey's nervous face as he waits for me to either confirm, deny, or side-step our connection, I realize I can't go on as I have been. If I'm going to start moving on with my life, if I'm going to make something important with Aubrey, then I need to start now by laying claim to him in front of my circle of friends. I open my mouth purposefully as Sylvia continues to look between Aubrey and me expectantly, and I do something I've never done before with Aubrey, something that a year ago I vowed I would never do again.

"Sylvia, everyone, this is Aubrey, my boyfriend. He is the park planner the Oakland City Council found to design the new space on Danbury Avenue." My words come out in a rush, too quick, but everyone heard that one little word. Eight sets of eyes bore into mine, but I am looking at one face only. And that face breaks out into a sunshine smile brighter than I have seen since our fight outside this very building, possibly brighter than I have seen it since the day Aubrey and I met. Luckily for me, my friends understand the import of the moment and murmur greetings to Aubrey as the two of us stare at each other. When I return Aubrey's smile, it is not forced. It feels like the easiest and happiest smile I have ever had the pleasure to experience. No negative thoughts intrude, no harsh reminders of a past and pain better left hidden and forgotten.

For the first time, I feel no trepidation about my feelings for Aubrey, and the moment is liberating. My hands shake a little as I clasp his hand and place a soft kiss on the back of it. We aren't alone, but the moment feels private, and I try to memorize the details of his face, his hair, his eyes, his lips, as if this is either the first or last time I will ever see him.

"And second place goes to," the announcer fumbles with the list, even though he just read off places fifth, fourth, and third, with little problem, "The Sirens Motorcycle Club! Co-sponsored by Tilly's Bar & Grill. Congratulations!"

Our entire group groans before cheering boisterously. Apparently not that disappointed at having lost, yet again, to the local high school Gay-Straight Alliance, everyone jumps around and hugs each other. I laugh as Tilly picks up Kirsten and spins her around, despite the fact that Tilly is shorter than her by at least four inches. No one is paying attention to the announcer anymore as the music from a local band blares up.

Black was standing right beside me, but when I turn, I find he isn't there anymore. Panic bubbles up inside me for a moment, sending my thoughts into a tailspin. *He left because he couldn't handle it, not even for me.* But before I can freak out, I feel Black's strong arms around my waist as he picks me up and spins me around. He kisses my neck and mumbles something I don't understand in my ear. As I start to turn to face him, I'm distracted by a series of loud booms and look up to see confetti raining down on us from above. Black spins me around to face him and peppers kisses all over my face as the colorful paper falls around us. Melting into his arms, I tug his head down for a real kiss, a kiss that contains my whole heart and soul.

When we finally separate, I can see the green and gold glitter I had on my face has now transferred to his. I swipe my fingers across his cheekbones and wiggle my fingers at him. He laughs and leans forward to whisper something else unintelligible in my ear. For once,

I don't mind not knowing what he said. From the happy look on his face, I interpret the message as good and just grin up at him. His hands come up to cup my face, and he kisses my lips softly while looking me directly in the eyes. I know I see joy there and I hope that I see love in their dark chocolate depths. It is no secret to anyone how hard I have fallen for Black. His friends even expect me to come around with him now. The only question that remains is whether or not Black will let me in enough to really love him completely. But, I refuse to let such thoughts mar our celebration or this moment with Black, so I just kiss him deeply again and giggle hard when he starts to tickle my belly.

"Stop!" I somehow manage to giggle out.

Black shakes his head and spins me around again. The street has erupted into a rowdy dance party here at the end of the parade route. It is the last day of Pride celebration in the neighborhood and everyone seems to be living it up. By the time we part ways with The Sirens, it is well past two in the morning. Black practically carries me to my hotel as I had one too many cocktails and also managed to dance myself to exhaustion.

As Black carries me into my bedroom, I remark on how the room is spinning. He laughs. "No, Aubrey bear, it's just your head."

I gasp. "You have to call me that again. I love it!"

Black chuckles as he lays me on the bed, removes my shoes, and pulls the covers up over me. I suddenly need him beside me more than I need breath. "Please," I plead, "stay with me."

His smile is beautiful in the dim light of my room. "Of course, Aubrey bear, I am not going anywhere."

I am already falling asleep, but I still mumble out, "You better not." I hear the soft rumble of his laugh against my neck as he pulls me to him and drops a kiss on my cheek. "Perfect," I breath out with my last conscious breath, "perfect."

CHAPTER 17

I'm still racking my brain for a way to make up for the pain I caused Aubrey over Pride. Sure, we had a fabulous time, but I can feel he has pulled back a little, like he is guarding his heart. Even though I identified him as my boyfriend to The Sirens, I can tell he is still afraid, still waiting for the metaphorical other shoe to drop. I sigh as I acknowledge to myself I really cannot blame him for it. I've hurt him badly, twice now, both times when the past came roaring to the surface and overwhelmed my growing feelings for the auburn-haired beauty. And, oh god, is he beautiful. It's not his alabaster skin, his light freckles across the nose and cheekbones, freckles you cannot even see unless you are within kissing distance of them. It's not his clear green eyes that sparkle with open mischief and love. No, it's the fucking sun blazing from inside him, and I'm like a light starved plant, arching myself closer and closer to him, all the while afraid I'm going to burst into flames and burn out. Not because of him, no, absolutely never because of Aubrey. But because of my own gaping hole inside. A hole I can never seem to seal up, no matter how hard I try.

And, damn it all, I have been trying every single second since I laid eyes on Aubrey. I'm trying to move forward, so hard, but then some shard of the painful truth intrudes upon the perfection of joy and calm Aubrey offers me so freely, so willingly, so beautifully. Kissing his glitter covered face as the confetti rained down on us at the end of the parade route had been a moment of absolute perfection. A moment that has me resolved to show him how much I want him in my life. It will take more than acknowledging our obvious romantic relationship to my friends to show him I want to keep him in my life. As I stare into my cup of coffee as it sits cooling on my kitchen island top, I hear a faint scratching. I smile fondly, recognizing the sound Benny's claws make as he climbs up the patio fence. I make my way through my living room and out onto the patio. Benny is sitting on the top rail with his head cocked as he looks at me quizzically.

"What, Benny?" I ask the furred miscreant. "What do you think I should do?" Benny twitches his tail and actually chatters at me! My eyes are about to bug out of my head. Benny is talking to me. Since he seems up for conversation, I continue with a sigh.

"I broke Aubrey's heart. Carelessly. Thoughtlessly. I didn't mean to, but I did. Again. So what do I do, Benny? What do you when you've made Mrs. Squirrel upset at you?"

As I wait not so patiently for the damned squirrel's response, I think about how quiet Aubrey has been since our fight several weeks ago. Sure, he still messages and teases, and even seems to forget about my outburst most of the time. Then a haunted look will pass over his face, and I know exactly what he is thinking. He doubts what I feel for him. It's not like I've said anything more than that I like him, even though I know my feelings are far deeper than that.

"And that is my fault, Benny. I've given him plenty of reasons to doubt me. So help a brother out, huh?"

Benny looks contemplative for a moment as his dark eyes stare into mine, unblinking. He makes another chattering noise at me, flicks his tail with flair, jumps off the side of the patio, and hightails it straight to the bird feeder. I'm sure he has lost interest in the boring human, but after he scrambles on top of the pile of bird seeds, he glances back over his little squirrel shoulder and chatters again.

"Oh," I murmur as the solution, so simple and so obvious, comes to me in a flash. "Thanks, Benny," I call out to the fat little mammal, but he is no longer paying me any attention as he stuffs seed after seed into his fat little cheeks. Saved by the squirrel, I think as I chuckle to myself. I know exactly what to do to show Aubrey how much he means to me. I just have to figure out how to surprise him with it.

Over the course of the past few months, Aubrey and I have developed a routine of sorts. And that routine involves coffee. Every weekend day, and as many weekdays as I can manage, I meet him at the coffee shop near his hotel. Today I arrive early, fussing a bit at my clothes. I have opted for a cerulean blue T-shirt instead of my usual black. I've been told it highlights my coloring well, and I cannot argue that this shade of blue pairs nicely with the black of my hair. Grinning, I shake my head at my nerves. Just then, Aubrey pushes open the café door and beams when he sees me. He glides over to me and raises his lips to mine for a kiss. I love how he does that, and I don't miss the sparkle in his eyes when he pulls back.

He bites his bottom lip and gives me an appreciative look up and down. "I like the blue. To what do I owe this sudden change in your sartorial choices?" His grin spreads wider as he pats his hands across my upper chest and shoulders. He raises his eyes from my chest and lifts his right brow, clearly waiting for my answer. Whatever I intended to say has fled my mind, but luckily, we are interrupted in the moment by a cackling laugh. We both turn our heads, and I spy my elderly neighbor, Mrs. Watson, standing a few feet away, clad in bright pink and purple athletic wear, holding small weights in her curled fists.

"I guess I know where you have been spending all of your time lately, Black," she chortles at me, "or should I say, with whom." I laugh, and Aubrey glances at me curiously. I take his hand and kiss it, and Aubrey's eyes widen. He seems surprised at my public display of affection in front of someone I know, and I guess I have given him reason to wonder about my feelings of late. But no more.

"Aubrey, this is my neighbor, Mrs. Watson. Mrs. Watson, this is

Aubrey. He's the planner for the new park the city is putting in over on Danbury Avenue." Even though I told The Sirens what Aubrey is to me, I don't use the word now. But Mrs. Watson always knows what's up, and the smile she favors both of us with is full of mischief. Aubrey turns to face her and offers his hand. After rearranging her weights in one hand, she takes his hand in her strong grasp.

"Pleasure to meet you, young man."

Aubrey looks at a loss but manages to reply, "It's a pleasure to meet you as well."

I'm sure it's mean and just a little bit like throwing Aubrey to the wolves, but I take this opportunity to say, "I'll get our coffees, Aubrey. You can chat with Mrs. Watson."

Aubrey shoots me an incredulous look and I almost burst out laughing. Yeah, he wasn't expecting that. But the momentary breather will allow me to gather my wandering thoughts, and since Mrs. Watson *is* my neighbor, I have an even better segue into inviting Aubrey to my house today than I did before. Leaving him staring at me like I've gone crazy, I rush to the counter.

Watching Black's retreating back, I'm at a loss for words. Turning my head back to Black's elderly neighbor, I rack my brain for a suitable topic of conversation. My gaze must have fallen to the floor because suddenly a warm soft hand touches my arm. Mrs. Watson has stepped closer to me, and she is smiling gently at me when I raise my eyes.

"It is wonderful to meet you, Aubrey. How long have you and Black been together?"

I swallow hard at the question and glance over my shoulder again toward the counter where Black is currently trying to order from the bored teenaged barista. They really should hire better staff here. I return my gaze back to Mrs. Watson. We have not discussed our relationship status which we probably should since Black told The Sirens I'm his boyfriend. To say my heart bloomed with joy at those words would be a pale description of how I felt in the moment. But

Black didn't repeat the declaration with Ms. Watson a moment ago when he had the opportunity. That worries me, and I am at a loss as to how to respond to the kindly older lady. But, like every other woman in my life, his neighbor has bypassed the technicalities of relationship labels, acknowledging what she can clearly see with her own eyes.

I can't help but smile back at her. "Almost three months," I answer honestly. She squeezes my arm, her eyes warming even more.

"I'm so glad to hear it. After a loss like that, I'm just so happy he has found you."

I'm startled by her words. Once again, one of Black's friends is giving me a hint about the dark cloud that shadows Black, that unspoken something that keeps surfacing between us. An iceberg lodges itself in my chest, and I almost ask what she means. But Black rejoins us at that moment, so the opportunity is lost. He brought her a bottle of water, and she drops her hand from my arm to take it.

"Aren't you a good boy, Black? Taking care of old ladies and bringing coffee to beautiful young men." She winks at me then before taking a drink of water from the bottle.

Black laughs softly, surprising me. The incredulous look on my face must be amusing because his smile widens, and he drops a kiss on my forehead. To say I am surprised by the behavior of both of my current companions would be an understatement. Black turns his attention to Mrs. Watson.

"Out for your daily powerwalk, Mrs. Watson?"

She grins and points the water bottle at him. "It's how I stay so fit and spry, young man. Speaking of, I better go. I just popped in here for a bottle of water, and you took care of it for me. I wouldn't want Gladys to lap me too many times around the block." She pats my arm again but speaks to Black, "Don't be a stranger, Black. Drop by and see me soon."

Black nods and she power walks herself back out of the coffeeshop at a brisk pace. I'm still reeling from the weird encounter when Black touches my arm, returning my attention back to the present.

Black scatters whatever thoughts I have managed to corral back into my mind with his next question. "Now that you've met my neighbor, would you like to see my house?"

I can sense that Black wants to jump out of his skin and run away. With everything that has gone on since we met, I'm floored Black wants me inside of his home, a place that is clearly his sanctuary from the world. Perhaps some things really are changing for him. I feel the effort to pull me closer in everything he does lately. First, he declares me his boyfriend in front of his friends; then, he takes me to Pride even as it was clear so many memories of Pride parades past still haunt him. Now, we are here in his home, and I can almost see his skin crawling at having me in his space.

Mrs. Watson's statement from this morning filters across my mind, "After a loss like that, I'm just so happy he has found you." His elderly neighbor's words keep circling my brain, but unlike a sink, it has no drain and the undercurrent is drowning me. I already knew Black must have lost someone close to him, as close as me, or closer still. Many of his friends and acquaintances I meet drop unhelpful little hints about it. I want Black to tell me what's wrong, what causes him to hold part of himself away from me too much of the time. I want him to share those fears that strangle him at inopportune times, threatening our happiness, but most importantly his happiness. There are more and more moments in which I can tell he is right there with me, swimming in the deep end of the ocean. Then, suddenly, a haunted look will flicker across his face, and he withdraws from me, from our connection, and my heart cracks a little more each time.

Shaking my head at that thought, I refocus on the man who is currently describing something about his warm, inviting home. I want to make this more comfortable for him, but I'm at a loss as to how. As he points out the features of what admittedly is a gorgeous cottage style house, I have found my gaze falling to the floor as my mind wonders how to make him feel better about this. I must have been quiet too long as Black suddenly speaks my name, and I find myself looking up from the neutral beige carpeting in the living room to gaze into his dark brown eyes which have gone tense with unnamable emotions. I drop my hand from my mouth where I'd been unconsciously worrying my bottom lip. I flash him jaunty grin and grab his arm, tugging him into my chest. I bump our noses and breathe in his breath but hold my lips back from his.

"It's gorgeous, but what on earth made you go with bland, beige carpeting?"

"Bland?" he chokes out, clearly confused as to my meaning.

"Yeah, you are the artist here. Where is the adventure? Where is the style? Nah, beige is just not your color, man." I keep grinning, and finally, the tension seeps from his shoulders and he wraps his arms around me, pulling me in tighter.

"So, you're an interior designer now too? I thought you designed parks and playgrounds. Since when are you a carpet color coordinating expert?"

"My, my. That was a bit of a tongue twister."

"I have a very talented tongue."

I feign a scoff and look at him skeptically.

"Oh, do you need proof now?"

I hum and cock my head to the side, pretending to be thoughtful.

"I'm not sure I have the data to back up your claim, sir..."

Black cuts me off with a searing kissing, using said talented tongue to lick my bottom lip until I open my mouth. Then he swirls in, taking away the last vestiges of thought from my mind. My last cogent notion is one of joy and triumph at distracting him. Then, my mouth is too busy to care about anything other than what Black is doing to it.

As I kiss Aubrey breathless, I marvel at what this man does for me, and to me. I had meant this invitation into my home as an apology for my strange behavior, as a sign to Aubrey that I am in this thing as deeply as he is. I am well and truly fucked as it is impossible to keep myself from loving this man. And there it is. As I pull back from kissing Aubrey, I know I can't keep lying to myself. I love him. I love everything about him. I love his scent, I love his eyes, I love his nose, I love his mouth, his hair, his laugh, the way he absent-mindedly hums when he is thinking or when he is innately happy. I expect the realization to flood me in terror, but instead, I feel relieved. I pull myself from Aubrey's lips and a slow smiles creeps across my face. Aubrey latches his eyes on to my lips, licking his unconsciously. I just can't help but laugh and pull him into a tight hug against my chest.

Leaning forward, I whisper into his ear, "Let's go explore the backyard."

CHAPTER 18

"*B*enny's been back," I comment as I inspect the bird feed holder in my backyard. Aubrey comes up to stand beside me and looks at me quizzically.

"You have a cat? Or a dog?"

"No," I reply as I straighten up to my full height and grin at him. "What I have is a squirrel."

"A squirrel?" Aubrey sounds delighted, and he clasps his hands together underneath his chin, making himself look even younger than his twenty-nine years. "And you named him Benny?"

I smile at his reaction. "Yep. I will let you in on a little secret too," I murmur as I pull him into a hug there on my back lawn, the sunshine warm around us.

"And what is that?" Aubrey whispers, bringing his lips up to ghost against mine.

"He is the subject of the statue in my warehouse."

Aubrey's grin widens, and his eyes light up. "That is why you won't sell him."

I'm mesmerized like I always am by Aubrey's special brand of sunny happiness. "Yes," I whisper, "but I would never sell anything you love so much." Aubrey blushes prettily, and I give in to my desire by kissing the strawberry flush across first one cheekbone then the other. "Beautiful," I murmur against the colorful show of emotion. He huffs out a laugh and drops his head to my shoulder then cocks his head so he can see me out of his right eye now.

"You just love making me blush, don't you?"

"It is one of my favorite things."

Rolling his face into the crook of my neck, he laughs then pulls his face up. He slides his hands down to mine and takes one hand into his. He steps back as he laces our fingers together.

"Did you name him after Benedict Cumberbatch?"

I laugh at the unexpected question, and Aubrey's eyes twinkle with humor. "I'm right, am I not? You have a crush on Sherlock Holmes."

"No." I chuckle as I pull him back into me by our clasped hands. I nip his bottom lip because I can and hear him sigh in contentment which sends a shiver of anticipation through me. The sun is shining down on us, the weather mild for the beginning of July. Birds twitter in the trees in the woods just off my backyard, and there are only white puffy clouds in the sky. The day would be perfect, but with Aubrey standing in my backyard, kissing me, teasing me, loving me, "perfect" seems like a pale imitation of what this moment means to me.

Aubrey shakes me from my reverie by prompting, "You lie. Everyone has a crush on Sherlock Holmes. Unless you like Dr. Watson better?"

"I do have a thing for redheads." We both laugh, and I kiss his lips again before tugging him along, back to the patio. "I named him after that Elton John song, actually, 'Benny and the Jets.'"

"Benny, Benny and the Jets," Aubrey sings out in a high voice. "Did you know the reason we have so many squirrels in cities is because early twentieth century park planners thought people needed some sort of animal entertainment? No joke, they started importing them and bam! Now we have squirrels everywhere."

I laugh at how he related the little tidbit of park planning history. Every subject leads to another when I talk to Aubrey, and eventually winds back to parks which I already know are his true passion. I lean my head against his shoulder for a second before pulling him up the patio steps and back into the house, sliding the glass patio door closed behind us.

"How did you meet Benny?" Aubrey's question amuses me. His curiosity always leads me to consider how the various aspects of my life tie together. I never really thought about it before Aubrey. As I lead him through the living room and back to the kitchen, I relay my first encounter with the furry miscreant.

"Benny broke into my house and stole a candy bar off the kitchen counter."

"No way." He laughs, looking at me suspiciously.

I raise my right hand, three fingers up. "Scout's honor." He settles himself on one of the bar stools next to my kitchen island, favoring me with an amused glance.

"Were you a Boy Scout?"

"For about two years, but I never made it far. As much as I love the great outdoors now, I found all of the knot tying and survival training boring. I bailed right before a big canoeing trip. To say my father, who was an Eagle Scout through and through and my den leader to boot, was pissed would be an understatement." I chuckle at the memory, now turned bittersweet so many years after his death. "He took the troop anyway and didn't speak to me for almost a whole day afterward. Maybe I was a bit of a space cadet, my mind already too wrapped up in drawing and all things art related, because I didn't even realize he was trying to give me the cold shoulder until my mom called him out on it at dinner the night after the trip."

Aubrey is smiling, such a sweet look on his face that I have to lean across the island to kiss it off. "Would you like some iced tea? Or water? It's a bit early for wine."

He sighs, sounding long suffering and put upon. "Since you refuse to contribute to my lush-inspired living, I will take some tea. Thank you very much." He is giggling by the end of that statement, and I am struck at how good having him in my home feels.

I turn away, retrieving the ice from the freezer and the tea from the fridge, and fumble around in my cabinets for glasses. Reality intrudes upon the moment, sending a spike of pain through my chest. *You can't do this*, my brain tries to tell me. *It's too much. You can't risk his heart like this. What do you have to offer him that hasn't already been taken, used up, burned out, torn out of you, body and soul?* I am gripping a glass tumbler too tightly in my hand as I set it down with a hard bang against the counter. The jolt of sound shakes me from my emotional spiral. I breathe deeply for a moment, closing my eyes, trying to center myself.

"Black?" Aubrey's voice sounds close now and worried. I turn around to find him standing just a few feet from me. "Are you all right?"

I force out a laugh I am not feeling. "Yeah, just wool gathering for a moment. Did you say something?"

Aubrey doesn't look convinced, he may even look a little disappointed. Damn it, he is much too adept at reading my moods. "I asked if you needed some help."

Pushing some semblance of a grin onto my face, I shake my head. "No, I can handle a couple of glasses of tea." Desperate to change the subject, I pick up my story about Benny where I left off as I put ice in the glasses then pour in the tea. "As I said earlier, Benny, the miscreant thief of a squirrel, stole a candy bar off this counter right here."

Aubrey smiles softly, knowingly at me, but follows me for the subject change. "How did he get inside?"

I laugh. "I accidentally left the sliding door to the patio cracked open for some fresh air. I must have forgotten to close it before bed. When I walked into the kitchen the next morning, he was sitting on this counter with the edge of the candy bar wrapper wedged into his little mouth. As soon as he saw me, he took off. I followed him through the living room and saw him dart across the patio, through the yard, and off into the woods." I'm laughing at the memory, though a small part of my mind keeps niggling worries at me. I glance at Aubrey, who is grinning widely.

"So, Benny is a thief squirrel, then."

"He sure is. He eats most of the bird seed I put out for the warblers and wrens."

Aubrey winks at me. "I bet you put out extra just for him."

"Me?" I gasp. "Why I do no such thing. I refuse to contribute to the delinquency of squirrels. Or to their dietary misbehavior." Aubrey and I are both giggling now. Motioning toward the living room, I hand him a tall glass of iced tea. "Shall we?"

He takes the glass with one hand and twines his other arm through mine as we walk toward the living room. "Yes, we shall." We spend the day talking, laughing, and drinking iced tea. I make us grilled cheese sandwiches for lunch. Aubrey is surprised I cook, and I amuse him with stories of desserts gone wrong and burnt casseroles that set off the fire alarm. According to him, he can make anything coffee related and he is an ace with breakfast burritos, but that is the extent of his culinary excellence. I try to ignore how much I enjoy having Aubrey in my house. But deep down, I know I can't deny just how right all of this feels.

CHAPTER 19

"What do you want to do tonight? Watch a movie?"

"Are you inviting me for a date? A date in your house? My, my, Mr. Black, you do move fast. Next thing you know you will be inviting me over for sleepovers."

"Now that sounds like a good idea."

Aubrey almost chokes on his sip of iced tea. He sets down his glass on the coffee table, and I pat his back, trying hard not to grin at his reaction. Well, not trying too hard. He leans over his legs, resting his head on his knees, with his face turned toward me.

"Are you serious?" His voice sounds hesitant, so I pet his hair as I watch his face.

"Yes, we can order some pizza, Netflix and chill."

Aubrey laughs deeply. "Netflix and chill, huh? Aren't you romantic?"

Though I know he is teasing me, I still ask, "Is that okay?"

The smile Aubrey favors me with is sunshine, sending fuzzy happiness through my system the way it always does. "I would love that." His head is still on his knees, and I am now rubbing circles on his back through his periwinkle button down.

"Me, too," I murmur as I lean forward to kiss him lightly on the lips. I can't count how many times we have kissed today, but it is seriously the only thing I want to do right now. Okay, it is not the only thing, I think as I press butterfly spot kisses on his mouth, on the corners, on his cheeks, on his nose. Aubrey is laughing under his breath, and I want to record the moment, for replay for the rest of my life. This day has been good, so far, far beyond good, absolutely perfect. When my mind tries to wander off to darker thoughts, questioning why it feels so wonderful to have Aubrey here, reminding me why I can't do this, I take in a deep breath and push it all aside. If I don't have any space in my mind for doubts, fears, and past pains, then I can fill myself whole with Aubrey. And that is exactly what I want to do.

We are quiet for a few minutes as I continue to rub Aubrey's back.

"What do you want to watch?"

Aubrey winks at me. "How do you feel about teen romantic comedies?"

I laugh, patting him on the back as he rises up to a seated position. "Sure, why not?"

Aubrey giggles and taps his finger against his chin. "Have you ever seen *Ten Things I Hate About You*? It's an early Heath Ledger movie. You know, the guy who was the Joker in the Batman movie with Christian Bale."

"Sure, that sounds fun."

"Does it really, or are you just being nice so you can make out with me later?"

"I plead the fifth."

Aubrey laughs. "You've never seen it, have you?"

"Nope, but I can't pass up any movie you recommend."

"Aww, aren't you sweet. But it's the Heath Ledger movie you can't pass up."

"So you say."

Aubrey pokes me in the ribs and tries to tickle me. "I do say."

"Then we better check it out."

As I call in our pizza order, Aubrey finds the film on Netflix. By the time Kat is defending her violent self-defense against handsy boys, the pizza has arrived. We feed each other gooey slices, and the film turns out to be just as fun as I would expect of a favorite of Aubrey's. When the movie ends, it is still early, but Aubrey keeps kissing me and before long we are both sans clothing in the middle of my bed. He pushes me onto my back and kneels between my legs.

Aubrey greets my now naked cock, talking to it as if it might respond. "Well, hello, Reginald's quivering member!"

I howl with laughter. It takes several long moments to get myself under control. Aubrey sits between my legs the whole time, grinning manically, so clearly pleased with himself and his movie related cock joke. Propping myself up on some pillows, I play along, enjoying this playful and explicitly sexual side of Aubrey's personality.

"So, what is your name then, if I'm Reginald?

"You are Sir Reginald."

"Oh, I am, am I?"

"Absolutely. The best knight in the land."

"I think you might be mixing up two Heath Ledger movies. Yeah, *A Knight's Tale*, or something like that."

"Shh. Lie back and think of England."

I really do fall backwards now as I once again collapse into a fit of laughter. Still he sits between my legs, grinning as I struggle to regain some semblance of composure.

"So really, if I am Sir Reginald, then who are you?"

"Why, of course, I am Renaldo, Sir Reginald's loyal squire!"

"And what does Sir Reginald's loyal squire do for him?"

"He bathes him and cares for him. Makes sure his skin is soft and supple."

"And how does he do that?"

"Mmm… wouldn't you like to know, Sir Reginald?"

"I would, my dear Renaldo."

"Well, I think you will have to experience it to believe it."

With that Aubrey takes my "quivering member" into both of his hands and gently blows on its head. My member is now definitely quivering, and I bite into my lip, muffling a curse. Aubrey sighs a throaty laugh and continues with his torturous ministrations. Taking the crown of my dick into his mouth, he sucks while the fingers of both of his hands trip up and down my thighs, across my groin, and back again. He watches me the whole time. He is sucking me like a lollipop, and I can barely breathe.

Though we have had quite a lot of sex in the last few months, none of this ever gets old. Every time is fresh and new, every time is deeper, more real, more personal. As Aubrey gives me the mother of all blow jobs, I come apart inside as much as I do physically.

After I have come down his throat, he pops off me with a dreamy and very self-satisfied expression on his face which makes me want him all the more. I pull him up to me and kiss him until he is breathless. When I roll him beneath me, I cannot take my eyes off his. He seems to see into my soul with his jewel green eyes. Smiling softly as he winds his arms around my neck, he sighs, his eyes fluttering shut for a moment. I take the time to memorize his face, hoping I never have to recall him as a distant memory. My heart throbs and my hand shakes as I bring it up to touch his face. His smile deepens, and he pops his eyes open.

"So, Sir Reginald," he teasingly whispers, "what did you think of your Renaldo's performance?"

"Perfect," I whisper as I drop my lips to his, "perfect as always."

He hums then, thrusting his hips against mine. "Then you ought to repay the favor."

I cannot help but laugh softly, nor can I disobey his demand. I kiss him deeply before showing him with my body just how much he means to me. Even if I cannot say any of the most important words, I try to worship his beautiful body with my own. I can only hope that he has even the smallest clue what he means to me. When we reach our climax, I watch his face awash with pleasure and know I will never be more whole than I am with him.

CHAPTER 20

*J*uly heats up, pun intended. Work on the park keeps Aubrey so busy we don't have lunch or dinner together nearly as often as we did before. My work on the sculpture is progressing more slowly than usual. The designing stage took twice as long as it should have then I had to scrap my first two attempts because of little errors I usually don't make. Such ridiculous little delays have forced me to work later than normal for the past two weeks to try to catch up for the mid-August deadline. Even though I am behind on work and could use the weekends to get ahead, Saturdays and Sundays have become our days to hang out. I haven't let Aubrey know how behind I am because I don't want to miss any time with him. Per his official job requirements, he does receive updates. But, because he is Aubrey, he always turns those updates into an excuse to visit my shop. I haven't let on that the sculpture is behind schedule. Aubrey seems awed by it every time he visits, and his dreamy expression of appreciation delights me too much for me to let him know how far off my original timeline I am.

As with everything, we don't discuss our weekends together, we just do it. Nothing interrupts our routine of a visit to the coffee shop first thing on Saturday morning until halfway through the month.

Without even a small discussion, we have fallen into the habit of Aubrey staying at my house on Friday and Saturday nights. Unfortunately for this Saturday, we end up at my shop for an emergency repair job much too early.

"Now why did you have to do this at," Aubrey pauses to turn his wrist dramatically and squint at his watch, "the butt-crack of dawn?"

Laughing, I unlock my shop door and flip on the lights as I enter the warehouse. "You didn't have to come with me. I told you that you could sleep in. I even offered to bring you coffee and pastries when I came back."

Aubrey pats my ass as he brushes past to sit at the nearest workbench. "Un-uh, you said this was an *emergency* repair job. That could take *hours*."

"Yes," I reply as I walk to my welding corner. "Exactly, that is why you should have stayed in bed."

"But it would be time for lunch by the time you came back to me."

"So? I could have brought you coffee, pastries, and a BLT."

Aubrey laughs as he folds his arms on the table and lays his head down on top of them.

"Wasn't my coffee enough for you?" I tease, amused he seems to be settling in for a nap at my work bench.

Aubrey shakes his head and yawns.

"Don't you start that. I won't be able to work if you put me to sleep by yawning."

Aubrey yawns again, even wider, before giggling. At that moment, a knock sounds against the front door. Aubrey lifts his head to look in that direction, and I cannot help but tease him.

"Don't worry, dear, I'll get the door."

"You ought to. It is your door."

I'm laughing as I open the door for my neighbors, Ron and Lisa. Surprisingly, they have their eighteen-month-old daughter, Sarah, with them in a purple stroller. Ron is carrying the broken lawn cactus in his arms, though it looks like he might drop it on someone's toes if he is not careful. I motion him toward the back corner, and he waddles the ornament over and clunks it down hard on the concrete floor. He straightens up and wipes his hand over his brow as if carrying the cactus caused him to sweat profusely, though I see no evidence of this and suspect he is trying to act manly in front of his wife who is not even paying attention to him. She and Aubrey are cooing at the baby, and I can't help but laugh. Ron pulls a spiky saguaro arm out of his back pocket, which is definitely not a smart place to store a sharp piece of metal sculpture. He sets it on my welding supply bench and straightens up looking pleased with himself for no clear reason I can determine.

"So, one of the arms broke off? How did that happen, *Ron?*"

"Well, *Ian*, I was mowing the lawn and hit a rock. The damned thing spun out and knocked the arm completely off."

I freeze as soon as he says my first name, missing whatever came next entirely. I must have been standing there motionless for longer than I thought because suddenly Aubrey is beside me, looking into my face with concern. He pats my arm and smiles gently at me but doesn't say anything. Ron continues to ramble on and Lisa is too preoccupied with their baby to notice anything amiss with me or the conversation. I close my eyes for a moment and breathe deeply.

"It's Black," Aubrey says to Ron quietly, taking the burden off of me. "He goes by Black. You know how artists are, particular about their names." He tries to pass off as a joke, an artistic quirk, and the gambit works.

"Oh, yeah. I forgot, Black." Ron pauses and looks at Aubrey as if he is just now seeing him. "Who are you?"

If I weren't still reeling from the terrible onslaught of painful emotions and memories, I would have snapped at Ron for being rude to Aubrey, but Aubrey takes it in stride like he does everything. He holds out his free hand to Ron, leaving the other on my arm.

"I'm Aubrey. And you are?"

I would laugh at the slightly snide tinge to Aubrey's tone, but I can't do anything right now but try to pull air into my lungs. Ron does not seem to hear it, so he makes a big deal out of shaking Aubrey's hand then introducing himself, his wife, and their daughter. He almost launches into a long story of how we met four years ago, but I have now recovered enough to interrupt.

"Ron, I think this might be a bit more complicated than I thought. I can't fix this today. Why don't you give me a call on Monday afternoon? I will know by then if this is going to require more than a resoldering."

Ron does not seem to care one way or another which leads me to wonder why he insisted on bringing it in this morning. Why call someone at seven on a Saturday morning if it didn't really matter? Knowing Ron, he was trying to show off for Lisa. For a man who has been married to the same woman for close to decade, he always seems to be in impress my girl mode. Aubrey saves the day for me by ushering them out while I sink down on the bench where he was sitting before. I lay my head on the table in the same place he had laid his and pretend it is still warm from his skin.

"So, that was awkward."

I turn my head so I can look at Aubrey. I don't reply because I honestly don't know what to say or how to explain myself. At least, not without telling him so much more than I ever want to share.

"How long have you known them?"

My voice sounds hoarse when I reply, "About four years."

"You would think he would know your preferred name by now."

I sigh and push myself up to sitting and scrub my hand over my face. "Yeah, but as you might have noticed, Ron is not the most careful person. Unless, of course, it comes to impressing Lisa."

I can tell by the look on Aubrey's face he wants to ask me more.

"So, you don't let anyone call you Ian?" he asks softly, coming to sit down beside me on the bench. My jaws clench involuntarily, and I don't realize I have scrunched up my fists, until Aubrey takes one into his hands, prying my fingers apart gently, then intertwining them with his own. I dare to look at him, and he is smiling softly, patiently at me. But I can't stand the sound of that name, nor can I handle the memories it stirs up inside me.

My voice is hoarse, croaking like a frog when I finally manage to squeeze out, "Please, Aubrey, just don't call me that name."

Aubrey is contemplative for a moment, and I hope that he is going to drop the subject, but he does not. Cocking his head to the side, he studies my face before replying, "But you seem to have no problem with it in the professional sense. You use your full name in your work."

"It's not the same," I reply lamely.

He softly asks, "It's the intimateness of it, isn't it?"

I nod shakily, wishing this conversation were already over. "Please, I just can't. . . hear it, not from you." When I realize what I've said, I'm horrified. "I didn't mean it that way," I stammer. "You just can't say it, please!"

Aubrey looks hurt, his mouth downturned in a way I've never seen it before.

"Someone special called you that, didn't they?"

I nod wearily. I no longer want to talk about it. Hell, I never wanted to talk about it, not with him or anyone else.

"Did they hurt you?"

I close my eyes at the pain in his voice. I know what he is thinking and shake my head.

"Not in the way you're thinking."

"Then in what way?" Aubrey lets go of my hand and his hands come up to cup my face.

I barely stop myself from jerking away, but he notices the flinch and drops his hands. I bring them back and clasp them to my chest. I look directly into his pure green eyes and do something I haven't done in almost two years. I beg.

"Please. I just can't. Please, I know I can't..." My voice drops off, and I don't even know how to finish that sentence.

"Okay," he suddenly relents, pulling his hands free and wrapping his arms around me tightly. He lays his head against my collarbone, and I can do nothing but sigh.

"It's okay," he murmurs even though I'm the one who just wounded him. I want to cry, but instead, I pull Aubrey into my arms and drop my head into the crook of his neck so I can draw his calming scent into my lungs. I pull him as tightly against me as possible and he lets me, though I am sure I'm practically crushing him.

"I'm sorry," I whisper against the soft skin of his neck.

"It's okay," he whispers again, placing a kiss against the side of my neck.

We stay there, holding each other, for a long time. I feel like I'm cracking apart inside, and Aubrey is the only thing holding me together.

CHAPTER 21

*A*s if I weren't already feeling guilty about my freak out over my name, my trip to the grocery store the next day made everything exponentially worse and yet, exponentially better at the same time. I was determined to make Aubrey something special to make up for yesterday. After we left my workshop, we picked up BLTs to go from the diner. Aubrey kept watching me with a serious, but soft, expression on his face, an expression that made me want to die inside. He didn't seem hurt or offended by my refusal to explain why hearing my first name sends me into an emotional tailspin. I know I should tell him, but it would be impossible without explaining everything. And, I'm still sure I cannot share any of that with him. Not because he wouldn't care or wouldn't understand, but because I literally cannot do it. I cannot explain the last two years of my life or what events shattered it completely apart. Reliving the pain even momentarily threatens to kill me. I would never survive telling the whole story. Aubrey stayed with me all day yesterday and we watched old movies and went to bed early. This morning, he claimed to have work to do even though it's Sunday. But since he promised to return for dinner, I didn't fuss over it even though I did not want him to leave my sight.

As I look at the various boxes of brownie and chocolate cake mixes, my eyes are about to glaze over. I actually like to bake, but I just cannot decide which Aubrey would like better. He is a chocaholic through and through, but I don't know which he would prefer. Suddenly I remember the brownie recipe on the back of the Nestle's baking chocolate box. Last time I was craving chocolate, because I'm honestly a bit of a chocaholic myself, I added mini-marshmallows to that. Yeah, that sounds perfect. I straighten up and push my cart further down the baking aisle. I locate the Nestle's baking chocolate with ease. Now, where do I find the marshmallows?

"Black!"

I startle and almost drop the box of chocolate when someone yells my name. Glancing about, I find the source of the disturbance: Mr. Owens, the chairman of the Oakland City Council. My heart is beating rapidly in my chest. The old man must be deaf if he thinks that level of volume is appropriate for the grocery store.

"Mr. Owens, you startled me."

Owens, a pudgy octogenarian with thin, but fuzzy, white hair sticking out all over his head, grins at me, waving off my admonishment. He looks a whole lot like that famous photograph of Albert Einstein with his tongue stuck out. But he doesn't have the personality to match. I am surprised he is standing there grinning up at me. Usually he looks like he has been sucking lemons all day long.

"Black," Owens practically yells again. Clearly, he needs to turn up the volume on the huge hearing aid in his ear. "I am so happy to see you. I've been meaning to drop by your studio since that park planner presented your proof of concept binder. It was brilliant. The whole committee loved your passionate words about our ecosystem and the importance of celebrating natural wonders."

"Okay." I have no idea what the man is talking about. "When did Aubrey give you the binder?"

"Oh, way back in April. As soon as you backed out on the new cowboy sculpture."

I'm frowning now because nothing of the sort ever happened. "I don't know what you are talking about, Mr. Owens. I never agreed to do another western themed sculpture. I made that quite clear to both you and Aubrey."

Owens guffaws, slapping me a bit too hard on the shoulder. Ow, I step a bit farther out of his reach to avoid any other "friendly" pats on the back. I really don't have time for this distraction if I want to have brownies ready for dessert tonight. "Well, it was nice to see you, Mr. Owens."

"Hey, don't run off just yet young man. I didn't tell you the best part. None of us were too keen on your native plant idea and were on the verge of demanding a face to face meeting. But that park planner, what did you say his name was? Arty?"

Now that makes me bristle. Owens has been working with Aubrey for months. The least he could do is get Aubrey's name right. "No, his name is Aubrey Davies."

"Yeah, yeah," Owens continues, "that guy Aubrey spoke so passion-ately in favor of your design and the proof of concept binder convinced us you were right. From the updates he keeps sending over, we are just pleased as punch we let you follow your own artistic incli-nations, young man."

Let me follow my own...what? "I'm sorry, Mr. Owens. I'm not really sure what you are talking about. What binder? What updates?"

Owens chortles. "You been sniffin' the welding gases, boy? The binder we asked for when you cancelled the original sculpture. It had all those pictures of your other plant sculptures. Those added with the historical significance that young buck pointed out, well, we just couldn't say 'no,' now could we?"

Owens continues to chuckle under his breath, and I feel like I've had the wind knocked out of me. I'm starting to understand that Aubrey had to present an extra file on my behalf to convince the council to approve my plant sculpture. Owens pops me rudely out of my thoughts by slapping my back extra hard again.

"Well, it was good to see you, Black, keep up the good work."

"Wait, did you say something about updates?"

"That Aubrey kid sent us one just last week. We sure were impressed to hear the sculpture is so close to completion. We cannot wait to see it. Anyway, Black, I have to run. Like I already said, keep up the good work." Owens rushes off down the aisle before I can object.

Everything comes together in my mind in one rush. Aubrey had to go to bat for my design. I almost drop the box of baking chocolate again. Putting it into the basket before it ends up all over the floor, I push the cart forward absentmindedly. A couple of aisles over, I find the mini-marshmallows and throw them in the basket. Aubrey has been giving them updates too. I knew he was, but apparently, he has been doing it more often than I thought.

For the binder, he must have pulled the photos of the previous plant sculptures from my website. But why did he do it? Why didn't he say anything? Then I remember our conversation the night after our wine bar date. He mentioned some "petty squabbles," but didn't elaborate. My chest is aching with a sudden realization: Aubrey has been taking care of me from the start. He didn't even mention the council's objections. He just took care of it, as he has been trying so hard to take care of me ever since.

Tears push at the backs of my eyes and threaten to embarrass me in the middle of the grocery store. And what have I done for him? I've freaked out on him and pushed him away. Repeatedly. And every time I apologize, he forgives me without hesitation. I look down at the brownies and marshmallows in my cart. I really don't know how I am going to make this all up to him, prove to him that I am worth all of the trouble. I am not actually sure I am.

Pain laces through my entire body on the heels of that thought. As has happened so many times since I met Aubrey, my brain argues with my heart. But after hearing what Aubrey did for me, quietly, without any expectation of return, I know which part I'm going to side with. I sigh heavily, threading my hands through my hair in a familiar attempt at soothing my nerves. Brownies are a good start. With that thought in mind, I move my cart toward the checkout line.

I might not be able to say what I feel, but I can show him some extra care. Just like the care he has shown me from the very beginning.

I am a little bit hesitant as I knock on Black's front door. After yesterday's kerfuffle over his name, I thought Black might want some time alone. But then he practically begged me to come back for dinner, so here I am.

When Black croaked out, "Please, I just can't...hear it, not from you," my heart dropped out of my chest. For a long time, I have suspected Black's loss was of a lover, and yesterday's incident did everything to confirm that. Only the death of someone profoundly important could elicit such a reaction. And it hurts far more than I want to admit that he clearly doesn't want me to know anything about it. Everyone arounds us knows what is going on and I, the other person smack dab in the middle of the situation, know close to nothing, just tiny hints from Black's friends. The hints aren't even helpful. All they do is remind me that Black won't tell me...anything.

I sigh and glance around Black's front lawn as I wait for him to answer the door. He is usually right on top of it. Maybe he changed his mind? Maybe he thought better of his invitation? Damn it, all of this not knowing is driving me up a wall. I turn from the door, considering walking back to my car. My heart hurts at the thought, but if he doesn't answer the door soon, I won't have a choice. Then Black's door opens, and I turn around to see him standing in the doorway with Santa Claus oven mitts on his hands.

"You came back!" He exclaims and a bright smile cracks across his face.

His joy at seeing me burns away my anxiety, fear, and pain. I smile back at him and nod toward his oven mitts. "Baking?"

His eyes sparkle, and he laughs. "Yes, I made you something special."

Flip-flop goes my heart in my chest. "You made me dessert?"

Black steps back, making room for me to enter his home. "And dinner."

His happiness is infectious and soothing. Maybe I am making too much of yesterday. After all, we spent the rest of the day together, and he seemed to want me here desperately. I shake my head at myself and step through the door. The smell of dinner wafts from the kitchen and my stomach rumbles. Black leads the way toward his kitchen and dining area, and I shut the door behind me.

"Did you get a lot of work done today?" He throws the question over his shoulder, and I can hear some hesitancy in his tone. So I decide to answer honestly. If I want honesty from him, I should give it right back.

"No, mostly I worried about you. I wasn't sure if you really wanted me to come back."

Black turns into his kitchen and nods his head toward the dining nook off of the room. "Have a seat. I will have everything ready in a few more minutes."

Not pleased he didn't respond to my leading statement, I walk through the kitchen to the set the table. I pull out a chair facing the window to the backyard rather than the kitchen and plop down, uncharacteristically morose. I hear Black chuckle behind me, and I turn in my chair to watch him carrying a pot of spaghetti to the table. He sets it down on another Christmas themed pot holder. Going back into the kitchen, he returns with a basket full of sliced garlic bread, complete with cloth napkin. On his last trip to the kitchen, he slips off the oven mitts and sets them on the kitchen island before retrieving two wine glasses and a bottle of red wine from his countertop wine rack and returning to the dining table. Before sitting, he uncorks the bottle and fills both glasses, setting one in front of me and one in front of his place setting across the table from me.

There are no candles, but the meal is definitely intended to be romantic. Black finally settles in his chair and raises his glass toward me. I raise mine, feeling curious and a bit suspicious. We clink the glasses, but Black doesn't say anything, so I don't either. I cannot decide if this whole encounter is interesting or incredibly annoying. For the moment, I am siding with interesting.

"So," I say, no other words coming to mind.

Black takes a drink of his wine and holds his hand up to stop me. "No, I owe you an apology, Aubrey." He sighs and looks down at his plate for a moment before busying himself with filling my plate with spaghetti, salad, and garlic bread. I watch him without speaking as it is clear he wants to do the talking here. After filling his own plate, he takes another drink of wine before leaning a little forward, putting his elbows on the edge of the table. I quirk my eyebrows up at him and can't resist teasing him.

"My Aunt Patty would chastise you for putting your elbows on the dinner table, though my Aunt Susan would just join you."

Black smiles and nods, taking another drink of wine.

I can't help it now because this is becoming amusing. "Are you going to say anything or just drink your wine?"

Black looks a little sheepish then he grins and downs the last of the wine in his glass. He refills his wine glass and quirks his brows at me. Then we are both laughing, the tension breaking. I pick up the garlic bread from my plate and take a bite, chewing slowly. Pointing the end with a bite out of it at him, I declare, "Make with the rest of the apology."

Black laughs and blushes which makes me giggle as I am trying to take a sip of wine.

"I made you my special brownies."

I giggle again and wink at him as I set down my wine glass, "How special are they?"

His grin pulls wider. "Not that kind of special. You will have to wait until you have finished dinner to find out."

I wait until he is taking another sip of wine before remarking, "So you made me your special brownies. They must be very good if you think they will get you out of trouble." I wink at him so he knows the last bit was mostly a tease.

He sighs, serious again. "Aubrey, I know I am difficult. I promise it's not on purpose."

"You are not particularly difficult."

"Yes, I am, Aubrey. I promise it has nothing to do with you."

I nod, watching him thoughtfully. I expect him to say something more, but he does not. I am not sure how to proceed. Pushing for an explanation seems like the wrong choice, but honestly, I am not sure how much longer I can put off the inevitable. We fall to eating and the food is really nice.

"Great wine pairing, Black," I compliment him.

"Just wait until you taste the brownies. It is my secret recipe."

I grin at him.

Black sets down his glass of wine, pushing his now empty plate aside. "I am sorry, Aubrey. Ron made me upset yesterday, and I snapped at you when I shouldn't have."

I frown. "That is not exactly what happened, Black." When he just stares at me with a somewhat panicked look without saying anything, I continue, "You know you can tell me anything, right?"

He drops his eyes from mine and nods. I am trying so hard to tread carefully here. I want to know everything about what haunts Black, but it becomes clearer every day he doesn't want to tell me what is wrong. So, I give him an out, even as I chastise myself for doing it.

"And you will, when you are ready."

Black raises his head, his look surprised then thoughtful. He watches me for a long moment, and I hold his eyes and smile softly. I need him to understand I want this. I want, no need, everything from him. He sighs, a small smile on his lips now. He nods firmly once then smiles. Pushing back his seat, he rises and takes up both of our plates before walking into the kitchen. I turn in my chair to watch him.

"The meal was wonderful, Black. I hope you know I can't return the favor, unless you want breakfast burritos. Beyond scrambling eggs and reheating tortillas, I burn boiling water."

Black chuckles as he retrieves a glass baking pan from the top of the stove where it was cooling. I watch as he cuts the brownies and plates us each one. He brings the desert plates back to the table. After setting mine in front of me, he asks, "More wine?"

"I never say no to more wine."

"I know. So do The Sirens."

"Hey," I exclaim, "I was not drunk on wine, thank you very much, just lots and lots of cocktails."

Black laughs, and I take a bite of the brownie which has an oddly bubbled up top crust. The first bite bursts flavor on my tongue. "Wow, what does this have in it?"

Black takes a bite of his own, chewing slowly, then pointing his fork at me. "Mini-marshmallows."

Taking another bite, I savor the flavor. "These are so good."

Black rises from his seat and leaves the table. I am too preoccupied with my delicious brownie to pay any attention to him anymore. Heavenly. Just as I finish my brownie, a cup of coffee appears near my plate.

"Would you like another one?"

Looking up, I find Black standing next to me with the pan and a spatula, smiling broadly.

"Yes. And just for the record, you can apologize to me with brownies any day."

Black chuckles as he offloads another brownie on my plate. Before taking the pan back to the kitchen, he leans down and kisses me softly on my brownie crumble covered lips. When he stands back up, he licks his lips to catch the crumbs and winks at me.

I wave him away with my fork before I dig into another delicious marshmallow laced brownie. He laughs, returning to his seat to finish his own brownie, and he watches me wolf down my second one with a happy gleam in his eye.

"Happy now, Aubrey?" Black goes for a teasing tone, but of course, there is an underlying current of tension below the words.

"Deliriously. Now carry me to the couch. I'm going into a brownie coma."

We both laugh then I help Black clean up the dining room and put the dishes in the dishwasher. We settle on the couch to watch some old movie, and I put my head on Black's leg. I drowse my way to sleep with a happy heart and a full stomach.

CHAPTER 22

When Aubrey asks if I want to run errands with him the following Saturday, I am ridiculously excited. It is such a domestic thing to do together, but despite my fears, I'm very pleased to spend the day with him. I try not to think about what any of this means, we are just running around town after all. I feel extra skittish today for no apparent reason. Though, if I am being honest, I do know the reasons why. But I'm outrageously happy to be doing this nonetheless.

"I hope you don't mind some music."

"Not at all."

"Even if it's Celine Dion?"

"Well, I might draw the line there."

"Luckily for you, there's no Dion on my playlist."

"Thank heavens."

He laughs as he messes with his iPod which is connected to the radio of the car. "Aubrey's Playlist One: Classics," he declares as he hits the play button. "You better be buckled up."

"I got it."

He nods at me then checks his mirrors before putting the car in reverse. Just as with everything else, he is very meticulous with his driving. He pulls the car to the parking lot exit, checking both ways more than once before turning into the street, and I'm mesmerized by the sun glancing off of his hair through the windshield. The rays of sunlight reveal the brilliant red within his auburn fall of hair, sparkling the strands with a shimmer of gold. It creates a halo type of effect such as you find in medieval paintings of the baby Jesus.

I'm so entranced by the play of light over his hair and his face that I miss what songs are playing. He is unabashedly singing along, and I finally recognize Freddie Mercury and David Bowie as Aubrey gives "Under Pressure" his vocal all. He looks so boyish and charming as he throws me the occasional surreptitious glance. When he finds me grinning at him, he smiles wider and sings the songs to me. I'm enjoying the 80s and 90s retrospective of his playlist until about six songs in. He doesn't miss a beat as he segues into "This I Promise You" and then "I Want it That Way" right after that. I'm thoroughly amused by the switch from classic rock to pop, from Queen and Spin Doctors to late nineties boy bands.

"I can certainly go along with Queen, but NSYNC and Backstreet Boys?"

"Hey, they were hot boy bands, and I was going through puberty."

"You do realize you're not in puberty anymore."

"Shut up!"

Aubrey pauses to glare at me since we have pulled up to a stop light. I'm trying not to laugh, but I can't help it. Nor can I help teasing him.

"You look cute when you're embarrassed about your lackluster song tastes."

He narrows his eyes at me. "You recognized those songs immediately. What does that say about your secret musical preferences?"

"They played those songs everywhere."

"Mmmhhmm... says the self-professed hermit who has never liked gay bars or dance clubs. I'm not sure I'm buying your act. Where exactly was 'everywhere' if you spent the whole of the late nineties in your bedroom?"

"I plead the fifth."

Aubrey outright cackles at that. He snags his hand out and grabs my neck. He pulls me forward for a fast kiss, but we don't part until the car behind us starts honking incessantly.

"All right, all right!" Aubrey waves a hand at the back window as he hits the gas to move along. "Jackass."

I'm laughing again, and Aubrey throws me a dirty little grin and a wink before returning his eyes to the road. I can't believe how happy I am, and I refuse to question it. I just lean back in my seat, close my eyes, and listen to Aubrey as he starts singing along with his playlist again. Luckily, we are back to something civilized and his voice blends effortlessly with Halls' as he declares that my kiss is on his list. I open my eyes, and he throws me a gentle, loving glance; I take the look and hold it in my heart to cherish forever.

The months of June and July were up and down emotionally speaking, really forcing me to think about how I've been treating Aubrey. I have to think about what I want in the future and how I will handle things. It is still impossible to talk about the past. I have to shut it up and wall it off. I can't go through those emotions again: the grief, the devastation, the all-consuming uncertainty of not knowing. Shaking my head, I lift my coffee mug to my lips again and take a small sip as I watch Benny the squirrel eat way too many seeds for his tiny little body. Just thinking about the past this much almost spins me into a panic attack. July was, overall, a better month than June. I cannot believe how wonderful having Aubrey in my home has been. I pause in my thoughts a moment and think about that. He's not in my home all the time, obviously. But having him here, in my space, rights my world as if it is tilted without him in it. So the times when I am alone are far more obvious and uncomfortable. It may be it is just more obvious being without him makes me lonely and unhappy.

My work on the sculpture is coming along. There's a little bit of a snag because I just cannot seem to finish the thing. The deadline for the sculpture is officially mid-August, but the park opens on the first of September. Technically, I have more than enough time to finish if I could just concentrate. I decided to go with an incredibly large aloe plant, even though it is technically a succulent, not a cactus. It will be more than eight feet tall and ten feet wide. I've struggled with it even though it is not a particularly difficult plant to draw or reform into metal art. Every time I go to work on it, I'm conflicted about the little things. Should this leaf bend this way? Is the aloe flowering? Then I'm unsure of the whole project. Should I have gone with an aloe? What about an agave? Or a saguaro? Every time I think I'm making progress, I wander off into distraction. And, I have to admit, a lot of times, my distraction is Aubrey. Worrying about questions I do not have the answers for, I spin out scenarios in my head, scenarios that usually end with Aubrey leaving me…or worse.

Shaking my head hard on the heels of that thought, I take another sip of my coffee which has gone cold. Rising from my patio chair, I sling the coffee out on the lawn. There, now the grass is caffeinated. Pausing, I reflect on that. Yes, it was an Aubrey type thought. I smile softly. Walking through the open patio door, I close it securely behind me. I don't need any more intruders of the furred variety or any other type.

I am supposed to be working today, but I woke up discombobulated and worried. Throwing myself on my couch, I wiggle around until I am comfortable. An unwelcome new thought rises in my brain: Is Aubrey even here permanently? Fuck! How could I have not thought about that? We have known each other for four months, and it has never occurred to me to ask, "Are you staying after the park is built?" Probably not. It seems to be the nature of his work that he moves around a lot. I sit up and run my hands through my hair. But could he have Oakland as a home base? He is from Chicago, so I guess it is his current base of operations. Could he move here? Would he even consider it? Suddenly, my stomach knots painfully. I lie back down trying to calm my nerves, my stomach, my entire being.

Who am I to consider asking him that? When I won't, *no can't*, tell him about my past, how could I expect a commitment like that from him? And how am I even considering it? My head is spinning, my whole world tilting on its axis. I cannot believe I am thinking about these things, thinking about Aubrey, thinking about a *future*, a *future with Aubrey*, for fuck's sake! My mind twirls and my stomach keeps trying to revolt. What will I do when he leaves? My heart cleaves open at the word *when*.

I take deep breaths and try to settle myself, but it is not working. *Calm the fuck down, Black!* Belatedly, I realize I have thrown myself into another panic attack. Breathing deeply, I allow myself to clutch my hair too tightly. I count to ten, then fifty, then two hundred. When I have pulled two hundred calming breaths into my lungs, I don't feel quite so sick anymore. I feel hazy and weak, like I always do after a panic attack. Tears leak out of the corners of my eyes, and I try hard to just blink them away. Seemingly out of nowhere, a snippet of a poem I read years ago, wanders through my mind: "But at my back I always hear / Time's wingéd chariot hurrying near."

I jolt up to sitting. Fuck it all. No matter what Aubrey is doing next, I have to show him how much he means to me. *Now!* I, of all people, know time is not guaranteed. Breathing deeply again, I shake my head to declutter my brain. A new, happier thought creates itself out of the gloomy clouds and cobwebs in my brain. I know when Aubrey's birthday is. *And*, it is next week. My face almost hurts when I smile. Reaching up to my cheeks, I massage them a little as I contemplate what to do. Making my way up to my temples, it seems like this impromptu face massage is helping me think. I laugh and consider sending Aubrey a text about it. *Impromptu facial massages help me think.* Grinning, I decide against it.

The only reason I know Aubrey's birthday is August fifth is that Chuck's new bartender, Rylan, has turned out to be a stickler about carding people. Everyone, he cards everyone. He cards the baby-faced teens trying to pass off fake IDs and even grizzled old biker dudes who have his age on them by a factor of three. While Chuck would have just given the misbehaving teens a bit of snide side eye and thrown their cards in their faces, Rylan confiscated three IDs right in front of us last week. After he chewed them out in a fashion worthy of a fed-up school teacher, Rylan threatened to call their mothers. At that point, the boys ran out, red faced and almost crying. Chuck had laughed his head off and clapped Rylan on the back, much too hard, of course. After he was through wincing, Rylan grinned at Aubrey and me, putting his hand out in a "give-me" gesture. While he shined his penlight on our IDs and scrutinized them closely, Aubrey just laughed and went to find us a booth. When Rylan handed them back to me and took our order, I looked at Aubrey's and was delighted to see I had not missed his birthday.

Tapping my chin, like Aubrey does, I contemplate what Aubrey would like best. A surprise party? No, too public. I smile when I remember Aubrey's favorite sculpture, and the prize he won me that sits on top of it. I know exactly what I am giving Aubrey for his birthday.

CHAPTER 23

"No, you can't open your eyes yet."

Leaving my eyes closed for the moment, I bat at Black's hand when I feel him try to put something on my head.

"Hold still! This is a surprise."

"You putting something on my head is a surprise? No, you greeting me at the door with a glass of wine would have been a surprise, a very pleasant one." I bat his hand away again when I feel it against my chin.

"Aubrey! Come on!"

"What are you trying to put on my head, and why does it have a strap that feels suspiciously like a rubber band?"

"You would already know that by now if you would stop fidgeting."

I sigh, and then sigh again, heavily, to indicate how very put-upon I am by whatever Black is trying to do to me. When he greeted me at his door with the order to close my eyes and keep them closed, I thought we were playing a kinky game and my cock was immediately all for that. Instead, Black led me into the living room and sat me on the couch where he has had me for the last five minutes as he has shuffled around the room, obviously adjusting things. Now he is trying to put something on my head and this no longer seems like a sexy scenario.

When he tips up my chin with his finger this time, I let him and sigh extra loudly. Something that feels like a weird circle rests on my hair. "If this is not a tiara, then I don't want it."

Black laughs. "Oh, I am sure you will love what you see. When I let you open your eyes, that is. But you look cute there with your eyes closed. Maybe I should have gone with the blindfold."

"Black!"

He laughs again, and I feel the couch cushion sink in as he sits beside me on his couch. I turn myself toward him and he takes my hands in his and finally says, "Open your eyes, Aubrey."

Black is grinning like a mischievous elf with two brightly colored gift bags in his lap.

"Happy Birthday, Aubrey!" he yells out, and I cannot help laughing.

He puts my hands back in my lap and passes me the smaller of the two bags, a shiny silver one with a profusion of rainbow-colored ribbons curled around the silver fabric handle.

Joy bubbles up inside of me, and I cannot contain it. I jump toward him, wrapping my arms around him, not caring about mussing up the presents in his lap.

"Wait! You'll wrinkle the bags!"

I laugh as I pepper his face with kisses. "Thank you, thank you, thank you! How did you know today is my birthday?" Pulling back, I release him and snatch the smaller bag back, attacking the ribbon which stubbornly clings to the handle.

Black smirks at me and hands me a pair of scissors, god knows from where. Snatching them out of his hand, I cut the ribbons off and toss them into the air with a flourish. I hand the scissors back to Black and pull the rectangular package from the box. I can't believe my eyes. I look up at Black who is smiling softly at me with an expectant look on his face.

Overcome with a mixture of joy and surprise, I barely manage a whisper, "You bought me *We Bare Bears*?"

Black's grin grows wider. "Do you like it?"

"I love it!"

"Seasons one and two. Three is not out on DVD yet."

"I can't believe it."

Black shrugs and leans forward to peck me on the cheek. I blush, and he laughs, swiping his thumb across the color on my skin.

"No one has ever given me a present before."

"No one? Not even your aunts?"

"You know what I mean, Black." I try for stern, but I cannot contain my excitement. "Oh, my god! I love it!"

Black sweeps the empty silver bag out of my lap and deposits a cobalt blue one in its place.

"There's more?"

"Yes, of course there is, Aubrey. You only turn thirty once."

I look at him sternly, closing one eye and squinting the other. "How do you know my birthday and age?"

Black chuckles and gestures toward the bag in my lap. "I sneaked a peek when Rylan insisted on carding us at the bar last week."

I nod and turn my attention to the much larger bag now on my lap. Scissors land on the palm of the hand I hold out to Black and I clip the ribbons, this time taking the bunch of them and trying to put them on my head. My hand bumps against an object and I remember that Black put something on my head.

Pointing up at it, I ask, "Is this a birthday hat?"

"Yup, complete with ears."

"Is it a *We Bare Bears* hat?"

"Yup, can you guess which bear I gave you?"

"Ice Bear!" Squealing like a little kid, I drop the bag back into Black's lap and run to the bathroom to look in the mirror. "I'm Ice Bear!"

Black's chuckle follows me from the living room, and I rush back, throwing my arms around his neck from over the back of the couch. I kiss his cheek before running back around and sitting next to him again. I snatch the bag from his lap and pour the contents out on couch. There are two more party hats, one Grizzly and one Panda. There is a stack set of mugs, a T-shirt with Ice Bear holding an axe in his mouth with the caption "Ice Bear will take care of it.", a set of socks with each bear's face represented, a book of Mad Libs, and a book, *We Bare Bears Go Everywhere Handbook*. I run my hands over everything and look up at Black. Joy overwhelms me, and for a moment, I think I am going to cry. No man has ever given me a present; no boyfriend has ever shown up for me in this way. I'm almost overcome with tears, but one look at Black's happy smile brings out a laugh instead.

"I cannot believe you did this. I love it all. This is the best birthday ever!"

Black stands up and walks to the fireplace mantle where a third bag sit, this one purple with purple curled ribbons. I didn't even notice it there before.

"I have one more present for you. It was too hard to decide which one you would like best, so I bought both. But this one seemed most like you."

He comes back to the couch, handing me the bag before sitting down beside me. Once again scissors appear, and I clip the ribbons, this time tucking them into the breast pocket of my button down like a flower, "Purple is my favorite color, you know."

"I do know."

Pulling out the tissue paper, I find a T-shirt in baby blue, with Ice Bear standing above a mountain range on the front. The graphic reads "Ice Bear will protect you."

Before I can react, Black asks, "If you are Ice Bear, who am I?"

I'm distracted by the reverent tone in Black's voice.

"I don't know. I guess we will have to watch these to find out." I hold up the season one DVD box.

Black nods as I unwrap the box and open the case to retrieve the first disk. Black turns on the TV and DVD player, slipping the disk into the slot when it pops out.

"Why do you like Ice Bear so much?" Black asks as I arrange my presents on the coffee table. He laughs when I pull the baby blue T-shirt over my head, sliding it on over my button down.

Cocking my head to the side, I hum a moment before answering. "Because he takes care of his brothers. He is cool and smart and wicked talented in everything he tries. But he can cook, and I can't." I laugh. "I guess cooking is where the similarities end."

Black hands me the TV remote then pulls me closer to him after slinging his arm around my shoulders.

"You do take care of me, Aubrey," he whispers in my ear before kissing it softly.

Emotions strangle up in my throat and I turn to look into his eyes. *I love you.* The words beat against the back of my throat, but I smile instead of saying them as I kiss him softly on the lips. Winking, because it is easier to be silly than to reveal my heart, I reply, "That is Ice Bear to you."

"Which episode do you want to watch?" Black asks.

"Some people would go with conventional wisdom and start with the first episode, but now that I think about it, I want to start with my favorite episode."

I pick up the season two DVD set, unwrap it, and give Black a different disc. "Swap it out."

"Yes, sir." Black winks at me and follows my command, bringing me back the other disk which I put carefully back in its case. Picking up one of the birthday hats, I crook my finger at Black, and he dutifully bends forward to receive his hat.

"I think you should be Grizz," I say as I deposit the Grizzly hat on Black's head. He adjusts the rubber band strap and turns his head side to side as if modeling it for me. I make an okay sign with my fingers and nod my appreciation. Turning toward the TV, I flip through the episode menu until I find "Losing Ice Bear." After I press the start button, I snuggle in against Black's side and he wraps his arm around my shoulders. I watch Black's face and am pleased he seems as enthralled with my favorite cartoon bears as I am. My heart throbs with a special kind of joy and I snuggle into his side, content and so thoroughly in love it does not even bother me that neither of us have said the words.

Aubrey and I watch Ice Bear leave his brothers, become a sushi chef, and finally return home to his family after they apologize for taking him for granted. I cannot help but be impressed by the cartoon and its themes of family, love, and acceptance of differences. Aubrey really is like his favorite character, with the very obvious exception of cooking. After we watch a few more of Aubrey's favorite episodes, I whisper in his ear, "Would you like a cupcake?"

Aubrey giggles joyfully. "You bought me cupcakes?"

"No, I made you cupcakes."

Aubrey smiles, sending sunshine through my bloodstream, and I'm mesmerized by the light of his crisp green eyes. He shifts out of the crook of my arm and kisses me suddenly. I grab him around the waist to pull him halfway into my lap. When he kisses my lips again, I murmur, "Are you sure that you're Ice Bear?"

Aubrey jerks back out of my lap, plopping down hard on the couch. He levels a stern look in my direction. "What could you possibly mean? I am the epitome of Ice Bear."

I can't help grinning and teasing him, "But you are so much more like Grizz."

"How dare you? Next thing you know, you will be comparing me to Panda."

"Well…"

Aubrey tackles me, pushing me back against the cushions and pulling my arms above my head. "Take it back."

I lick my lips and reply in a naughty tone, "What are you gonna do to make me?"

Aubrey grins wickedly and lowers his face toward mine. Before our lips can touch, he replies, "Absolutely nothing."

Then he jumps backward, off the couch and away from me, practically cackling.

"Oh, no you don't," I growl, jumping off the couch and chasing him as he dodges his way out of the living room and into the kitchen. He runs to the other side of the island, and I strut forward, throwing my hands down on the island counter. "Now whatcha gonna do?"

He feints right, and I fall for it. He runs left, but instead of running out of the room, he follows me around the island and jumps on my back, piggyback style.

"Gotcha!" He yells in triumph. "Say it!"

"Say what?"

"You know!"

"Uncle?"

He growls and takes advantage of his position by nipping me in the ear and whispering threateningly, "I do know where you are ticklish."

"No," I howl as I gallop us back to the living room. I dump him off on the couch and jump on him. "You win! You're Ice Bear!"

Aubrey is giggling so hard he can barely breathe, and I take full advantage because I know *his* ticklish spots too.

"No," he pants out breathily. He squirms as I run my fingertips across his belly where his shirt has ridden up to show it. Laughing, I kiss the complaint away and his laughter turns to a groan. I lean my elbow into the couch, so I can look down into his face.

"Whatever am I gonna do with you, Ice Bear?" I ask, immediately wishing I hadn't. I want to tell him I love him, but I can't. The words clog in my throat and my tongue lays flat in my mouth and refuses to move. I hope Aubrey cannot see my struggle to reach out to him, past my fear and panic. He smiles up at me softly.

"Anything you want, Charlie." And just like that he makes it all better without even knowing it.

Hope blooms in my chest even as I respond with feigned indignation.

"You did not just call me a Bigfoot!"

"If the foot fits." He giggles as he kisses my face and neck with little butterfly kisses. I growl and kiss him back, hoping and praying I really can keep him forever.

I could *feel* the words on the tip of his tongue. I would swear on my whole heart Black was about to tell me he loves me. But then a look of panic flashed across his face, lighting up his eyes with fear when they had shown only delight this afternoon, and I gave him an out. Continuing our cartoon joke, I called Black the neighborhood Bigfoot from *We Bare Bears*, Charlie. Relief shoots through Black so fast and hard I am both ecstatic to distract him and so sad not to hear the words I could see on the tip of his tongue. Then I kiss the love of my life with all of my heart and soul and hope it will be enough to fix whatever is broken inside of Ian James Black.

Our make-out session on the couch is interrupted by my need for cupcakes. I push up against Black's shoulders, forcing a little space between us. I look Black directly in the eye and say in a solemn tone, "You need to feed me my cupcakes."

Black's grin is quick and happy, and a touch wicked. He licks his lips and slips his fingers across my belly again in another attempt to tickle me. I laugh and push against his chest again. He growls, swooping forward to nip my bottom lip before jumping up from the couch. It takes him no time to return with a plate full of chocolate frosted cupcakes. He hands me one, and I wait until he is seated with his own before I pull the edge of the paper wrapper down so I can bite into it.

"Happy Birthday, Aubrey," Black murmurs then the glorious taste of chocolate icing, cake, and strawberry filling burst across my tongue. Closing my eyes against unexpected tears, I savor the taste, chewing slowly before swallowing. When my eyes finally reopen, Black is watching me with an intense look of longing and what I believe is love.

I've never believed in love at first sight, but I know that is the closest possible description of what happened to me the very first moment I saw Black. The connection had been so instantaneous and overwhelming. Everything we have done in the past four months has strengthened the connection, tipping it over from lust and infatuation to affection, longing, desire, and need. I know Black feels the same. If I hadn't known before, today would have told me. This private birthday party was filled with personalized touches, details personalized by Black for me alone. My heart throbs in my chest, beating a bit too fast as I swallow my mouthful of cupcake. I nod and smile at him before I shove the rest of the cupcake into my mouth. Black laughs, not knowing that I did it so I wouldn't have to speak, so I wouldn't tell him I love him because I am afraid it will scare him away.

Something holds Black back, I muse as I watch him bite into his own cupcake. He is so happy with the little party he threw me. I am almost overwhelmed by the care and attention. I snatch up another cupcake because they are glorious and because my feelings are too much for me at the moment. I bite into this one gently, and Black's face is sweet and soft as he watches me eat it. Whatever happened to Black, whomever he lost, shattered his soul, fundamentally altering who he was. Closing my eyes briefly so I don't cry from the mixture of joy and sadness that courses through me at the moment, I savor the taste of the chocolate and strawberries. After finishing the last bite, I open my eyes to find Black looking at me with longing. I smile, leaning forward to kiss the crumbs off his lips.

"Thank you," I whisper against his lips as I push him back down on the couch, shuffling forward so I can straddle his lap. "This was the best birthday ever, Black, because you made it so." We kiss for a long time, feeding off of the chocolate, strawberries, and love on each other's lips, even if we don't yet call it love.

On Tuesday afternoon, I receive a weird text from Aubrey as I am smoothing the outside metal of my aloe plant with a blowtorch. Hearing the message ding on my phone, I turn off the torch to check it.

You named your statue "Monstrosity." This is followed by a laughing face emoji and a puppy dog one with a bewildered face.

Before I can answer, he messages again.

Alluding either to the raging bronco being busted or the cowboy doing the breaking. OR... Lol.

I laugh and type him back a quick message.

How did you find that out? Did you go see it? WITHOUT ME???

Nah, Grizz, I saw your neighbor, Lisa, and baby Sarah. Lisa told me about it. Apparently, it's a big hit!

Groooooaaaannnn. Can you hear me groaning from here????

Another laughing emoji lights up my screen. We message back and forth for a few more minutes before I return to the sculpture with far more energy and inspiration than I had a few moments before.

CHAPTER 24

I usually grab lunch at the diner near my shop. But as I am hours late, it is packed, so I bypass their parking lot and go for the nearest drive-thru. I am making good progress and wanted to grab a BLT and get back to the sculpture, so I don't want to wait while blue hairs contemplate their orders of hash browns and coffee. Taco Bell is the closest place, so I slide my car into the thankfully empty drive-thru.

"May I take your order?" A whiny teenaged voice crackles through the order box.

"Yeah, I will have a number two and a Mountain Dew Baja Blast."

"Will that complete your order?"

"Yes, and I need some Fire sauce."

"Pull up to the window, sir."

I do as commanded and am rewarded with my drink, tacos, and sauce. After paying the bored teen his money, I drive back to my studio, wishing Aubrey could take a lunch break with me. But he has been preparing a presentation for another city all week and I do not want to disturb him. After arriving back at my studio, I eat my less than stellar tacos morosely as I ponder the progress of my sculpture. Honestly, the whole thing is almost complete, but something is lacking. I shake my head. It is so weird how my indecision about Aubrey is affecting everything, from my work to my appetite. I have a sudden horrifying thought. Does he know how discombobulated I am? Has he started to feel my struggle? I want him so much. I care about him so much. Fuck!

"Fuck!" I yell out loud. I pick up one of my workshop rags to wipe my hands on it and find myself wringing the life out of it within seconds. Damn it, I'm so in love with him, though this is not the first time I have realized this. No, I have known for a while, for far longer than I have been willing to admit to myself. I have known since the day I brought him into my home. I have realized it over and over again, acknowledged it in the back of my mind as we kiss or make love or eat popcorn or drink coffee. I realize it every single time I lay eyes on him, and the feeling just grows beyond all bounds, beyond all of the walls I hastily try to erect in myself. I almost told him on his birthday. There on the couch with him laughing beneath me the words were on the tip of my tongue, and I swallowed them. Shame floods me at the memory. How long can I keep doing this to myself? To him?

"I'm in love with Aubrey." I say it aloud, testing the words. No, I can't. I cannot do this. Not again. I sit down at my bench with my head in my hands. I am trying to deep breathe my way out of loving the man, but it obviously isn't working. I raise my head and spy one of the leftover sauce packets. "I will if you will" it declares, and it feels like a positive sign. Maybe, maybe I can. I stare at the sauce packet as if it will tell me what I should do. The two parts of my heart are at war, but I'm finally beginning to realize I have no hope of holding my soul back from him. And the thought eases the tightness in my chest.

I snap a picture of the taunting little sauce packet and send it to Aubrey, a smile hovering on my face as I try to guess how he will respond. Hopefully with something kinky, though I do love it when my man gets silly. I roll my eyes at myself even as my heart clenches. *You cannot call him that, Black,* I admonish myself internally. *He is not your man and he can't ever be.* My heart slices open with that thought. I try hard to ignore reality's intrusion. I am intensely watching the screen on my phone, expecting a speedy and witty response. Nothing.

I toss my phone on my bench. He must be busy – with the next project that will take him far away from me. Pushing the thoughts aside, I sigh, and amble up and over to my metal monster. I pat one smooth side then pick up my blow torch, gloves, and safety helmet. Settling the helmet over my face, I light the torch and try to work out some of my angst on this gigantic aloe plant that I just cannot seem to finish.

Three hours pass in a blink. I turn off the torch, remove my gloves, and helmet, setting them in their proper places on the workbench. I stride up to the table, expecting to find a host of suggestive messages on my phone. Clicking it on, I find…nothing. That is strange. Even when he is busy, Aubrey always responds, even if it is to say "Shh!! I'm workin' here!" a response I absolutely adore which thrills me beyond words every time I receive it. It feels like a special, secret communication between us, and it never fails to lighten my overly heavy heart.

Hey, good lookin, what ya got cookin?

I try for Aubrey style corny, pop culture reference, knowing I will never have the skill he has at it. No response. I should give it a few minutes, but this is so out of character for Aubrey I am panicking after two missed messages.

Aubrey? Everything all right?

I try the direct approach and hit send. I put the phone down so I do not ceaselessly check it. I watch the clock on my back wall for sixty whole seconds. No beep. No message. I switch to the call screen and hit number two, Aubrey's speed-dial, the only speed-dial in my phone. It rings until the voicemail switches on. Now I am seriously worried. Damn it. I am going to hunt him down. I check the gas bottles before I go, making sure they are turned off, flick out my lights, slam the door too hard, and lock up. It is just after five when I pull out of my shop parking lot.

Luckily, Aubrey works out of his hotel suite, so there is really only one place for him to be. I park in the hotel lot and walk briskly inside to the elevator. It seems to take forever to arrive, so I can hop on and ride up to Aubrey's floor. I impatiently tap my foot until the door opens. I don't have a key to Aubrey's hotel room, so I am wondering how I will get in. But, when I arrive at his door, I grin because the plastic "Do Not Disturb" sign is wedged between the door and the frame, keeping it open. I knock softly then open the door. All the lights appear to be off, and I do not hear any sounds. Frowning, I am instantly concerned the propped open door was not an invitation to me but an indication something was wrong inside. Heart pounding in my chest, I yell out his name.

"Aubrey!"

I hear a thump then; it is coming from the bedroom. Making my way through the kitchen, I flip on all of the lights as if they will provide clarity for me.

"Black, I'm in here," Aubrey calls, but his voice is muffled.

When I walk into the bedroom, all I see is an Aubrey shaped lump under the bedspread.

"What are you doing under there, sleepy head?" I ask teasingly as I walk to the bed and sit on the end by his blanket covered feet.

"I don't want to get up. And you can't make me."

"Oh really?" I reply as I lift up the edge of the covers so I can tickle the bottom of his foot.

He squeaks, throws the covers off his head, pulls himself up to sitting against the headboard, and glares at me. I cannot help but laugh at his mutinous expression.

"What's up, buttercup?"

Aubrey huffs and tries to slide back down the bed and under the covers. I catch his hand just as he tries to bring the blankets over his head again. I still want to laugh because he is just so damned cute. I have never seen him quite this way, clearly pissed off about something and trying his best to pout it out.

"Aubrey," I say in a soft and hopefully soothing tone as I scoot myself down the bed toward him. He curls his legs up under himself and arranges the covers around his body, straightening them and refusing to look at me.

"What's wrong, Ice Bear? Did no one like your sushi?"

A smile peaks out a moment before a scowl falls down his features like a thunderclap.

"No," he replies mutinously as he crosses his arms over his naked chest. I wonder if he is wearing any clothes at all. I lick my lips and stifle the groan that wells up in me at the thought of his naked body just beneath the covers.

"No one likes your sushi?"

A small laugh forces its way out of his throat. He doesn't look at me, but his face softens as he sighs and uncrosses his arms, so he can clasp his hands together. He mumbles something, but it is unintelligible.

"What, Ice Bear? I didn't understand that."

Aubrey finally looks me full in the face and sighs. Tear tracks run down his face as if he just recently stopped crying. I move closer toward him and lean over to touch his cheek with my thumb.

"What's wrong, Aubrey? Are you okay?" My heart is thumping in my chest. I've seen Aubrey cry once, during our fight outside of Tilly's. Swallowing the lump in my throat, I voice my sudden fear. "I didn't make you cry, did I?"

Aubrey's hand comes up to cover mine against his cheek. He turns, placing a kiss against my palm, shaking his head.

"No," he croaks out, his voice sounding hoarse and dry.

I scoot even closer to him on the bed until I can softly, slowly take him into my arms. He leans his head against my shoulder and winds his arms around my back. As he sighs and sniffles, I pet his hair and murmur in his ear.

"Whatever is wrong, we can make it better, I promise."

Aubrey nods then pulls back and studies my face for a moment. Seemingly satisfied with what he sees, he nods again, then fall dramatically over on his side.

"I lost Palo Alto," he mumbles morosely.

"You lost Palo Alto? How do you lose a whole municipality?"

Aubrey makes a scoffing noise in his throat as he scrubs his face against the sheets and blanket. Sighing, he rises back up to sitting.

"My bid for a park project in Palo Alto was rejected. I didn't win it."

"Oh, I'm sorry. Was that the project you have been working on for the past few weeks?"

Aubrey nods and leans back against the headboard again. He rubs his eyes then blinks at me. "It was supposed to start in October, two weeks after the opening of the park here. It would have been the perfect job to do next. I wouldn't even have to leave Oakland. But now that is down the toilet and I have to start searching the available contracts again. Damn it!"

Aubrey thumps his head against the headboard twice then stares up at the ceiling. I am speechless because of what he said about not having to leave Oakland. Considering my own thoughts on my feelings for Aubrey today, I am both gratified and a little bit petrified to hear Aubrey wants to stay in Oakland. I want to believe I am the reason, but I'm honestly too scared to let my thoughts wander in that particular direction. Aubrey breaks me out of my reverie by lowering his gaze from the ceiling to me.

"I want to be grumpy. Why are you being so nice to me?"

I have to chuckle. "Why wouldn't I be nice to you, Aubrey?"

He looks startled at my statement, and I have to admit it hurts. Why is he surprised that I care? I don't know what to say now, feeling suddenly uncertain. I try to corral my thoughts back into some sort of shape. He looks so sad sitting here, in his bed, shirtless, his hands listlessly linked together in his lap. I clear my throat to push down my fears and try to think of a way to make him feel better.

"You've lost bids before, I'm sure. You will catch the next one." He shakes his head, and I bring my hand back up to cup his cheek. "Yes, you will. You are very good at your job, Aubrey."

He shakes his head again. "No, you don't understand. I've never lost a bid before."

"Never?"

"No, never."

"Well, that is even more impressive. You founded your company right out of college, right?"

Aubrey sighs and rubs his face vigorously with both hands before nodding. "It is my first loss in eight years. I have worked so hard, Black." A sob wells up and spills out of Aubrey's throat. I pull him toward me, into my chest, and stroke his beautiful hair. He continues to choke out words against my neck.

"I took every internship opportunity. Every single job that came my way, I picked it up, no matter what it was, no matter where it was. I was so afraid I would fail, Black. I wanted to be the best." He chokes a bit on the words as his tears coast down my neck, down my shirt, and over my clavicle. He is crying harder now and whatever he is saying doesn't make sense anymore.

"Shush," I murmur into his ear and rub his back in long strokes up and down. When he has calmed a little, I kiss his hair.

"It's alright, Aubrey. You will find another job."

I stop and think about how to phrase my next question. I don't want to be intrusive as Aubrey and I have never discussed money. But, besides the disappointment of not landing a bid he clearly wanted, Aubrey seems especially distraught.

Lowering my voice, I ask the question despite my trepidation, "You're not worried about money, are you?"

Aubrey laughs against my throat and kisses my pulse before pulling his head up to kiss my lips. "No," he murmurs as he flops back over on his side. "My business is really successful. In fact, I am at the point where I need to establish a permanent home base and hire a second designer. Because I have done nothing but work for the better part of a decade. I actually have multiple bids waiting for me." He pauses, worrying his lip as he steals a glance up at me as if wondering if he should share whatever he is on his mind.

I smile down at him as I turn so I can face him more easily. "So, what's stopping you?"

He narrows his eyes at me. "From what?"

"From starting an office and hiring a second designer?"

He sighs and closes his eyes. When he doesn't answer me, I drop the question because I know I am part of the problem. If I could just… my mind draws a blank. I don't know how to make this better for him, or if I even could. Since I can't help on the job front, I try to soothe him in the here and now.

"How long have you been under these covers, Aubrey bear?"

He cocks one eye open at me. "Hours."

"You should probably get up. Have some dinner. Come on, I'll make you something."

Aubrey gives me a glare with his one open eye. "Why do you get to saunter in here and make me get up? I wanted to pout some more."

"How do you know I was sauntering when I came in here? You had your head under the covers."

While he is looking at me suspiciously out of the one eye he is showing me, I sneak my hand under the covers and run my fingers over his ticklish belly.

"No," he howls and tries to burrow deeper under the covers.

Chuckling, I draw my hand back and rub it over his exposed back. "Come on, Aubrey. No one wants to go to Palo Alto. Too many techies, too much pollution. You're not missing much by staying here."

I'm surprised at how I phrased that, but I don't regret it. I lean forward and kiss his cheek. He rolls onto his back, and I put my hands down on each side of his torso as I lean down to kiss him more thoroughly. When I pull back, Aubrey has a tentative smile on his face. I smile back and some of the tension that has held my heart since I couldn't contact him earlier finally breaks.

"Okay, you have me convinced. I'm not too sad to lose Palo Alto. Who wants to go to Palo Alto anyway?"

"No one, ever." Black leans in again and brushes his lips across mine. He still has me caged in, his arms at each of my sides on the bed. I take a deep breath because as I look into his eyes, I know how deeply I love him, and I can see the familiar pain he has thus far refused to share with me lurking in his eyes. I sit up a little and whisper against his mouth, "Your turn."

He blinks, twitching his head to the right, creating the tiniest bit of space between our faces. "For what?"

I sigh and lean my forehead against his and look into his eyes. They are so beautiful, with a deep sadness in their depths, a sadness he has yet to share with me.

"You know."

Black looks confused for a split second then utterly panicked. He tries to pull back, but I have anticipated the move and am holding his wrists to the bed by my hips. He looks down at his hands surprised and when he whips his head back up, I can tell he is shocked at both the position I have him in and by the look of determination he sees on my face. He is clearly at a loss for words and his facial expression has turned from panic to absolute desperation.

"Please, Aubrey, don't."

I sigh again but don't lean back or reduce the pressure with which I am holding his wrists down and his body to me.

"It really is okay," I murmur, but he drops his eyes and shakes his head vehemently. This is the first time I have come so close to confronting him about everything he holds back from me, about the moments when he withdraws, and I feel a bitter chill at the loss. This is the first time I am demanding a real answer, even if I am doing it subtly without articulating the question. Black knows exactly what I am asking. But as his look of anguish does not abate and he tries to pull himself away from me, my heart starts pounding hard in my chest, and I'm sure in that moment I'm going to lose him. Desperate now myself, I change tactics. I surge up as I drag his arms down further on the bed. I catch his mouth in a demanding kiss, shoving my tongue into his mouth and forcing his to duel back. He is clearly shocked, and I take advantage. I kiss him hard, brutally, in a dominant way I've rarely displayed or felt before, only ever with him. He is mine, and I am showing him. I pull back enough to take his bottom lip between my teeth and pull it a little before letting it go with a snap.

"You will tell me," I practically grind out, surprising myself with how I've gritted my jaw, my voice dropping into a deep demanding tone I barely recognize. I pull his arms again, forcing him down on top of my chest as I lean back into my pillow. I release my left hand and snake it around his back, caging him to me with that arm as I still hold the other wrist to the bed, now closer to my armpit. I kiss him again, as hard as before, showing him that I own him, that he is mine.

He finally rouses from his shock and growls, kissing me back with as much ferocity as I am giving him. He yanks at his left wrist, but I won't let it go. I've already released his right hand, so he threads it behind my back and into my hair, his grip so tight it's almost punishing. We are fighting for control, not of the kiss, but of our destiny. Our hearts are beating so hard I can feel his against my bare chest. As neither of us is relenting in our desperate demands, for him to give over or for me to back down, everything blazes purely carnal in an instant. Thank heaven I went to bed in the nude, I think as I begin tugging at the back of his shirt.

"Off!" I grind out against his lips. The look on his face stays desperate for a second then he lights up, a wicked grin forming against my mouth.

"Oh, you're gonna pay now," he growls, and I know he means it in more than one way. He tugs on the hair in his right hand, thrusting my head back, revealing my throat which he immediately bites into, hard. I shout out the pleasure coursing through me. I let go of his back but not his wrist. He pulls back, rising off the bed as I throw the covers from between us and sit up. He tries to pull his hand away so he can throw his clothes off, but I refuse to release his hand. He looks up at me, his right hand stilling on his jeans button. I am looking directly into his eyes as I put his other hand on his waist band. I let it go, but do not remove my hand fully from his. I skim along the back of it as he unbuttons his pants, lowering the zipper with his other hand. My right hand stays on his as he pushes his jeans down, taking his underwear with it. I don't break our intense eye contact. Somehow, he manages to remove his shoes without me releasing him. When he is finally as nude as I am, I twine my hand with his and yank him into the bed on top of me. Threading my hand through his hair, I kiss him hard, biting at his bottom lip, making him growl and moan.

"The lube," I grind out against his lips, and he reaches blindly for the bedside table, almost yanking the drawer off its hinges in his haste, our haste. When he finally manages to grab hold of the bottle, I've moved on to try to suck a hickey on his neck, a claiming mark as if the bruise would somehow show him he belongs to me, with me. He fumbles the bottle open, pouring some into his only free hand before dropping it on the floor.

"Now!" I practically yell in his ear then I feel his slick fingers between my cheeks. I thrust my hips up at him as he circles my hole with his index finger. The shift forces him inside of me, and I groan against the sensation, the burn, the need rising inside of me.

"Black!" I am panting now as he settles himself more fully on top of me, taking his weight on his one elbow, finger fucking me hard and fast as he nudges my head to the side roughly and bites down where my neck meets my shoulder. One of my hands is threaded through his hair, and I hold him tight against my neck as he bites and sucks while his fingers work me open, quickly but oh so thoroughly. I hold him to me with my other arm, my hand splayed across his back as if I could pull him inside of myself, into my chest, inside of my soul. But he is already there, inside my heart, and I claw at his back as I try to pull him into the part of me he can enter. Black tries to pull back, perhaps to look at my face, but I don't let him.

"Now," I scream in his ear before biting down on his earlobe, almost hard enough to break the skin, definitely hard enough to bruise. Black finally succeeds in pulling away a moment, and I don't understand where he is going until I hear the crinkle of a condom wrapper. Even in our haste to join ourselves, Black tries to take care of me. Tears prickle the backs of my eyelids, and I bite down hard on my bottom lip to keep from crying at the care. Moving himself back into the position, I feel him pushing into me, but my emotions are more intense than the sublime physical sensations. As he sinks into me, I pull his head up by his hair, forcing our gazes to meet.

"You are mine," I tell him in that demanding voice I never knew I had until today. He nods shakily, clearly overcome by what is passing between us. His free hand comes up to brush across my cheek before he slides it under my shoulder to pull me tighter against him.

"Everything about you is mine," I continue to growl, my hold tightening in his hair as he finally joins us completely. My back bows in violent pleasure as he pulls out, only to shove back in much more forcefully than before. I slip my legs up his thighs and around his hips, squeezing him, pulling him into me more tightly. His thrusts inside of me grow harder and more frantic.

"Yes," I say, demanding he repeat after me.

"Yes," he half sobs out, his arm holding him up suddenly giving out, so he collapses hard against me, driving into me further. I scream, my back arching in pleasure. I draw my legs up around his waist, propelling my ass higher into his thrusts, clenching him to me as I pull his lips to mine and kiss him like I'm dying tomorrow. Everything I am is in the kiss and I take everything from him. I can tell he knows it; he is trembling so hard even as he fucks me with a ferocity we haven't reached before. And then I'm coming, my orgasm sudden, hard, and never ending. I scream and scream as wave after wave of pleasure rushes through me. His climax barrels through us both in the next instant, throwing me into a plane of sensation I have never reached before. I tighten my arms around him, hold him to me as we both shudder and twitch under the onslaught of the physical and emotional violence of our release.

"Aubrey," he croaks out, his voice sounding broken. We may have fucked down a barrier today, but so much still remains between us. "Shhh," I soothe him, "sleep." He nods his head against my chest, the first time we've slept in this position, with him curled into me, not the other way around. "We can talk tomorrow." He nods, but I know it's not that simple. As he drifts off to sleep, I consider the events of the day. I hope we've reached a new place, a place where he can trust me with whatever truth is paralyzing him and holding us apart. But deep down, a part of me is afraid all I've done tonight is delay the inevitable; his ultimate refusal to let me in and my own unending heartbreak.

CHAPTER 25

I make us coffee with Aubrey's tiny hotel suite coffee maker, feeling both hollow and full of hope. When I rose from the bed this morning, Aubrey barely stirred, mumbling the word, "Coffee." I kissed him on the forehead, murmuring, "Your wish is my command." I think he chuckled, but he could have been snoring. The machine beeps to signal the end of its cycle, and Aubrey stumbles out of the bedroom wearing a soft pair of gray lounge pants and no shirt. His hair is sticking up in all directions, and he looks adorable. I motion him toward one of the bar stools on the other side of the island from where I stand. Taking a mug from the counter rack, I pour him a cup before I pour my own. We drink in silence for a few moments. Absentmindedly, I rub my hand across my chest where it both hurts and feels next to unbearably full.

Aubrey notices the movement then flicks his eyes up to mine. "Do you remember what you promised me?" he asks calmly before taking another sip of coffee.

I nod, still feeling shell shocked from last night. He sips again, watching me, before he grins.

"Good, glad to hear it. Do you remember what else I told you? You can have slow."

Nodding again, I feel relieved. I'm not sure if I would have been able to talk about anything today anyway, and I'm glad he's given me an out. But another topic is on my mind, and I press on before I can second guess myself.

"You're thinking about establishing an office here, in Oakland."

He takes a larger gulp of coffee as if fortifying himself. He nods and simply answers, "Yes."

I reach across the counter and grasp the hand sitting on it, giving it a little squeeze. I can't speak, but I hope he understands what this means to me. *Too much Black,* my evil inner voice reminds me. *He means too much, you stupid motherfucker. You fucked up and now you love him. All you are going to do is ruin his life.*

"Black! Black!"

I come back to myself to find Aubrey pressed against my side, his hand on mine where I am gripping the edge of the countertop. I don't recall pulling away from his hand or clasping the counter, but as the emotion boiled through me, I must have stepped back. Releasing my hold on the edge, I take another step back, and Aubrey hugs me tight, trapping my arms against my sides. I feel dizzy and dazed.

"Are you okay?" He whispers against my neck where he has nestled his face. I pull breaths in and out of my lungs. It is painful. He doesn't wait for an answer before he loosens his grip enough that he can steer me around the island toward the small couch in the even tinier living space. He never lets me go, and I'm relieved, though I don't want to explore that thought. We sit on the couch awhile, just breathing while Aubrey holds me. A few more minutes pass before I can speak.

"Aubrey," I start, but he shakes his head where it is against my shoulder.

"Shhhh, just...rest. I have enough for now," he murmurs, snuggling his face into the curve of my neck.

Inwardly cursing myself for my fears and my cowardice, I pull my hands into my lap, threading and unthreading my fingers with each other. Aubrey's hand reaches down and stills my restless fingers.

"I said, it is enough for now."

I nod again, but yet another concern niggles at me. I withdraw my hands from his so I can press my fingers against my eyelids before dropping my hands back into my lap. We shift on the couch so we can see each other while still leaning against the cushions.

Aubrey tilts his head down so he can meet my gaze, since I have dropped my eyes from his. "What is it, Black?"

"Last night," I pause, feeling dumb and purposeful, "we almost forgot condoms." When I thought about it this morning as the coffee brewed, I was both horrified and filled with a curious and surprising longing. Aubrey laughs softly, using his finger to tip my chin back up so my eyes meet his. Smiling, he shakes his head and takes both of my hands in his again. His eyes shine like emeralds. It is his sunshine smile, warming me inside and out.

"No, I forgot. You, however, remembered. Thank you." He leans forward and kisses me softly, a bare brush of his lips against mine. When he pulls back to watch my face, I blurt out my thoughts, "I think we should get tested."

Gobsmacked, I'm absolutely gobsmacked at the sentence that just fell out of Black's mouth. I must look shocked because Black takes one glance at my expression and hurries forward his explanation.

"I just want to protect you," he confesses, the look on his face indicating he is surprised by his own statement. He has just openly indicated a level of commitment to me, to us, I did not expect, but I sure as hell want. I nod my head emphatically to accept what he is offering me. It has little to do with whether or not we ditch condoms and everything to do with what we want together; what Black wants together with me. Relief washes over Black's features, and I'm smiling so hard my face feels like it might crack. After the heavy emotion of last night and the last twenty minutes of this morning, this fizzy joy bubbling up inside of me is bright and welcome.

Black sighs and I draw my attention back to him, away from my scattered but joyful thoughts. He reaches up and runs one of his hands through his hair, just as he does so many times when he is nervous. His eyes drop to the hands we still have joined in between us.

"It has been a very long time, Aubrey. Two years," he confesses on a whisper. I bring up our joined hands and kiss the back of his hand. From the look on his face, he cannot handle more than that monumental confession.

"You've been quite the monk," I tease, hoping he won't mind. When he gives me a tremulous smile, I know he's okay with it. I laugh, poking fun at myself now, "I've not exactly been a player, but you have me beat."

His smile remains soft and I see a hint of sadness there too. Not wanting him to focus too long on the emotions that paralyze him, I wink at him as I suggest how we might accomplish his suggestion.

"We can make a date of it."

Black huffs out a surprised laugh, "What?"

"We cannot lose that much blood without refueling ourselves. Come to think of it, we could do it today, grab some breakfast afterwards."

Black nods and his smile is happier, the sadness having retreated, I hope because of our current conversation. When I walked into the kitchen this morning, Black was leaning against the island counter wearing just his jeans, slung low and sexy on his hips. For once, I didn't feel bad or hesitant about pressing him for the answers I need. Honestly, we both need the truth, whatever it is, to be aired: what hurt him, what keeps him apart from me, and why he refuses to be called by his first name. But his confession about how long he has been alone and his suggestion we get tested has upset the apple cart of my mind, and I'm rolling with the change. I stand up and pull Black to his bare feet.

"Shower. Tests. Breakfast. In that order," I declare.

Black laughs softly again and pulls me into a tight hug before dropping a kiss on my forehead. He is not much taller than me, but he really does enjoy doing that.

"Lead the way," he quips, and I pull him by the hands toward the shower and, hopefully, our future.

After a surprising quick stop at Planned Parenthood, we decide to play hookie. Since it is Friday, I can get away with it as I have no meetings scheduled. Black sets his own hours, so we are free to stroll around the streets of town, hand in hand. I was surprised to find out Planned Parenthood does the Rapid HIV test, so we were both cleared of that particular hurdle, negative tests in hand, within half an hour. We went for the complete slate of tests to be on the safe side, so after our blood sacrifices, we end up at Shelly's Diner. Kirsten is not working today, so we have a no-nonsense waitress in her fifties who barely speaks two words to us. When we finish breakfast, we pick up the stroll we started earlier.

Our results for all of the other common STDs won't be in for a week. But it is clear neither of us is in a big rush. While bare sex will likely be the eventual result of our decisions today, it was not even half of the point. I could tell Black suggested it for both the reason he stated and the one I read in his eyes. He wants to protect me, and he wants to do that because our relationship matters. Even if the tests had turned out differently, I know I would still be here, holding his hand. The thought is comforting, and I lean my head against his shoulder as we stop in front of a store display. Black explains something about metal toy trains as we watch an old-fashioned train set wind through a miniature village, but I'm not really listening. I feel, for the first time, I don't have to question Black's feelings for me. His decision to suggest testing, with all of the implications surrounding it, showed me the evidence I have been searching for, the proof I longed for that Black cares for me as much as I care for him, that Black loves me, even if we do not seem close to verbalizing those three little words.

The weather heats up fast, not surprising for the middle of August.

Black's hair waves up and my hands keep creeping up to thread through the dark strands. Black chuckles when I swipe a lock behind his ear, tucking it in after I caress it between my fingers for a long moment. The day passes quietly and beautifully. I have never been as happy as I am in this moment.

CHAPTER 26

I hear a knock on the front door from my place on the couch in my living room. I'm covered in papers, most sent over by my assistant Monica. Orders for small sculptures, an invite to speak at a local community college art symposium. Since I finished my aloe vera sculpture last week and the unveiling is not for another two, I finally have time to tackle some of the business backlog that has been waiting for my attention. The knocking is loud with an insistent rhythm. Recognition sparks on the edge of my consciousness and I feel rather than know I have heard this knock before. Fear shimmers through my chest. I'm paralyzed in place, weighed down by the emotions roiling through me.

There's a slight pause and I hold my breath, hoping against hope the knocking has ceased permanently. I jerk when the knocking begins again, just as insistent, just as familiar, just as absolutely terrifying. No, I murmur to myself. Not again. My conscious mind has finally caught up with my lizard brain, somehow managing to calm my fight, flight, or freeze response. My feet are leaden in my shoes as I brush the papers off my lap and watch as they fall to the floor. I rise and lumber my way toward the front door. I see everything so clearly as I make my way through the hall then the kitchen. Aubrey's sunglasses are on the kitchen island. My heart clenches so hard that I clutch my chest, almost unable to breathe.

The knocking has not stopped, and it will not stop ever. I finally make my way to the door and watch in that familiar slow motion as my hand reaches for the bolt, flips the lock, and grasps the knob. I do not hesitate now, knowing the worst is before me. I yank open the door and a familiar pair of dark blue eyes meet mine.

"I'm sorry, Black," he murmurs, his expression pained. I nod and gesture him inside, my heart shattering like so much glass.

As soon as Aubrey comes home, to my home, he knows something is wrong. He makes no move to ascertain what or why. He just collects me in his arms and holds me tight. With one look at my face, he knows my world has crashed in on me. He just didn't know why or how bound up with it all he is. I let him hold me for a long time as the sun sets through the bay windows of my kitchen. The lights hit Aubrey's hair, and for the first time, the sparkle makes me wince. Because I don't deserve to see it. I don't deserve to have him here with me. But I take the care, *the love*, he offers me. We don't talk. We don't eat. We quietly retreat to my bedroom when the sky grows fully dark. He holds me while I cry, never asking why. His soothing murmurs put me to sleep, and when I awaken a few hours later, he kisses me softly, soothingly, *lovingly*. He undresses me, touching me everywhere, including my heart, holding me together with the magic of his touch, the glory of *his love*. Quiet tears stream down my face as he makes love to me softly, slowly, kissing the tear tracks from my cheeks, sharing the salt with my lips. I fall asleep in his arms, cherish, *loved*, and dying.

I run through the kitchen, searching, searching. The living room is empty. I throw open the glass patio door, my eyes scanning my backyard that butts up against the edge of a small forest. Nothing, no one. Not no one. No Aubrey.

"Aubrey!" I scream. I'm running out of air. "Aubrey!"

A familiar voice greets my ear, even though the person who owns it does not appear to accompany it, "I'm sorry, Black."

Not again. No. No. No. NO! NO!

"Aubrey! Aubrey!"

Sobs wrack me now as I find myself on my knees in the wet grass. Not again, I can't do this again. I will die. I'm dying right now. My heart thumps hard in my chest, and I clasp at my breast, looking down, horror dawning as blood pours from no visible source. I cup my hands, trying to catch my blood... No, his blood, Aubrey's blood. It pours out of me, overflowing my outstretched hands which shake so violently they feel like they might shatter. I try to hold on, but the blood slips through my fingers, dripping on the grass, staining it a dark, rusty red.

"Aubrey!" I scream again.

Then another voice, which sounds suspiciously like my own, mocks me, taunts me. "Shouldn't you be calling another name, Ian? Or have you forgotten already?"

Jerking my head up, I search out the voice, but no one is there. I'm no longer on my knees in the grass. I'm in my living room, looking into a pair of dark blue eyes as a soft voice whispers, "He's not coming home."

My own screams reverberate throughout my house as I violently awaken in the sweat soaked sheets of my own bed. I struggle to breathe, my heart galloping in my chest. I turn to my side and curl up into the fetal position. Hot tears wash down my face, and I couldn't stop them even if I tried. Everything is tangled in my mind. Aubrey is him, and he is Aubrey. Both of them are dead and it is my fault. Scrunching up my eyes, I wage a losing battle with breathing and my head spins.

I must have fainted because the next moment I am aware, I'm struggling in the sheets that have wrapped themselves around my arms and legs. I don't know what to do now. Not about Aubrey, not about my love for him, nothing. I know nothing, and I desperately wish I could feel nothing too.

Unfair, I have been downright unfair to Aubrey and I simply do not know how to stop it. The past no longer lingers on the periphery of my mind but invades the whole landscape of my life. Even when we are together, I am distant now. It didn't happen gradually. After kissing me goodbye in the morning, Aubrey left for work. I didn't leave my house at all that day. After falling asleep only to awaken within my nightmare, the loss of Aubrey and the one who came before tangling in my mind, I cannot leave my bed. When Aubrey texted to check in on me, I responded in one word replies because I could not manage more. I couldn't think. I can't think. He brought over my favorite Italian food and a bottle of wine from Tilly's which means he talked to her. I can't bring myself to think what he said to her. I can't be sure she won't tell him the whole, sordid truth. But when he shows up, I can tell by his demeanor, cautious but caring, that she did not. If she had, well, I can't say what he would have done. Part of me knows he would have come to me anyway, but the part writhing in pain and fear knows no such thing. *He would never speak to you again,* my own insidious, punishing voice whispers to me. *And you would deserve it. All you have done is lie and cheat to catch him and to keep him.* I can't argue with that because it is the God's honest truth.

Barely able to swallow a single bite, I push my food around on my plate while Aubrey watches me with mounting concern. I manage a single glass of wine even the oblivion of alcohol not appealing enough to reel me in, to entice me to partake. Aubrey cleans up the kitchen and puts me to bed, slipping in behind me, spooning me. I clasp his hands to my chest, allowing myself the one small gesture even though I shouldn't. No more crying, but I don't sleep. When Aubrey slips away to work, I barely move. When he calls me later, I decline the offer for dinner. I cannot see him right now. It hurts too much. Everything bleeds together in my mind, a jumbled chaos, and I'm no longer sure I can ever make sense of it again.

When I awaken the next morning, there is no message from Aubrey. My heart cracks further when I thought it was already broken beyond repair. Later, he again offers dinner, and I decline. I can't keep doing this. But I don't honestly know what *this* is. Do I mean reliving the pain, anguish, and horror of the day my life ended two years ago, or do I mean my love for Aubrey? I don't know. I fist my hair at the roots as I lie in my bed during the middle of the day. I don't know anything. But loving Aubrey can't fix this. I doubt anything can or will.

On the fifth day after my world crashed in on me again, I have to crawl out of bed. Work obligations force themselves upon me, and I should be happy for the distraction, but I am not. It is not a very good distraction anyway, just meeting with someone who picks up a dozen small sculptures for various buyers. I don't care about it; I don't care about anything but the pain radiating from my heart.

Once I'm upright, I stay standing and begin to move again, slowly and without direction. Aubrey still texts to check in on me, and I answer even if I can't put more effort in than a single lie. *I'm okay.* Of course, he knows I am not, but he never calls me on the blatant fabrication. He seems to be waiting me out, but I don't know if I will ever be okay again. And I doubt I should let him wait for that unpromised day anyway.

But… I am slowly coming back to myself. I hope I can come back to Aubrey, yet I don't know how. It should be simple. It should be easy. I could call. I could show up at his suite. I could text an invitation to dinner. Nothing seems right. Everything is still out of place, and even though a few clouds are finally starting to lift, I remain unconvinced that this is my reality. If I try to pull him back to me, I will most assuredly lose him, only this time, permanently. A week after the past came barreling back into my life, I text Aubrey. A simple message, but it bears a far greater weight than the words themselves:

Would you mind coming to dinner at my house tonight?

Aubrey is prompt in his response. *Yes, I will see you at six.*

I don't know what I am going to say. I don't know what I am going to do. But one thing is for certain, I will see Aubrey tonight.

———

I'm not going to tell him I love him until he is ready to tell me. A sickening thought curdles my stomach. What if Black never says it? I'm sure he feels it. Maybe, I'm not so sure, I realize. I had been sure until this past week, until the walls slammed back up again, severing our connection. I want to cry onto my laptop keys when my email icon flickers. The from line reads "Chicago City Council" and the subject line spells out the worst possible solution to my problem; it is a bid request.

While my decision had been obvious before this week, now I'm not so sure. Hell, Black even indicated he would be on board with my business relocating to Oakland. But the past week has been pure hell with Black pulling further and further away from me. He is clearly far from okay, and every time he offers me that lie, I feel another drop of acid on my soul. Maybe Black expected this to be short term. No, it's not that. If anyone is almost deadly serious about intimacy, it is Ian James Black, owner of my heart. I know something happened. After the emotionally tumultuous experience of our conversations after I lost the Palo Alto bid, from Black suggesting blood tests to promising me, however tenuously, he would tell me about the problems that cause him to panic, everything was moving forward. I can't wrap my mind around how he went from asking me if I intended to stay in Oakland once the park is finished to avoiding me and lying.

It has to do with what Mrs. Watson said to me in the coffee shop and the salt 'n' pepper haired fox I saw leaving Black's house last week. I'd planned to ask who he was, but Black had looked shattered when I walked into the kitchen. In a blink, he'd shuttered his expression and forced a smile that was more of a grimace onto his face. I had quietly walked over to him, kissed him gently on the lips, and hugged him, leaning my head onto his shoulder. He stayed rigid in my arms for long moments then sighed and slipped his arms around me. He snuggled his head into my neck, and I could feel him breathing in against my skin. I smiled, loving how he does that almost every time we hug. It makes me feel cherished and wanted and loved. Even though he has never said the words, that is what Black's need to breathe me in means to me, love. I snuggled my head into his neck, drawing his scent fully into my lungs. We held each other for a long time, standing in the kitchen silently as the sunset streamed in through the bay window, throwing shadows and ghosts upon the floor.

I shake the memory from my head and I know what I have to do. Black has to tell me the truth, whatever is wrong that separates him from me. Whatever happened this week to put him into a deep depression, I have to know everything now. He promised me after all, and as much as I hate to do it, I have to call in the marker now. I cannot handle the distance he has put between us even as I have tried to show him the care I so desperately want to offer him. Threading my fingers through my hair, I shake my head. Everything was going so well. Every day seemed to bring me more confirmation Black loves me in the same way I love him. I shove back from my desk and pace around it for a few minutes before flopping down in my chair again.

I have a clue, honestly, far more than a clue, about what haunts Black. But as much as it breaks my heart to acknowledge this truth, I can't go on if he won't tell me what tightened the vise around his heart again one week ago today. The thought freezes my breath in my lungs. But even so, I can't deny my own truth; if he doesn't love me enough to tell me what or who he lost, I can't let it go. And I can't stay with him. My phone buzzes on my desk, startling me. It is a text from Black, inviting me to dinner. Simple and straightforward, the words reveal nothing, but I know what I have to do. Agreeing quickly, I know I will have the answers tonight. My heart squeezes in my chest. Or I will have nothing.

CHAPTER 27

*A*ubrey greets me at my front door with the worst sentence in the history of the human language, "We have to talk."

In the eons of people talking to people, no sentence is worse to hear and probably to utter. But he didn't have to say it. He doesn't have to ask this of me. Because I already know what he wants, and I cannot give it to him. I won't. A coward's way out, I think, but I shake my head. No, I can't. I can't let Aubrey love me. And I can't love him. Even now my heart and soul both call me a liar, but my mind is resolved and has been since before we met. I cannot let anyone that close again. Because to do so is to kill him. I thought I could do this, but I was wrong. This is all going wrong and I have no way to stop it.

I meant this invitation to dinner as a way to bridge the new gap I created between us over the past week, but one look at his face, and I know he wants answers. No, wants is not the right word. The need on his face is clear. But I also know I won't give those answers to him. I had considered telling him everything, but looking at his face now, love shining through his bright green eyes, I know I've made a mistake. Aubrey wants everything, and I have nothing to give him. Opening my door wider, I step back to allow him to pass by me. He walks directly to the living room and settles himself in the middle of the couch, leaving me no option other than to sit next to him. I hesitate a moment, and Aubrey's eyes meet mine with a determined look. With heavy feet, heart, everything, I drag myself forward and sit on his left side. He angles himself so we are facing each other, even though my eyes have dropped, and I cannot meet his gaze.

"What happened this week, Black?"

His directness startles me for a moment then I almost smile because what else would Aubrey do? I clear my throat, but I have no words to explain myself, so I shake my head. Aubrey sighs, ducking his head down so he can look me in the eyes. Without a word, he gently picks up my hand, threading his fingers through mine.

"You have wonderful friends, Black," he states softly, solemnly. He sighs and scrubs his free hand over his face.

"They've been giving me hints for months." I must look horrified at the revelation.

"I never took them up on it," he says, rushing forward, "I wanted you to tell me. I want you to tell me right now. No, I need you to tell me right now. I've been waiting patiently, but I can't go on like this. I already have a strong idea of what the problem is. The reason why you pull away suddenly, the reason why it took forever for you to bring me to your home. The reason why you don't like me calling you by your first name. I even have a good idea as to why you pulled back this last week. It was the guy who visited you, wasn't it?"

I cannot even form a response as I am shocked at how much he has put together, how much he already knows about what I've tried so hard to hide from him, from myself. He smiles sadly in response to my silence.

"I know it was." He swallows hard and picks up his previous train of thought. "Your friends love you, Black, and they have been trying to take care of you through me. But I need to be able to take care of you myself and I can't if you won't even promise to tell me the truth someday." He sighs heavily again. "I'd even take that even though you don't seem willing to uphold that same promise right now," he admits dropping his eyes from mine and sighing again.

When his eyelashes flick up, I can see a hint of tears on them. My heart drops out of my chest. He's really doing this, making me confront the truth and my past. A small part of me feels relief while the yawning hollow hole inside of my mind and soul screams at me to stop him. And like the coward I've been since the beginning, I follow that impulse even as the choice claws at my insides. Aubrey's hand tightens around my fingers and the look he favors me with is soothing, understanding, encouraging.

I screw my eyes shut and rip out my own heart. "No."

It comes out hoarse, and the silence that follows is like nothing I'd ever heard while Aubrey is around. Flicking open my eyes, I see the despair descending on Aubrey's face as he gazes at me with those soulful green eyes. Slowly, he withdraws his hand from mine and stands up. I follow his lead, rising from the couch as well.

Aubrey scrubs a hand over his face and does not raise his eyes to meet mine just yet. He sighs, fiddling with the hem of his button down, which is uncharacteristically untucked from his slacks. Aubrey never shows anxiety through his appearance, and I want to cry because I know I am the one causing his distress. I am the one hurting him...again.

"Another bid offer came in today." He finally lifts his eyes to mine, and they are so sad my hands twitch with the desire to reach out and touch him, but I stop myself.

"In Chicago." He doesn't say anything else, just watches me with his crystal-clear green eyes shining with sadness and pain. "Before the past week, I would have declined immediately. It would have been a very easy call," he continues softly. "But now, I don't know if that's right answer anymore."

"What do you want to do, Aubrey?" I shock myself with the question because I already know what he wants, and here I am, refusing to give it to him.

An uncharacteristic flash of anger rushes across his features, followed by an accompanying flush of color. He fists his hands at his sides, closes his eyes, and breathes deeply for a moment.

When he answers, his voice is low, gravely, and full of passionate anger, "You know very well what I want, Black." His eyes pop open and they glitter beautifully, fire and anger flashing in their depths. "I want you, but I want all of you."

As I don't have an answer to that, I don't respond.

Aubrey's face hardens for a moment. "What would you have me do?"

"Do you want to take the job? Do you want to go back to Chicago?"

"No!" He exhales sharply, dropping his head and running his hand through his thick auburn hair, and I am reminded of how the sun glinted off of it the first moment I met him. He looks up again, his hand worrying his bottom lip for a moment before he drops it back down to his side.

"But I may not have a choice. It all depends on this. This moment right now. Because I'm going to choose with my heart, I have to. Do you want me to stay?"

"Yes! Of course, I do!"

"Then you know what I want, what I need."

"What if I can't give you that?"

A flush of anger rises on Aubrey's skin, running up his neck and across his cheek bones. Beautiful. When we first met, he only ever blushed with embarrassment. While the effect of the strawberry hue against his alabaster skin is the same, the emotion behind it is not, and I swallow hard at the difference. I'm the reason he is angry now, not flushed with excitement and need. No, I did this to him.

"You promised," he whispers.

"I know."

He swallows hard and I see his Adam's apple bobbing in his throat. Time has slowed down for me, and I see every little flash of emotion that rolls across his features and flows through his body.

"So you won't keep your promise then?"

I cannot believe the words that are coming out of my mouth. "No."

Aubrey visibly shudders, but when he speaks again, his quavering voice jabs the knife deeper into my chest.

"I know you lost someone close to you. Will you please tell me what happened? Please, Black, you promised."

His eyes, glittering, so ready to shed tears, of betrayal, of pain, of all the emotions I am causing him right now, bore into mine. His voice drops to a barely audible whisper, "You promised."

I flinch, but my voice when it comes out is hard. "No."

"It's a choice you're making, Black!" Aubrey practically yells.

Even now, in his anger, he is trying so desperately to reach me, but I can't bridge the gap. I can't reach across the divide and take his hand. I cannot die again when it all inevitably comes crashing down. I thought I could, but a single reminder of the past showed me just how wrong I was. I feel the blood drain from my face as I realize I don't have any way to stop this, not any way that I am willing to take.

"You either choose me and the truth or…"

Aubrey's voice trails off, but his eyes don't leave mine. He's pleading with me to walk off the cliff with him, but I can't see him bloody and broken at the bottom. That's where he will end up, either figuratively or literally… *NO, NO, NO.* I shake my head furiously. If I tell him, this is real, and I can't risk it. I can't risk his very life. I clamp my mouth shut and pray he stops. I clench my fists, so I don't reach for him. Grind my teeth so I don't tell him the truth, so I don't call out my love to him and ruin his life forever. *Please, God,* just let him drop it as he has every time before. I can't risk it. I won't risk it. *Please don't leave,* I plead in my head, willing him to hear what I cannot say out loud. But my breath stops flowing when I finally comprehend the look he has had on his face since we walked through the door. Resignation.

"I'm asking you for you, Ian."

I flinch involuntarily at the name, and Aubrey's shoulders roll forward slightly, as if he is caving in on himself.

He looks away, swallowing hard before he continues, "And, yes, I know you don't like me calling you by your first name. But it's your name, Ian, and I want all of you. Maybe you have a really good reason for holding me apart from you, for not allowing me to call you that, for not allowing me to know what hurt you so badly in the past. And you don't have to tell me today. It is not a smart decision on my part, considering you just broke that promise to me within the last five minutes. But I will do it for you, Black."

Turning his head to meet my gaze again, his eyes flit across my face, looking for any change, any shift in my resolve. He sighs again, heavily, with a sound full of longing. Shaking his head, at himself or me, I'm not sure.

"But I have to know you will tell me, you will share whatever the dark secret is with me, because without it," Aubrey pauses before continuing, "you are still not mine and never will be. I might as well be in Chicago for as far apart as we are in our hearts."

Black stares at me, his expression flitting between hard resolution to pained shock and back again. It's a look that says he isn't budging. And my heart breaks, feeling quite literally so in my chest. If I didn't know better, I would think I was having a heart attack. He won't tell me, he won't give me that part of himself, and I know I can't stay. Whatever haunts him clings to him tighter and with more weight than the love I am trying to offer him and whatever amount of love he feels for me in his heart. It would break me every day, knowing he was holding so much of himself back. Knowing I don't matter enough for him to risk it all. He knows by now, or at least he should, I will be there to catch him. But he won't even allow me the chance. The knowledge is already breaking me which is why I am here, trying to reason with him, trying to draw out the littlest crumble that will allow me to stay.

I thought things were changing, his walls were coming down, brick by slow brick. But, if I am completely honest with myself, I've felt it for a while, this seemingly insurmountable distance, perhaps even right from the start. I knew the first night we were together. The last week reminded me of what I had forgotten, reminded me of what had seemed to change, for a short while anyway; Ian James Black really isn't mine and he won't let himself be.

"I knew." I sigh, looking at his beloved face, knowing he won't ever tell me why he doesn't love me enough to give me everything.

"I knew the first night, when I called you Ian," and he flinches at the name just as he's done every single time I've said it, though it couldn't have been more than a dozen times since I met him.

"And," I continue sadly, "if you can't even acknowledge I already *know* part of what is wrong, if you can't even ask me to wait, to give you just a little bit longer, if you can't even ask me to stay now, well then, I have my answer, don't I?" Surprisingly, I'm not crying, though I'm dying as surely as if he'd plunged a knife into my heart, into my soul.

"Goodbye, Black." I look directly into his eyes as I say this, giving him every opportunity to stop me, to say anything, anything at all. I know I'm not strong enough to resist even his voice, and I can't help holding out even this last opportunity. I press my lips firmly together as we stare at each other, to stop myself from begging. I know this is the last time I will see him, and even with everything said, even if it's just my part given, I linger, trying to convince him, just with my presence, just with my eyes. But my shattered heart knows it's no use as his expression, even his stance, his fists balled at the ends of his loose arms hanging at his sides, tells me he will never let me truly have him, his full self. I sigh, turning away from the only man I've ever loved and likely will ever love. Even as I turn to walk out the door, I can't stop myself from saying, for the first time and the last time, "I love you, Black." I slam the door behind myself and walk away.

CHAPTER 28

My feet are so heavy, my eyes are so heavy, my heart is so heavy as I trudge through the airport baggage claim. I pull my phone out of my pocket to check and see... What, Aubrey? He's not going to call you now. I press the on button and wait while the lock screen loads. I tap in my code and my phone lights up with the voicemail message icon. I have the unreasonable hope that it is Black, even though I know it isn't. Even though I admonish myself not to allow it, hope ticks up in my chest. I swallow hard and press the one to take me to voicemail and press my phone to my ear as I try to juggle my jacket and my carry-on bag. I slow down and pull myself out of the flow of people, finding an empty spot next to a pretzel shop that is closed for the night.

"You have one new message."

I hold my breath and then pain sears through me as the voice on the line does not belong to the only person I want to hear from.

"Hey, Aubrey. It's your Aunt Susan. No Patty, he can't hear air quotes around the word aunt. Anyway, before your Aunt Patty Cakes so rudely interrupted me, I was trying to leave you a message saying we haven't heard from you. We miss you and need you to give us a call. Also, we're a little bit worried. The last message you left didn't sound happy. Give a couple of old hens a break and call us okay? Love you!"

I pull the phone from my ear, and the tears I had managed to hold back on the plane are sliding down my cheeks. They are hot against my skin and I cannot stop them. I hang up on voicemail and slide my phone back into my pants pocket. I'm crying so hard now that I can barely see. I stumble my way toward the sign that says "Restrooms." I barely make it inside of the men's room before the sobs start.

Shoving my way into a stall, I collapse against the back wall as I slam the stall door shut behind me. I'm making terrible noises, but I don't care. My heart is well and truly broken, and I don't know how I will ever move past his rejection. I sink down on the toilet seat and let my bag slide to the floor as I drop my head into my hands. I give into the sobs and within seconds I am shaking uncontrollably. I am choking and sputtering, snot starting to run out of my nose. Grabbing some paper from the roll, I shove it against my face.

I cry into my hands for God knows how long. I'm totally exhausted now, and the toilet paper in my hands is soaked through. I have just the sniffles now, though I feel quiet hollow inside. A tentative knock rattles against my stall door. A deep, gruff voice asks, "You okay, man?" I swallow the lump from my throat then clear it. It hurts, and I suddenly feel completely dehydrated.

"Yeah," I respond softly. I think for a moment to make up some lie, but the idea makes me immediately pissed off. I don't care who I am talking to through the stall door or what he will think. I raise up my head and tell this stranger on the other side of the wall my earth-shattering problem.

"I left my boyfriend."

"I'm sorry, dude. That sucks."

I'm startled into a laugh, and I am not really sure why.

"Yeah, it does."

"Do you need anything? I got an extra bottle of water here."

"Other than a time machine?" I try to joke. "A bottle of water sounds great." I stand up, throw the wadded-up tissue into the toilet, flush it, and pull together my things. I unlock the door and exit. A gray-haired gentleman is standing by the sink holding two bottles of water. He sets one down on the sink counter and motions toward it with his hand. "I had an extra."

"Thanks," I sigh. I step up to the sink and set my bag and coat on the floor. I wash my hands and splash water on my face. A paper towel appears in my peripheral vision and I smile at the continued kindness. I take the towel and stand up, wiping my face. I throw the towel into the trash bin in the middle of the sink counter. I pick up the water bottle and take a long swallow. The man has not moved off, and he is watching me in the mirror. He seems to be about my Aunt Patty's age, and I feel a pang of remorse that I didn't call her and Susan before I left Oakland.

"You gonna be okay?" he asks in a soft voice.

"Yeah, it just hit me, you know. I hadn't cried yet, and I guess I had to let it all out."

"Mind if I give you a piece of advice, son?"

I grin at his choice of terms. He certainly does remind me of Aunt Patty.

I wave my hand in the air at him. "Sure, why not?"

"Keep moving forward. If it's supposed to be, it will work itself out."

I sigh and bend to pick up my jacket and bag. Rising back up to my full height, I shake my head.

"Unfortunately, I don't think it's going to work out."

"May I ask, why not?"

"Sure," I laugh weakly. "Ian," I pause at how much pain saying his name sends through my chest. I actually lean forward a little. Sighing, I pull in a breath, so I can continue discussing my love life with a complete stranger in an airport bathroom in the middle of the night.

"Ian won't tell me the truth about something." I see the guy's frown reflected in the mirror and I hurry to explain, "It's not cheating or anything like that. In fact, I have a very good idea of what the problem is. But," I pause because this is just so hard to articulate aloud or even inside of my own head, "I can't live with him knowing he won't let me share the burden. He won't tell me what the problem is. He doesn't want me to even know about it, and he certainly doesn't want my help. He wants to pretend that nothing is wrong. But I've always known something stands between us."

I sigh and take another drink from the water bottle. The older man crosses his arms across his broad chest and leans against the wall by the air dryer.

"His elderly neighbor dropped hints about something bad happening to him. When we started dating, random strangers would come up to me and make cryptic comments about how happy they were that Ian was out and about again. I know, I could have looked it up on Google. He's an artist and popular enough in the area that I'm sure there was some news story about whatever happened to him. But I didn't want to find out that way. I wanted him to tell me."

"So, what happened? I'm guessing you just flew in from somewhere."

"I insisted that he tell me. Something else happened in the past week, and he pulled away. I had to make a decision about work and I needed to know if he wanted me to stay."

"And he didn't?"

I take another drink of water and wipe my mouth with the back of my hand. "No, he wanted me to stay. But I can't stay if he won't tell me the truth, and that's the one thing he refuses to share with me."

"That's heavy."

I laugh snort. "Yeah."

The friendly stranger shoves off the wall and pats my shoulder. "Good luck. I hope it all works out for you."

"Yeah, thanks, me too."

After he exits, I finish the bottle of water and throw the empty container into the trash. I gaze into the mirror, and I'm not shocked at what I see. I look like death warmed over and I just don't care. All I want to do is get home, crawl into my cold, lonely bed, and cry my eyeballs out. I have no plans beyond that. I can't think of anything but the broken look on Black's face when he realized I wasn't going to back down this time. He could have said anything at that moment, and I would have stayed. It probably would have been the worst choice, but he didn't allow me even that. I shrug my jacket on and adjust the strap of my carry-on bag over my left shoulder. I exit the bathroom and head toward the baggage claim. I startle a laugh out of myself. Now I have plenty of new baggage to carry around, and I doubt I will ever be able to rid myself of it.

CHAPTER 29

I cannot stop shaking my leg. It's my own damned fault for drinking so much coffee on the plane ride out here, my own damned fault for jumping right into a cab at the airport, and certainly my own damned fault for letting the love of my life leave me in the first place. Damn it! I can't ask the concierge to keep an eye out for Aubrey. What good would that do, except either get the cops called on me or cause him to be alerted to my presence . So he could hide, or run away, or avoid me? Nope, none of that is happening. I am sitting right here until he comes down that elevator, my bladder be damned, possibly along with my heart if he won't take me back.

Ding! The elevator bell grabs my attention and pulls it away from my leg and, thankfully, away from my bladder. This had better be him. I cannot take much more of this. Three hours on a plane and two hours in this chair. Multiple parts of me are about to explode, and the mess won't be pretty or easy to clean up. The door finally opens what seems like an eternity later, and there he is, stepping out, his auburn brown hair gleaming under the sunlight from the lobby's bay windows. I jump from my chair, stride across the glossy tile, grip Aubrey's face, and proceed to kiss the fuck out of him, tongue slashing through the lips that parted as soon as my lips met his. I pull back, resting my forehead against his, and I say to him what I've been dying to say for the last 5 hours. "I love you, and I have to fucking pee!"

To say you could've knocked me over with a feather would have been a massive understatement, so understated it might, in fact, qualify as a reverse hyperbole. Shocked by his presence, shocked by his kiss, shocked by his declaration of love, I am absolutely gobsmacked by his declaration that he needs to pee.

"What?" I squeak.

Black practically growls as he hustles me backwards, back into the elevator I have just stepped out of, his larger mass and height propelling me even as his hands and forehead never leave my face.

"I love you," he snaps, "but I have to piss so damn bad that if we don't get to your bathroom in the next five minutes, I'm gonna pee on your leg like a dog claiming its territory. And if you haven't realized already, that's exactly what I'm doing right now," his voice dropping even lower than his usual growl. "I'm claiming you."

I'm finally breathing again. I swear I did not take a single breath in the time it took to punch the number of my floor on the elevator and ride up the seven flights, with Black's hands still clasping my cheeks and his dark eyes boring into mine. He did not so much as blink for the whole eternity of the ride and my lungs just gave up the ghost right then and there in the elevator. I could barely disengage myself from his hold in order to exit on wobbly legs, trip my way down the hall, and fumble my keys out of my pocket and into the door knob. Black leaned over me from behind, bracing himself above me with his hand planted firmly on the door frame, level with my head. I could feel his body heat, and all I wanted to do was sink back into it. But the man had to pee. The laughter started in my throat, and I couldn't stop it bubbling out. I flung the door open and motioned down the hall.

Finally gasping oxygen into my starved lungs, I managed to squawk "Down the hall, on the right." at Black as he rushed past me like his ass was on fire. I guess it would be more appropriate to say his bladder was on fire.

And that was it. As I slammed the door shut behind me, I fell against the wall and collapsed into a fit of laughter. After a few moments, I managed to get myself under control, so I shoved off the wall and went to listen at the door. Yes, I was listening at my own bathroom door to make sure he was really peeing, as if he would have had some other reason to fly three hours here other than to use my facilities. And then I heard it–that sigh of relief, and I just lost it. Gales of laughter rumbled through my chest and out of my throat, and I sank against the bathroom door in an effort to keep myself upright.

"You're gonna pay for this." I hear him call through the door, and I just cannot help it. The giggles won't stop, and I slide down the door to the floor, belatedly thinking to scoot out of the way, so he can open it once he is done. Turning to look in that direction, I collapse back against the wall as Black exits the bathroom, my sunflower hand towel still in his hands. I'd just started to recover, but seeing him there, in his black jeans and his black shirt and his black boots, drying his hands on my sunflower print towel made me howl with laughter once again. This really can't be happening, can't be reality. He has not come all this way for me, it was just too absurd.

I flop over onto my back on my hallway floor, covering my eyes with my hands as I try to get myself under control. Deep breaths in and out, in and out. I can tell he is standing at my feet now, and by the way my skin is prickling all over, his dark, hungry eyes must be roaming all over my body.

"Why?" I manage to sigh, not removing my hands from my eyes.

"Why what?" Black asks, sounding oddly amused and for what reason I am sure I don't know. Even though I've barely stopped laughing myself, this is not amusing at all, not even in the slightest.

"Why are you here? Why did you come?" I'm still not looking at him. To do so might break me, and I can't handle that again.

"I told you why," he grumbles, and I can tell by the sound of his voice that he is on his knees by my feet now. His hands encircle my ankles, pulling my whole body toward his a few inches.

"I needed to fucking pee."

That snapped something inside me and I am howling again. Taking advantage of my laughter ridden state, he begins to crawl up my body slowly, his knees on the outside of my legs, his hands shifting up, starting at my knees. Sliding up my thighs, then a soft weight on my groin as I feel him kiss me through my jeans – his breath warming the fabric through to my skin. Another kiss on my left hip, then on my right as he keeps crawling forward as the laughter dies in my lungs. He nudges my knees apart with one of his and slowly settles his hips against mine. I give a little cry as our groins come into contact, his hard jean-clad cock resting ever so gently against my similarly clothed one. He lets out a little hiss between his teeth, but then his lips are back—kissing first the middle of my chest, then the left side of my collarbone where my shirt has pulled down to reveal it.

"And yeah," Black murmurs, making me realize I no longer have a clue what we are talking about. "I love you, Aubrey, and I came to claim you. *Claim you as mine,*" he growls, emphasizing the last four words as his breath puffs against my neck and the shell of my ear. Then he clasps his rough palmed hands against my wrists and lifts my hands off my eyes, placing them beside my head, not relinquishing his hold.

"I love you, and I was a fool to let you go."

I suck in my breath as I search his dark brown eyes for the truth. Does he really mean that? His eyes are more intense than I've ever seen them and his face serious, though I could swear I see the hint of a curve to his lips—a smile just waiting to spring out.

"Your immaculate bathroom with the sunflower theme was just an excuse," he murmurs as he finally presses his lips against mine.

"It's you. It's always been you," he breathes against my mouth.

I can't take a breath for wanting this to be real, for his words to be true. My voice comes out in a broken whisper:

"Are you sure? Cause I can't—" I almost stop breathing again and I have to swallow down the sob in my throat as my voice cracks on the words. "I can't—"

I search for the right vocabulary to explain what I mean, what I truly feel.

"I can't die again like I did when I left you," I somehow manage to get out as tears begin to trickle from the corners of my eyes against my will.

"Please," I plead, baring my soul to the only man who's ever owned it, "please don't make me die again."

I knew I'd broken something precious when I'd allowed Aubrey to walk out my door. And why had I done that foolish thing? Why had I stood there mutely when he'd asked me for myself—refusing to speak?

"Fear," I say out loud, as I answer both his unspoken question and my internal one. "I was afraid, of what I felt, of what you wanted. You asked me for myself and like a fool I refused. That is the mistake I'm here to rectify."

My voice is dropping off, and I can't help it, can barely speak past the lump in my throat, the very knot of fear that tore him from me in the first place, trying to stop me from taking him back now. I manage to swallow, clearing my throat as I lay my forehead against his, his clear green eyes centimeters from my own.

"Fear of what I wanted, fear of what you were offering me, and asking of me in return. But it wasn't just fear, Aubrey." My voice drops down to a croaky whisper. I can barely force the words out of my mouth and off of my tongue. "I lost someone important to me."

I pull in another rough breath, steeling myself against the pain tearing across my soul, even as it heals me in the same instant. "It was my boyfriend, Vinny. It made me afraid to love you because…because I could lose you." I'm barely whispering now. "I knew that would kill me. I thought I couldn't do this again, love someone, love you. I thought this couldn't be real. Then the door slammed behind you, and my heart shattered."

I'd gone to my knees in disbelief on my living room floor.

"And I knew I'd made a mistake. But I couldn't move. I died too," I admit in a whisper. "I don't know how much time passed because my mind went blank, and I couldn't believe what I'd done."

I take a deep breath, cherishing his scent. And suddenly, I can't get enough. I duck my nose down to his neck and inhale. The emotions washing through me and over me are unreal, almost too much to bear. I can feel my bigger body beginning to shake against his smaller one. Suddenly, I am back there again—alone, on my knees, on that bland biege carpeting with my heart shattered in my breast. And I cannot stop myself as sobs tear through me. Then, miracle of miracles, he shakes my loose grip off his wrists and slips his arms around me.

"I love you too," he hoarsely whispers in my ear, and I can hear the tears in his voice. "Always."

I can do nothing but cry harder against his neck, tunneling my arms under his and crushing him to me.

"Please," I plead, not knowing anymore what exactly I am asking for, but knowing he hasn't given it back to me yet. "Please, Aubrey."

His left hand flies up my back and into my hair—his fingers grabbing it by the roots to thrust my head back so he can look into my eyes again.

"Yes," he states emphatically, nodding his head, his own tears streaming down his beautiful cheeks. "Always, yes. *Forever, yes.*"

And then we are kissing, our tongues dueling fiercely even as our joint sobs do not lessen. So we lie there, mating our mouths and crying, holding onto each other so tightly, because it really is for dear life.

Somehow, we fall asleep on the floor. Or rather, Black fell asleep on top of me after our crying slowed and finally stopped. I am a mess. He is a mess. But looking down at his face where he's pressed it into my chest, I haven't seen anything or anyone more beautiful in my life. And he is mine now, truly, and I won't be letting him go again no matter what. With a few simple words, he has given me what I asked him for, and even though I know there is much more to come, my heart is lighter than it has been in weeks. For the first time since I left him, I feel whole again. I bring my left hand up to brush his black hair off his face, the long strands tangling a little with his heavy five o'clock shadow. Speaking of five o'clock anything, I have no idea what time it is or how long we have lain here on the plush brown carpeting of the hallway outside of my bathroom. I stroke my left hand through Black's shoulder length hair as my right stays splayed against the middle of his back. I can feel his breath coming in and out of his lungs. I gather him more tightly to me, dropping kisses on the top of his head, on his ears, anywhere I can reach from beneath his very welcome body which is currently pressing me hard into the floor. I don't want to move, but now I have to tell him something.

"Honey, I have something I need to say."

Black stiffens in my hold as he comes awake immediately.

"What?" he murmurs, sounding somewhat suspicious and even a little bit scared.

"Umm. . . *I* have to pee now."

He slow smiles at me, blinking his warm brown eyes as he comes more fully awake.

"Luckily for you," he murmurs as he brings his head up to ghost his lips across mine, "I know the best bathroom in town. And it's right off this lovely hallway we are currently lying in."

"I'm so lucky," I sigh dreamily against his lips.

"No," he whispers back, "I'm the lucky one."

He licks his tongue against my bottom lip, teasing the corner of my mouth which I gladly open to him in invitation. Scooting his hand up into my hair, he swirls his tongue into my mouth, licking against mine in a kiss that starts off sweet and tender but turns heated fast. Suddenly he jerks away.

"Damn it. *You* have to pee now."

I laugh, my throat feeling dry and achy from what came before.

"Yep," I reply as I nip at his lips as he pulls back. Taking my upper arms into his hands, he pulls me to my feet with him as he rises. I can't help winding my arms around his neck and kissing him again, only removing my lips from his, my tongue from his tongue when we are both breathless.

"It's just another thing we have in common."

He chuckles as I release his neck and turn to saunter into the bathroom. I flash a heated glance over my shoulder as I kick the door closed behind me. I hear him groan through the door and I cannot help but laugh again as I take care of business.

CHAPTER 30

"How long does it take?" I fake grouse at him through the door, leaning my hip against the door frame, crossing my arms against my chest. I've seriously gotten lucky here today, and there is no way I'm waiting more than a few minutes longer to claim the man as mine again. But just like every other time, I am left with too many feelings on my mind, I start to worry. What if it's not enough? What if he hasn't really forgiven me yet?

I'm going to have to tell him everything now. I straighten up and drop my hands to my sides. I try to take a few deep breaths, but the nerves are truly taking over now. How am I going to do this? How will I bear it? How will I reveal the worst moments of my life to the man who has given me so much happiness?

I worry my lips between the fingers of my left hand. Deep breaths, deep breaths, I try to encourage myself. I hear a shuffle from behind the bathroom door, and I feel paralyzed by the same fear that held me mute at such an important moment before. I feel like I might faint. The bathroom door finally flings open and I look up, feeling like I am going to face my executioner.

When I fling open my bathroom door and reveal my completely naked body to him, it doesn't quite elicit the reaction I was expecting. Black looks nervous and scared, so I look around as if to see what has happened in the less than five minutes it took me to go to the toilet and strip off my clothing. It's just him in the hallway, so the fear I feel rolling off him doesn't make sense to me.

"What's wrong?" I ask, feeling puzzled.

"I have to tell you," he stammers out, "I have to tell you everything."

I sigh, realizing the problem.

"Yes, Lucy," I say in a completely terrible, fake Cuban accent, "you have a lot of 'splanin' to do, but can it please wait?"

He looks totally befuddled, and I have to kiss the puppy dog expression off his face before I laugh which, considering how he is obviously feeling, would be the absolute worst reaction to have.

"But... you left because I wouldn't tell you, Aubrey." His tone changes from anxious to almost accusatory. "This is what you said you wanted."

I have to kiss him hard this time and nip his bottom lip extra sharply to get his attention.

"Yes, I want absolutely everything. But at this precise moment, I want you to fuck me in my shower. Because you broke my heart then flew all the way out here to fix it, nearly breaking your bladder in the process. You *finally* tell me you love me, and now what I need for you to do is prove it to me with Reginald's quivering member." By the end of this absolutely ridiculous tirade, I'm yelling, and he's grinning like an idiot.

"Okay?" I huff out even though I'm already grinning too.

"More than okay. Absolutely perfect."

I take Aubrey's face into my hands and kiss him tenderly. I can tell Aubrey was expecting me to ravish him, and I will, but first, I will worship him body and soul.

"Take your clothes off," he demands, and I kiss him again before I comply, just because I can. I walk him backwards into the bathroom, my hands never leaving his face, my eyes never dropping from his eyes. I brush my hands down his neck, across his naked clavicle, down his arms and twine my fingers with his hands which I bring up to my mouth so I can kiss his knuckles. I open his hands in mine, and I kiss his palms too. His breath is coming in heavy pants, and the look on his face can only be described as ecstatic in the near religious sense, happily overwhelmed and content like the looks of the saints as they gaze upon the face of the messenger of God in Renaissance paintings.

I bring his hands to the belt on my jeans, leaving them there for him to do with as he pleases as I reach behind my head to tug my black T-shirt off. I throw it on the floor, and Aubrey has already loosened my belt and is drawing down the zipper of my jeans. He shoves his hands down the back, into my briefs, and clutches the cheeks of my ass, hauling my half-undressed body against his completely nude one. Aubrey hisses as the rough fabric of my jeans presses against his dick. I let him take control as he shoves all my clothes down, dropping toward the floor with them until he reaches my boots which are my heavily laced combat style ones that will require more of his attention than he clearly wants to pay to them.

"Fuck it," he grumbles as he settles on his knees between my booted feet. He looks up at me with a surprisingly serious face. "One day, you are going to take me wearing just these boots. But not today."

I smile at the image that conjures in my mind and at his clear aggravation that his goal, my complete nudity, is being thwarted by my boots. The wicked glint has returned to his eyes, and he slowly lowers his mouth toward my throbbing dick while his eyes never leave my face. Lightly running his hand up my length, he presses my cock against my stomach, and licks up from the base all the way the head which he takes into his mouth and gently sucks. My hips buck up involuntarily and he drops me from his lips and grins wickedly.

"Again," I whisper hoarsely, and Aubrey's grin spreads impossibly wider before he complies with my order, licking me again from base to tip and sucking just my head into his mouth, this time with slightly more pressure.

"Umph!" I make an inarticulate grunt-like sound and lace my hands through his hair, holding him gently. This is his show, at least for the moment, and I don't dissuade him from his goal, whatever it might be.

Apparently, the goal is to deep throat my cock which he accomplishes with one slick glide of his mouth down until his lips meet the hair at my groin. The picture he makes is so incredibly erotic and turns hotter still when his green eyes flick up to mine. I'm going to come in his mouth any second now if he keeps this up, so I gently tug on his hair, encouraging him to release me and rise up my body. But, of course, he does it his own slow and torturous way, sucking harder on me as he rises, his mouth making a popping noise as he finally releases my head. Even though I have him by the upper arms as I tug him upward, he kisses my left hip, then my belly button, up my sternum, and licks my left nipple as he glides up my body. When I finally pull him to his complete height, he grabs my head, slamming our mouths together as he plunges his tongue into my mouth. I cannot help but groan as I wrap my arms around him, crushing him to me as if my hold can keep him with me forever.

"Damn it!" he suddenly curses, and I pull back to see what's wrong. I look down where his gaze has fallen and laugh when I see that my boots are still on.

"You could sit on the toilet."

"Well, that's not very attractive."

His face is growing more annoyed by the second, so I cannot help but laugh at our predicament.

"I will take them off," he huffs as he tries to slide down my body again, but as I still have hold of his arms, I stop him and kiss his mouth again until he sighs and links his arms around my neck.

"It was never going to be easy," I say against his lips.

Aubrey tilts his head to the left, raising his eyebrows at me, "That is entirely your fault, mister. I am easy. Very, very easy."

We both laugh now at the words he said to me once before, and Aubrey shakes my hold off his arms so he can flop to his knees and untie my shoes. He pauses slightly in his work to address my cock.

"Soon," he coos at it, pressing a gentle kiss to the middle of my shaft. "Soon."

Once he has disposed of my shoes, socks, and all the clothes that had pooled at my feet, he practically jumps back up and throws himself into my arms. I pick him up by the back of his thighs and he wraps his legs around my waist as he plunders my mouth with his. I stumble us toward his shower. It is an open floor plan bathroom with the large shower embedded in the corner, the rock façade walls making up two sides and a third glass wall separating it from the deep jacuzzi bathtub. As I carry him toward it, I see a recessed shelf for soaps and bottles as well as a bench made of the same rock material. A rainforest shower head sits in the center of the shower ceiling and two regular heads also protrude from the wall.

"This place is built for company," I remark.

"Shhh. Talk later, sex me now."

I set him down so he can turn the shower on and adjust the temperature. While Aubrey is distracted, I drop to my knees and swiftly take his cock into my mouth, his warm soft skin gliding across my tongue, my goal to have his head at the back of my throat in one move. He jerks and whimpers, his hips shifting forward as he leans against the rock wall in an effort to stay upright. The warm water is cascading from the rainforest shower head now, drenching us both. I slide slowly off him, swirling my tongue up his length as I withdraw. I turn him so his back is against the wall, and once again suck him fully down, relaxing my jaw so that the head hits the back of my throat and my lips kiss his groin, his curly pubic hair tickling my lips and nose. I alternate between gentle glides of my lips, loosely holding his cock in my mouth, and full on suction as I bob up and down on his dick. His taste is addictive as I taste his precum on my tongue as I swipe it over the slit in his head. He is trembling now, murmuring incomprehensible noises, the only recognizable sound is my name. "Ian, Ian."

If at all possible, hearing him call my name, in passion and desire, drives my need higher. I hold the base of his dick in one hand while the other moves lower to gently fondle his balls. I slide my hand up and down with my mouth, covering his whole cock as my other hand

DREA ROMAN

slowly moves back farther still until my fingertips gently tease his taint.

A groan rips from his throat, and he arches his back, thrusting his hips forward and his cock further down my throat. I could make him come this way, but I know it is not what either of us want. I slide my fingers back further still as I slow my plunges down his cock. My index finger brushes his hole, and his body ripples with electricity.

"Ian!" he cries out, his voice echoing off the walls of the shower. Hearing him call my name sends a happy ripple through me. Now that I am here, now that I have finally given in to my love for him, I crave hearing my name falling from his lips. I take one more plunge down then up his cock with my mouth, sucking his head hard so it pops as it leaves my mouth.

"Where is your lube, Aubrey?" I take a commanding tone, and his skin flushes all over from his thighs to his face. His head is thrown back, his eyes are closed, and his body is trembling so hard that I take hold of his hips, pressing him into the shower wall as I rise to my feet. I kiss his lips tenderly as the warm water flows down my back. His eyes flutter open, taking a moment to focus, and he smiles dreamily at me. "The lube, Aubrey," I repeat.

"In my shaving kit on the counter by the sink."

I kiss him one more time, making sure he won't fall when I release him. I retrieve the dark purple bottle of lube from his bag, and when I return to the shower, he has not moved and his eyes have drifted shut again.

"You're not going to fall asleep before I make you come, are you?" I drawl as I kiss his lips again.

He laughs softly, reopening his eyes. "No, I'm memorizing this, just in case it's a dream."

My heart cracks a little at that. I set the lube in the wall shelf and pull him into my arms. "No dreams, Aubrey bear, I'm right here, and I always will be. I love you, Aubrey."

He smiles and kisses me tenderly. "I love you, Ian."

"Thank God, you do."

He chuckles softly, but it quickly turns into a moan as my hands have migrated south and are cupping his ass cheeks, massaging them open and closed.

"Are you going to touch me or not?" he asks as he begins to trail kisses down my neck.

"Oh, I'm gonna touch you all right," I growl as I take advantage of exposed neck and bite down hard on the spot where his neck meets his shoulder. He shudders against me, and I release his ass so I can clasp his hips and turn him around.

"Face the wall."

He whimpers a little as he turns around. I place his hands on the wall where I want them, chest high, about a foot apart so he can hold himself up. I slide my hands down his sides and grip his hips, pulling them back toward me so he is bending slightly toward the wall. He shuffles his feet back, and I nudge them apart with my foot, giving him a solid stance. His breath is coming more heavily.

"Okay?" I whisper, leaning forward over his naked back to press my lips against the shell of his ear. He nods, and I nip his ear lobe, eliciting a little squeak from his throat.

"God," I groan heavily, "you make me want to come just looking at you."

He wiggles his ass at me, and I smack his cheek lightly with my right hand. The sound reverberates off the shower walls, mingling with the sound of the water falling, and our harsh breaths. I grab a bottle of shower gel from the shelf as I drop to my knees behind him, trailing my other hand over his ass then down his thighs to his knees. I crack open the bottle and pour some into my hand before setting it on the bench to the side. Using the water still pouring down on us, I lather it in my hands and start rubbing it into his skin, starting at his ankles. I move my way up his legs, across his ass cheeks which I crack open and slide one soapy hand down his crease, across his taint, and around his balls, all the way up his cock and groin on the other side. Aubrey is groaning and panting as I continue to soap him up, up his defined abdomen and his chest then around his waist to his back, sliding my hands up his spine to his shoulders. The shower is washing it all away, but it does not stop me from my ministrations.

"Mine," I growl and Aubrey answers with a breathy moan. "Mine to take care of." I kiss him on the right shoulder blade then the left. "Mine to protect." My hands and mouth slip down his back, sliding down his spine and over his ass as I lower once again to my knees. "Mine to own." With that, I pull his cheeks apart as I glide my tongue from his taint all the way up his crease.

"Oh," Aubrey moans.

I've positioned his stance wide enough I can easily see his hole from this angle. I swipe my tongue across it, and he jerks. I still his hips with my hands and run my tongue around him counter clockwise, lapping gently. I moan in the back of my throat as I kiss his hole again and again, now with my lips, now with my tongue. My hands are on his cheeks, holding them apart. I cannot help but inhale deeply. He smells like the strawberry body wash and him, just him, the intimate smell only a lover ever knows. With that thought, my dick swells even further, and I'm harder than a rock. But I don't rush anything. I am worshipping him because he deserves it, because he saved my soul.

"Ian," he whispers hoarsely. "Please."

I kiss his asshole one more time as I slide my right hand from his cheek to his perineum and rub him gently there, knowing his prostate rests on just the other side of the muscle.

"Oh, oh, don't stop."

I blow air across his hole as I slide my hand all the way around and up his cock. He trembles a little as I stroke his hard shaft lightly with my fingertips.

"Oh, oh, oh," he whimpers.

I kiss him again and circle his ass one more time before pressing the tip of my tongue inside of his hole. I am rewarded with more whimpers and his ass shoved back against my face.

"Please, Ian, I need more. I need you."

I snag the bottle of lube from the recessed shelf and pour a generous amount on my fingers. It smells of grapes which makes me smile. It is so very Aubrey to have grape scented lube.

Sliding the lube across my fingers, I smear plenty on his asshole, circling it with my index and middle fingers. I begin to slide my index finger inside of him slowly. He's so tight around me, and suddenly, I'm in much more of a hurry to get my cock inside of him. But I don't rush. I turn my finger inside of him, brushing along the walls, past the ring of muscles until I'm all the way inside. He bumps his hips back against my hand, and I curl my finger forward searching out that special place.

"Oh!" he practically shouts as my finger finally grazes his prostate, "more. Oh, my God, more!"

I slowly remove my one finger and my middle finger joins it as I carefully push back inside and return to gently stroke that spot inside of him. His back arches as electricity shoots through him.

"Now, Ian, now!"

I can do nothing but obey his command. I remove my fingers slowly, turning my wrist back and forth as I exit his body. I grab the lube again and slather a generous amount on my throbbing dick. This is the first time we are coming together naked, bare, and my hands tremble as I touch him gently, fingers trailing over one cheek on their way to his hip.

"Aubrey," I whisper, and it is the only thought my addled brain can produce. "Aubrey."

I grasp his hips with one hand and guide myself to his hole with the other. I slowly push inside, the heat, his heat, engulfing my length, centimeter by torturous centimeter. I tighten my hold on his hips, so he can't thrust back. I'm claiming him slowly, even as the desire to thrust all the way inside of him rushes throughout my entire body. I angle myself so I brush across his prostate and his knees nearly buckle from the pleasure. I snake my arm around his hips as I lean forward over his beautiful back.

"Aubrey," I whisper again, the only word I know anymore.

As my thighs meet the back of his and I'm fully seated inside of him, a moan escapes his lips, his breathing ragged. I slide my other hand around to his cock and balls, lightly gripping him and holding him against his own body. I am holding myself purposely against his special spot, and his trembling increases twenty-fold. I see his fingers trying to grip into the stone wall. He is starting to pulse around me, and his cock jerks in my hand.

"Oh, my God!" he wails. "I'm gonna, I'm gonna, oh, my God, I'm gonna come," he screams, and I pull back almost all the way out and slam back inside, his tight heat claiming me again. Over and over, I plunge in and out of him, gliding over his prostate again and again, holding his cock and balls against him. His penis pulses to the same rhythm as the muscles surrounding my cock, and he screams as he finally does come, his orgasm sending me over a moment later. Waves of pleasure pulse through me, through him, and I feel like our bodies are united as one and our souls meet.

"Aubrey!" I scream as I empty myself inside him, the waves crashing through me as I hold myself tighter to him, my hips still thrusting as hard as possible into him. His knees finally buckle, and I pull him up, pressing him against the wall with my larger body, kissing his shoulders, his neck, his ear, his cheek, and finally his mouth as he turns his head to claim mine. Our tongues touch languidly as we try to catch our breaths. One of my arms is around his waist, and my other still cups him against himself. My hand is covered in his cum. As I slide out of his body, I pull my hand around his hip and slide it up to cover his hole as my cum drips from it. I lower my other hand from his waist and gently cup his balls and still pulsing dick.

"Mine," I growl against his lips as I hold the evidence of our love-making against the most intimate parts of his body. "Mine."

Aubrey sighs, kissing me again. His sparkling green eyes open and a soft smile forms against my lips. "Mine," he repeats, "all mine."

CHAPTER 31

"Where were you going when I accosted you in front of the elevator?" I ask Aubrey as we lie cuddled in his king-sized bed. After our reunion sex in the shower, we toweled each other off and fell into his bed. We have lain here for a while, just holding each other, not talking, but touching, kissing, and slowly coming back to earth.

Aubrey chuckles. "Coffee, I was going to get coffee because I have none in the kitchen. It was not a very pleasant surprise this morning to find myself devoid of caffeine." He laughs again. "You know, I still haven't had coffee, and it's past noon now."

My stomach takes this opportunity to rumble. Aubrey laughs, ghosting his lips across my chin and down my neck. He turns in my arms, snuggling deeper, before whispering in my ear, "Do you want to order room service?"

"I thought this was an apartment."

"More like a long-term hotel suite. And this hotel serves food." He pulls back and grins, and I am so relieved that his smile makes it all the way to his eyes which are now twinkling with mischief. "Do you want breakfast?"

"Hell, yeah, I do. I swear, the airline coffee did just about break my bladder. I think it's currently burning a hole through my stomach."

Aubrey pecks me on the lips before disentangling himself from my arm and sitting up. "Poor baby. Don't think I've forgotten how much 'splainin' you have to do, Lucy." His expression turns guarded for a moment, so I sit up swiftly and gently take his face in my hands. One kiss on each eyelid, one kiss on each cheek, and I look him straight in the eyes as I kiss his lips softly.

"No worries, Aubrey. I am going to tell you everything." My stomach rumbles again, and Aubrey laughs, shaking me off so he can lean over me to grab an old-fashioned desk phone. He dials room service and orders us enough breakfast and coffee for four people.

When he hangs up, he smirks at me, and says, "Don't think you are allowed to leave this bed until I am satisfied."

I can't help but grin at that and tumble him back down to the mattress. The food takes no time to be delivered, probably because we were too busy making out to pay attention to the time.

"Breakfast in bed," Aubrey announces as he rolls the food cart directly into the bedroom and motions for me to lean back against the headboard. He places a breakfast tray over my blanket covered lap and whips the lid off.

"Bon appetit!" he declares before settling himself beside me against the headboard, his own tray over his lap. We eat in companionable silence, occasionally feeding each other bacon and sausage from our plates. When we finish, Aubrey whisks the trays and cart away. We resettle in the bed, full and drowsy, our arms wrapped around each other as we lie on our sides. I kiss Aubrey's brow before putting a little more distance between us so I can look in his beautiful eyes.

"It is hard to know where to start."

"The beginning obviously," Aubrey responds dryly before giggling.

I growl at him playfully before I continue. Taking a deep breath, I launch into the story of Vinny with so much trepidation that my voice quavers at first.

"I was your age when I met Vinny, just on the cusp of thirty, a bit more like you than you might believe. This was four years ago. I went for what and, more importantly, who I wanted. I didn't believe in cheap hookups, not for myself anyway. I wanted the whole shebang: a whirlwind romance, courtship, flowers. I wanted to give that to my man, surprise him at work with lunch and planned vacations. Vincent was my opposite. Some might say he was controlling, but it was more a matter of everything having its place. He liked ordering the chaos of life."

It is incredibly hard to say the words, the rest of the story. I have to take another deep breath at this moment.

"Saying Vinny died is both truthful and not the whole truth. But to say the whole truth threatens to rip my heart out of my body. Vinny didn't just die. He was murdered."

Now that I've said it, I feel light-headed. I take a deep breath as a shocking realization washes through me, freezing my heart in my chest.

"I never realized it until just this moment, but after his murder, I became Vinny in lots of ways."

Though he knew at least part of what was coming, Aubrey still gasped as soon as I uttered the word murdered, as if he couldn't help it, his left hand coming up to cover his open mouth, his right gripping my hand tighter.

"He was murdered," he whispers through his fingers, still too horrified to drop his hand from his mouth. I pull him hard into my chest, burying my head in his neck. I have to breathe in his scent because the memory of that day is drowning me again.

"It was the most horrendous day of my life," I say as I hold him tight against my chest. I know I have to hold him close in order to tell him this. There's really no other way for me to relive that horror. I take a deep breath of his pure, clean sent from his neck where I've lodged my face. I am sure I am squeezing the life and breath out of him, but I just can't help it. He soothes me by snuggling impossibly closer and petting me, his hands sliding up and down my back and it is very comforting gesture.

"I was painting," my voice is barely above a whisper. I am sure that it is cracking, and it is a very good thing my lips are next to Aubrey's ear, or I'm sure that he wouldn't hear me. But I can't bring myself to speak any louder. I've never spoken of this moment with anyone.

"I don't even remember the subject of the painting. I just remember I heard a knock at the door, so I put down my paint brush and palette on my work table and grabbed a rag to clean off my hands as I walked down the hallway to the front door. The person was knocking so loudly I really thought that it had to be Mrs. Watson which made me smile."

Aubrey makes a muffled noise against my cheek as he kisses it before pulling back to look me in the face. "You knew Mrs. Watson even then?"

A little laugh bubbles out of me. "Yeah, she saw us at the park one day and took us under her wing. We really didn't have a choice in the matter. As soon as she introduced herself, she claimed us, and she treated us fondly, like grandchildren." I sigh before continuing, "We lived one street over from her then. It wasn't until after Vinny's death that I moved next door to her."

Aubrey's expression is soft and sad. Wiggling his arm loose, he brings his hand up to stroke my jaw. My shadow is practically a short beard now, since I have not been concerned with grooming for the past week. When his fingers press softly against my lips, I kiss the tips.

Paused for the moment, I'm awash with memories both bitter-sweet and joyful. I swallow hard and Aubrey presses his lips gently against mine. I smile against Aubrey's soft pink lips. His hair is adorably mussed, and I want to laugh at how light my heart feels as I hold him here in my arms.

"What?" he mumbles, clearly picking up on the lightening of my mood. I've told him so little, but my chest becomes lighter as I stare into his brilliant green eyes. Sighing, I cuddle my face back against his neck and just breathe him in.

"Mmmm... I love when you do that," he mumbles.

I smile into the crook of his neck, pressing my lips gently against his pulse. "Why?" I murmur against his skin.

He makes a satisfied groaning noise and I can't help but laugh. His voice comes out huskily, "Because it makes me feel cherished."

My heart flips over in my chest, and I feel like my adoration of Aubrey knows no bounds. Aubrey hums and I feel it in his throat. I give his neck a few light kisses, knowing I can't get too distracted. Not right now.

"Later," I whisper against his warm skin and steady pulse. I pull back a little and settle my head on the pillow beneath it, returning my gaze to Aubrey's eyes.

"Thank you," I breathe out, and he takes my right hand in his and kisses my palm before entwining my fingers with his.

"Always, Ian. Always."

I shudder at that sound of my name from his lips, unable to deny the wave of relief that flows through me. Breathing deeply, I return to the story of the worst day of my life.

"I remember putting my right hand out toward the door, touching the knob, and turning it. I can see the whole scene in slow motion. I have orange paint on the back of my hand and fingers. As I pulled the door back, I saw a man about my height, wearing a dark blue suit and a loosened yellow tie over a white shirt. His knuckles seemed to have paused in the air, poised to rap on my door again. He dropped his hand slowly. I'm sure this didn't really happen in some weird slow-motion, but it's how I always remember it."

I swallow hard, those remembered emotions as clear to me now as they were then.

"When I said hello, he flashed up a badge in his other hand, and I had a weird momentary fear he was there to arrest me. I don't know why, but I've had this fear since I was a kid of the police showing up and carting me off. The look on his face was nervous, sad, and weary at the same time. He looked tired, and his brown salt and peppered hair was messy, like he'd been running his hands through it. All of my senses were keen, and I could smell his aftershave. Sure, I do tend to notice more sensory details than other people, but in this moment, it was heightened ten-fold. Not in hindsight, it was literally this way for me in that moment. I knew by the way he held his dark blue eyes something was very wrong."

Panting hard now, like I've run a marathon, I have to consciously slow down my breathing. Aubrey pulls my face from his neck again and seeing his sparkling eyes calms me. Aubrey's gaze never drops mine as his one hand tightens around mine and the other continues to gently rub my back.

"I was momentarily distracted by the blazing sunset behind the cop's back. I'd gotten lost in the painting, hours must have passed since Vinny left. And then I knew. I'm sure my eyes were horrified as they met his again and he gave the slightest, almost imperceptible nod, and my chest caved in; I knew Vinny wasn't coming home."

Tears are trickling out of the corners of my eyes. Aubrey takes a tear drop, smudging it on his fingers before rubbing the tears that have escaped my eyelids off my cheekbones with his thumbs.

"Then what happened?" he asks.

I clear my throat, Aubrey's care and patience finally soothing me enough to reach the most horrible part of my story.

"They never found his body."

Aubrey jerks in my arms, then props his head up on his elbow. "What?"

I blink my eyes clear of lingering tears. "He disappeared."

"Then how do you know he is dead? How do the police know?"

A shudder ripples through me as I recall David's words from that day.

"The police detective, David Derricks, informed me they found Vinny's car, still running with the tank almost empty, in an alley miles from where he should have been. It was in a bad part of town, rumored to be mob territory."

"There are mobs in Oakland?"

"Apparently. The front seat was covered in blood, too much blood. According to David, no one could lose that much blood and survive." Pausing, I breathe deeply for a few moments before I continue.

"I thought it was my fault."

Aubrey shakes his head and clearly wants to interrupt. I interrupt *him* with a quick kiss and say, "I know it makes no logical sense. But Vinny was out buying painting supplies for me. Plus, I was painting at the moment he disappeared."

Aubrey makes a quizzical face, cocking his head to the right. "You used to paint?"

I laugh, love for this man flooding me with warmth. I grab his face and kiss him languidly just because I can but pick up the conversation where we left again as soon as we part for air.

"Yes, I was a painter and a sculptor at the time. My career was starting to take off, and Vinny was just so proud. Whenever I needed something when he was free, he would insist on fetching it for me. Called himself my 'gopher.'"

Aubrey laughs too, and God, but I adore that sound.

"There was an art supply store a few blocks from our apartment. We'd moved in together after six months because we just knew."

At that Aubrey gives me an "oh, really" sort of look and raises his eyebrows.

"Six months, you say? Hmmm..."

I retaliate his subtle tease about the length of our relationship, almost six months, by tickling his stomach where his shirt has ridden up to reveal it.

"No," he howls, overcome with laughter, my sexy little ticklish man. Despite the fact he looks good enough to eat up right now, I have to tell him everything and answer any questions even if it takes days because I owe him that. And, because, for the first time in over two years, I really do want to share myself, and Vinny too, with someone who will understand.

Lightening my brushes across his belly so I am caressing rather than tickling him, I lean in close enough to kiss his lips again.

"Thank you," I sigh against his lips.

"For what?" he whispers back.

"For allowing me to share him with you."

Aubrey makes a surprised noise in his throat. "What? I thought you didn't want to share him with me. That is why you wouldn't tell me."

Huffing out a sad laugh, I sigh. "No, Aubrey, I was scared to relive all of this, all of my feelings, all of my guilt over his death. Scared to risk my heart again then scared to risk your safety."

"Why are you okay with it now?" His expression is so serious it looks haunted. A little bit of fear sparks in his eyes.

"Because I love you, Aubrey. After you left, I realized keeping all this inside was what was killing me, not falling in love with you. And, I had no hope of not falling in love with you, Aubrey. You're everything anyone could ever want, everything I have ever wanted. Smart, funny, kind, *forgiving*."

Aubrey giggles at my emphasis on the last word, freeing me to laugh too.

"Yes," I murmur, "I think the forgiving part might be the most important."

Aubrey kisses me then, nipping my lower lip. "You are a scoundrel."

"That is why you love me."

"Keep telling yourself that," he laughs.

A sudden insecurity lodges itself in my chest. "Why do you love me, Aubrey?"

Surprised by my question, he cocks his eyebrow up. "Have you had a look at yourself, Ian?"

Laughing, I ask again, "Why?"

Sighing, he rubs his nose against mine in an Eskimo kiss. "Because I do."

When I grumble at that, he smiles. "But if you must know, it is your hair."

Leaning my head up off of the pillow, I shake my tangled hair at him.

"Shake not thy gory locks at me, Banquo."

"See! You even quote Shakespeare while lying in bed with me, forcing me to spill all of my guts everywhere. What's not to love? But you haven't answered my question, Aubrey bear."

"You are more than the sum of your parts, Ian, even though I do love your parts." He winks at me lasciviously. "I love your heart, your charm, your acceptance, and if I am being honest, knowing you were afraid telling me this would hurt me endears you to me more. But most importantly, I love you for the sculpture of Benny the squirrel."

Laughing, I nip at his lower lip. Sighing, I drop my head back to my pillow. Aubrey rearranges himself in a sitting position with his back against the headboard. Shifting myself so I am lying perpendicular to him, I lay my head in his lap. He strokes my hair for long moments, and I almost drift off to sleep.

"Ian?"

"Hmm?"

"Are you asleep?"

"Yes."

Aubrey laughs softly.

"There is one thing I don't understand," Aubrey confides, his voice unsure as if he is afraid he will scare me away like the last time.

I smile sadly even though I know he can't see my face. "It's okay. You can ask anything you want. Anytime. Anywhere. Like for instance, if we are standing in line for popcorn at a Heath Ledger movie marathon, you can ask me then, in front of couples with children and old ladies with walkers, when I first knew I loved you. And I will answer you right then and there. Because I'm tired of hiding... everything," I finish lamely, shaking my head against his thigh. "Everything."

"So, when *did* you first know you love me?" he asks, his curiosity so predictable and beloved to me.

I sit up and cuddle into his side before I look into his eyes.

"Well, I guess you will have to find a Heath Ledger movie marathon to find out."

His mouth falls open before a huge smile settles on his mouth, the first sunshine smile I've seen since I broke his heart several days ago.

"Why were you so scared to tell me all of this? Did you think I wouldn't be able to accept how much you loved Vinny?"

"No, Aubrey. I spent almost a year and a half limping along, pretending my life was just fine. Any time I thought of Vinny, I would shove my sadness and grief into the back of my mind. I pretended I was okay for so long that I started to believe it. Then, I met you and everything blew apart."

Aubrey looks startled, so I nip at his chin before leaning back against the headboard. Slipping my arm around his shoulders, I pull him closer to me so his head is leaning against my shoulder.

"It wasn't your fault, of course, but I think some small part of me did blame you."

Aubrey slides his hand up my chest and pats me over my heart. I clasp his hand to that spot, taking a moment to savor the heat of his palm against my skin.

"I wanted you as soon as I saw you, but immediately I knew you would be more and deserved more than I was willing to give. And, that scared the fuck out of me." I sigh and Aubrey giggles.

"Such a way with words," he teases me, trying as always, to put me at ease.

"I wanted more but lied to myself about what it meant."

"Okay," he murmurs, bringing his head up to look into my eyes. "I think I get it."

Smiling, I turn and peck him on the cheek. "If not, I will just keep explaining until we straighten out this mess of spaghetti noodles that is my mind."

"Grief does tend to fuck you up."

"Yeah, especially if you are in denial like I was."

Aubrey shifts so it is easier to look me in the eyes. "Are you comfortable?"

Laughing, I respond, "Yes, why?"

He pats me on the chest, right over my heart, sending it tumbling with happiness.

"Just making sure you were happy with your confession bed."

Chuckling, I can't resist kissing him.

"As long as it is not a 'death bed confession,' I have no problem staying right here with you all day," he whispers against my mouth.

"Nope, I think it's a 'starting my life over confession.' And, I'd like to stay in bed with you all day too."

Surprisingly, Aubrey does not laugh like I expected. He looks serious. "You're starting your life over?"

"Yes, Aubrey bear, though," I scratch my chin and feel like I need to shave, "I have already started over with you."

A whoosh of air leaves Aubrey, indicating he must have been holding his breath.

"Good," he replies, "I'm glad to hear it."

Startled into a laugh, I gaze down into his relieved face. "Were you concerned about that? I thought I was being pretty clear here, what with the flying half-way across the country, the bladder busting, and the confession bed I'm lying in with you."

He giggles, a faint blush falling across his cheekbones. His eyes sparkle. "I had to make sure."

"Oh, I'm sure," I growl as I tumble him over and stretch above him, grinding my hips against his.

"I need you," he whispers against my lips before claiming them.

"I always need you, Aubrey," I whisper back before we kiss until there is nothing left between us by the touch of skin, the rustle of sheets, and love in physical form.

CHAPTER 32

When we wake from our sex-induced napping, it is time for dinner. Our shower takes far longer than is necessary since we refuse to make ourselves behave. By the time we finally stumble out, the sun has set, and we are both starving.

"Do you want to go out for dinner or order more room service?" Aubrey asks as he walks into the bedroom, gloriously nude.

"Room service. I'm too tired to make it past the elevator, I'm afraid. Besides, I have plenty more to tell you, and…"

"And you don't want an audience for that?" Aubrey helpfully provides.

"Yes, but you better put on some clothes or we are going to end up in the confession bed again, 'confessing ourselves' over and over."

Aubrey laughs and throws a sock at me. "I can behave. You are the one with 'Russian hands and Roman fingers.'"

A sharp bark of laughter leaves my throat, "I cannot believe you just used the oldest double pun in the book. My dad used to say that!"

Aubrey grins, glancing over his shoulder as he pulls on a pair of lounge pants. His brow cocks up at me before he walks over to where I am standing in the bathroom door. Putting his hands over my naked chest, he doesn't seem too much in a hurry to do anything other than touch me. While I can't blame him, the desire to tell him everything burns under my skin. So I tip up his chin with my finger and kiss him softly before raising my head.

"Sooo…" I mutter.

"Sooo… What?" Aubrey's face is alight with mischief which I can barely resist. But at the moment, the need for everything to be open and free between us presses at me more than my ever-present desire to make love to him.

"I don't have any clothes."

Aubrey cackles, throwing back his head. The light from his bedroom lamps casts a warm glow around him, catching the sparkle of shimmering gold in his auburn hair. Bringing my hand to his face, I caress his cheekbones then his lips while he stares into my eyes, a slow smile spreading across his face.

"You forgot to pack."

"Well, yes. I was a bit more concerned with catching up with you. I really did stay on my knees in my living room for an hour after you left. I had torn out both of our hearts, and if it were possible to die from a heartbreak you caused yourself, then I would have right then and there."

Aubrey reaches up to cup my chin. He runs his nails through the beard I have going, his eyes shining with understanding.

"I'm going to shave it."

He smiles and nods before patting me on the chest again and stepping back. "I'm sure I have something that will fit you. God knows why, but my aunts can't get my size right no matter how many times I tell them." He waves a hand toward his dresser as he walks forward, clearly expecting me to follow. "Drawers full, I have drawers full of pants and shirts two sizes too big."

"Maybe they are sizing your clothes according to your personality, not your waist measurements."

He hums a little laugh as he pulls open a drawer, shuffling through the contents until he pulls out a pair of gray pajama bottoms a similar shade to his own. "I think these will fit."

Taking them, I slip them on and tie the drawstring. "Perfect. I knew you would have everything I need."

"Including food service. The kitchen has an Italian menu. Do you want some pasta or something easier like pizza?"

"Pasta sounds great, thank you."

Once our dinner arrives, we settle on the couch to eat. In some sort of unspoken agreement, we eat before we pick up our confession conversations. After clearing away the dishes and returning the cart to the hallway, taking the one from breakfast out as well, Aubrey comes to sit on the opposite end of the couch as me. He settles in so we are facing each other. Never one to beat around the bush, Aubrey throws down a gauntlet of a question.

"What happened last week, Ian?"

Even though the question is a hard one for me to answer, I smile because Aubrey called me "Ian."

"David," I sigh then clarify, "Detective Derricks visited me again. I hadn't seen him in a year; not since the case went officially cold. Gloria, Vinny's mom, has petitioned to have Vinny declared dead. She wants the closure. I have no rights in the matter as I was just the boyfriend. We weren't married. Hell, we barely could have been. Gloria asked David to let me know." I sigh again and look down at my hands in my lap.

"Why didn't she tell you herself?" Aubrey asks with a quizzical expression on his face.

Scrubbing a hand over my face, I take a few deep breaths before I continue. "I stopped speaking to her a few months after Vincent's death. I just couldn't do it. Her sympathy, her kindness, it burned me up inside. The last time I saw her, I screamed at her to leave me alone, it was my fault that her son was dead, and she should hate me. Now, I realize I should have talked to her. It would have been better for both of us, and the rest of his family, if we had mourned together. But, I just couldn't."

Aubrey leans toward me, scooting forward on the couch until he is next to me. Taking my hands in his, he holds them, settled as they are in my lap.

I look into his eyes, so open and loving. I can't help but smile. Aubrey just waits, letting me have a moment to calm the jumble of feelings inside of me.

"When I saw David, it brought everything back. You came in right after he left. You have no idea how much you helped me that night, Aubrey. I have no idea what I would have done if you hadn't been there."

"But it wasn't enough, was it?" he asks in a sad, solemn voice.

Pulling him into me, I hold him tight as I whisper in his ear. "Yes! Yes, it was. You were enough for me that night and are enough for me every other night. It's my fault I didn't let you help me. As soon as you left the next morning, the same depression I felt when Vinny's case was declared cold descended on me. And, I couldn't deal with it." I huff out a breath against his ear and kiss the skin behind it, making Aubrey shiver from the tickle my beard creates against his skin.

"I resorted to the same tactics of withdrawal and disconnection that hadn't worked so well for me the first time around." I release him from my tight hold so that I can see into his face. "But it didn't work at all this time, Aubrey. Because I needed you. By the time I realized it, I tried to reach out, but…" Pausing, I take a deep breath. "But even then, I couldn't, no, wouldn't, allow myself to bridge the gap between us. I should have told you everything then, Aubrey. I should have kept my promise. I'm so sorry I didn't."

"I should have waited, Ian."

"No, Aubrey. Absolutely not. It never would have ended. I never would have had the courage to force myself to face reality if you hadn't confronted me. Walking out my front door was the best thing you ever could have done for me. Because I would have kept hiding. I would have kept fighting my need to be with you, to tell you everything. It wasn't until you left that I could realize and understand I had to change. I had to face my fears, and let the pain go or it would kill me and kill any possibility I had of you loving me back the way I love you."

Tears slip down Aubrey's face even as he smiles at me. "I mean that much to you?"

I shudder because I cannot believe he doesn't know. "I love you, Aubrey, so much. You make every day happier and easier. With you, I can breathe again. And, for the first time in two years, I really want to breathe again."

Aubrey leans into me then, putting his arms around me, nestling his face in my neck. I can still feel tears against my skin, and I make murmuring noises to soothe him, rubbing circles on his back. We sit there a long while as the night closes in on us softly and quietly.

"I know what you did for me, Aubrey."

"Oh, you do, do you? Do tell."

Aubrey and I have not left the couch. We cuddled for a while, but now I have remembered something I want him to explain to me. He wiggles around in my hold until I release him so he can sit up.

I laugh at his answer. "I don't think I have heard the word do used that many times in a sentence before."

"It is a versatile word. Spill it. Tell me what I did for you." Aubrey's eyes flash, and he smiles a naughty little smile.

I can't help myself. I have to kiss his laughing face. When I pull back, he eyes me suspiciously.

"So, what did I do for you?"

I grin and pull his upper body into my lap so I can look down into his face. "According to Mr. Owens, you saved my bacon."

Surprisingly, Aubrey blushes. I laugh. "Ha, ha! I made you blush. Now let me kiss it to see what it tastes like." Bending forward over him, I kiss his cheekbone then nibble at it affectionately. "Mmmm... Definitely strawberries over cream."

Aubrey's smile is somehow both beatific and shy. He sighs, just looking up at me, waiting expectantly. My heart throbs, this time not with fear but with absolute joy.

"I love you," I murmur, my voice low with emotion. Aubrey's eyes are bright then a mischievous look settles on his face.

"So Mr. Owens told you that, did he?"

Laughing, I shake my head. "No, but he did tell me about the proof of concept binder, the updates, and how hard you had to fight the council to gain approval for my sculpture. What I want to know is why? We barely knew each other at that point."

Aubrey laughs, pulling himself out of my lap into a seated position facing me, his back against the armrest of the couch. He leans forward to kiss me on the cheek before putting his feet in my lap and nodding at them, clearly signaling me to massage them. I fall to the task while waiting for him to answer my question.

"You were pretty vehement about not wanting to do another cowboy and horse statue. You never did fully explain why you hate the piece so much."

I sigh as I remove his socks. He wiggles his toes before I start kneading his arches.

"That feels good."

"Ummhmm. Continue with your confession."

Aubrey winks at me. "We had already made out in the back seat of my rental car."

"So, you did all that work just to keep the sexual favors coming? Wait, I seem to recall you put the brakes on such activities, presumably to protect my virtue."

Aubrey giggles and pokes me in the ribs. "Keep kneading, and I'll tell you all of my secrets."

I hit a knot, and Aubrey groans. "That's it. I am your slave forever."

"Spill it, oh virtuous protector of the sexually innocent."

Aubrey howls, and I tickle his foot. "No, no! No tickle torture. I will spill my guts." Once he catches his breath, he grins at me.

"Jenene called me the morning after our backseat adventures to say Mr. Owens and Mrs. Swift were having conniption fits over the change. I just pulled some of your photos from your website and put together a proposal. Bing, bang, boom! Approval."

I shake my head at him. "Mr. Owens said it was a little more complicated than that. You had to argue for it. He also said you were sending him updates on my progress."

Aubrey cocks his head to the side. "Yeah, I'm supposed to do that."

"The point is, Aubrey, you went above and beyond for me, after knowing me for about twenty-four hours. Why?"

"I also drank wine with you then threw you up against the side of a building so I could kiss you silly, all before I had known you a day."

"So, you are just a friendly and accommodating dude, huh?"

We are both laughing now.

"No. But it seemed really important to you. I already liked you. I didn't want you to lose the job just because some council wanted you to do the same thing over and over again. That would be bad for you and for the park which means it would be bad for me." Aubrey pauses for a minute.

"Now that I have told you my big bad binder secret, you have to tell me why you hate that statue so much. It's not just that it is a cowboy and horse, is it?"

I smile. "You know me too well, Aubrey."

Aubrey leans back on the arm of the couch. "Do tell."

"Since you asked so nicely, I will oblige." I sigh. "You are right. I don't like "Monstrosity" and it has nothing to do with the theme, the quality of the work, or the difficulty level, which was rather high in the end. While I do believe that western style sculpture is played the fuck out, I hate or rather hated it for an entirely different reason. It just took falling in love with you for me to realize what that reason was."

Aubrey smiles softly at me, just waiting for me to continue. I love that about him, how he just lets me think a moment, gives me space to breath, not feeling the need to interrupt with questions or guidance.

I look down at Aubrey's feet and continue my massage up his ankles to his calf muscles. "It was the first big deal I took after Vinny disappeared. I needed something to pour my soul and my grief into. Objectively speaking, it is some of my best work, but once it was finished, I couldn't bear to look at it again. It holds too much pain, too much anguish and longing. It was a large, labor intensive project that took nearly a year to complete. The year just happened to coincide with the year when the police searched for Vincent everywhere. Nothing concrete happened, nothing was found. It was a terrible year of waiting and yearning. Then, the day after I finished "Monstrosity," David came to tell me the case was officially cold, closed for all intents and purposes. Nothing, I had nothing left. I didn't spend another night in our house. The house next to Mrs. Watson was up for sale, so I jumped at the chance to start fresh. Or," I shake my head, "the chance to pretend to start fresh."

I pause for breath and shake my head. "I guess I associated the two in my mind. I haven't seen it since the day it was unveiled."

Aubrey pulls my arm until I release his leg. He intertwines his fingers with mine.

"Would you show it to me when we go back to Oakland?" he asks softly.

Relief and joy flood through me, and I stare at Aubrey for a moment before I can catch my breath. "Yes," I somehow manage to choke out. Clearing my throat, I ask the most important question, "Are you coming back to Oakland with me?"

Aubrey laughs as he tugs me up from the couch. "Someone suggested I make my office in Oakland. I think it was a great idea, don't you?"

No one could break the smile on my face off, not even with a crowbar. "I do."

Aubrey leads me to the bedroom, where we snuggle in to sleep, ecstatic to be back in each other's arms.

CHAPTER 33

"*I*an," Aubrey whispers in my ear, "do you want breakfast?"

Rolling into him, I glance past his shoulder at the clock. 10 a.m. "Coffee," I grumble out. He laughs, his breath puffing across my face before he gets out of bed.

"I will take that as a yes."

"Is it okay if we stay in bed again today?"

Aubrey looks over his shoulder at me from where he is standing by the dresser. "That probably would be best as you have no street clothes to wear until we wash your outfit from yesterday."

"That's not why I asked."

Aubrey laughs softly and throws a blue pair of pajama pants my way. "I know, Ian."

"It's just easier talking about all of this when I can hold you. Is that okay?"

"More than okay, it's wonderful. Go shower and I will call for some breakfast. At this rate, my bill this month is going to be outrageous."

"I can pay for it," I say as I walk past him toward the bathroom, pausing to drop a kiss on his forehead.

"It is no problem. I was just joking."

While Aubrey orders us another monster sized breakfast, I quickly shower, contemplating shaving my face but leaving it until later since I don't want to spend the time on it right now. Despite everything I revealed to Aubrey yesterday, so much still weighs me down and my reflection in the mirror looks nervous. When I finally emerge from the bathroom, I find the food has arrived.

"Come sit," Aubrey pats the bed next to him.

I comply, and Aubrey passes me a plate of breakfast after I have settled in the bed next to him. But I don't find myself very interested in the waffles and bacon. So many things rush through my mind, making it difficult to know where to pick up the thread of my story, also making it almost impossible to eat.

"Can I ask a question?" Aubrey's voice startles me from the reverie I have fallen into as I stare at my breakfast. I nod to encourage him to continue.

"I can't think of a polite way to ask since I am already so impatient to hear the answer."

"I'm curious now. What do you want to know?"

He looks down for a moment, a frown on his face, then he shakes his head and looks up.

"Your name, Ian James Black. Why didn't you want me to call you Ian? And why do you seem to be okay with it now?"

I'm relieved even though the answer will probably seem convoluted. Laughing lightly, I run my hands through my hair a few times before meeting Aubrey's gaze again.

"It is sort of a weird story. Even though my parents named me Ian, no one called me that growing up. Everyone called me James. But after Vinny died, everything became bound up with his death, from the horse and cowboy sculpture to my first name." My anxiety is ratcheting up again, and Aubrey lays a gentle hand on my leg.

"It's okay, we can get to later, if it is too hard right now."

Nodding, I try to eat a little bit of the breakfast, and somehow manage to get part of it down. My stomach is tied in knots now, but there is only one solution: to tell Aubrey everything.

Looking at him, I realize he has his hand out for my plate. I hand it over then scoot down in the bed, pulling Aubrey down with me after he sets the plate aside. Kissing the side of his head, I take a deep breath of his scent to calm myself.

"You don't have to talk about it right now," Aubrey offers, but I shake my head.

"No, I have to do this, Aubrey. All of this has become like a cancer inside of me. I have to get it out. But in order to explain my own name, I need to start with Vinny's name."

Taking a deep breath, I close my eyes. Aubrey snuggles in next to me with his head on my shoulder.

"I called him Vinny, mostly so I could introduce him as "my cousin Vinny" to unsuspecting people. No one else called him Vinny, so it was incredibly special to me that I could. Vinny was an attorney and wasn't particularly fond of the film. He couldn't help pointing out how many things the movie had wrong about his profession."

I turn my head, so I can look at Aubrey's face, and he's smiling as if he understands what the little joke meant to me and Vinny.

"He thought it was a dumb film, and no matter how many times we watched it, he'd always declare that Vanessa Redgrave had been robbed at the Oscars. Then we would play-argue, with me taking up Marisa Tomei's case, Vinny-style. We'd end up laughing so hard as we made up outrageous arguments and counter-arguments, presenting them so boisterously once a nosey neighbor knocked at the door to ask if she needed to call the police because we were having a domestic row. Of course, it was Mrs. Watson, who heard us 'arguing' as she cruised by our house on her nightly power-walk."

Aubrey surprises me from the silent reverie I did not realize I had fallen into by wiping tears from my cheeks, tears I didn't even know I'd been crying.

"He called you Ian?" Aubrey asks gently, still holding my face in his hands.

I nod in his hold, still having a hard time maintaining eye contact with this man who owns my heart. The tears begin to flow harder, and Aubrey tips my chin up so I can meet his gaze again, surprising me because I hadn't realized I had lost hold of his steady eyes until that moment. He leans forward, his eyes watching mine as he gently kisses my lips, then proceeds to start kissing the tears. I move back slightly, and his hold shifts, his hands sliding into my hair to pull me forward again. He rests his forehead against mine in what is quickly becoming a go-to gesture between us, a momentary pause, a rest, a small window of respite in which we look into each other's eyes, and it feels like we are gently holding each other's souls.

"It's okay," he murmurs to me gently. I pull his entire body into me, marveling at this man, marveling that he really is mine.

"I love you," I whisper raggedly against the lips I've pulled to mine. I feel like I need to explain that Vinny is the past and Aubrey is my future. My heart squeezes with fear he'll misunderstand and think I wished Vinny were here instead of him. But as always, Aubrey already knows me and what I need. He smiles against my mouth, surprising me by nipping at my bottom lip with his teeth.

"It's okay, Ian," he says calmly, gently, and I shudder, reveling in the fact he hasn't called me Black since I accosted him in front of the elevator yesterday morning. I let him hold me for a while until I have enough calm to continue my story.

"Vinny called me Ian right from the start. I never corrected him, never told him no one else calls me that. It felt so special to me, and I wanted to have something special with him. He always insisted everyone else call him Vincent, but he let me call him Vinny. It felt wonderful to call each other names no one else ever used. Not a pet name, but a unique name with a personal meaning. I was his Ian and he was my Vinny. We and our names didn't belong to anyone but each other. When he introduced me to his family, it was as Ian. But the first time his mother, Gloria, called me that after Vinny disappeared, I went into a panic attack. I never had anxiety issues before, but in that moment, I felt like my heart cracked open and I couldn't breathe. I couldn't keep seeing her. I couldn't see his family. I couldn't bear to see anyone at all for a long time."

Breathing heavily now, I open the eyes I had not realized I had squeezed shut. Aubrey has rearranged himself, lying on his side, his head propped up on the pillows so he can look into my face more easily. As always, his sweet gaze calms me, and after a few moments, I feel like I can continue again.

"I didn't even know my first name wasn't James until I did a middle school family tree project. My mom gave me our family birth certificates and I was confused. Apparently, Ian is a family name on my dad's side. My mother didn't want to name me that, but dad insisted. She won though. No one ever called me Ian until Vinny came along. In high school, I went by Black. It fit who I was better, an artist, with one name. You know, like Madonna."

Aubrey giggles, and I can't help but grin at having amused him in the middle of my far too heavy story. "Once I went to college," I continue after a moment, "I thought using my full name would make me stand out, like Frank Lloyd Wright, I guess. The people at the top always have three names, like Franklin Delano Roosevelt."

In the pause of silence, Aubrey replies, "Or Lee Harvey Oswald."

Laughing, and quite relieved for the levity, I scoot onto my side to face him.

"Exactly like Lee Harvey Oswald, only I was painting and sculpting, not assassinating anyone."

Aubrey giggles, smiling his beautiful smile at me, keeping me calm as I pour out these stories I've kept locked in my soul for two years.

"Almost six years after I finished my MFA, I was invited to be part of gallery showing at my alma mater, Stanford. Vinny saw my paintings in our college art museum on the first day of the show and tracked me down. It was the annual alumni retrospective and since Vincent had gone to law school there, he was taking a nostalgia tour. Vinny got what Vinny wanted, and with one look at my art, he wanted me. I don't think it ever occurred to him the painter he was stalking down might not be gay."

Aubrey and I laugh at that for a moment. "That was definitely Vincent for you. He was a few years older than me, almost a decade out of law school and established in a local law firm. He was so damned determined about everything. I used to tease him that his to-do lists had to-do lists. He planned everything down to the letter. I think I was one of the few things he didn't plan."

"But once he decided I was his, well," I grin at the memories, "he set out to woo me. What's funny is that half of the time, the plans did not work out how he intended. To say he was frustrated would be an understatement. He planned everything so carefully. One time, a hot air balloon ride went awry, and we landed in a cornfield. The farmer was not pleased to have us as guests in the middle of his harvest time."

Stalling out a moment in the bittersweet memories, I don't realize I've stopped talking again until Aubrey brushes his hand against my cheek.

"Where did he stalk you down?" Aubrey asks, and I laugh, so pleased to be asked for a detail I never would have thought to share otherwise.

"Since it was an alumni retrospective, there was an evening event in the gallery auditorium. All of the artists introduced the piece they were showing then the guests browsed the gallery. I was talking to another artist when I felt a tap on my shoulder. I turned around and there he was, an incredibly attractive dark-haired man in a three-piece suit. I was confused for a moment and thought he was looking for one of the event coordinators. Then he flashed a smile at me, handed me his card, and asked me to show him my piece."

Chuckling a little as I recall the happy memory, I almost blush when I meet Aubrey's eyes. "I was floored by him and didn't understand he was flirting with me until we found my painting in the gallery and he asked for his card back, so he could write his number on it. 'But, it already has your number on it,' I replied in confusion. He winked at me, took the card, wrote his cell number on the back, and replied, 'This is my personal number, for personal calls, from sexy men who call me for personal reasons. I hope you will call me for personal reasons, Ian.'"

It felt a little weird to be sharing this private memory with Aubrey, but it also felt right. Tears glisten now at the corners of his eyes and he grins widely. "Wow, Vincent was... Wow, he was something else, wasn't he?"

Smiling, I snuggle myself closer to Aubrey and kiss the corner of his mouth. "Yes, he was. And so are you, Aubrey. How did I get lucky enough to meet both of you in one lifetime?"

Aubrey blushes, and I kiss the strawberry from his cheek.

"Thank you," he breathily replies, "for sharing this with me."

"Thank you, Aubrey, for giving me another chance. And for letting me share this with you. It has been so long since I've allowed myself to remember the good times. Everything was buried under the pain of losing him. Until you asked just now, I had not allowed myself to think of how we met and what he was like in a very long time."

We are quiet for a few minutes then Aubrey draws me back into it with a new question. "What did you do after Vinny disappeared?"

Blowing out a breath, I answer, "At first, Gloria and I were very involved in the case. For the first month, we relied on each other, kept each other upright. But once the leads started drying up, my guilt that Vinny was out purchasing supplies for me overwhelmed my mind. I started to withdraw from everyone. The only person I spoke to about it anymore was the detective on the case. I stopped by his office so often we were quickly on a first name basis, well, his first name and my last. I stopped speaking to Gloria after I screamed at her not to call me "Ian."

"But you know Mrs. Watson. She never let me go long without coming up with some reason she needed me. Tilly and a few others tried to do the same, but I wouldn't really let them. It felt like acid in my blood every time someone said 'sorry for your loss' or 'my condolences' or asked after my health. So I stopped going out. I didn't return calls. I just sculpted. I think some of that pain came out in "Monstrosity." Working on that statute felt like I was moving on without Vinny, and I didn't want to do it. Even when I moved out of our house, I took all of Vinny's stuff, though I haven't looked at it since. All of it is still in boxes in my garage."

Pausing, I take in a deep breath before continuing. "In the first few months after his disappearance, I looked at everything of Vincent's often, especially his shirts. They still smelled like him, the scent below the detergent that marks a garment as well loved. But after about six months, they stopped smelling like him. I tore apart the boxes, searching for just one shirt that still smelled like him. None of them did and I lost it. I wrecked my bedroom, throwing the boxes, tearing through them, and crying like I'd never cried before."

Tears start to trickle from my eyes, making my vision of Aubrey watery and blurry.

"Hey, you can cry whenever you want." Aubrey pauses oddly at the end of that sentence and I know why.

"Aubrey, I *want* you to call me 'Ian.' It means so much to me every time I hear it from your lips."

He smiles softly with those lips. "Now you are going to make me blush."

"No, you mostly blush when you are surprised." I pause. "Or angry. But you're not surprised that I want you to call me by my name. Well, I hope you are not."

"Why are you okay with that now?"

"It's special, it's intimate, and I want that with you. But mostly, after you left, I realized that I wanted to give you everything. I regretted holding anything back. I should have told you all of this when you first asked. So many opportunities presented themselves, and I ignored every one of them in favor of holding my pain inside. But it was the wrong choice, Aubrey."

He smiles at me and brushes his hand over my face. "Well, I'm glad you are making the right choice now."

CHAPTER 34

*A*ubrey sits up and stretches his arms above his head. "Do you feel like a walk? We are going to get too stiff if we stay in bed two days in a row." Though I'm not too keen on leaving his apartment, I agree. After dressing, we walk down the block from his hotel to the nearest coffee shop. Laughing when I see our destination, I tease him for it.

"You wanted better coffee."

"Yep, that room service stuff is not really up to my standards."

Bemused, I shake my head at him, pulling our clasped hands up so I can kiss the back of his hand.

"Besides, I need to pick up some for my coffee maker."

I nod and Aubrey orders for us. We are back in his apartment a half hour later, and I have to admit I feel better for the moment of fresh air.

"Hey! I was just wondering: How did you figure out my address?" He snaps his fingers before I can reply. "Wait, did Jenene give it to you?"

"Nope." I sip a drink of my coffee before continuing, "It is on the business card you gave me when we first met."

"You still have the card?"

"It's in my wallet."

"Let me see."

Surprised by his reaction, I pull out my wallet and hand it to him. He examines the card and a small smile forms on his lips. "You kept it."

"Why wouldn't I?"

Aubrey shrugs, seeming a little embarrassed as he hands back my wallet. "I just didn't expect it is all."

Chuckling, I pull him into my arms and kiss his cheeks. "Can we go back to bed now?"

A flush rises up Aubrey's skin, and I ache with how much I love him. We make our way to the bedroom, abandoning our coffees on the nightstand. After we have settled back into bed, with no other intent than to hold each other close, Aubrey asks me a new question.

"What did he look like?"

I smile and feel warmed to my soul. I look into Aubrey's eyes, his head resting on my shoulder and his body tucked up against mine in his bed. I can't resist brushing my lips over his then, when that's not enough, stealing into his mouth with my tongue. He groans against me, snuggling into me deeper, and I sigh as I pull back and smile at him again.

"Hi," I softly murmur.

"Hi," he murmurs back, the corners of his mouth crinkling up.

"Do you want to see a picture?" I ask, surprisingly overjoyed to share this with him.

"I do. Do you have one?"

"I have plenty. I took them off my media pages because I didn't want to share him with anyone else. But I want to share them, share him, with you."

"Really?" His smile widens and becomes beatific, like an angel in a Pre-Raphaelite painting. And suddenly, I want to paint him.

"Would you let me paint you?"

He gasps, his eyes going wide. "You want to paint me?"

I nod, settling myself better on my side so I can pull him closer.

"Yes, I do. It's been two years since I've picked up a brush. You make me want to paint again."

Tears form at the corners of his eyes, and I sip them up, replacing them with kisses, first the right eye, then the left.

"Yes, please, Ian, I would love for you to paint me," he declares in a soft but earnest voice.

"Without you, I'd have no reason to ever paint again," I whisper softly, every word coming from my heart. "I love you, Aubrey, so much." I place my hand over his lips when he tries to return the declaration. "Shhh. I need you to know you are the only one."

He shakes his head a little at that, making me chuckle.

"I know what you are going to say."

At this, his right eyebrow cocks up and his eyes seem to say "Oh, really?," amusement dancing in the clear green depths.

"Yes, really," I intone solemnly. "You want to say I don't need to tell you this. But Aubrey, I really do. I can't let there be the slightest possibility you wonder if I wish Vinny were here with me instead of you."

He pulls my hand away from his mouth. "I would never ask you that."

"I know. That's why I'm making a point of telling you myself. I don't regret anything in my life that brought me to you. I loved Vinny, and I would never diminish that wonder of my life. But Aubrey, with you, I feel even more. More than I thought possible. You're put me back together when I didn't even know I was so broken apart. I've lived an okay life since Vinny died. I managed to stay upright when, at first, I felt like I would have to crawl for the rest of my life. I refocused on my sculptures and my career expanded beyond what I'd imagined possible even a few years ago. But I was shattered inside. I hid it so well I even hid it from myself. I thought a lot about it on the plane ride here. I wondered how I could have been so confused about everything, about myself, about you, about us."

I shake my head before I continue. Aubrey's soft eyes hold mine gently and I gather strength from their warmth.

"His death killed part of me, the circumstances making it even worse. No body to bury, no person to punish, no closure whatsoever, except what we could make ourselves. And I couldn't make any sort of closure. I couldn't kiss his lips goodbye one last time or even see a casket lowered into the ground."

Quiet tears are sliding down my cheeks now, and Aubrey wipes them away. I lean my forehead against his and feel the comfort this gesture always brings me.

"I have closure now. I said goodbye on the plane. Luckily, I managed to book a first-class seat and the flight was practically empty, so only the poor flight attendant noticed my crying. He kept bringing me hot towels and cosmos."

I laugh a wet laugh. "God only knows why he thought I would want those. It sounds ridiculous now, but it really did feel like loving you would kill you. But I misinterpreted the feeling. I was actually afraid I would die again if I loved you and lost you. So I kept hiding it and denying it even as I took everything you offered. Some part of me knew you were right. But I couldn't let go of the fear. You were right to leave me, and I'm just so happy you've taken me back."

Aubrey's eyes are glistening with unshed tears. "Thank you for following me, Ian. I love you so much."

He holds my face, looking into my eyes for the longest time. Then he kisses me gently, almost reverently. "I think we should sleep now," he sighs, amusing me.

"Tired of my voice already, are we?"

He laughs softly, kisses my lips again, and settles his head into the crook of my neck, his right hand on my chest and his left arm slung over my side.

"No, never," he declares. "But it's been an emotionally draining couple of days, wouldn't you say? We have so much to talk about now, and I think we need to snuggle up right here and rest first before we talk about anything else." His breath is evening out, and he falls asleep in my arms. The smile that cracks my face is so wide I think my cheeks might split. I wind my free arm around his waist and he sighs in his sleep. Perfect, I think, as my eyes drift closed, this is my heaven.

CHAPTER 35

We have spent most of the last two days in my bed. When I awaken on the second day after Black stormed into my elevator and kissed me senseless, I have never felt more content in my life. But I'm still worried about Ian. *Ian.* I can call him that now, and I could burst with joy. But I have to make sure he is really okay. I don't want him worried about his security with me or something from the past coming between us again. The only way to ensure that is to make sure he really comes to terms with his trauma. He has to go to therapy to deal with this. I'm snuggled into his arm and smile at how I sound. Nah, a minor in psychology does not a therapist make, but I know I am right about what Black needs. I will just have to convince him of it.

"What's making you smile against my side?" Black had been sleeping. I had no idea he had awakened. And I'm surprised he knew I was awake.

"Really?" I ask, "You knew I was awake because you could feel me smiling against your side?"

"I always know when you're smiling, Aubrey. It's the most important look you ever give me."

My heart melts in my chest. If I weren't already so in love with this man, that statement would do me in.

"I was contemplating your future therapy bills."

A laugh is startled out of him. "Oh, really?"

"Come on, Ian. As helpful as the flight attendant was, you are going to need professional help. Don't even argue with me on that. You won't win."

He laughs and hugs me tighter. "Yes, sir, Mr. Davies."

"I'm glad you see things my way, Mr. Black."

"Can I keep telling you things even though you aren't a licensed therapist?" Black teases me.

"You better believe it. Keep spilling your guts. I think you still have more in there," I quip, poking him in the belly.

"Are you calling me fat?"

I giggle. "Yeah, right. You know you look like a Greek god. Stop stalling, make with more confessions."

"What if I am out of confessions?"

I laugh. "I quite doubt that, Mr. Black."

———

No one else in the world could make this as easy as Aubrey has. I snuggle into him a little more, his head resting on my chest.

"I didn't tell you the whole truth about the morning I left you."

Aubrey laughs and puffs air against my nipple. I squirm a little and say, "Hey, I'm ticklish."

He puffs air against my nipple again, as he laughingly replies, "No shit, Sherlock. It was pretty obvious when you tracked me down at the coffee shop. I knew you were not telling me everything."

I snuggle him closer into my chest. "Of course, you knew," I sigh before continuing. "Up until that point, I had done a rather remarkable job of keeping my despair and fear at bay around you. But it all rushed in on me that morning. You were so happy, and for a split second, I was too. I'm embarrassed to say," I look at him now, "but before the panic started in, I wondered if you had watched me sleep."

274

I feel a blush on my cheeks, but I don't drop my gaze. "I liked the idea. My heart warmed with it for a moment then guilt, shame, and fear hit me hard. By the time you were in the kitchen, I was in a full-blown panic attack."

Aubrey struggles up into a sitting position, pulling me up with him, linking our hands together. We face each other, crossed legged. Aubrey clutches my hands harder, tugging at my arms so I lean forward into his chest. I settle my face against his neck. "I'm sorry," I murmur against his warm, soft skin.

"Why didn't you tell me?"

I laugh, and it's muffled against his neck. "I couldn't."

"But why?"

I sigh. It's one of the few points he's pushed on since we started this overdue and very long conversation two days ago. We may have taken breaks, for food, for a sleep, for sex. But this is one long conversation, and it's far from over yet. Though I've talked for hours now, it seems like we haven't even scratched the surface of what I've kept from him, haven't bridged even half the distance I have kept between myself and him.

"I'm sorry," I breathe against him. Tears run again, hot against my cheek and a sob racks me. I pull back, so I can look Aubrey in the eyes.

"How can you forgive me? I lied to you."

"Ian," he sighs out, and he won't let go of my hands when I try to pull them from his.

"Ian," his tone turns firm, like he's speaking with a wayward teen with whom he has just become *fed up*. "Damn it, Ian." I'm shocked he's cursing.

His eyes turn hard and appear to be glittering in anger. "I love you, Ian. I'm disappointed, but not because you lied to me, you didn't."

When I move to argue, he interrupts, "Shush, Ian, just shush."

"I'm disappointed I didn't have the opportunity to help you. I'm not upset at you, okay? I'm relieved you are telling me now. Every new word that drops from your mouth slides another puzzle piece in place in my mind. I've spent the last six months so afraid I'd never know what was wrong, why you would never tell me. I'm beginning to understand now. But, please baby, you have to stop thinking I'm going to run away. I left because you would not tell me, remember? There is not anything in the world you could tell me right now that would make me leave you. Unless you are a cannibal. Or you're married with three kids and a Rottweiler in Boca Raton. I can forgive just about anything but Rottweilers and cannibalism. Are you a Rottweiler loving cannibal, Ian James Black?"

I'm stunned into laughter. Tears are still streaming down my face, and I'm laughing so hard I can't breathe. I tug my hands from his and pull him into my arms. I kiss his neck, the side of his face. I'm drowning in laughter and tears.

"Don't you get it, Ian?" I can hear the laughter, frustration, and the love that so surprises me in his voice as he speaks directly into my ear.

"No, apparently I don't," I mumble into his neck. I've stopped crying, but I'm suffering from some weird hiccupping sniffles now. Aubrey pulls me back and his eyes hold laughter now, and I'm so happy the anger is gone. He searches my face as if looking for something, some understanding I apparently don't have.

"I. Love. You. You. Idiot." He emphasizes each word slowly and emphatically, but he's laughing by the time he christens me an idiot. "That's not conditional, and I might actually be a little pissed you thought it might be. In fact—"

Grabbing him by the face, I kiss him. Because I can. Because I need to. And, perhaps most importantly, because he seemed ready to be mad at me again and that's the last thing I want. When I pull back, I whisper against his lips, "I believe you, Aubrey."

"Good," he whispers back, "I thought I was going to have to get mean to make you understand me. But," he sighs, causing me to sigh too, "I still don't understand why you never let me know about the panic attacks. Did you have more after that?"

I sigh again, feeling truly exhausted. "Baring your soul is hard work."

Aubrey laughs and pinches me on the inner thigh. "Ow!"

"It's your fault, mister."

"I know, just don't pinch me again."

He purses his lips and pinches me again.

"Hey!"

"Really, answer the question, or I will keep pinching you. I'll even move to the other thigh once I run out of space on this one."

"What was the question again? You distracted me with pain."

He glares at me and before I can react, slaps the same hand onto my other thigh and pinches it.

"Stop it!"

"You stop it! Answer the question. Did you have more panic attacks? I have to know, Ian. It breaks my heart to know what you were going through, that you wouldn't let me share it with you. You have to tell me now."

"I am! Just stop pinching me!" I push his hands off my legs because I don't trust him not to pinch me again. He wants the answers yesterday, and he's clearly not above retaliation when I become reticent about something. And no wonder, after what I put him through.

"The short answer is yes."

He narrows his eyes at me and slaps both hands down on my legs and pinches, even harder this time. When I try to jump back, he holds on to my legs.

"No, no, mister, you aren't going anywhere. Had I known this was such an effective method of torture for you, I would have started pinching your inner thighs months ago."

I can't help but giggle.

"Are you giggling?" He holds up his hand and makes a mock lobster claw with it. "Does this mean nothing to you? Do you like being pinched? Is this a kinky side you've kept hidden from me?"

We're both laughing now, and Aubrey launches himself into me, knocking me onto my back. I wiggle my legs lose, uncrossing them and stretching out flat beneath him. He looks down into my face, quite serious looking now.

"You have to tell me now, Ian. I can't wait. I have to know."

"Yes," I whisper because it's easier to say it this way. "But nothing like the first one. The two days I spent away from you were essentially one long panic attack which started that morning. After almost forty-eight hours, I realized it wasn't going to stop until I came back to you. It started because of fear: of betraying Vincent, of risking myself again, of risking you. But I came to understand only you could make it go away."

Aubrey's face is so serious as he stares down at me. "I won't ever hurt you, not on purpose. You know that, don't you?"

"Yes, I know. Even when you left me, I knew. It was about me hurting you. You had to leave because I wouldn't stop holding myself apart. No matter what you say, Aubrey, it was lying, even if only by omission. And I'm so sorry. I won't stop apologizing until I'm sure you know how much I love you and need you. I don't just want you, I need you. It's a matter of survival now. I need your love and your kindness and your forgiveness."

Aubrey drops his face slowly toward mine, finally touching our lips together and kisses me slowly, softly.

"I know," he responds when he pulls back from my lips. "I forgive you, this and anything else."

"Good," I lean up and he meets me for a second kiss, which turns into seven, eight, nine, ten until we lose track of counting.

CHAPTER 36

Something has been eating at me since our conversation yesterday. And suddenly, I remember what it is. I have to get it off my chest right now even while we are eating lunch in Aubrey's living room with *We Bare Bears* playing softly in the background.

"Fuck, Aubrey, I did lie to you. I'm so sorry. I can't believe I forgot that."

Aubrey looks at me warily. "Is it about Rottweilers?" That beatific grins stretches across his face, and he laughs. "We already talked about this, Ian."

When I shake my head, Aubrey looks concerned. "What did you lie to me about?" His voice is very low, and there's a little hint of sadness to it.

Sighing, I confess again, hoping it is the last time I have to admit to lying to Aubrey ever again. "What I told you about Pride was true, but what I didn't tell you was how important it was to Vinny. I purposely distracted you with a story about my mom because…" Pausing, at a loss as to how to continue, I am fisting my hands in my hair now because I want to get everything out in the open.

Aubrey smiles softly and places his hands on mine in my hair. He gently disentangles them and takes them into his lap. He finishes my thought with something I did tell the truth about. "Because it hurt too much. That's what you said that day, Ian."

I shudder in relief at hearing him say my name again.

He continues, looking me directly in the eye with a soft, caring look on his face. "I knew the statement meant a hell of a lot more than you wanted me to know." He shrugs. "I spent a lot of time thinking about it, what you really meant and what it meant for me, for us."

"I'm sorry I ruined your first Pride parade, Aubrey."

"You didn't."

"But I did. You spent the whole weekend so careful about me, around me. You put a subtle distance between us, and it hurt so badly. Even though I knew it was my fault, it still hurt."

"I'm sorry, I wasn't trying to hurt you." Aubrey sighs. "I wasn't sure we could continue." My heart beat speeds up now as I realize how close I came to losing him even earlier. "You have absolutely no reason to be sorry, Aubrey. That's when I realized that I had to bridge the gap I had created."

I shake my head and drop my eyes from his. "Because I'm an idiot, I still didn't think I could tell you about Vinny. My thoughts then make no sense to me now, but I guess I'd been hiding my feelings, even from myself, for so long, that it never felt like I could tell you."

I laugh at myself and raise my head to meet his eyes. "My fear of feeling that loss again, of processing everything, was too over-whelming for me to deal with."

Lifting our clasped hands, I kiss the back of his hand. "But I had no choice, Aubrey, I had to keep you with me. Benny helped me figure out what I needed to do."

Aubrey laughs softly. "What does Benny have to do with it?"

"He suggested I bring you home to meet him."

"Oh, he did, did he? And how exactly did your fat backyard squirrel 'tell' you to bring me into your home?"

"By chattering and flicking his tail, of course."

Aubrey laughs, and I can't help but kiss his lips. "So I brought you home, and I'm so very glad I did."

"I was very surprised, you know, to receive an invitation to your house. But it did show me how you were trying to be with me. And then I knew I couldn't keep any distance from you unless I wanted to leave."

Aubrey pulls our hands apart and puts my arms around his neck. He removes his plate from his lap, setting it on the coffee table next to my forgotten lunch. He crawls into my lap, his legs on the outside of my thighs and slips his arms around my neck as I slide my hands down to his waist.

He smiles at me again. "So Vinny loved the Pride parade. It's just another thing we have in common." I squeeze Aubrey's waist and kiss his lips.

When we come up for air, I lean our foreheads together. "He liked to help Tilly and her motorcycle club with their float."

A flash of surprise crosses Aubrey's face then he laughs. "Of course, they wouldn't tell me that, would they?"

"I was worried she might, actually."

"What would you have done then?" Aubrey laughs.

"Spilled my guts sooner, I guess."

Aubrey cocks his head to the side and studies me. "Maybe, or you might have run away. It doesn't matter anyway. I know now. Speaking of things I know now, if I'm moving my business to Oakland, I have a hell of a lot of work to do."

"Does that mean you have to go to work tomorrow?" I pull a pouty face, and Aubrey giggles at it.

"Yes, but it shouldn't take more than a few days to close up my office here."

"You have a real office here?"

Laughing, he smacks me on the back of the head. "Of course, I do. I just haven't been there since March."

"But you still paid rent?"

"Yes, but the office is shared with another civil engineer, a guy who designs city water systems. I have to let him know I'm leaving and set up all of my stuff for shipping."

Now that his thoughts are clearly on work, he kisses me one more time before slipping off my lap and going in search of a notepad and pen. When he returns, he proceeds to create a very long to-do list which reminds me of Vinny, and for the first time, I am okay with seeing similarities between the two men who have owned my heart. Aubrey chats at me about what needs to happen, but I am just watching him, completely content to witness his happiness, his drive, his enthusiasm. When he catches me staring, he just smiles. After about half an hour, he has a very long to-do list, and I have a question.

"Are you sure, Aubrey? Do you really want to move to Oakland?"

"Does this move to Oakland involve a move into your bedroom?" Though the question is at least partially serious, he waggles his eyebrows at me suggestively.

"Absolutely." I laugh out. "You better not expect to stay in that hotel suite again. Sorry, but the coffee maker sucked."

"Is that the only reason you want me in your bedroom?"

"Hmm…" I pretend to contemplate it as I lean back on the couch and drift my eyes over Aubrey's form suggestively. "You are awfully sexy. I might have other, more sensual, reasons for inviting you to stay," I pause, "in my bed… with me."

Aubrey cracks up, tossing his notepad and pen on the coffee table and launching himself at me.

"I'll take it!" he announces cheerily before kissing me passionately. We spend the rest of the day wrapped up in each other, and it couldn't be better if I dreamed it.

CHAPTER 37

*I*an meets me at my door with a devilish glint in his eye and that slow smile creeping across his face as soon as he sees mine. I've spent the last two days packing up my office while Ian has puttered around my house, doing God knows what.

"I have something I want us to do," he purrs at me.

I lick my lips in anticipation and his eyes zero in on my mouth.

"Oh, yes," he says, his eyes flicking from my mouth to my eyes, "my plans involve your pretty pink tongue."

He steps back from the doorway and forces me to brush past him since he gives me very little room. His eyes and stance are so dominant I anticipate being eaten right up. And God, will I love it. I walk down the hall, past the bathroom, and veer to the left, toward my bedroom. He is right behind me, his body bare inches behind me. I stop in the doorway and arch back, turning my head, and he doesn't disappoint me. He slides his hard body against mine, his hand coming up to clasp my chin as he holds it steady and takes my mouth.

I am completely owned as he slides his right arm around my body and splays his hand across my chest. His left hand still holds my chin over my left shoulder as his tongue slides in and out of my mouth. He nips at my bottom lip, and I tighten my grip on his left wrist where I have come to rest my right hand. My left is fumbling with my button, trying to free myself from my pants. He pulls back from the kiss and leans forward to look over my shoulder at the hand I have on my waistband.

"Eager, are we?" He drawls, and I laugh huskily in my throat. My head is still turned toward him, and his hand has not moved from my chest. I'm trapped in his arms and my libido is kicking into over drive. He shifts his right leg forward between my legs roughly, and I groan at the sensations running through my body. I love it when he takes control like this.

"Do you have any idea what you do to me, Aubrey?" He growls in my ear and my desire and breathing spike in tandem. His right hand slips from my chest downward, coming to rest on my fumbling one. He moves my hand aside gently and pops the button of my jeans open, grabbing the zipper tab and pulling it down slowly.

His lips touch mine and he growls out, "I had different plans for you, for us, this evening, but then you come home and offer yourself to me like this and I can't resist."

"So don't."

He groans, nipping my bottom lip and holding onto it for several seconds before releasing it. He drops his hand from my chin to my shoulder and begins to turn me in his arms. He starts walking me backward and a thrill rushes through my body.

"I adore when you do that."

"What?" he asks, his voice low and full of sin.

"Walk me backward like you know where we are going and how exactly we are going to get there, and I don't mean directionally."

He laughs low as he takes my face in both of his hands. We have hit the edge of my bed. I start to sink back into it, but he stops me by dropping his hands to my waist. He looks into my eyes as he kisses me again.

"Naked first."

He tugs impatiently at my jeans before stepping back to grab the back of his shirt and pull it off over his head.

"I love it when you do that too," I pant out as my eyes roam over the broad expanse of his chest.

He grins devilishly me. "I know you do."

I swallow hard. I'm so turned on by his dominance I can barely breathe, much less speak.

"Aubrey."

There is a level of command in his voice I have never heard before. And I love it.

"Take off your pants."

I shiver as I put my hands on my waist band and push my pants and boxers down. They pool at my feet, and I step out of them and toward Ian. I kick off my shoes and place my hands on his chest and run my fingers through the light sprinkling of dark hair. He's still clothed in his jeans and those damned combat boots that have thwarted my sexual intentions before. His eyes are so dark, and I feel like I am falling forward into them. His breath is coming harshly, and he brings up his right hand to cradle my face. I take the initiative now, the power in the room seeming to have switched hands, even if just for a moment. I swiftly undo his jeans but drop to my knees before pushing them off his hips. I make quick work of the laced-up boots and he compliantly raises his feet one at a time to let me pull them off. I rise and take hold of his waistband, shoving his jeans and boxers down hard.

He steps forward out of them, pushing me. I drop down on the bed and crawl backward. Our eyes never leave each other's as he follows me down on the bed. I lie back on the comforter and he settles himself on top of me, holding some of his weight on his elbows by my shoulders. Time slows as we stare into each other's eyes. Then Ian drops his hips against mine, rubbing our cocks together, and the insane heat and desire surge again. I cry out at the sensations, and Ian takes my mouth roughly. There is no control anymore on either of our parts. We run our hands all over each other, desperate to join ourselves as one.

"The lube," Ian gasps against my lips.

I curse in frustration. "In the drawer."

Ian leaves me but for a moment, and I want to keen at the loss. Then he is back, raising my legs and resting them on his shoulders as he kneels in front of my groin. I watch his every move as he lubes up his fingers, his eyes never leaving mine as he lightly touches my asshole. "Harder!" I practically scream, and he obliges me by sinking his finger inside me, first one, then two. We are rushed, but the tempo is just right. I'm writhing against him in seconds, raising my hips to capture more of him inside of me. His fingers curl up in a come-hither motion, stroking my prostrate and sending sparks throughout my body.

"Now!" I scream, as the waves build inside of me. He pulls out and with his eyes on mine, uses the leftover lube on his fingers to cover his cock. I'm stroking my own cock slowly, afraid of sending myself over without him. Ian moves forward, pressing his dick slowly inside of me as he settles his weight over me, my legs bending over his shoulders. He thrusts slowly at first, making his way inside me. He settles against his elbows again, leaning over me as I bring up my arms to twine around his neck. He finally bottoms out inside me and his groin settles against my ass. He holds there for a moment, leaning forward and kissing me tenderly.

"I love you so much, Aubrey," he gasps out as he begins thrusting in and out of me slowly.

I can't speak, so I nod my head vigorously, too overcome with emotion to assure him of the same. Our bodies rise and fall, the tempo picking up until we are slamming against each other. I'm clawing at his back, my entire body pulsing, and he pulls out, slams in hard, and holds against me, grinding his hips in circles. I scream his name as I come. He watches me with his dark eyes and the pleasure crashes through me and my cock empties against his muscled stomach. He stiffens in my hold, and I see his own orgasm take him over. His hips jerk against mine as I slide my hands from his neck to cup his face. His neck arches as he comes inside of me, his face a mask of bliss, and I see his heart in his eyes.

"Aubrey," he whimpers as he collapses forward against me. I kiss his face all over, finally capturing his mouth. Many moments later, when our breathing has finally slowed and the intense pleasure has receded to leave behind a warm buzz, he finally pulls from my body. I groan as he pulls out, still so sensitive to the intimate sensations. He kisses my lips gently and brings his hands up to hold my face, mirroring the hold I still have on him. He shifts his hips so I can lower my legs, and I wrap them around the backs of his thighs.

His voice is hoarse as he whispers to me, "You are my home."

Tears falls from my eyes then as I nod. I manage to croak out, "Home." His big, muscled body shudders against mine as he drops his full weight on me, his face nestled into my neck. I slip my hands from his face to wrap my arms around his body tightly. We continue to whisper in each other's ears until sleep takes us over, locked in each other's arms.

CHAPTER 38

I knew seeing Aubrey's aunts would be the final challenge in my quest to win Aubrey back. He would never think or say so, but as close as he is with these ladies, I know I have to make a better impression than the last one. Assuming Aubrey told them about our breakup. I turn in the passenger seat and stare at his profile. He immediately senses I am watching him and a smirk tugs at the corners of his mouth.

"What?" he laughingly asks without taking his eyes off the road.

"Did you tell your Aunts about leaving me? Are they going to hate me now? I don't want to mess this up, Aubrey. What if they don't like me?"

Aubrey laughs softly and pulls a sad puppy dog face at me. "Aww, you are so sweet."

"Aubrey," I almost growl now. "What did you tell them?"

He fully smirks then as he slides his gaze toward me. I laugh. "Now you are giving me side-eye. I should be worried, shouldn't I? Damn it, and this was all going so well," I whine as I throw my head back against the headrest. Aubrey practically cackles.

He glances at my expression and laughs harder. "Stop it or I won't be able to drive."

"What did you tell them?" I whine again. Suddenly I am enjoying my petulant child act, and I stick my lips out in an exaggerated pout.

"Nothing, actually. Until this morning when Patty called, I hadn't even told them I was in town."

I'm surprised to hear this. "Why?"

Aubrey sighs out a little laugh, "Because I didn't want to talk about it. And they would make me talk about it."

"So they didn't know you were coming home?"

This elicits a surprisingly sharp glance from Aubrey. "Just so we are clear," he states, his voice taking on a hard edge, "you are my home. Chicago was only ever the place I grew up. Besides Patty and Susan, I have nothing here."

The vehemence in his voice surprises me. I sit up straighter in my seat and once again angle my body toward his.

"Something happened."

Aubrey sighs. "No, not really. I wasn't happy here anymore. That's why I made the bid for Oakland in the first place."

"Why weren't you happy?"

"Weren't we supposed to be talking strategy on how to make my Aunts like you?"

"Nope, this is more important."

Aubrey's face shifts into a tremulous smile, and he paraphrases something I told him on our first date, "You sure are something, Black."

I purposely smirk and twitch my brows up at him. "And don't you forget it." Allowing silence for a beat, I continue, "Spill your guts. What happened?"

Aubrey laughs softly and shakes his head. "I'm not going to get out of this, am I?"

It's my turn to chuckle. "Considering how many revelations you have dragged out of me in the last few days, no. You will not get out of this. Like I just said, spill it."

He laughs softly again, then gives me an annoyed look before turning his gaze back to the road. "Fine. What do you want to know?"

"Argh! You are so frustrating."

"Turn about is fair play, mister."

"So, it's my fault you won't tell me why Chicago no longer felt like home?"

"Well, it's only fair that I make you work a little for it. You know, considering."

"What happened to the Aubrey who called himself, 'easy, very, very easy'?"

Sunshine, Aubrey turns to look me straight in the face and gives me his sunshine smile. The desires to cry with happiness or kiss him to death war inside of me momentarily. I settle for leaning over and pecking him softly on the check.

"Come on, Aubrey," I purposely puff my whisper against his ear. "Spill it."

Aubrey groans and a slight blush creeps up his neck and across his face. "No fair using your sex appeal to coerce confessions out of me."

I slouch back into my seat. "Aubrey," I say his name in a demanding tone.

He pretend shivers and wiggles his shoulders. "Oh, I do love it when you get all dominant on me."

I grin and wait in silence for whatever confession has him so reluctant to share. Aubrey is never reluctant to share how he feels. Though, I realize, maybe I just never noticed before.

"Aubrey, what happened?"

He sighs again. "Not much really. I couldn't seem to find my place here. Sure, my business is doing well, growing, gaining a good reputation. But, my personal life? Ha!" He laughs sarcastically. "There hasn't been one to speak of for a while."

"Why is that?"

"Building my company meant more to me than getting off. Besides, every time I tried, I ended up meeting assholes who wanted me to tone myself down or boring, country club types who wanted to impress me with tickets to the opera. Don't get me wrong, the opera is just fine. But there are more options for entertainment than that."

"What about the assholes?"

Aubrey throws an amused glance my way as we exit off the freeway. "More of the same, but they wanted to show me the backseats of their luxury cars as soon as we met."

Laughing, I point out the obvious. "I seem to recall someone introducing me to the backseat of their rental car pretty early in our relationship."

Aubrey laughs then blushes, and god, do I love it. I groan. "Stop blushing, sexy, or we'll have to pull off into some alley to make out."

Aubrey laughs and winks at me. Then I remember something else Aubrey indicated about his dating life in Chicago.

"I thought your aunts liked to hook you up with delivery men."

Aubrey laughs loudly. "No. I never took any of those numbers. The whole thing was just too creepy. What would I say if I called them? Hey, my aunt hit on you for me, I'm a cool guy, let's go have coffee?"

I'm laughing too hard to breathe for a moment. When I have recovered, I acknowledge, "That's a fair point. But are those the only reasons?"

Aubrey sighs and rolls his eyes at me. "I was bored here. As I said, my dating life was dead."

Something from his previous description clicks in my head and I sit up straighter in my seat. "Besides the fact I was an unforgivable ass, that is why you were so upset when I turned down Tilly's invitation to help with The Sirens' float."

Aubrey stiffens then nods. Keeping his eyes on the road, his fingers tighten on the wheel. I touch his arm lightly and he glances over quickly with a soft, shy smile. Clearing his throat, he says in an apologetic tone, "I may have overreacted a little bit. It reminded me of those assholes who found my personality too big. So, when you said no after already agreeing to go to the parade with me," Aubrey pauses blowing out a breath. "I felt rejected again. Since you had always encouraged me to be myself, I was confused and hurt."

Turning his luminous green eyes toward me again, he murmurs, "I'm sorry."

Patting his hand, I smile softly. "Not necessary. I'm sorry, Aubrey. I won't ever make you feel that way again, I promise, at least not ever on purpose."

A calm, comforting silence settles over us until I think of another question. "How did you end up in Oakland?"

"I was traveling most of the time for jobs anyway, even when I didn't have to actually be in whatever city I was working for most of the time. I thought I should check out life in a new place."

I sit up a little straighter at that. "Did you have to come to Oakland?"

"Nope, but the whole 'tired of my life here' feeling is what compelled me to go for the bid in the first place." He turns to me then, smiling his sunshine smile at me. "I'm very glad I did."

"Me, too, Aubrey. I'm so very glad you did."

If I thought I knew what Aubrey's aunts would be like, I was sorely mistaken. While Aubrey had told me a few stories about them, it was the difference between reading a synopsis and seeing the film. No wonder where Aubrey inherited his joyful personality and sense of humor. Within minutes of meeting them, I could already feel the love and joy the two ladies shared and imparted to their nephew. A short, dark-haired woman with a choppy bob flung open the blue door as soon as Aubrey's knuckles touched the wood.

"Aubrey!" she screeched then turned her head to yell over her shoulder, "Patty! He's here! And he brought company!"

While she grabs Aubrey in a bear hug, a taller, blonde woman with sparkling blue eyes comes to the door with a dish towel in her hand. Throwing the towel over her shoulder, she extends her hand toward me with a warm smile that reminds me of Aubrey's.

"Hello! It is so nice to meet you. It is Black, isn't it?"

Aubrey stiffens in his other aunt's arms and glances my way with a look that says he is at a loss as to how to introduce me. We haven't discussed it, but the choice is easy, just like it was once before.

Smiling, I take Patty's outstretched hand. "Please, do call me Ian."

The other aunt, whom I have deduced is Susan, has finally released

Aubrey. She makes a squee noise at my introduction and tackle hugs me, almost knocking Patty off balance.

"Susan!" Patty admonishes, but with a grin, and Aubrey laughs.

"Come in! Come in!" Patty invites as Susan finally releases me, patting my chest once and murmuring to herself, "Nice, very nice."

Aubrey groans and puts his arm around my waist. "I promise they are *always* like this."

Ducking down to his ear, I whisper in it as we cross the threshold. "I love it."

Chuckling, he shakes his head at me.

"Hurry up, you two!" Patty calls from inside the kitchen, which is to the right of the entryway. "I have fresh cookies waiting for you."

"You didn't have to go out of your way, Aunt Patty."

"No problem," she replies, waving us into the homey kitchen area. Gesturing toward the kitchen table to the right, she continues, "Sit. Susan is grabbing coffee mugs. Then we can all sit and chat."

"More like interrogate," Aubrey whispers in my ear, and I laugh.

"Tsk, tsk, Aubrey, I heard that," Susan responds, chuckling.

Once we are settled at the table with coffee and cookies, Aubrey's aunts sitting across from us, I feel a nervous anxiety descend on me.

Patty must sense this as she gives Susan a "behave yourself" sort of look before passing me a cookie on a dessert plate. "It is so wonderful to meet you, Ian. We were surprised to find out both of you were in Chicago." At that, she gives Aubrey a pointed glance. "Someone didn't mention he was coming."

Aubrey laughs, "It was sort of last minute."

"And why is that, Aubrey?" Susan practically purrs.

Suddenly, I realize we are woefully underprepared for this meeting, or at least I am. My foot is tapping involuntarily, and I feel Aubrey's warm palm on my thigh which calms me immediately. He smiles at me warmly, and the ice forming in my veins melts away. Returning his smile, I answer Susan's question with at least part of the truth.

"Aubrey has decided to move his office to Oakland." My eyes don't leave Aubrey's face, and I am rewarded with a sunshine smile.

"Oh, really?"

Huffing out a breath, Aubrey shakes his head. "Yes, aunties, I am moving to Oakland to be with Ian."

I can't help twining my fingers with the hand he has on my leg, raising it to kiss the back of his hand.

"That seems sudden," Susan replies, a glint of challenge in her eyes. I would have expected Patty, his biological aunt, to be the tough sell, but apparently, I was wrong. While Patty has a soft, comforting, motherly presence, Susan is like an eagle, with sharp eyes and even sharper talons with which to defend her family. I can feel the annoyance gathering in Aubrey; he is practically vibrating with it.

"Susan," Aubrey sharply responds, clearly ready to defend me and our relationship. From their reactions, I know Aubrey has shared at least some of our ups and downs over the last few months.

"It's fine, Aubrey," I assure him. "It's not like I don't have some explaining to do." Instead of reassuring him, that makes him even more annoyed.

"No, Ian. it is our private business," he turns to face his aunts, "and I quite resent the intrusion."

I can't help laughing which draws three glances of surprise my way. "I love you," I declare to Aubrey before kissing him lightly. "But it is just fine, Aubrey."

Aubrey huffs, clearly still annoyed. I clear my throat and look at Patty because Susan scares me a little bit if I am being honest about it.

"Aubrey is in Chicago because he left me. It was my fault." I pause considering how to succinctly tell his aunts what it took me three days to tell him. "My previous boyfriend, Vinny, died suddenly almost two years ago. To say it was devastating would be quite the understatement. I closed myself off to anything and everyone for a long time." Again, I pause and look at Aubrey's sweet smile. "When I met Aubrey, I just couldn't reconcile how hard I was falling for him with the pain I still feel over Vinny's death. So, I refused to tell him anything about it. But problems kept creeping up because of the distance I tried to maintain. Last week, we had a fight over everything

I was holding back. Aubrey was right to leave. I'm just glad he took me back when I followed him."

Susan clasps her chest dramatically, saying, "So romantic," causing the rest of us to laugh.

"No, not really. More painful than romantic I have to say," I respond dryly.

Patty reaches across the table and pats the hand I have on it. "I'm glad the two of you could work it out. I guess that means we will have to plan a visit soon."

Susan picks up her mug and winks at me over it. "Beach trip!"

All laughing now, we fall into an easy conversation until Patty asks Aubrey if there is anything he needs from his old room. When he goes upstairs to see what he has left here, Patty turns into the interrogator.

"You seem nice, Ian. But you better not hurt Aubrey again."

I can't help laughing. "I don't intend to, Patty."

"Aunt Patty," she corrects me.

Nodding my head, I decide to explain how important Aubrey is to me. "Aubrey brought me back to life. It's as if God hit me with defibrillator paddles the second I laid eyes on him. I was dead, and he has slowly awakened every part of me. But that initial jolt, when I saw him blowing on his coffee, consumed with his papers and work, was like nothing I had ever experienced before. It made me forget, at least for the moment, that I had reasons to hold myself back." I blow out a breath to calm my nerves. Patty smiles at me and a twinge of pain and guilt flutters through my chest. She reminds me of Gloria and my own mom.

"I didn't really stand a chance of not falling in love with him. I'm just lucky he finds something worthwhile in me."

It is Susan's turn to reach out to me. She pats my hand then slides me another cookie from the plate at the center of the table. Sitting here with Aubrey's wonderful aunts, I realize just how much I miss Gloria, and just how unfair I have been to her.

"I need to apologize to Vinny's mom."

I didn't realize I said this out loud until Patty softly asks, "Why is that?"

I blink at her for a moment. "I cut myself out of her life. I couldn't stand to be around any of Vinny's family. I know it was selfish and ultimately self-harming, but I couldn't stand their love and care. It felt wrong. My skin felt like it was on fire every time Gloria told me it wasn't my fault, that Vinny loved me, that she loved me."

Aubrey returns to the kitchen then and it's clear from his shining eyes he has overheard everything I've told his aunts. He sits down beside me and takes my hand from where I was resting it on my thigh. With his other hand, he brushes a lock of my hair back behind my ear.

Susan clearly wants more of the story though. "How did you know to follow him to Chicago?"

"He made it pretty clear he was coming back here if I didn't tell him everything."

Aubrey settles in his chair again, setting the box he was carrying on the floor. "I was wondering about that. How did you get to Chicago so fast? I had an open-ended ticket, so I was able to catch the next flight out when a seat opened up."

"As soon as I recovered enough from my own stupidity and fear, I tried to call your hotel room. It bounced back to the concierge who said you checked out and said you were going home. I checked the airlines, and everything was sold out. I knew I couldn't make it to the airport before the last flight of the night left. I thought you might be on the morning one."

Thinking about it a moment, I realize the chance Aubrey took on there being an open seat. "You were going to wait all night at the airport if you didn't catch that flight?"

"I knew if I stayed, I would go back to your house, and I couldn't do that when you wouldn't tell me the truth."

"I'm sorry, Aubrey."

"Shhhh, no more of that."

Surprisingly, I am not at all embarrassed we are having such an intimate conversation in front of his aunts. Though I am sure I blush a little when I see them both favoring us with approving looks.

"So," Susan drawls, throwing a side glance at Patty. "Does he get mad at you often?"

I'm surprised by the question, and it seems a little suspicious. Aubrey shrugs his shoulders, clearly used to his aunts' style of conversation. Despite thinking it is a weird segue of conversation, I answer anyway.

"Ugh, it's happened a few times. But like I said, it was my fault."

Susan and Patty laugh, eyeing each other conspiratorially. Susan leans over, lowering her voice, "Has he pinched you yet?"

I blush, and both of his aunts dissolve into a fit of giggles.

Patty remarks, "Susan, don't you dare ask where." Overcome as I am with embarrassment, I laugh too.

Looking at Aubrey, I notice a blush, indicating he is a bit embarrassed by this line of questioning. Always on board with teasing Aubrey into a blush, I watch his face as I ask, "Did he pinch everyone?"

"Oh, no, no, no." Patty laughs. "That punishment was reserved for when his closest friends misbehaved, which usually meant they did something Aubrey didn't like."

Aubrey is blushing hard now and glaring at both of them. He seems too flustered to defend himself, so he takes another sip of coffee.

Susan's eyes flash, a naughty twinkle to her eye, "Does he pinch you a lot?" She eyes me appreciatively and murmurs, "You look like you get into lots of trouble."

Finally shaken out of his embarrassment induced silence, Aubrey almost chokes on his coffee. "Oh my God, Aunt Susan! You *are not* flirting with my boyfriend!"

We are all laughing now at Aubrey's disgruntled face. Then he dissolves into laughter too.

"You did though," I say to Aubrey, "you've pinched me a lot."

"Once! I pinched you *once* and you deserved it."

"No, you pinched me many, many times. At least twelve!"

Aubrey huffs and narrows his eyes at me. "Only if you count them individually. I pinched you on *one* occasion." Then he grins, "On *one* occasion, multiple times."

We all laugh, and the conversation becomes easy and relaxed. Aubrey's aunts are warm and friendly. They insist on making us lunch, and we hang out with them well into the evening. When we leave, I make sure his aunts know they are welcome to visit us anytime. As we drive back to Aubrey's apartment, I slouch in the passenger seat and watch him in the fading light of the sunset. As always, I am struck, awed by his beauty.

He notices me watching him and twitches his lips. "What?"

"I love you, Aubrey. I'm glad you are coming home with me."

Aubrey grabs my hand, kissing the back of it quickly before returning his attention to the road. "I love you too, Ian."

Settling into the passenger side, I think about the future. And, for the first time in a very long time, I feel like everything will work out. As long as I have Aubrey by my side, I can face anything.

CHAPTER 39

A few more days of packing, delegating, planning, and general move preparation slide by before we can catch a flight back to Oakland. Ian is in no hurry, this being the first moment of vacation he has allowed himself since before Vinny died. While I packed up my office, said goodbye to my only officemate, and put all the moving preparations in place, Ian browsed the Newberry Library and several museums, including the National Museum of Mexican Art and the Chicago History Museum. He even managed to talk me into a weekend trip to the Rock 'n' Roll Hall of Fame in Cleveland. While he claimed that all of these tours gave him new inspiration for art, I suspect he wanted to go to Cleveland for the exhibits on Aerosmith and the Class of 2018 exhibit featuring Nina Simone. No wonder he wasn't too fond of my not so well-hidden appreciation of boy bands from my youth.

Now, bright and early, we are finally at the airport waiting for our flight to Oakland, browsing the shops and considering where to grab a bite to eat before take-off. Ian points out one restaurant, and it makes me smile.

Winking at me, he directs my attention to a Teppanyaki style restaurant and sushi shop. "I thought I might find you working at one of those, Ice Bear."

Laughing, I shake my head. "No, I would poison too many people."

Our flight is uneventful, though Ian playfully laments that no one brings him cosmos since he is not crying this time around.

"Did you actually drink those?"

"God, no." He laughs, turning to wink at me as I slide my seat belt off once the "Fasten Seatbelt" sign turned off. "I gave them to the guy across the aisle from me in payment for having to listen to me cry." A blush creeps up his cheeks, and he rubs the back of his neck in another show of embarrassment. "Not my finest moment."

Taking his hand, I kiss the back and shake my head. "I respectfully disagree."

"Oh, really? And why is that?"

Shrugging, I lean back in my seat and smile at him. "You had to be willing to let go of all that before you could move forward. You just picked an oddly public way of doing it."

He laughs, and our flight passes without any crying or cosmo-related incidents.

Having caught a morning flight, we arrive in Oakland in the afternoon. Ian seems very excited to welcome me into his home; he has not stopped beaming since the flight touched down at the airport. When we reach his door, he opens it with a flourish and waves me inside.

"Gentlemen first." Giggling, I step into his entryway and the whole place feels different because it is my home now too. Once he sets down my bags, I grab his shoulders and haul him forward for a kiss.

"Welcome home, Aubrey," he murmurs against my lips. "I'm so glad you're here."

"So am I."

After some lunch, Ian and I settle in the living room to relax. But he seems to have something else on his mind as he rifles through his bookshelves in the corner of the room after motioning for me to sit on the couch.

"What are you looking for, honey?"

Grinning, he finally locates the book he wants which turns out to be a leather-bound photo album.

With a shy expression on his face, Ian comes to the couch and sits next to me. Opening the album, he sets it on my lap.

"You asked what Vinny looked like. After the police declared his case cold, I printed these photos out and put them in here. I couldn't risk losing the digital copies. I had to have physical ones, I guess in some way to replace his physical body."

I'm overwhelmed by the trust Ian is showing me, how he keeps opening his heart, inviting me inside. Blinking away tears, I give him a small smile.

"Will you show them to me? Tell me what they mean?"

His shy smile spreads and he lets out a breath, as if he had been afraid to offer. "Of course."

We settle in on Ian's couch, the large album open across my lap, and he tells me more of the story of Vinny and their life together. As we flip through the pages and photos, Ian relaxes more, pointing out details in the photos, regaling me with funny stories and heartfelt recollections.

Later that night, as we lie in bed, Ian snuggles his face into the crook of my neck, kisses my pulse, and murmurs, "Thank you, Aubrey. I needed to share him more than I thought. I'm just so happy I can share him with you."

CHAPTER 40

*L*uckily for us, the park opening was delayed a week, so Aubrey and I did not miss the unveiling of my sculpture. There is a little surprise for Aubrey on it, and I am excited to see his reaction. The mayor and the entire Oakland City Council are involved in the presentation, so the whole event is longer and features more speeches than are necessary for the occasion. I am not so patiently waiting for the whole shebang to move along, and of course, Aubrey notices.

"Are you okay?"

Smiling, I take his hand in mine and sigh. "Yeah, just ready to get this dog and pony show on the road."

"Ponies? I thought you didn't sculpt ponies anymore," he teases me.

Laughing, I squeeze his hand tighter. "I'm excited to show you the finished product."

Aubrey tilts his head to look at me thoughtfully. "I didn't do the final check-in, did I?"

"Nope, so it will be a surprise."

Shrugging, he leans against my arm as we not so patiently wait for the introductions, explanations, and congratulations speeches to end.

"Finally, without further ado, I would like to reveal this fine native plant statue done by local artist Ian James Black. Mr. Black, would you like to do the honors?"

Aubrey looks surprised, and I can't help but grin. After letting go of his hand, I walk over to the statue's base where a sheet connected to a rope pulley covers the piece. Turning to face the crowd, but with eyes only for Aubrey, I introduce my work.

"This is a special piece for me, representing new growth, new life, and, of course, my love of the natural world. This piece could not have been completed without the support of my friends and family, and, most importantly, my boyfriend, Aubrey." When I gesture toward him, Aubrey blushes bright crimson though he also throws that sunshine smile my way. "So as the mayor said, without further ado, I give you "Aubrey's Aloe."

A single yank of the rope cord sends the sheet falling to the ground. The crowd claps, murmuring in appreciation, I hope, but I have eyes only for Aubrey. He ducks his head slightly, waiting for the city council members and the mayor to shake hands with me. When they have stepped away to admire the features Aubrey painstakingly planned and brought together, he walks forward into my arms, and leans his head against my collarbone.

"You named it after me?" he whispers, then glances up at me through the shadow of his eyelashes. His emotions shine so brightly in his eyes and across his face.

"Do you like it?" I murmur back, though by the look on his face, I am sure he does.

Laughing and tilting his head back to look me in the eye, he says, "Yes, I love it."

Taking his hand, I lead him around the park he designed. As he points out the fountain, the walking paths, the new plants and trees, I listen to the joy in his voice, watch the sparkle in his eyes, and drink in his enthusiasm and love for his work. People come up to us, congratulating me on the sculpture. Few know Aubrey's role in designing the park, so I make a point of highlighting it. He blushes a few more times, but when people ask about the details, his confidence and pride shine through. Sunlight highlights his hair, casting a halo around him, and I can't believe I get to keep him as mine.

Relocating a business halfway across the country has turned out to be an even bigger hassle than I imagined. Update this certification, file that request, find a permanent office space. Ian did offer me one of the rooms in his house, but I need a public space for meetings. I recall Ian's declaration when he made the offer, "It is our house now." I smile faintly, my heart overflowing with happiness as I pull my keys out of my pants pocket. The door opens in front of me and Ian fills up the space of the doorway, leaning against the door jamb and crossing his arms over his chest.

"You're late."

"Nice to see you too," I quip as I give him a quick peck on the lips. "Move," I admonish when he seems set on standing in my way. If I didn't have my briefcase in one hand and an armload of papers clutched to my chest, I would have shoved him out of the way. "I want inside. I need some wine and water, lots of water. It is humid as fuck here. I think I lost five gallons by sweating today. I'm gonna dehydrate on the doorstep." I'm starting to whine now, and he looks ridiculously amused.

"Do come inside and have some water. I have a surprise for you."

"Water and wine, first. Don't forget the wine," I reply as he shoves off the doorframe, and I follow him inside of the house.

"God forbid I forget the wine."

"No, I forbid you forget the wine."

He chuckles as we arrive in the kitchen. He takes my briefcase away from me first, laying it on the island.

"Sit down," he nods at the bar stools along the island, "I'll fetch you that wine."

"Thank heavens." I lay my papers on tops of my briefcase before sitting on the stool.

He laughs as he pulls a bottle of red from the countertop wine rack. "No, thank me."

I grin at that and say in my sweetest voice, "Thank you, Sir Reginald."

He throws a grin back at me over his shoulder as he uncorks the bottle. "You are welcome, dear Renaldo."

"Did I hear you say something about a surprise?" I query as he fills a wine glass for me.

He brings the glass to me and hands it over, "Yes, I do have a surprise for you in the living room." He turns away and retrieves a cold bottle of water from the refrigerator for me as well. I'm sipping my wine already, but he puts the bottle in front of me and says, "You have to drink this first before you can have it." I sigh melodramatically and set down the glass of wine in favor of the bottle of water. I purposely hold his gaze as I drink the bottle down. He is watching my throat as I swallow and just the lustful look in his eyes is turning me on. I set the empty bottle on the counter when I am finished and raise my eyebrows at him.

"All done. Now do I get my surprise?" He leans over the edge of the counter and kisses me gently on the lips.

"Yes," he breathes against my mouth, "yes, you do."

He pulls back and snags my right hand to pull me from the bar stool. I grab my wine glass up as he directs me toward the living room. "You have to sit and close your eyes," he murmurs as he stops at the edge of the room. I dutifully close my eyes and sigh, not because I'm pretending to be put upon, but because I'm happy to be home, to be home with Ian. He leads me around to the couch and settles me on the cushions. He takes the wine glass from my hand, and I hear him set it on the coffee table. He moves away, and I hear something electronic turn on with a little whine.

"You can open your eyes now."

I blink my eyes and discover Ian standing in front of the fireplace holding a microphone in one hand with one hand behind his back. A karaoke machine sits on the brick step in front of the fireplace grate. If anyone could pull off looking very proud of himself and just a little bit embarrassed at the same time, Ian has pulled off this look perfectly. He grins a little sheepishly before leaning over to hit the play button on the machine. He rises back to standing and shakes his shoulders a little which causes his black hair to sway around his face. I can't believe he's going to sing to me, but I have to admit he looks quite a bit like a rock god at this precise moment. I'm smiling so widely I'm sure my cheeks couldn't stretch farther, but when I hear the first strains of the song, my smile grows even wider, and I can't help but start laughing.

It's Cher's "If I Could Turn Back Time," and at the first words, his face turns from sheepish to sexily playful. He sings along with Cher, gesturing wildly with the lyrics, melodramatically acting out both his apology and hers; I'm laugh-crying within a few words. His stance is loose, and he sways to the music. I couldn't have imagined him like this before, the moment burning into my memory to forever encapsulate what and who this man truly is. After the first verse and chorus, he moves his hand from behind his back to reveal a second microphone. He tips it toward me, and I jump up to take it. Then we are singing wildly with abandon. I'm still half laughing, half crying, but by the time we sing the last refrain, I'm just singing, pouring myself into the words. As the music stops, Ian leans over toward me, and I tip my head up to kiss his waiting lips.

"I love you, Aubrey," he whispers between kisses.

I throw my arms around him and I'm smiling so hard now my face hurts, but I don't care. "That was some surprise, Ian. Thank you. I love you too." He sighs as his arms come around me to pull me close.

"You surprise me every single day, Aubrey," Ian responds with a soft smile on his lips. "I just have to keep up with you."

The moment is perfect, and I couldn't ask for more.

CHAPTER 41

$\mathcal{A}$fter a long day of welding on my next sculpture, a ten-foot-tall flowering saguaro, I am ready to come home and kiss Aubrey's pretty face. As I stride up the walkway, I notice the smell of popcorn and the sounds of laughter coming from inside of my house. Did Aubrey throw a surprise party? For what? My birthday is February. The weather hasn't even turned to fall even though we are well into October. Maybe an early Halloween party? Surely he would have mentioned that to me. Shrugging, I open my door and almost smack someone with it.

"Sorry," I call out to whomever is standing right behind my front door.

A cackling laugh greets my ear as Mrs. Watson pops out from behind the door.

"Black! Finally, you're home!"

"Mrs. Watson, what's up?"

I notice her leaning on a walker and worry spikes through me. "Are you okay? Did you hurt yourself?"

She waves my concern off. "Nope! Aubrey told me to come over for some Heath Ledger movie marathon. He insisted I bring a walker.

I had to borrow one from my *older* sister. I'm too young for that jazz, you know. Seventy-five and fit as a fiddle. Come on, feel my biceps."

She holds her right arm out toward me, making a muscle. Touching it with my finger, I have to admit it is impressive. "Wow, Mrs. Watson, remind me to never to meet you in a dark alley."

Satisfied that she's proven her prowess to me, Mrs. Watson waves me toward the kitchen. "Your man is in there. You ought to go see what he's up to."

Following her advice, I turn into the kitchen to find a crowd of people. My neighbors, Ron and Lisa are showing off baby Sarah to Kirsten and Tilly, who are cooing at the toddler and trying to tickle the socked feet she keeps kicking out.

Aubrey stands by the counter, scooping popcorn into paper bags, which he then hands to our guests. When he looks up, he catches my eye and sends me a sunshine smile.

"Oh, great! You are home. You can finish setting up the projector in the living room."

"What's going on?"

"I'm creating your scenario for you. Don't you remember what you said you would tell me while we were getting popcorn at the Heath Ledger movie marathon?"

I laugh and shake my head at him, wondering why I'm surprised he would do this.

"You are certainly a keeper," I tell him.

"Thank you! I went for authenticity to your idea. We have couples with children," he says, as he gestures toward my neighbors and their toddler. "And Mrs. Watson is here with a walker. Kirsten and Tilly love popcorn, so they had to come along. The more the merrier I say."

"The walker is borrowed," I point out as I decide to play the contrarian.

"It doesn't matter," he replies breathily, waving his hand as if to wave away my objection. "You didn't say the walker had to be hers."

He puts the last scoop of popcorn into a real movie theatre bag, drops the scoop back into the machine, shuts the door, and hands me the bag.

"Where did you get all of this from?"

"Later," he replies, "stop stalling."

"Stalling about what?" I ask as I purposely delay his satisfaction.

Aubrey links his free arm through mine and pretends to look at an imaginary concession stand board near the ceiling.

"Yes," he tells the imaginary clerk, "I think the popcorn is all we need."

Our friends have stopped milling around and are giving us their full attention. Even the baby looks at us expectantly.

"Mr. Ian James Black," Aubrey addresses me formally and loudly enough for our guests to hear, "When did you first know you loved me?"

I smile at his beautiful face and say without hesitation, "The first time I saw you, sitting alone at that table in the coffee shop. I thought I'd never seen a more beautiful man, and I must make him mine."

Our captive audience "oohs" and "ahhs," and Aubrey kisses me, then whispers in my ear. "I know you just lied."

I turn my head to whisper in his ear. "Well, I couldn't very well say the first time you called my dick "Reginald's quivering member," now could I?"

He blushes furiously then laughs, dropping his face to my neck and hiding. I drop a kiss on his head and hear him grumble into my skin, "I'm gonna get you for that."

"Tell me later," I quickly say as our guests begin to demand the return of our attention. "Yes, Sir Reginald," he whispers, raising his head to look into my eyes. "Make sure you have that 'quivering member' ready."

"Oh, don't worry, he's always quivering for you."

BONUS DELETED SCENE

{THIS WAS THE ORIGINAL OPENING}

The first thing I plan to do this morning, just like every morning, is check my to-do list. I roll out of my bed, throw the covers back off my naked body, and rise to stretch my hands far above my head.

"Arck!" I make a very unattractive moose-like noise as I look out my window at the sunny day outside. Some people think artists are flighty, and I have certainly cultivated that image in the last few years, with the public at least. Give the people what they want, I think. Give them what they expect, and they will love you for it. But in reality, I've always been a planner, through and through, in all aspects of my life, from my sculptures to my daily trips to my local coffee shop. Even my dating life is planned out. *Okay, dude, stop lying to yourself. You haven't had an actual date since...*

Sucking in a deep, painful breath, I banish the thought from my head, locking the memories away in a dark corner of my mind. Wishing for the billionth time, at least, I could wash those memories out of my mind, like washing paint out of my work clothes.

Not that you paint anymore more. Not since...

"Damn it!" I accidentally yell out loud, startling myself and scaring away the fat gray squirrel that had been sitting on my outside window ledge.

"Sorry, Benny!" I call out after the fluffy, fleeing miscreant, but it is too late. He took off like his tail was on fire. His is probably up a tree a block away by now. Great, he won't come back for days, I grouse internally. Is that damn squirrel my only friend?

"Fuck! Why am I so morose today? Coffee, I clearly need coffee."

I glance at my night stand, expecting to see my daily to-do list, but it is not there. Bending over, and not caring that my ass could be clearly seen from the window if anyone did happen to be in the woods behind my house, I feel the unwelcome rush of blood to my head as I look under my bed. "There it is!" I shout in victory as I practically jump back to standing. "My life is not ruined by the lack of my list!" Then, I'm embarrassed by my own ridiculousness and my own addiction to having a plan for everything.

You weren't always this anal retentive, my brain reminds me, *you used to be spontaneous. You used to be a free spirit. Sure, you liked a good five-year plan, but there had been room for play, for other people, for sex with people who matter, for happiness.*

I try to shake the thoughts physically from my head. "Argh!" God, I am full of too many painful thoughts and too many weird noises this morning. I take the list in my hand as I stretch my back again, flexing my muscles loose in preparation for the day ahead. Good thing I don't have any backdoor neighbors, or I'd end up in jail for indecent exposure for sure.

As I walk into my bathroom, I peruse the list, my eyes stopping on the first item:

9 a.m. Coffee meeting at the café with Park Planner, Aubrey Davies.

"Shit, is that meeting today?" Great, just great. No grousing, I remind myself. New work is new work. Maybe I can convince them to go with a native plant sculpture this time, not a stupid cowboy on a horse. I shudder at the memory as I drop the list on my bathroom counter and turn to get the shower going.

"Hell yeah," I declare, pumping myself up for the day. "Native plants all the way, baby." I chuckle at my own ridiculousness, immediately quashing my sudden wish that I had someone to share this silliness with. "No time for day dreams now, Black. We have work to do." I nod my head as I step into the shower, the hot water a welcome shock to my system. Yeah, today is gonna be a good day, I try to convince myself. Grabbing my shampoo bottle, I start to plan how I'm going to accomplish my goals.

ABOUT THE AUTHOR

Drea Roman is an over-educated lady with cats, ferrets, lizards, a fiancé, a sister, and a wonderful village of like-minded friends, authors, and artists. There are two things in this world that make me feel authentically myself: dance and writing. I feel so blessed to have begun this writing adventure. *Loving Him* is book 1 in the Hearts Intertwined Series. Book 2, all fingers and toes crossed, will publish in 2019. A novella, *Saving Him*, is book 1.5 in the series. It will be available in early 2019. Writing plans for the new year also include two omegaverse/mpreg series. All of this coupled with too many day jobs makes Drea a ridiculously busy woman.

Connect with me!
I can be found on Facebook, Twitter, and Instagram under Drea Roman. Join my FB reader group, Drea's Dirty Divas, for special stories and reading opportunities.

Sign up for my newsletter for updates and exclusive story snippets.
http://bit.ly/DreaRomanNewsletter

www.ingramcontent.com/pod-product-compliance
Lightning Source LLC
Chambersburg PA
CBHW070915260626
47162CB00007B/2678